ALL THE DEVILS ARE HERE

MICHAEL SAAD

Michael Saad

ALL THE DEVILS ARE HERE
MICHAEL SAAD

Tumbleweed Books
Tumble through the pages of our books
HTTP://TUMBLEWEEDBOOKS.CA
An imprint of DAOwen Publications

ALL THE DEVILS ARE HERE / Michael Saad

ISBN 978-1-928094-17-3
EISBN 978-1-928094-18-0

Cover art by MMT Productions

10 9 8 7 6 5 4 3 2 1

Acknowledgements

This story was literally 25 years in the making. Beginning as a short story in my Writing 11 class in 1991, I would like to thank the following people for helping me bring it here. The late Ron Basarab, my Writing 11 teacher, who challenged me to take this story further — it took 25 years to do it. I only wish you could have seen it in this stage. Thanks for introducing me to Robert Frost, George Orwell, and Oscar Wilde as well.

To Mr. John Gill, another bright light taken too soon, for all the legal and crime advice on procedure, courts, and sentencing, and for your ever kind patience with your busy schedule to walk me through my questions. To Kevin Anderson, for your ongoing insights into police and tactical procedures. I would also like to thank the Alberta Federation of Police Associations and the RCMP, for their prompt responses to my questions about the various elements of policing handled in this book. Any inaccuracies or errors in this story fall on me, not these fine gentlemen and organizations.

To my friends and volunteer editors on early, shorter drafts of this story — Lesley Little, Sjoerd Schaafsma, and Melvin Roth — thank you very much for your time and feedback.

And, of course, to my wonderful wife Jodi and my two kids, M & M, who continue to support me with love and grace in this often solitary vocation of writing. I love you all very much.

To Mr. Ron B,

This is the one you said I should write. Thanks for everything.

Prologue

Age 23

"You realize you're holding the future of your family in that envelope," Diane told him as he sat at the kitchen table, wrestling with the decision of whether to seal it or not.

"I know." Radley leaned forward, hands over his eyes. "Believe me, I know."

Diane motioned to the sliding glass doors that led to their outside patio. "Does it make any difference that she's sitting on our deck right now sipping lemonade and working on a puzzle, while you sit here humming and hawing over that letter?"

"It makes it so much easier," Radley said, letting out a heavy breath, "and a billion times harder."

"Why don't you wait until later?" she chastised him, the only person on the planet who could. "I don't understand why this has to be done right now. Especially with her —"

"I'm going to the mail." Radley shot up, cutting her off. He took the letter and marched out of the house. Envelope in hand, he trudged across the lawn and the dry, yellow birch leaves that peppered it. Approaching the postal box, he paused, uncertain.

Do I mail this damn thing or not? The simple act of dropping the letter into the postal slot was killing him, each minute spent agonizing over it was like a subtle but precise pinprick into his beating heart.

That was the power of decisions. The power to shape destinies, to confirm or deny fate. Radley wielded this power once before in his life, and the consequences were monumental. He had wielded this power impulsively yet cleverly, on a whim, yet with careful premeditation. What he needed to decide, once and for all, was whether it was *truly* worth it.

Dammit, you gotta think this through.

He stopped in front of the mailbox, returning back to that critical moment one decade ago, when he turned his life upside down and inside out. Leaning against the cold metal of the box, he looked up at the birch trees above him, their gentle rustling reminding him of his horrifying childhood, and the events that led to the most fateful decision of his life...

PART I

Chapter 1

Thirteen Years Earlier - Age 10

Radley stood outside the perimeter of the campfire, lying among the brown, crinkly leaves that fell from the thin, crooked birch surrounding him. He looked up at the length of the trees, the tops of which were barren, extending outward like angry, witches' claws clasping at the autumn sky. Radley imagined himself swinging from the treetops, bellowing like Tarzan in the cartoons, his only care was grabbing the next branch, then the next, keeping himself off of the ground.

"Radley, get outta those shit leaves," his mother called from the campfire where the adults sat. "Come here and have a toke with your mommy."

"Oh Carla, don't," Aunt Dulcie warned, but the other adults laughed. They were sitting in lawn chairs around the fire they'd set in the early afternoon. There had been a lot of weed smoked and alcohol drunk in that time, and the more they consumed, the bigger the fire got. By four o'clock, it became a raging inferno, and Radley didn't want to sit around it because of the immense heat. The black smoke from the rotten wood only made it worse.

His mother was stoned – Radley could tell by the red in her eyes and the squeal in her voice. She also laughed a lot more when she was high, and that was okay, because that meant she was happy. Drugs made you happy.

"Radley, come here honey," his mother repeated, leaning forward in her chair. She wore a red-and-grey checkered hunter's coat, and the bangs of her flat, brown hair clung to her forehead in a mat of sweat. She was redder in the face than Radley was used to.

"Stop it, Carla, the boy's only ten," Aunt Dulcie repeated. She herself had been smoking, but was nowhere near as wasted as his mother.

"Shut up," Carla spat. "He's my fucking kid and if I want ta smoke a dube with him then I'm going to do that. Radley, come here, son."

"Hey Mama," Radley said, approaching her slowly. The drugs didn't scare him – he was used to those. They had been around since his earliest memories, and he could name different types. What made him cautious in approaching his mother was the way she acted. Normally she didn't want him in the same room as her when she smoked, and now here she was calling him over to her like she was giving him a chocolate bar.

"Come here, baby." His mother put her arm around him.

She smelled of skunk and sweat, which made Radley want to pull away, but he didn't. "You're gonna have your first toke, honey bun."

His older brother emerged from one of the RVs parked around the campsite. As though possessed of a sixth sense, Dustin bolted to the fire, straight to his mother.

"Aw, you're lettin' Radley have that?" Dustin complained. "I was supposed to get some."

"Shut up, you little asshole." His mother swatted him away. "I'm going to let Radley have a try, right honey?"

Radley didn't know what to think. He'd never had a toke before.

"You can't let him smoke that," Dustin said with an exaggerated whine to his voice, "he's too young. Gimmie that doobie."

"Get away from me, you little pothead!" His mother cussed at him. In the next breath, she turned her attention back to Radley, hugging him while trying to hold the fat, grey joint between her shaky fingers. She held it up to his lips.

"Breathe it in slow, sweetheart," his mother said.

Reluctantly, Radley put his lips around the joint and breathed in. He inhaled too deeply and burst out coughing. Hunched over, he spit on the grass.

"Radley, you're not doing it right!" Dustin yelled at him. "You took in too much smoke, you idiot!"

"Shut the fuck up." His mother stood up and slapped

Dustin on the arm. "Leave him alone, it's his first time!" She put her arms around her youngest son and started chuckling like a girl in his Grade 6 class. "You breathed in too much, honey. It's okay. We'll let you try again."

"Hey, you're becoming a man now, Radley." His dad's friend Cyclo came up from behind and roped his arms around Radley's midsection then picked him up. The sudden jolt across his belly almost caused Radley to throw up. "Your first joint – we all been there buddy."

He set Radley down, allowing the boy to compose himself. Radley felt like he'd gotten off a roller coaster – his head spun.

Is this what drugs do to you? The burning sensation coated the inside of his lungs. His brain boiled. *They turn you into the devil.*

His mother gave him a kiss on the cheek, then handed him the joint.

"Here, take another puff, this one slower," she said.

Radley did so, and felt the earth spinning off its axis. He stumbled a bit, and then the buzz really set in.

"Whoa, I feel like a helicopter, twirling around," he said. The adults around him laughed, but he wasn't trying to be funny. They seemed like dull blurs.

"What the bloody fuck is going on?" an angry voice called out from behind him. The voice stuck fear in Radley's heart. He spun around, terrified to see his father behind him, kneeling down to look at Radley's face.

"What did you fucking imbeciles do to my kid?" Tavis

Wycliffe yelled at the people standing around his son. He was a tall man, well built, with a pig shave, a bushy goatee, and splotches of freckled skin on his arms. Two tattoos graced either arm — one a medieval lance wrapped in a vine of roses and thorns while the other was the face of a red, sinister looking dragon-like creature his father said was a demon. His dad glared at the people around him with slitted eyes.

"We let him have his first joint," Cyclo answered. "Hey, it was your woman's idea."

"His first joint?" Tavis looked into his son's eyes. "Radley, is that true?"

"Y—yes," Radley answered. He felt like he was in a beehive with the constant buzzing.

"Well, did you like it?" his father asked, a smile forming.

"Yes," Radley replied. What else could he say?

"That's my boy!" Tavis Wycliffe shouted, picking up his son in a fireman's carry. His smile now full-fledged laughter.

He spun Radley around in circles. Radley closed his eyes — he felt tingly all over.

"Tavis, ya stupid shit," Carla said. "Put him down or he's gonna hurl all over ya."

Tavis stopped on the spot, stumbling backward. Cyclo caught him. Radley thought like he was going to barrel backward into the fire.

"Whoa, easy, man," Cyclo said, grabbing Radley and setting him down, then taking Tavis' arm to prevent him from falling into the fire pit. "The kid is fine. Your woman's had too much weed."

Tavis ignored his friend and glared at his wife. "You fucking bitch." He pointed at her. His words slurred, which they often did whenever he was angry – and high to boot. "You give our nine-year old son weed, and you fucking tell *me* I'm going to make him sick? Because I'm spinning him 'round the way I did when he was a baaaby!"

"Our son is ten, asshole," Carla replied. "And yeah, I gave him weed, but I don't expect ta spin him around like a fucking helicopter after I give it to him."

"Hey, come on, you guys don't fight." Radley saw where this was going. He stood up straight. "Look Mom, Dad, I'm fine. I'm not gonna puke!"

"Spin him like a fucking helicopter, hey?" Tavis said, raising his fist. "Maybe I ought a spin your fucking skull like a helicopter, hey bitch?" He made a lunge for her.

"Dad!" Radley yelled.

"Whoa, hey, Tavis." Cyclo stepped in, blocking his buddy from charging his wife. "Everybody's had a little too much right now. Let's all calm the fuck down, okay?"

Aunt Dulcie stepped in. "Come on, Wycliffe family. This is supposed to be a happy time. We're here to party, not fight." She took out her .35 mm camera. "Dustin." She turned to her nephew. "Come over here, Dust, get a picture with your mom and dad."

Dustin sat by the fire, taking a sip of beer from a bottle left open on a cooler. "I'm not going in no picture!"

"Hey, yeah, you wanna take our picture, Dulce?" Tavis said, bumbling. He gave Cylco a hug. "Hey, man, you know I wasn't gonna hit her, right, buddy?"

"Yeah, of course I know that, man." Cyclo sounded unconvinced. He held Tavis, who clung all over him. Whatever drug Tavis had taken, it was starting to mellow him out.

That was the devil acting. The sudden thought surprised him. *This is why Mom and Dad fight. It's the drugs that makes them do it. Everything at home is quiet when my parents aren't using.* The revelation hit him like a bullwhip snap.

"Why don't you let Dulcie take a picture of you with your wife and boys?" Cyclo said. "Come on, it'll be nice, hey buddy?"

"Yeah, yeah. Course it will." Tavis pointed to Radley. "Hey, come here, son o' mine. Get in this picture, okay son?"

Radley immediately skirted over, knowing not cooperating would only set his father off even further. *Yes, because Dad is still high.*

"Come on Carla, you slug–faced bitch," Tavis said to his wife, motioning her over. "Come take a picture with your stud muffin."

"Stud muffin, my ass," Carla said with sneer, but got up at her sister's prompting. She stood next to Radley and kissed his cheek with her rough dry lips. "Hey, Radley baby." She caressed his cheek. Her hands were miraculously soft, but she rubbed them in lotion and had them in mitts for most of the weekend. His mother was meticulous about keeping her hands lubricated and moist. "Mommy came into the picture to be with you, baby. Nobody else."

"Dustin!" Tavis shouted for his oldest son. "Get your ass over here, boy!"

"Come on, Dust," Dulcie goaded. "We finally got all four of you together in front of a camera. This ain't gonna happen ever again."

"Yeah, and I wouldn't want it to," Dustin said. He never left his chair. "Why the hell would I want a picture with them for?"

"BECAUSE I'll FUCKING KICK YER ASS IF YOU DON'T!" Tavis shouted at him, spittle flew from his mouth along with his anger. He waved his arms in the air and looked ready to charge at his son.

"Hey, hey, I got it, man," Cyclo said, holding his palm up to keep Tavis in his spot. "I'll get him, okay?" He made a lunge for Dustin, snatching him in the rocking chair. Pinning the boy's arms in a bear-hug, Cyclo dragged him towards the fire where the rest of his family stood.

"Get the fuck off of me!" Dustin thrashed, trying to pry his fourteen-year old frame against the massive fortress that was Cylco. "Fuck you, you fucking goon."

"Shut up and get a picture with your old man." Cyclo set him down next to Tavis, and threatened to backhand him if he tried to bolt.

"Come here, you little quiff." Tavis pulled Dustin toward him.

"Get off me, Dad!" Dustin tried to break away, but his father's grip was too strong.

"Just take the fucking picture," Cyclo said to Dulcie, shaking his head.

"Okay, Wycliffes, smile!" Dulcie took the picture.

"Aw, fuck I don't want be in no picture!" Dustin broke away, running toward their tent.

Radley had his mother's face pressed against his for the picture. He felt her matted hair against his cheek and she smelled like wet grass.

I'm probably not smiling in that picture. It's a sure bet Dustin won't be either.

"I'll get these developed and make doubles," Dulcie said, putting her camera away. "I'll give you guys one of them."

"Good picture," Tavis said, seemingly oblivious to everything. "Thanks, Dulcie honey. The Wycliffe clan, one big happy family." He stumbled over to his tent, ignoring his wife and youngest son, which suited Radley just fine.

"Oh God." Carla tried to rise up from her knees, her right one cracked. "Oh shit, I'm an old lady. Radley baby, bring your mommy her lawn chair, okay honey?"

Radley ran and brought it over. His mother slumped into it like a sack of flour.

"Cyclo, Buddy!" Tavis shouted out from the tent entrance. "Where's our weed? Time for a toke, you and I, eh Bud?"

"Hey, where's my joint?" Carla blurted out. Radley saw it, smoldering on the plastic table, next to where her chair had been.

Aunt Dulcie brought it over to her. "Here, shut your yap."

Radley skirted away from the party, and made his way back to the pile of birch leaves he lay in earlier, hoping his brother wouldn't see him go. Only his mother watched him leave, despite his best efforts to sneak away. He noticed her eyes were fixed on him as she reclined in her lawn chair with her joint.

"Radley baby," she called out in a croaky voice a couple of minutes later. She was happy, chirpy, and utterly stoned.

"Hi Mom," Radley said, knowing he needed to acknowledge her, if only to shut her up. He lay on his back — his head pressed against a pile of crackling leaves, the playful sound of which helped him manage the buzz–like sensation in his head and the early start of what felt like a headache. Staring up at the darkening sky at the treetop claws above him, Radley wallowed in thought.

The devils are here, in the forest. They come out whenever Mom and Dad and Cyclo are high. I get it now.

He pretended to grab up at the demon claws and swing

from branch to branch like Tarzan the Ape Man. The rhythm and pattern he visualized for himself provided a sense of calm, granting him a temporary recluse from the partying and chaos around him.

Chapter 2

Age 12

Radley sat on the floor in the living room, playing video game wrestling with Dustin on their 40–inch, box-screen television. The TV was so wide their mother had a shrine of framed pictures on top of it – mostly those she'd taken as a photography student in high school – flowers, an orange sunset over a mountain landscape, a weird one of a paper cup on a barbed wire fence post. The only family picture on the TV was the one Aunt Dulcie had taken two years ago at Windbender Valley, where they camped amongst all the birch trees.

Radley vaguely remembered the picture being taken. What he recalled came from what the picture itself showed him. Dustin refusing to be in it – his scrunched-up, red, angry, face as their father held him in a headlock. Radley, on the other hand, looked squeamish as his mother forced her head against his. Whenever Radley looked at the picture, he could still catch a scent of the wet grass-like stench of his mother's breath.

"Wham! Nailed you to the ground, you little dildo." Dustin laughed, having his character pile drive Radley's into the mat. Radley frantically tapped on his controller's buttons to get his character to stand back up. He did, and put Dustin's wrestler in an arm bar.

"There … got you," Radley said.

The beautiful part about their giant TV was it made Radley forget about the photo. It got so that when the TV was on, whether Radley watched The Simpsons, an Indiana Jones VHS, or played Sega Genesis, the photo was non–existent. The second best part about having the TV was having friends over and listening to them gawk about how awesome the big screen was, complete with the two, giant stereo speakers their father had at the corners of the living room. The only problem was the boys weren't allowed to have friends over very much. They hadn't had any over in almost a year.

"You're getting better with your holds, kid," Dustin said to Radley, trying to fight out of the arm hold. "But you still suck." Dustin wrenched his wrestler free, hoisted Radley's character above his head, and threw him over the ropes, outside the ring, onto the concrete floor.

"Hey, you jerk," Radley muttered. "I hate it when you do that."

"Ha–ha, you little dweeb," Dustin said.

With an inkling of energy left in his life bar, Radley's wrestler bounced up. Radley sent him back into the ring, where he stood up on the apron, waiting for Dustin to follow him.

"Come here, you chicken-shit," Dustin said. His character jumped onto the apron, but Radley used the kick feature to knock Dustin's wrestler to the floor again.

"You're not doin' that again!" Dustin cursed. "You're gonna get me counted out."

"Only 'cause you cheat," Radley shot back. His brother was notorious for throwing him outside of the ring, pile driving him repeatedly on the cement, then throwing him back into the ring for an easy three count. It wouldn't have been so annoying had Dustin not done it every *single* time they played. So Radley developed this strategy to keep Dustin from getting back in the ring each time he pulled that stunt – and it drove his brother batty.

"You friggin' pussy!" Dustin said when the count hit ten and the match was over. He slammed his controller to the floor and punched his brother in the arm, hard.

"Get outta here!" Radley tried fighting back, but his brother had four years on him, and was developing into a bulky sixteen year old. Radley had just turned twelve, and had a lot of growing to do.

"Quit yer cry'n, you faggot," Dustin repeated, pinning Radley to the ground.

"Hey you little assholes, stop it!" Their mom charged into the living room from the hall. "Your father just pulled in – hurry up and help haul in his stuff." She had the usual sense of urgency whenever her husband came home with the "stuff."

"Mom, Dustin hit me again," Radley said, showing his mother the welt emerging under his left shoulder. "I think it's going to bruise."

"It's not gonna bruise as fast as your ass if you don't get out there and help your Daddy!" Carla held her hand up, threatening to swat him.

Dustin was already outside to greet his father. It was the

usual time of night when Tavis came back from the industrial yard, where he made his pickups. The sky was dark but not quite enough for the street lamps to come on. Tavis pulled his sedan into the garage and did not unload until the door was completely closed.

Their father, as usual, was all business. He dressed in his drug-running outfit – black pants, dark grey hoodie concealing his tattooed arms, and an LA Raiders ball cap. He did not say hello to the boys or to his wife. Instead, he got out of his vehicle, opened the back hatch and immediately started handing the "Loney's Bakery" boxes to Dustin and Radley, who knew their jobs. Take each box, walk it to the basement, and place it directly in front of the large black curtain draped across what used to be Dustin and Radley's play area. Since the boys had grown up, their father's work area gradually swallowed up the free space in the basement, forcing both boys to spend time upstairs.

The rules were specific – leave the boxes at the base of the curtain so their father could slide them into his work area. Under no circumstances were they to open the boxes, or go behind the curtain.

The boxes were heavy, but Radley was used to the lifting, in spite of his sore arm. They took the final two boxes into the basement and set them at the base of the curtain.

"Hey Rad," Dustin whispered. "Dare ya to look. How much weed do you think Dad's growing right now?"

"I don't know." Radley shrugged. It was no secret what their father was doing behind that curtain. Their parents had been more open about it in recent years, but the boys were still not allowed back there.

"Come on, I dare you to look," Dustin said.

"No way, Dad'll kill us."

"Boys!" Tavis shouted from the garage. "I gotta get this shit outta my car. Move it!"

Dustin bolted up the stairs.

Radley stood alone in the basement. He could smell the plants behind the curtain — a smell as familiar to him as the scent of cookies baking. Like a cat, Radley skirted behind the curtain to peek at his father's grow op. The plants, as they were the first time Radley saw them, were ordered in even rows underneath the lighting rack Tavis set up overtop them. But the room had an entirely different look than the last time Radley peeked at it. There were dirty glass jars, pipes, metal cylinders, some kind of heating contraption, and loads of banded wire around the room, as well as two new tables. The only things Radley recognized were the plants and marijuana-leaf banner hanging over the only window in the room, blackening it from outside viewers. His father's room looked more like a science lab than the "greenhouse" Tavis often called it.

"Radley, get yer ass up here and help us out!" Tavis barked from the garage.

Radley closed the curtain, then scooted up the stairs to prevent any suspicion, but one thing was clear, his father's operation had gotten a lot more complicated than it used to be.

Age 14

"Your brother Dustin's a freakin' monster," Donny Greyus said to Radley. Donny was his Grade 9 buddy. "I wouldn't wanna fight him."

"He's a sour puss." Radley tried to sound tough, but did a double take in the hallway in case anyone he knew overheard. "You should hear him whine when I beat him in videogame roller derby. He pouts worse than a girl."

"You're crazy, man." Donny laughed. "Your brother's gotta be one of the meanest kids in the whole school."

Leading his friends, Radley walked through the Grade 11 wing to get to third period science class. Mayer Cross High School, where Dustin and he attended, was the largest in the city. They didn't have to go there, it was an extra 15 minute walk from their house, but Tavis and Carla liked it because it was big, and kept the boys invisible. Yet neither brother wanted to be invisible – both yearned for attention, even the negative kind, which they often got from their teachers. Not openly belligerent like his older sibling, Radley wasn't eager to please either. His misbehaviour came as the result of being lazy rather than defiant.

This marked the only year in which the two brothers would attend high school together. Radley was in Grade 9 while Dustin, held back one year, was slated to graduate, though the chances of that were touch-and-go.

The boys walked up the Grade 11 stairwell. It was always intimidating for niners to enter a senior–high wing, yet Radley did so with confidence. The rest of his buddies were uncomfortable, nervous about getting hazed, but Radley basked in security, knowing he was the brother of the toughest kid in school. He knew most of the Grade 11s through Dustin, so Radley didn't feel intimidated by them.

Except one. Posko Scandrovich, one of the bad apples known around the school for having ties to the *Knights of the Apocalypse* gang on the South side. Only the kids knew this — the teachers seemed oblivious about Posko's connections.

"Hey, kid." Posko stopped the boys as they were coming down the stairs. He honed in on Radley and motioned for him to come over. "I wanna talk to you."

"Me?" Radley asked, feeling knots twist in his stomach. Posko was muscular, tall, seasoned — he wore an oversized hunting coat and a bandanna that made him look like a player. Radley's friends stared wide–eyed at the conversation.

"You're the young Wycliffe kid, right?" Posko said.

"Yeah." Radley swallowed.

"Your dad is *Cabana,* right?" Posko whispered.

Radley had no idea what he was talking about. He shrugged his shoulders, looking like a deer lost in headlights.

"Good answer," Posko said with a smirk, reaching into his pocket. "Listen, give him this cell number — tell him it's from King Arthur." He leaned into Radley's ear. "Tell him the Knights want him to cook for him. Everything would be under the table."

Radley took the note. To his astonishment, Posko rubbed his hand over Radley's head, a playful sign of acceptance.

"Good man. See to it that your dad gets this message, okay?" He turned and headed down the stairs, blending into the mass of students making their way to class.

Radley's friends looked at him in disbelief.

"Crap, that was Posko," Donny said, "You're friends with that guy?"

"Yeah," Radley answered.

"That's wicked, man. What'd he give you?"

"Nothing," Radley said with a shrug, reveling in the newfound notoriety, which he owed completely to his father's business.

Chapter 3

"Hey, let me play the game with you, dweebs," Tavis slurred as he stumbled into the living room and plopped on the floor next to where Radley and Dustin sat playing video Motocross.

"Come on, Dad, you can't play," Dustin grumbled. "You're stoned–stupid."

Tavis leaned over and pinched his oldest son, far harder than he should have.

"Ow!" Dustin cried. "Bugger off, you dumb druggie."

"Don't talk to yer old man that way," Tavis said, oblivious as to how hard he pinched him. "I bought you this damn game system, didn't I?"

"We're playing Motocross!" Dustin snarled. "You can't even walk a straight line, how you gonna steer a motorbike?"

"Give me that friggin' controller," Tavis said. "I'll show you how ta steer a damn motorbike."

Dustin wrenched the controller away from his father's grip. "Screw off. Take Radley's controller if you wanna play so bad."

Hey, I was playing this game first, Radley was about to say, but didn't get it out.

"QUIT BEING SUCH A GODDAMN PUSSY!" Tavis exploded, slapping Dustin across the head. The wallop had a hollow, echoing sound that killed all other noise in the room. The sheer shock of the moment sped Radley's heart tenfold.

"What the fuck are you doin, Dad?" Dustin's voice wavered.

"YOU WANNA GO WITH ME, BOY!" Tavis screamed, shooting up to his knees. He was centimeters away from Dustin's face. "COME ON, LITTLE BABY. I'LL FIGHT YA RIGHT NOW, MR. LIP–OFF!"

"No, I don't wanna fight." Dustin's eyes watered. He jolted up, and threw the controller into his father's lap, then stormed out of the living room. Seconds later, his bedroom door slammed.

"Yeah, that's right, Mr. Pussy!" Tavis shouted down the hallway, then stumbled back to his knees and grabbed the controller. "Go cry in your room! I'll play this game with my boy, Radley. He's a real man, not like his big, sissy older brother!"

Radley stayed quiet as his father patted him on the back. Tavis started moving the controller like a steering wheel, which was exactly what you weren't supposed to do with Motocross. His bike went all across the screen. *You're supposed to tilt the controller dad, not steer it,* Radley wanted to say, but knew better, keeping his character in the center of the road, and racing alongside his father. Recognizing his father's high was more than just weed, Radley learned just to keep quiet than to chastise Tavis when he was in this state, something Dustin clearly hadn't figured out yet.

"Nothing like playing a video game with my boy, Radley," Tavis repeated, steering his bike off the track and into the spectators, sending a crowd of digital onlookers scattering.

"Uh-oh, call the Pigs," Tavis chuckled, his eyes narrowed into slits. "I just drove into a whole crowd." He grabbed Radley by the arm. "I guess that's why they say you shouldn't toke and drive, hey son?" He blew a snot bubble from his nose as he laughed.

"Yes sir," Radley said. "Why don't I get the ottoman for you to lean on?"

"Good idea. Now that's a good boy, see?" Tavis said with a dopey smile. "Unlike your retard brother." His racer was back on the track, but his motorbike kept slamming into the side rail.

Radley dragged the leather stool across the floor and wedged it behind his father's back. Tavis leaned against the stool. A dopey expression permeated his face.

"Good job, Rad," Tavis muttered. "Now we can finish this race, hey son?"

It was only a matter of minutes before Tavis slumped forward, passed out with the controller in his hands.

Radley shut off the game and put it away.

"Come on, Dad, you gotta get off the floor." He helped his father up, and guided him to the sofa. "You gotta work nightshift."

Tavis collapsed on the couch – Radley positioned him diagonally across the cushions so that he wouldn't roll on the floor.

Five hours later, Radley lay in his bed, listening to the fighting. It was midnight. He'd only been asleep for an hour when the screaming started.

His father was still passed out on the couch, the effects of his latest binge lingering. Radley and Dustin had worried their father may have been done for the night. They could have run him over with a semi-truck and he wouldn't have known it.

Their mother, on the other hand, never learned that lesson. She had come home from her evening shift and doused water on him with her spray bottle, trying to pry him off of the couch.

"You have to start your shift in two hours, asshole!" she shouted, holding the sprayer inches away from his face and shooting him with it. "I'm not covering for you, and I'm not going to spend the rest of the night waking you up, so get your ass off that couch!"

"Fuck off with that thing, already!" Tavis swatted the spray bottle away from his face. The tone of his voice indicated he was still buzzed. "I'm fine – it's not like I haven't done this before!"

"You promised me that you wouldn't get stoned on work nights!" The sound of his mother throwing the spray bottle against the living room wall echoed through the house. "What kind of example are you setting for your boys?"

"Don't fucking give me that shit!" Tavis snarled. It sounded like he was starting to get off the couch, but must have thrown a cushion at his wife and knocked a lamp over.

"If this is all you're going to do – rely on those damn drugs to support this family – I won't have any part of it! I swear to God I'll smash all that shit of yours downstairs!" She stormed into the kitchen, straight for the pantry door.

Radley's heart sank. Whenever his mother threatened to smash the equipment, the altercations always turned violent.

"Radley." Dustin snuck into his room. He knew Radley wouldn't be sleeping. "If he starts hitting her, I gotta go in. You stay here, but if it gets out of hand, run over to Cyclo's to get help."

"Don't go in there, Dustin," Radley pleaded. Tavis was already mad at Dustin, given the chaos that happened with the Motocross game.

"Don't you dare go down into that fucking basement!" Tavis shouted.

"Let go of me, you bastard!" Carla wailed.

The sound of loud clashing, thumping, and screaming jolted both boys. Radley shot up in his bed. Dustin charged out of the room and down the hallway.

"Get the fuck off her!" Dustin shouted. He must have tackled his father. One of them fell into the kitchen cabinets, rattling the whole house.

Radley sat frozen on the edge of his bed. He couldn't bear watching his father beat his mother and brother. Dustin had told him to get Cyclo – he would be physically strong enough to restrain Tavis, but Radley had learned from experience that was a pointless venture. Cyclo's house was ten blocks away, and the guy either wouldn't be home, or was probably stoned himself.

Instead, Radley turtled under the covers, his eyes closed with a pillow covering his ears, trying to drown out the sounds of his mother and brother being slapped, punched, and thrown against walls.

"Owwww, no don't, please!" Dustin wailed. "Get off of me."

"Tackle me, hey, ya little fuckface!" Tavis snarled. "I twist a little more, I break your arm. What do you think of that, huh, ya little dickweed!"

Get up and do something. But the fear paralyzed him. He shook under the covers.

"Tavis, you asshole, let him go!" Mom shouted, her voice hoarse and pained.

"Ow, you Goddamn bitch!" Tavis' curse was followed by a loud slap, then the sound of his mother sobbing.

This is not the way life is supposed to be. The thought entered Radley's head as he heard his brother cry out in pain, and his father threatening to knock his mother's teeth out.

Chapter 4

"God, I hate frickin' health class." Radley sauntered down the Grade 9 hallway.

"Geez, dude," Donny laughed. "What class do you like?"

"Nothin' that's got book learning in it," Radley said.

"I hate ta tell you this, Rad"–Donny slapped him on the shoulder–"but that's pretty much everything."

"Tell me about it," Radley said. "I hate reading and I don't understand a thing in math. Social is garbage. Science is gay. What the hell's the point of school?"

"What about options?" Donny asked. "Woodwork and welding? We always got those, right?"

"Ah, they're okay." Radley gave in, only because it was cool to say that. The truth was Radley didn't like those classes either. He never understood dodo joints and the other fancy wood cuts, and didn't have a clue how you were supposed to forge two pieces of metal together wearing a helmet you couldn't see a friggin' thing out of.

There could be no disputing his hatred of school, but he absolutely despised health class, and that was where they were headed to.

"Health is the most pointless class they can make you take," Radley muttered. "Eat apples and broccoli, don't eat chips, do lots of exercise and don't drink-and-drive. I mean, do they really need ta teach this stuff? It's friggin' retarded."

"Doesn't help with that hose-bag Macklin teachin' the course," Donny said. "We're doin' the anti-drug unit right now, and if I hear one more thing about how 'drugs destroying your destiny,' I'm gonna puke."

"Yup," Radley said. "She's some weird church lady." *What the hell does she know about drugs? My dad grows weed, makes meth, and sells it for big time cash. Cyclo too — the guy's got two houses, a wicked car, and the best friggin' entertainment centre you've ever seen.* "Macklin doesn't know a bong from a blow horn."

"She's an airhead." Donny nodded, then stopped just short of the classroom door. "Hey, what are we even going to class for? Let's skip."

Radley paused. The thought appealed to him. The only thing he ever did in health was draw marijuana leaves and skull and cross bone designs inside his binder. The problem today was that he didn't even bring his binder.

"Let's do it, man, let's skip." Radley turned and started walking away.

"Not so fast, gentlemen." Miss Macklin stepped out of her doorway. "If you're gonna cut, at least have the intelligence to do it before you approach my classroom doorway."

Radley wanted to tell her off but he never could muster up his brother's belligerence. He turned around and followed Donny and Miss Macklin into the classroom. The second he entered the doorway he jolted to attention in complete shock.

"Hello guys." A police constable, in full uniform, greeted

them with a nod.

Radley felt like he had walked into an electric fence. The constable watched them sit in their seats. He was a husky man with broad shoulders, a dark crewcut, and hawk-like eyes that seemed to peer into the soul of every kid in the room. Radley had never been this close to a police officer before and stared in fascination at the officer's handgun, pepper spray, and baton strapped around his waist. There were so many questions Radley wanted to ask the cop – was his gun loaded? Had he ever shot anyone? But instead Radley sat quiet, sheepish.

"Alright, everyone," Miss Macklin called out, "this is our first visit from Constable Roake – we'll see him a couple more times before the semester ends. He's here to talk about his experiences in dealing with drugs and the people who use them."

For the next twenty minutes, Constable Roake spoke to the class – he was candid, talked openly about individuals he saw who had become drug addicts, and broken the law to get their fix. Many were people you wouldn't expect – lawyers, engineers, athletes – while others were teenagers – some the same age as Radley, who became full-fledged addicts.

Roake walked around the room. "The common mistake these kids made was that they got caught in the idea that drugs are cool … fun … something you can control.

"But you can't control drugs," he continued. "We can't control the effect they have on our bodies. Imagine common street drugs like marijuana, cocaine, or ecstasy. You take them to get high, to experience a rush, but you can't control what else that drug is doing to your lungs, your blood vessels, your heart."

Donny watched the presentation with his arms folded. He whispered to Radley, "You and I done weed before and we ain't addicted, Rad."

"You got something to say there, bud?" The Constable glared at Donny.

The moment was awkward – Donny had been talking out of turn.

"Yeah, okay." Donny decided to be defiant. "I heard you can't get addicted to pot, is that true?"

"I can tell you this much," Constable Roake challenged, "whether or not you get addicted to a street drug isn't your decision to make. We can't order our bodies not to become addicted to any drug that we choose. If you continue to take that narcotic regularly, you will work yourself into a habit – a habit where the drug slowly takes over your mind. Soon your decisions will be whether to get high or eat supper, get high or go to work, get high or be with your family. Before you know it, 'getting high' no longer becomes a choice anymore. It's your only option."

The Constable surveyed the room, looking at who was paying attention. Donny still looked unimpressed, but Radley listened.

"Let me introduce you to some people." The Constable signalled to Miss Macklin to turn on the projector. A school photograph of a pretty, young, blonde-haired girl popped up on the screen at the front of the classroom.

"This is Danielle," he said. "She was a Grade 10 honours student, interested in modeling. She tanned well, had perfect white teeth, a pretty face and a warm smile. She's not even wearing make-up in this picture."

He clicked to the next picture – a mug shot of the same girl, presumably a couple of years later. The same shaped face was there, but her hair was scraggly and unkempt. She looked haggard and stressed, as if she had escaped a burning building.

"Unfortunately Danielle believed she needed to lose weight to be a model – that only skinny models would be successful. She started using cocaine at raves, and continued using it in the belief that it would help control her appetite, and get her to eat less. Well, as you can see, she was right. When this photo was taken, she weighed only 98 pounds."

It was clear that her physical beauty went down ten notches. Bloodshot eyes, a gaunt face, unkempt hair. Her skin looked bumpy, rough – like the underside of a carpet. Two noticeable pits had hallowed into her cheeks, and her skin and hair had a greasy sheen to it.

"Gross," a student spoke up. "That chick needs a shower, badly."

"She looks like a witch," another student commented, provoking laugher among the class.

She looks like my mother's party friends. Radley held the words inside.

Constable Roake went through three more sets of pictures, displaying individuals who were clean cut, respectable looking young men and women, only to show them two or three years later looking like death-warmed-over. Almost all of them degraded to the point where their physical demise seemed irreversible. The most noticeable trait they all had were the discoloured blotches on their faces, dry, withered skin, and dopey, sad, strung out expressions.

My mother has those blotches. Radley bit his lip. *Her eyes have that same, dazed, stupid look whenever she gets stoned.*

"Gimmie a break." Donny leaned over and whispered to Radley. "I heard about this crap the cops do – they take pictures of these losers right when they arrest them. These people are so spun out at the time that they don't know which way is up. Most of them just need a shower and a nap, and they all turn out fine."

"Yeah," Radley muttered. He looked at the next picture – a mug-shot of a thin, pale-faced man who the Constable explained had been arrested at a party for hitting another man with an umbrella stand. Both men had been high at the time, and neither man could remember what the fight was about. Radley had never seen that photograph before, it was dated several years ago, but it caused him to do a double-take. Roake only showed it for a few seconds, so Radley couldn't be sure, but the picture immediately after caught Radley like a snare – it was the same individual, this time as a junior-high school student who had won second place in a science fair for building a greenhouse out of pop bottles. The boy smiled, proudly holding his award as he stood alongside his science teacher. Radley knew the picture well – he had seen it several times in a photo album in an old cardboard box that had been tucked in the corner of his closet.

Oh God, Radley's heart thumped through his chest. *That's my Dad.*

He glanced around the room, praying no one would know. They didn't, not even Donny. Radley cowered in his seat. Roake had only identified the man in the pictures as "Tyler," a talented honours student who got caught up with a bad crowd in high school and started experimenting with drugs that brought his life into a downward spiral. Tyler had spent time in-and-out of in jail, often letting his temper get the better of him, especially when he drank or was high.

"I didn't know Tyler," Roake said to the class. "But the really sad part about his story is that he had two little kids at the time of his arrest. I can only hope he's turned his life around, for their sake."

This cop has no clue, Radley realized. It was also clear the Constable was going off of a recorded script.

"Okay guys." Constable Roake finished his presentation. He picked up his police hat and a small stack of paper notes from the front desk. "If you have questions, write them down on this slip of paper and I'll try and answer each one."

Several of the students submitted questions. Radley left his slip blank.

"I ain't submitting no question," Donny whispered. "We've done all this cow shit before, hey Rad?"

"Yeah," Radley nodded, looking down at the floor. "It's a load of B.S."

Chapter 5

"Radley, baby," Carla whined from the couch, "turn off your video game so Mommy can watch her talk show, 'kay sweets?"

Radley sat on the floor playing Motocross by himself in front of the big screen. He ignored his mother, who lay on the couch. She'd been smoking pot when he got home from school and instantly started badgering him to go downstairs to bring her some of his Dad's 'green bud'. Radley knew better than to comply, as that was his father's high quality weed. *'Tell her to smoke her own Goddamn schwag first!'* Tavis would say. To make matters worse, his father was currently in the basement with Dustin making meth, and would have gone ballistic had Radley disturbed him for any reason whatsoever.

"Radley, baby," Carla spoke with the pitchy wail she often used when high. "You won't get your mommy a joint, at least turn the TV on for me."

"No, Mom," Radley shot back, refusing to take his eyes off of the game. "You're too spun out for another joint, and your talk show's not even on. The news is on now."

"Bastard child," Carla muttered, rolling onto her side. "I should've smothered you in your crib." Radley ignored her. She drifted in and out of consciousness. After a couple of minutes she was asleep, her head wedged uncomfortably against the arm of the couch.

His mother's comments did little to faze him – she often

insulted or threatened her boys whenever she toked up — that was nothing new. *It's just the devil talking,* Radley told himself with a smirk. It had become a quip that only he used and repeated to himself whenever his parents were high and said nasty things to him. He never shared the quip with Dustin or anyone else.

Aw frick, that smell is as bad as it's ever been. His thoughts returned to the present and the piss-like reek that kept coming up from the basement. The smell of weed was something Radley had become accustomed to at an early age, but Tavis' newest venture, the manufacture of crystal meth — and particularly the cat urine smell that accompanied it, grossed Radley out.

Tavis had been experimenting with different types of meth lately. According to Dustin, it was an easy drug to get supplies for, but a complicated one to make.

"Why bother?" Radley had asked his brother. "It makes your house smell like a urinal."

"It's the money, bro," Dustin told him, flashing Radley a stack of ten and twenty dollar bills. "It's a quick high, and the users need it bad. You can make a killin' off it. See this?" Dustin fanned the bills in Radley's face. "All mine from Tavis' last sale. And this was only a quarter of the coin he made."

Radley ignored his brother's ribbing. He was glad he didn't have to go downstairs and help his father. His parents fought over whether the boys should be helping manufacture the drugs or not, but Tavis insisted he needed help. Radley had no interest.

"He needs me so we don't blow up the whole friggin' basement," Dustin proclaimed. The trade-off of course, was that Dustin also got to rake in some of the money when Tavis made a sale, a fact that suited Radley just fine. With Dustin taking such an active interest in his father's business, Radley was getting more time to himself with the video game system, which he was perfectly happy about.

Dustin emerged upstairs, sweaty and annoyed. He made certain to shut the basement door before entering the living room.

"Let me have a race before Dad calls me down again," Dustin said. He grabbed the second controller and reset Radley's game, plopping himself on the floor. Dustin had become a boor since their father recruited him. Normally Radley would have put up a fight, but his brother was starting to grow into a real powerhouse. His shoulders expanded like blown-up balloons and his arms looked as though they were made of fine-cut marble. Radley was getting to the point of being scared of him again.

"Man, I'm sick of that cat-piss stench. Our basement smells like a fucking litter box," Dustin cursed, as his car raced around the track.

For the next game, Radley joined his brother and the two boys were on the same team. Their object was to score as many points as possible on the track. They had to work together, running other cars off the road and taking turns rounding corners. It was nice actually, the two of them in sync, cooperating with one another to achieve a common goal.

They completely lost track of time, until Radley looked up and saw the night sky out of the front room window. Their mother had gotten up, turned on the living room lamp, and started clanging pots in the kitchen, putting supper on the stove.

"I'm making spag again," she said bluntly.

"Oh good, I thought she was dead," Dustin said.

The two boys laughed. Radley was getting hungry, and figured his mother would be done for the night. He didn't care so long as he didn't have to hunt in the fridge for food. He could now concentrate on edging out his brother – his partner – on the final point total.

"Watch it, gimp-boy," Dustin smirked, as Radley tried to cut him off. The two boys laughed some more. It was fun.

The front door smashed inward, slamming against the landing wall. The broken hinges exploded out of the door frame, sending a shockwave through the entire house.

Three gigantic men stormed into the living room. Their eyes furious-wild.

Radley's heart scurried into his throat. He'd never seen these men before in his life.

"Where's Cabana?" A bald man with a pock-marked face, black sweater, and blood-shot eyes ran up to Radley. He didn't seem the slightest bit fazed that he was screaming at a 14-year-old. "Where the fuck is he? I know he lives here!"

"What the– Who the hell are you guys?" The boys' mother lunged into the living room. "Get the fuck out of my house!"

A short, tanned man in a hunting jacket grabbed her. She

tried to claw at his face, but he held her arms down.

"Get off her!" Dustin bolted up from the floor, charging the man. He was immediately cut off by the crazy, bald guy, who cuffed Dustin in the jaw. Dustin collapsed to his knees, holding his mouth.

The third individual, a rough, salt-and-pepper haired man with a slash across his face, from the top of his right eyebrow down to his left cheek, spoke to Carla calmly, as if they were old friends.

"Carla, Carla," the man spoke over her shouting, "I need to know where Tavis is. I know he's running with the Knights. I wanna talk to him."

"You, I recognize you," Carla shouted, her voice trying to hold a threatening tone. "Don't you bring this shit into my home!"

"Carla, I want to help Tavis," the man spoke, though he was not at all convincing in his words. "But I need to know what's going on. Why the double standard?"

"Where is he?" The bald man charged at Radley, picked him up by the scruff of the neck. He frothed at the mouth as he spoke, breathing hot, angry air on Radley's face. Radley was paralyzed with fear. "Tell me where he is, now!"

"Don't tell him anything, Radley!" Dustin shouted, spitting blood onto the carpet.

"Shut up!" The bald man spun around angrily, kicking Dustin in the midsection.

The door to the basement burst open. A crazed-looking Tavis ran into the living room with a baseball bat. Like a lightning bolt, the small tanned man shoved Carla to the floor and tackled Tavis against the far living room wall. The bald man bolted over and clawed Tavis across the face. The three men stumbled across the living room, where the bald man grabbed Tavis by the hair and threw him head first into the big screen TV, shattering the picture tube. He kicked the video game console across the room, knocking the top right off. A mess of circuit and wire spilled onto the floor. All of Carla's framed pictures fell backwards behind the television in a crash of frame and glass.

"Tavis, Tavis, Tavis." The scarred man spoke as if he were talking to a small child. "Look at the grief you're causing your family. It doesn't have to be this way."

Tavis pulled his head out of the broken television. He had a nasty gash on his forehead. "Go to hell." He spit blood.

"Why are you running with the Knights? Your operation, all of your contacts, they were set up by us. We funded your equipment. We made you, and now you underhand us by selling our product to a bunch of punk kids? Tavis, Tavis, Tavis."

"You son-of-a-bitch!" Carla screamed. "I'll go to the cops; I swear to God I will."

"You go to the cops, Carla," the scarred man said. "You do that and we'll send them right back here to your husband's pissy little meth hut, then we'll see how long you last!"

"I don't care. I'll fucking turn you all in!" Carla replied.

"Sure you will," the man goaded. "And we'll cut off your supply so bloody fast you'll be whoring off your boys to get a fix."

"I don't care about my damn coke! You can take it all! I want you out of my house!"

"Shut up, you stupid bitch!" Tavis screamed at his wife. He tried getting up, but stumbled to the floor.

"Now you know what happens when you run with the competitors, Tavis," the scarred man said. He motioned to the tanned man. "Rolly, go to the basement, find whatever you can."

"No!" Tavis shouted, "You can't do that – that's my speed!"

"I'll do whatever I want," the scarred man said with a shrug. "I'm not the one who broke our agreement."

"You won't find half my stuff, I've got it all hidden," Tavis challenged.

"I know you do," the scarred man replied. "That's why you're going to tell me where it is. All of it." He motioned to the balding man. "Chain, get me the lighter please."

"Screw you." Tavis tried to get up and run, but Chain pressed him to the ground. Scar Man grabbed the right sleeve of Tavis' T-shirt, and pulled it over his shoulder, revealing the crimson red, demon tattoo.

"Goddamn it, Tavis, you listen to me," Scar man said, "that is our tattoo. Our colours. The *Rouge,* man. Don't you get it? We don't give that to just anyone. The *Colaberro* gave that to you. He owns you."

"Nobody owns me," Tavis hissed. "I wasn't sellin' the same stuff to the Knights as I was sellin' you. I honored our agreement. You guys weren't payin' me enough. I couldn't keep up."

Scar man let out an exaggerated, phony sigh. He turned to the balding man and shook his head. "He really doesn't get it, does he?" He snapped his fingers. "Chain, hand me your lighter, please."

"No fucking way!" Tavis wrestled free of Chain's grasp and tried to lunge upward. Like a cobra, Scar Man struck Tavis in the throat, collapsing him to the ground. He started flicking the lighter in front of Tavis, who was heaved over, gasping for air.

"Tell me where my merch is!"

"F-fuck you!" Tavis wheezed.

"Have it your way, then friend." The scarred man grabbed Tavis's right arm and held the flame over his wrist. Tavis let out a bloodcurdling wail that sounded nothing like him.

"Where's your drugs?" The scarred man shouted with a vicious ferocity that chilled the room. "Tell me now, you Goddamn rat!" He ran the lighter over Tavis' fingers, hand and forearm. The two boys and their mother sat in terror as they watched Tavis scream out in pain. Chain looked them over like an angry Doberman, daring them to intervene.

"I'm not telling you anything!"

"You're breaking your bond, Tavis." The scarred man's tone went soft again. "Paulo, give me your knife."

The other goon opened his switchblade and handed it to his boss. Tavis responded by spitting in the leader's face.

The scarred man calmly wiped the spit from his eyebrow.

With the knife blade, he pointed to the Crimson Devil on Tavis's arm. "See that Tattoo, Tavis," he said. "That's our property. We're gonna want that back."

"Give me that knife - I'll shove it down your throat!" Tavis tried kicking at Scar Man's feet. Chain held him down, pinning his arms and torso to the ground with his hands and knees. Scar Man ignored him, and instead held the lighter up to the blade.

"Paulo, get the family out of here. This is gonna get ugly."

The Wycliffes were motioned to the master bedroom. They could hear Tavis wailing away, intermixed with the sounds of loud crashing. In a few minutes the wailing turned into horrible, painful, god-awful screaming. Radley sat on the floor next to his parents' bed, huddled with his mother. It took him a few minutes before he realized that at some point in all of the mayhem, he had wet himself.

Chapter 6

Radley sat in third block health class like a zombie. He almost skipped today, and would have for sure, had he known it was health this period. Having only been to school a handful of times this past month, he had lost track of his schedule.

The attack on his father still haunted him like it happened yesterday, even though a month passed since the *Rouge* sent in their "goons" to terrorize his family. Radley never wanted to see that scarred monster again – the sounds of his father howling in pain had burned into Radley's memory in much the same way that the scarred man's lighter and knife scorched his father's flesh. Tavis suffered second degree burns to his hands and right arm from the incident. He eventually succumbed to the torture, telling the scarred man the exact location of the drugs in the house, but not before launching a series of painful shrieks that kept Radley awake and horrified every night since.

Not a moment slipped past when Radley didn't think about the events of that evening. After his father cried out the location of his secret stash, the *Rouge* stormed into the bedroom and cut up the Wycliffe's mattress. They even went into Radley's room and tore out the register under his bed, which to Radley's amazement, didn't lead to a vent at all, but rather to a secret hollow that had bags of drugs stuffed inside it. The thugs then smashed up the basement, trashing his father's meth lab, and smacked a couple of holes in the walls, pulling out stashes of cash, cigarettes, and drugs. The men were in the house less than an hour, but it felt like an eternity.

When they finally left, Carla, Dustin, and Radley ran to Tavis, who lay writhing in pain on the kitchen floor, his arm and hands badly blistered and waxy. He had grabbed a dishtowel left hanging on the oven door and used it to cover up his arm. Radley was told to run a tub of cold water, which he did. The scene turned out to be just as chaotic as the home invasion. Tempers quickly flared up between Tavis, Carla, and the boys.

"I'm gonna kill those guys," Dustin shouted. "I'm gonna get Cyclo's gun and I'll blow their fucking heads off, every one of them!"

"Shut up you idiot," Tavis barked at his son, grasping his strong frame for leverage. "Those guys'd chew your balls off before you'd even have time to get your knees up."

All three of them carried Tavis to the tub – Radley couldn't tell if his father was bleeding or burned. Regardless, he was in tremendous pain. He screamed as they set him in the tub and the cold water engulfed his wounds. Tavis peeled off the dishcloth that seemed to embed itself on his right arm. His skin bubbled from his hands to armpits, but Radley could see that was the lesser of his worries. The dragon tattoo on his father's right shoulder was nothing more than a waxy, bloodied blotch of red and black, like strawberries that been mashed up against a piece of coal.

They peeled my Dad's tattoo off with a knife. A ball of panic and dread swept over him. He had never seen anything like that before, didn't even think it was possible to do such a thing.

"I think we should take him to the hospital," he spoke up, his voice quivering.

"No hospital!" Tavis glared at his son. "What the fuck are we going to tell them, Radley? That a bunch of drug dealers came into our house and burned off my gang tattoo? Use your fucking head, boy!"

"Leave him alone, Tavis, you're the bastard who brought this into our house!" Carla yelled, pressing a white facecloth to the clotted gash on his forehead. "Why did you have to start running against those guys? You're so Goddamn stupid!"

"Shut up and go downstairs, arrrghhh!" Tavis wailed as the water started to aggravate his burns. He knocked the cloth into the water. "Go and see if they took the stash I wedged alongside the furnace filter."

"Christ, Tavis, that's not important right now—" Carla cursed.

"DO IT!" Tavis screamed, grabbing a block of soap and hurling it against the bathroom mirror, cracking the glass.

"Fine, I'll go!" Dustin got up. "Where the hell is the furnace filter?"

"Ah, boy, you're so fuckin' stupid!" Tavis yelled. He was agitated, angry – though Radley wasn't sure if it was from the pain, or from the fact that his drugs had been taken away. "If I could get out of this tub, I'd pull out that filter and beat your sorry ass with it!"

"Whatever, I'll find it." Dustin muttered, leaving the bathroom. He looked at his brother, in particular the stain in

Radley's pants. "Jesus, Radley, did you wet your pants? Get changed, you wuss!"

Radley looked down at his jeans. He had forgotten about it.

"Did you piss yourself?" Carla looked disgusted. "Change your fuckin' clothes, boy — you smell worse than your father's drug lab!"

Running to his room, Radley bit back tears. They finally gushed out when he started thrashing through his drawers, searching for a clean pair of pants. Even then, he muffled his sobs.

Get changed, you wuss. Dustin's words stung as much today as they had a month ago. Radley's mind returned to third period health class, as disconcerted and antsy as ever. There was no question he was a different kid than the one before the attack.

He was surprised, then, to feel his chest tighten up when Constable Roake walked into the room. Once again, he was in full police uniform, exactly like he was when Radley saw him a month earlier. The Constable was there, Miss Macklin announced, to continue his lesson.

"One of the things we as a police force do is to follow-up in our community," Roake explained. "We don't just come out and tell you 'hey guys, don't do drugs.' We want to know what's going on in your homes, schools, and communities."

The Constable spoke for thirty-five minutes, discussing with the students specific strategies for saying no — whether it be at parties, at school, or on the Internet. Much of what he said was beyond anything Radley could comprehend – Constable Roake spoke of drug use as if it were a choice a young person could make.

I don't get it. I don't have a choice. What the fuck is he talking about? He had grown up with drugs in his house. It was as much of his environment as eating or sleeping.

But my life isn't normal. The thought struck Radley like a bullet. He knew not all families were into drugs. Maybe more than half of the kids in his class? He didn't know. Were some families like those he'd watch on TV shows? Radley sometimes wished he were a member of one of those families – never any worry of people storming into your house, threatening your father. There was never any yelling or swearing, or parents passing out on the floor before they were supposed to go to work.

Constable Roake walked around the room, passing out the half slips of paper for kids to write their questions on. Radley took the sheet and stared at it. Every night for the past month he'd been too scared to fall asleep – worried that the *Rouge* would barge into his house again, burn him with the lighter or blow-torches or something worse.

"Those losers won't come back here," Tavis told his son earlier in the week when Radley refused to go to bed. "I ain't involved with those guys anymore; they've got all the stuff they want." The words weren't very comforting to Radley, especially after Dustin told him his father was continuing to produce for the Knights.

"Quit being a baby about it," Dustin told Radley the following evening, when Radley again refused to go to sleep. "The Knights know those French freaks are after Dad, so they offered to protect us. They gave Dad a tazer-gun, so if those guys come back, we can shoot them and claim self-defence. The key is to not act like a pussy if they do come looking for us, because if they grab me or Dad, you gotta use it."

"I don't know how to use a Tazer," Radley said.

"I'll talk to Dad, get him to show you," Dustin replied. "Mom wants to keep you out of things, but you gotta grow up sometime, especially if you're gonna go on runs with Dad and me. He's been taking me more and more, and I tell ya, some of those guys are frickin' maniacs."

But I don't want to go on runs. Radley wanted to lash out, but kept quiet, fearful of his older brother's reaction. Dustin had been hard on him the past month, more so than ever, almost to the point where Radley didn't want to say anything for fear of being called a "pussy" or a "baby."

Which left Radley sitting in the classroom, with the blank slip of paper in his hands. He couldn't handle living like this anymore – physical pain from the fear now welled up in his body.

"You don't want to get caught up in the drug world," Constable Roake continued his talk. "It's a scary, dangerous, and deadly place."

The Constable's words rung true more than any other concept, any other lesson, Radley had learned in fourteen years of schooling. On a whim, he took his pen and scribbled on his slip of paper:

Dear Constible,

My dad dos and sels durgs. I don't no how to git him to stop. Plse help.

Before Radley had time to think about what he was doing, Constable Roake stood at his desk, ready to take in the paper. Radley folded and gave it to him, and the Constable dropped it in his hat and went to the front of the room. He read through each slip of paper handed to him, addressing each student's question.

"Here's a doozy," Roake read the first slip. "Dear Constable Roake, I think my sister is stoned all the time, she has rocks in her head." The class laughed – Radley laughed with them, but he didn't hear the joke. He only mimicked the laughter as he watched Roake skim through the rest of the questions.

"Okay, here's another one," The constable continued, "Dear Constable, my dad ... dos – no, *does* – and sells durgs – drugs, excuse me. I don't know how to ... get him to stop. Plis – sorry, it's hard to read this writing – *please help*."

"Sounds like whoever wrote that is on drugs," a prep on the far end of the room blurted out, garnering more chuckles among the class.

Radley's heart frozen in his chest. He had difficulty laughing along, but mustered enough effort to do so.

Constable Roake played along with the class, reacting to their mood.

"Okay, I know you guys like to try and rattle my cage, I've seen it all before." The Constable smirked. "But I take every question seriously, okay? And this question deals with some serious stuff. Now, if any of you were in a situation like this I hope you would make an effort to get some support – either through the teen crisis line, or by contacting your–"

Radley tuned out the rest of the Constable's answer, trying to deal with the awkward mixture of disappointment and relief that stirred inside him. Staring down at the floor with his arms crossed, he pretended not to care about anything else being said in the class.

Chapter 7

"Man, the fucking waiting is what I hate the most," Dustin whispered as he slouched on the mat of damp yellow and black leaves. They were in the rural outskirts of the city, an old, abandoned mining area embedded in the Dregs hills, a site not far from the wooded area Tavis did most of his drug dumps, where Radley and Dustin helped him get rid of the overused paraphernalia and by-products from his lab that they literally dumped down a wooded slope, or buried under loose dirt. The hills had largely been overgrown by hedge grasses and pine trees, both of which lasted into the winter. The cold weather had taken its toll on the poplar trees that surrounded him and his brother. Thankfully, they weren't out here to dispose of any materials or chemicals, the ethics of which Radley struggled with; instead they were both brought out, on their father's insistence, to assist with a drug run, something Tavis had promised would be 'quick and easy' but was proving to be anything but.

"How long do we have to stay out here?" Radley asked shifting his position on the incline of the hill they hid behind. His lower back hurt from kneeling so much. He could feel the gravity pull on his ankles and knees — it wouldn't take long before they'd start to ache as well.

"I told you for the 200th time, when the deal is done," Dustin growled. "Now lie back on the hill and quit yer fuckin' whining. That's more annoying than the waitin'."

Radley sighed as he slouched down. He couldn't see what was happening on the other side of the hill where their father and Cyclo were parked in the mini-van. The two men sat silently in the vehicle, about half a kilometer away from the boys' location, awaiting the arrival of their buyers — members from an inner city gang called the Militiamen.

"How come Dad's dealin' with this new gang, anyways?" Radley asked ten minutes later, breaking the lull the boys had fallen into. "Won't the Knights get mad if they find out he's doin' business with another gang?"

"That's why we're doing this real quiet-like," Dustin said, rolling his eyes. "Besides, these guys contacted Dad, not the other way around. And from what I heard, you don't turn down the Militiamen. They're crazy, they drill holes in their enemies' heads n' stuff."

"What?" A surge of panic welled up in Radley's throat. "Why the hell is Dad doing business with these guys, then?"

"Because he doesn't want to be their enemy," Dustin said, speaking to Radley like he would a five year old. "*And* they're willing to pay a gazillion times more money than anyone else Dad's dealin' with."

"Why are *we* here then?" Radley pressed, his voice shaking. "Why do we have to hide behind this hill?"

"For the umpteenth time, we're back-up in case anything goes wrong. Dad's never dealt with these guys before. We don't know what to expect, so we gotta keep watch."

And just what are we supposed to do if something goes wrong? But didn't dare say anything as he watched his brother skirt up to the hill's summit, binoculars in hand. Dustin peered through them. The two boys had been recruited by their father to go on a shopping trip to the sports wholesaler, at least that's what Radley had been told. Along the way, Radley was informed by his father he was about to enter manhood, he was about to go on his first run with his Dad, Dustin, and Cyclo.

"And not a word to your old lady," Tavis had warned Radley. "The last thing I need is for your mother to start bitchin' to me about dealing with these French Freaks, okay?"

"Just wait till she sees the cash you'll be haulin' in," Cyclo said to Tavis from the passenger seat, punching him in the arm. "She'll be beggin' you to build a new lab and give the Militiamen their own account."

At the time, Radley had thought it would be a quick run, something he could brag he had been a part of. Instead they drove out to a heavily secluded, wooded area, not a single vehicle in sight. Tavis handed Dustin a duffel bag with the binoculars, and ordered him and Radley out of the van and down the hill where the boys lay.

"You know what to do," Tavis told his oldest son. "Now get outta here. Go!"

Forty minutes later they watched the overcast afternoon sky darken. For whatever reason, the Militiamen decided to make Tavis wait.

"Still no sign of them," Dustin said. "What's keepin' them?"

Radley slumped back on the hilltop and gazed up at the

night sky. He noticed the thin, wiry poplars. Their leaves stripped away by the elements, cold and harsh, left to fall in the damp, decayed mat that lay around them. Radley grabbed a yellow poplar leaf off of the ground. He ran his finger along its serrated edges, and attempted to brush the film of ice that covered it. It was so brittle that it came apart in layers as his skin came in contact with it. Radley remembered playing in birch leaf piles as a kid, kicking them around, jumping into them, hiding from his brother. Colourful and bendable, the leaves were his only toys whenever his parents took him on one of their fall "camp-outs." He found them fascinating. They were alive, even though they were technically dead. To Radley they represented a life cycle, all part of a larger process at work. The trees from which they had fallen looked barren and naked, but the very next year, during their spring "camp-outs," Radley saw the same trees again – budding, green, full of new, growing, green leaves and sprouting buds. He remembered pretending to swing from the tops of them, like Tarzan or Spiderman.

The sound of a vehicle jarred Radley's attention. He edged to the top of the hill next to his brother.

"Finally, about friggin' time." Dustin took a breath, then signaled to Radley. "Alright, stay low."

Radley spotted the vehicle. It was a dark-coloured SUV, and blended in with the dense bush behind it. It travelled with headlights off and parked two meters away from their father's van.

"Why do they have their lights off?" Radley panicked, the

fear a lead weight in his stomach.

"They don't want to bring any attention to this area," Dustin answered. "Now shut up and be quiet."

Two men emerged from the SUV. Radley couldn't make out their complexions, but didn't think they were white guys. Both men dressed casually, in jogging pants and T-shirts. They were both heavyset, certainly a good match for his father and Cyclo, who appeared cautious getting out of their mini-van. Tavis carried a blue duffel bag over his shoulders.

"Dad's got his dope in two bags," Dustin reported. "He always leaves one in the car until he gets his money and counts it."

Radley couldn't see with the detail Dustin could, but he heard the voices of the four men, making out the odd word from their conversation.

"Arrgh," Dustin cursed under his breath. "I told the old man these guys don't like to be screwed around with. Just give them the merch already."

Radley squinted, desperate for more information. He could tell the conversation between the two parties had escalated, and both Cyclo and a Militiamen member began shoving one another. Tavis and the other gang member stepped in to intervene. Radley could clearly hear the yelling and swearing.

"Damnit, this isn't good." Dustin dropped down the hill, tearing into his duffel bag. "Radley get down here, quick."

Radley slid down the hill, his heart hammering. The yelling continued over the summit.

"Hurry, take this." Dustin handed him a thick, black pistol

with a grooved handle and rectangular barrel. "You're gonna have to hit these guys if I can't take 'em myself."

"What? The Glock?" Radley panicked. "Uh-uh. No way. I don't want that."

"Radley!" Dustin hissed. "We talked about this. You gotta use it! Just like Dad showed you at the range!"

"That was supposed to be to protect you or mom." Radley shook his head, backing away. "I'm not shooting anybody for real!"

"Radley, you little fuck, this is for protection!" Dustin's eyes grew wide, his voice a harsh whisper. "If Dad, Cyclo and I can't take those guys, you gotta do it. Now take the fucking gun! What the hell's the matter with you?!"

"I'm not taking it." Radley turned away from his brother, refusing to look him in the eye. "I didn't want to go on this stupid run in the first place!"

"It's a last resort, you idiot!" Dustin said. "If those guys beat the three of us, do you think they'll stop there? They'll gut us like pigs, and string us up in the trees, then they'll come after you!"

Radley stared at Dustin, and his wild, vicious eyes. There was something in his brother he had never seen before. A desperate ferocity that scared Radley to death.

"We're going on runs like this in the future," Dustin warned his brother. "Some of these guys Dad is dealin' with are ten times worse than the *Rouge* and the Knights combined! You gotta shape up and grow a set of balls, Radley. Like it or not, this is our life now, and Dad needs us to do the job."

Radley read between the lines. "Fine, give me the gun." He took the Glock. "Are you still gonna charge those guys?"

"I have to." Dustin's anger rekindled. "That's the plan. I help Dad and Cyclo fight those guys. Use the Tazer if I have to. If we don't take 'em, you gotta come out with that gun blazing."

"No," Radley said, tucking the gun behind him "I won't do it."

"Fuck, Radley!" Dustin spat. "Do you want us all dead?! Give me that fucking gun."

"No," Radley replied, his voice leaping out of his chest. "I'm not letting you kill anybody either."

"You fucking moron!" Dustin lunged at his brother, and tore into him, pelting Radley with punches. Radley turtled over the gun, refusing to let Dustin get at it, letting himself get pummeled with painful blows to his head and upper arm.

"You fucking imbecile!" Dustin foamed at the mouth – Radley couldn't tell anymore if his older brother whispered or not. He started burying the Glock into the dirt to prevent Dustin's vice-like grip from prying it out of his hands.

"Boys!" A voice called out above them. "What the hell are you two dipshits doing?!"

Dustin and Radley both shot up in a fit of panic to see Cyclo peering over the top of the hill where they were hidden – an angry, perplexed look covered his face. Both boys were too stunned to speak.

"Come on, let's go! The *Militiamen* are gone. Get your asses to the van!" Cyclo spoke, the agitation in his voice was obvious. "Your Dad and I are waiting! I thought you two were getting mauled by a friggin' grizzly bear with all the noise you were making!"

"I almost left you on the fucking hill," Tavis chastised his two boys as they entered the back of the van. Sitting on the driver's side, he was sorting a pile of cash from a burlap bag on his lap. He glared at them through the rear-view mirror. "What were you two fucktards doing out there?"

"Fighting, like two little girls," Cyclo said as he hopped into the passenger seat.

"It wasn't my fault," Dustin said, his voice pouty. "Radley wussed out on the plan. Don't bring him on any more runs, he can't handle it!"

"Well, it's a good thing you didn't carry it out," Tavis shot back. "If you'd been paying attention, you'd of seen us go back to the van with our money."

"We thought Cyclo was going to fight that guy," Dustin said. "You were pushing and shoving with them. I thought they were going to jump you guys."

Cyclo turned in the passenger seat. "They might of, but changed their minds." He flexed a bicep at the two boys, then winked at Radley.

"It's a good thing we brought Radley," Cyclo continued, speaking to Tavis. "If we'd a let Dustin run the show he'd a shot those two guys, started a gang war between the *Militiamen* and the *Knights,* and put us on the run from every cop, crook, and crony from here to Timbuktu."

"I'm frickin' serious," Dustin shouted. "You can't bring Radley anymore! He's got no guts! He'll get us all killed!"

"Oh, shut yer yap." Tavis threw the burlap sack into Dustin's face, sending him back in his seat. "Show your old man how high you can count."

Dustin immediately opened the sack and pulled out a handful of brown bills. "Hundreds?" His voice dropped. "Holy crap, how much money did you pull in?" He started counting. Radley couldn't help but stare at the cash in front of him. He'd never seen so much.

"Twenty grand." Tavis smiled. "Jackpot boys. Can your old man do business or what?"

"I told ya that ya should be dealin' with those guys." Cyclo looked smug.

"Aren't the Knights going to find out?" Radley blurted. "Won't they be mad?"

The question dampened the excitement. Tavis and Cyclo glanced at each other. Dustin groaned, a pile of ruffled cash strewn about his lap.

"See what I mean." Dustin groaned. "The kid's a paranoid freak. He's too scared to do this stuff."

Tavis started the vehicle and looked into the mirror at his youngest son. "Rad, buddy, Dad appreciates everything you did tonight, okay? I'm gonna get you boys something cool with this money."

"He's not ready to do this, Dad—"

"Dustin, SHUT the hell up!" Tavis said, then turned back to Radley, his voice returned to a soft, encouraging tone. "Radley, Dad needs you now, okay? We're gonna toughen you up. Cyclo and I gotta do more runs like this in the future, and we need you and Dustin as back up, alright, partner? Don't worry about anything – not the Knights, the *Rouge,* the cops, or anyone. I'm gonna show you again how to use the guns and the Tazer, and you'll see that everything we do will be exactly like tonight. You won't ever have to shoot or zap anybody, but you'll know how to just in case, kay, bud?"

"Okay," Radley said. It was the only answer he could give. He slumped into his seat.

"Good man." Tavis pulled out into the makeshift trail that led into the wooded abyss. "And remember boys, not a word of this–"

"–to our mother," Dustin finished for him, still sifting through the cash. "Yeah, we know. She'll want to blow it on coke or something."

"Don't be a smart-ass." Tavis looked dismayed. "I don't want her knowing we did this deal, period. Especially now that Radley's joined us."

The van was quiet until they scuttled on to the highway, heading back home.

"Okay Dust, put the money away." Tavis glared at his son. "Stuff it under the seat."

Dustin had sorted the money into piles along the backseat. He didn't appear to be counting it. Instead, it was more like he was enthralled, playing with the bills like they were individual toys. Radley wasn't sure if Dustin could count that much money.

"Man, this is awesome," Dustin spoke in a soft tone, mixed with awe and excitement – nothing like the way he had spoken to Radley an hour earlier.

"Yeah, well, it won't be so awesome if the cops pull us over and ask why you're sitting there with twenty grand on your lap," Cyclo said. "Now listen to your old man, and put it the hell away."

Radley slouched back in his seat and watched his brother stuff the cash back into the sack. He could feel the bruising form on his arms, shoulders, and upper back where Dustin had battered him. Looking out the window to his right, he stared at the withered poplars racing by in the dark. They stood like watchmen along the highway, their empty and prickly branches pointing upward into the open night's sky, begging for the warmth of spring to bring them back to life. As he watched them, Radley thought about the single, solitary leaf that had crumpled to pieces in his right hand. Its dark stain still ingrained in his fingertips.

Chapter 8

"Like it or not, this is our life now." Dustin's words, spoken a full week earlier, burned Radley's mind like a brand. *"And Dad needs us to do the job."*

There was no question as to what "the job" entailed. Shooting someone. Preventing his father, Cyclo, or Dustin from being killed.

Is it all worth it? His father promised to buy the boys a brand new, big screen TV and entertainment system, but said he needed to wait awhile to do so. He and Dustin got some handheld video games to hold them over. Radley hadn't even taken his out of the box. He didn't want to.

Constable Roake entered the classroom. He was a few minutes late and apologized to the class. His health teacher wasn't worried – she let the kids chit-chat while they waited. Radley tuned everyone else out, slumped in his desk in the far row against the wall. Roake announced it would be his last visit. He made some joke about there being a final exam, but he had forgotten it in his car. Some kids laughed. Radley pretended to. The rest of the Constable's talk had something to do about drugs and alcohol and adulthood. It was all a blur.

"Okay, question time," Roake held out his hat. "I don't want to hear any more questions about 'my grandma's weed garden' or 'how many stoners does it take to screw in a lightbulb?' Serious questions today, okay guys?"

Roake walked around the room with his cap, letting the kids drop their paper in. Radley crumpled his blank slip and stuffed it into his jacket pocket. Leaning against the bulletin board behind him, he removed a folded paper from the back pocket of his jeans. Compelled by the need to check it over, to make sure it was the very note he was going to give the Constable, Radley glossed over it again, rereading the carefully printed sentences he'd written:

Dear Constable,

My dad is Cabana he sells crystal meth, coke, and high qulety crack and sometimes heroen. He oprates frum the basmint of are house he runs for the Milta men and nites His drug runs are threw Lonys Bakry and the pickup points are at Barlow's Cliff out in the Flats his next one will be at the Flats Saturday night with the nites Ples dont tell my dad i wrote this letter. i just want to protct him and my mother and brother frum getting hurt but i know they will hat me if they new i told yo this stuff.

When the Constable came to his desk, Radley refolded the note and dropped it into the hat. The Constable walked to the front of the room, mixed the papers and cracked some more jokes before reading about three or four questions. There were some funny ones, some that he took seriously, but the mood and atmosphere was playful.

Then the Constable read Radley's question. He jolted a bit, his eyes shot up, and he started scanning the room. His eyes met Radley's, who dropped his head. The Constable looked like he'd swallowed a watermelon.

"Okay, more silly stuff, don't have to read that," the Constable said, laying the note face down on the table. He closed his talk by answering a couple more questions, but he seemed distracted. Roake watched Radley leave the room at the period's end, but didn't say anything to him – Radley knew the officer couldn't because the questions were supposed to be anonymous. That fact did little to stop Radley's heart from racing like a stock car. He appeared to have gotten what he wanted – the Constable's full-fledged attention. Whether or not the man would do anything about it was another matter entirely.

Three days later, Radley sat on their messy living room floor, watching television. Since the *Rouge* attack three weeks earlier, their house went into a nosedive in terms of messiness. Baseball bats, dirty hoodies, jackets, marijuana magazines, and fast food take-out containers laid strewn about the living room and kitchen. Even his parents' meth bong sat on the kitchen table, and they had always made sure their paraphernalia was never out in the open.

The room reeked of meth and marijuana smoke. A small 13

inch TV sat on top of their cracked big screen, a torrid reminder of the assault on his father. The family picture of his Dad, Mom, Dustin, and him at Windbender Valley sat out of its frame, propped up against the only photograph that didn't get smashed in the *Rouge* attack — his mother's black-and-white picture of the Styrofoam cup on the barbed wire fence post. At least Cyclo was kind enough to lend the boys the smaller TV, which was annoying, but better than nothing. Radley looked behind at his mother, who'd fallen asleep on the couch a second time.

"Mom, you awake?" Radley crawled on his knees over to the couch to jab his mother in the ribs. She lay, her eyes shut — humming softly, but stopped, prompting Radley to check on her. "Come on, Mom!"

"What?" His mother stirred, the smell of speed on her breath and oozing from her skin. "Fuck off, Radley."

"Mom, you and Dad told me to keep an eye on you," Radley said. "Make sure you didn't fall asleep. You're spun out."

"Is you father home?" his mother asked. "Are the bunnies home?"

"Who?" Radley replied, not surprised by the bizarre question. His mother had smoked meth — typical for her on a Saturday night, though he was starting to worry. Meth was definitely stronger than the cocaine or weed she typically used. Radley was supposed to go on a run with his father, Cyclo, and Dustin, but managed to convince his dad he should stay at home and watch over his mother, who'd been using since the early afternoon.

"Make sure she stays on the couch," Tavis said after assessing her condition. "Don't let her walk around or she'll go fucking AWOL."

"Hum, with me Radley." She started humming softly. When he was a child, Radley's mother had taken his hand and hummed with him. Such memories were few and far between.

"Hum, Radley baby," Carla asked again. "Hum with the bunnies."

Radley held her hand to humour her – part of him thought she might even think he was four years old again, hence her bunny comments. He wanted to pull away from her – the problem was he didn't know how she'd react. He took confidence in her dazed, dopey expression – confidence that the humming would soon lull her into a trance, and Radley could go back to watching TV.

"Hmmmm-Hmmmm." Radley tried to keep sync with her. He craned his head toward the TV to watch a clip from Saturday Night Live.

The battering ram barreled through the front door, knocking it completely off its hinges – Radley's worst nightmare renewed. The sound speared him through the heart.

"Freeze, police!" The TAC Team stormed the house and spread into the living room in seconds. "On the floor! Hands on your head! Both of you!"

All Radley saw were four helmets, the transparent plastic of two face-shields, and the barrel of a gun before he dove to the floor, his hands over the back of his head.

"Lady! On the floor! Now!" The officer shouted.

"Those damn bunnies are back, cutting holes in my roof. Fucking rabbits!" Carla screamed. She shot up from the couch.

"Lady get down!" The officer repeated, holding his gun up. "I'm warning you!"

"Please don't shoot her, she's high on meth!" Radley screamed, trying to raise his head up but not provoke the officers.

"Hold up, hold up," one of the officers said. "Grab her, she's unarmed." Radley kept his head down as one of the officers wrestled her to the ground. Radley burst into tears on the floor.

"Fucking rabbits!" His mother screamed again as she fought with the officers, kicking the clothes and garbage that had been left strewn about the floor. As they pinned her down, her voice fell, and she started to sob. "Please don't hurt my bunnies. Please."

"Your husband's been arrested, lady — we're here for his drug lab," an officer said.

"It's alright, Radley, you're going to be okay," another officer, who knelt next to him, said through his helmet and face shield. The voice sounded awfully familiar.

Part II

Chapter 9

Nine Years Later - Age 23

"Are you ready for this?" His foster mother, Diane, asked.

Radley took the duffel bag and threw it over his shoulder. "Yes, for the umpteenth time." He rolled his eyes at the overprotective guardian.

"You know where I'm coming from," she replied, forcing him into her arms for a hug. Her head just touched the bottom of Radley's burley chest. He could smell the jasmine scent of her short, silver hair – she was so unlike his birth mother. "You don't have a good track record with family reunions."

"I know," Radley said. "But it'll be different this time. My brother, he's married with a family. I got along with him, for the most part. I think he's cleaned up his act."

"Your father told you the same thing." Diane gave him a skeptical look. He hated it when she looked at him that way. She could sense he wasn't sure what to expect. Ever since he became part of their family, Diane Trillamede understood Radley – his fears, anxieties, what made him angry, upset. She and her husband, Doug, were the best foster parents Radley could have asked for. Warm, free-spirited souls, tough when they needed to be, and committed to welcoming Radley into their home, providing him with the rules, structure, and the safe environment he so badly yearned for. Diane was a counsellor and academic advisor while Doug taught English Literature – both worked at the city's university and couldn't have been anymore different than Radley's biological parents.

"Yeah, yeah, you're right – as usual," Radley said. His birth father had indeed told him the same thing, a year ago, when Radley mustered up the courage to contact him. Serving a twenty-year sentence for drug trafficking and selling to minors, Tavis Wycliffe had been moved to a minimum security prison on account of good behaviour, and permitted visitors under controlled conditions. Every Christmas and the occasional birthday he sent a letter to Radley, asking forgiveness and pleading for a visit. The first few years, Radley's foster parents and social worker both forbade him from doing so, and Radley complied.

After his first year in foster care, Radley wanted nothing to do with his birth family, coveting only the fresh start he was getting with the Trillamedes. Once he became accustomed to his new life, Radley revamped his entire history. For his final year of high school, he went by "Radley Trillamede" and severed all contact with his Wycliffe relatives.

Within the past two years, however, his attitude changed. Whether he became more forgiving or sentimental in his adulthood, he couldn't say, but he responded to one of his father's letters and agreed to meet with him. He was encouraged by the news that Tavis had become a reformed Christian. The two corresponded for about three months before Radley decided, one fall afternoon, to pay his father a visit. He hadn't seen the man since Tavis was officially charged in court, eight years ago, and deemed an unfit parent whose presence presented a danger to his two children. Tavis went berserk in the courtroom, and threatened to cut the throats of the judge and crown prosecutor and had to be restrained by three bailiffs, earning him contempt-of-court and uttering-threats charges which tacked on another two years to his sentence.

The Trillamedes supported Radley's decision to meet with Tavis, and offered to accompany him. Radley declined. The meeting with his father began formally and friendly – Tavis even got teary eyed upon seeing Radley. He proclaimed he was drug free, and looked forward to building a new relationship with his "long, lost son." It went so well that Radley visited his father a second, third, and fourth time, enjoying a new found perspective on the man he knew so little about growing up.

Then came the fifth meeting, and everything went to hell.

"Radley, buddy," Tavis whispered through the glass a week before Christmas. "I need you to do something for me, son."

"Yeah, sure Dad, what is it?" Radley replied. He wanted to do something for him; Christmas was in two weeks.

"There's a package in the north end of the city I need you to pick up." Tavis' voice dulled to a whisper. "It's got stuff in it, you know, merchandise for a wood-carving business I'm gonna start once I get outta this place. I need you to pick it up for me, 'kay? I'm in a bind on how to get it."

"Sure," Radley said. "Do you want me to bring it to you

here in the prison? Am I allowed to do that?"

"Oh God, no," Tavis replied. "I need you to bring it to Cyclo, you remember Cyclo, right?"

"Of course I remember Cyclo." Radley's voice stiffened. "He's out now?"

"Yeah, yeah, he's out." Tavis seemed pleased. "He's been out almost two years. He served his time, you know?"

"Right, okay," Radley said, recalling how the sentencing went. They arrested Cyclo as an accomplice, but Tavis refused to turn him in, taking the fall for the entire operation. Cyclo's sentence was considerably shorter – a fair deal, Radley knew, because his father had done all of the manufacturing on his own. "But why do I gotta bring the package to him? *I'll* keep it for you."

"No, leave it with Cyclo," Tavis said. "I don't want you getting caught with it."

"If it's wood-carving tools, what's the big deal?"

"Keep your voice down, son." Tavis' voice dropped to a whisper. "It's business merchandise. Let's just leave it at that, alright?"

"Well, where is this place that you want me to go to?"

"Ruzzo's Pasta Factory. It's the old Loney's Bakery. Remember when I used to take you boys there as kids–"

"Forget it, I'm done!" Radley slammed his hand on the table and stood up.

"Radley, wait a minute!" Tavis yelled at his son. "No, wait! Let me explain. It's not what you think. Radley! Where are you going?"

"I'm done," Radley repeated, leaving the room and not looking back, not ever again.

Radley walked down the lane, duffel bag over his shoulder. A row of weeping birch trees ran along both sides of the road, shading the street from the Western sun.

Tarzan, Radley thought as he looked up at the yellow, drooping flowers and imagined himself swinging from the lively, curved branches that just begged to be swung from. *My favorite part of those camping trips.* Radley shook his head and smirked at the memory, albeit a painful one.

It doesn't matter anymore. The present mattered, and that was what he wanted to focus on.

Dustin's place was easy to find – an older, one-level, beige stucco house with a separate, doublewide garage that started in the middle of the driveway and extended to the end of the lot. All of the windows and the large, bay door of the garage stood open. A red Ford Escort sat in the left side of the garage, while the right sat empty. No one was inside.

The driveway led to a small, covered porch on the left side of the house. Radley entered and rang the doorbell. A heavy-set woman with shoulder-length sandy hair and round glasses answered.

"Hello, Radley." Jezzelle smiled. A little girl, six years old, with long, auburn hair and a lace headband peeked around her mother's hip. Jezzelle placed a hand behind the girl and gently stroked her hair. "Abigail, you remember Uncle Radley, don't you Sweets?"

The girl instantly retreated behind her mother's arm, glaring at Radley cautiously. Radley laughed – the girl's unmistakable eyes reminded him so much of her father.

"Silly monkey." Jezzelle scooped up her daughter. "We've been waiting for Uncle Radley, haven't we? Come on in. Your brother's just washing up."

"Hell, never mind I'm right here." A hulking figure charged through the porch and tackled Radley in the midsection. Before Radley even had a chance to resist, Dustin scooped him off his feet and twirled him around, similar to the way Dustin did when they were young.

Dustin set Radley down and gave his younger brother a noogie. As always, Radley could do little to resist – his older brother had always been more powerful. But Radley relished it today because – from Dustin – it was playful and done in affection.

"Welcome, brother." Dustin knuckled his head once more. "Welcome to my home."

Chapter 10

Jezzelle made an excellent supper: chili, bread, salad. "Nothing to shake a stick at," as Radley's foster dad was fond of saying.

Radley talked to everyone for three hours at the dinner table, reminiscing with Dustin about times past, catching up on the last eight years, and having a staring contest with young Abigail. Radley had only been around his brother three times in the past eight years – the first time, four years ago, for a reunion at a local A & W. Dustin had got a hold of Radley through social services and wanted to introduce him to his girlfriend and their new baby girl. Radley had been so shocked to hear the news he absolutely had to meet with Dustin – the Trillamedes agreed to take Radley to the restaurant and sat with him at the table.

The second meeting occurred last year, when Radley was invited to Dustin and Jezzelle's wedding. He decided to go alone, and thoroughly enjoyed himself. It was after a long hug in the receiving line, and again during the dance in the evening, that Dustin invited Radley to stay with him some time.

"I'm glad you took me up on the offer, kid," Dustin said to his brother. "There's so much to get caught up on."

"Yeah." Radley eyed Abigail once more, making her laugh. Though his niece was finally starting to warm up to him, Radley had a difficult time warming up to his brother. Dustin now sported bulging muscles, a plethora of tattoos on his shoulders and arms, and a Van Dyke that gave him the look of an adult. His gravelly voice sounded deeper now, but retained the rough edge that reminded Radley of their childhood.

"I'm not on any fixed schedule," Radley continued. "I can stay so long as I'm not in the way."

"You're not in the way, man." Dustin shook his head. "Stay as long as you like."

"You're not working?" Jezzelle asked. "I mean, you say you're not on any schedule?"

Radley smirked, realizing he just set himself up for the very same questions that the Trillamede's constantly barraged him about. "No, I'm not working right now. You could say I'm between jobs. I have no freaking clue what I want to do with my life."

"Uncle Radley, spin me again," Abigail shouted in the living room. She clung onto Radley's legs like a leech.

"Oh, it's that pesky mouse again." Radley flipped Abigail upside down. Grabbing her hips, he spun around like a top, whisking her through the air. Her excited screams pierced through the house.

"Abigail, quiet!" Jezzelle chastised her daughter from the kitchen. "You're going to blow everyone's ears out!"

Over the past two days, Radley became Abigail's instant favourite uncle. They played board games, dress-up dolls, and the mouse-spin game, which they invented together. *She's adorable.* Pride welled up in him for his brother having such a nice family. Unlike Radley, Dustin refused to live in a foster home, and lasted less than a month in the two he was forced into, before finally living in the unfinished basement of their older cousin Galen's flat. Radley wasn't surprised by any of that – Dustin had never bothered with rules much. Dustin finally lived on his own when he turned eighteen and got a job in a mechanic's shop. Less than a year later, he met Jezzelle, the daughter of his boss, and six months after that, got her pregnant.

Jezzelle stepped outside, leaving Radley with Abigail. Radley imagined what must have been going through Dustin's mind when he found out he was going to be a Dad. *Ya stuck it out, Dust. You stayed with Jezzelle and became a family man. Good on ya, bro.*

"Radley, Dustin wanted me to ask if you could give him a hand in the garage?" Jezzelle asked upon returning a few minutes later. "He needs help with a jack or something."

Radley headed to the garage. Dustin had done quite well for himself, having become an auto-body technician. Apart from his regular job, Dustin had a small part-time business refurbishing cars, old and new, which he did out of his garage. He and his father-in-law put up the garage over the course of one summer – Jezzelle's dad wanted a place to store his RV for the winter, but added the extra space to support Dustin's business.

Knowing little about mechanics, and even less about body work, Radley spent the day with Abigail instead, and it was a nice change to get outside. Dustin had been bugging Radley to help him in the garage, and learn about cars.

"Here I am," Radley said as he walked into the bay. The doors and quarter panels of a gray car Radley couldn't tell the make of leaned against the garage wall. The hulled out car reminded Radley of a skeleton.

"Hey buddy," Dustin rose up from the right side of the vehicle. "I need help propping up this car's ass end."

Radley helped move the jack to the car's rear, something he was sure Dustin had done hundreds of times before. He suspected it was a ploy to finally get Radley alone in the garage, but he didn't mind. Fascinated, he watched his brother work – Dustin had become proficient with cars and body detail. It was so unlike the Dustin he had grown up with – that boy was angry, bitter, focused only on drugs and being the tough guy. This Dustin seemed under control, poised, a true *craftsman*.

The boys worked for two hours, replacing the old panels on the car with a similar, but more stylish, set. After supper, they began work on the other car delivered that morning – a gray Honda Civic. They needed to sand the entire car and prep it for a repaint.

"Why would somebody want to repaint this?" Radley asked. Apart from some minor rock chips, the car appeared to be as good as new.

"Big city money." Dustin shrugged. "Some people need to change their car colour like their underwear. That's the way big city people are, you know."

By the end of the day, the sanding was half complete. Radley's arms ached from the work — he couldn't believe how meticulous auto-sanding could be, everything had to be smoothed to the bare metal in order for the new paint to hold, but he enjoyed the time with his brother. With the half-stripped Civic in front of them, the two sat on an empty work shelf in the garage, drinking the beer Jezzelle brought for them. It didn't take long for the inevitable discussion Radley had braced himself for all week — the discussion that compelled Radley to visit his brother.

"So, you see much of Dad lately?" Dustin asked, sipping his beer.

"Yeah," Radley nodded. The adrenaline surged into his chest, his heart racing, as his guilt came to the fore. He had no idea if Dustin knew Radley had turned them in. "I saw him a month back."

"Did he ask you to go to the 'Pasta Factory'?" The question surprised Radley.

"Yeah. He asked you too?"

"Oh yeah." Dustin chuckled to himself. "Told me he was clean, and was getting his life back together, then drops the bomb. Friggin' loser." He shook his head in disgust.

"I feel bad he got caught," Radley answered, sipping his beer slowly. He knew he was treading on dangerous territory, but he needed to have this conversation. "But maybe it was for the best, you know."

"Aw, he had it comin'," Dustin said with a snort. "If the cops didn't get him, the Knights or the Militiamen would have."

Radley held his breath. "So, do you think it was for the best? That Dad got caught, I mean?"

Dustin shrugged his shoulders, "I honestly don't care anymore. Things turned out okay for me. Looks like they turned out okay for you. Maybe not for Mom, but she's so fried now, she doesn't know which end is up anymore." Dustin stared at the wall as he spoke. He guzzled the rest of his beer.

Radley tried goading his brother once more. This time, he pushed the envelope further. "I remember the day they arrested Dad. That was scary, cops bursting into the house."

"No doubt." Dustin took a swig of his beer. "I was actually with him when he got busted. We were doing a run with Cyclo, and the two Knights we thought we were dealing with turned out to be undercover cops. Dad walked right into that one."

"So …" Radley chose his words carefully. "That's how Dad got busted? The cops were undercover?"

"Yeah." Dustin looked surprised. "Didn't you know that? Well, I guess not, since protective services sheltered you up pretty good. I wasn't so lucky. The cops grilled me for the trial proceedings, since I was with him when he got caught."

And with those words, Radley had been given the answer he waited for eight years to receive. Neither Tavis nor Dustin had any idea what Radley had done. There'd been enough hard evidence to convict Tavis – the prosecution never needed statements from Radley, nor any explanation of why he wrote the letter. Child Protective Services simply wanted Radley out of the picture, safe in the foster home the Trillamedes provided for him. But in the back of Radley's mind, his split-second decision to hand his letter to Constable Roake gnawed at him. In that one instant in Health 9, he condemned his father to prison, sent his mother to drug rehab, where she remained to this day, and brought about a complete transformation in his life and his brother's. This visit to Dustin was as much a journey of penance for Radley as it was a chance to reconnect with his brother.

Well, I guess I got away with that one. If I play my cards right, my family will never know what really happened. And even if they did, Dustin just told me things turned out okay for him. Who gives a crap what Tavis and Carla think? I don't.

"Things turned out well for me, too," Radley said. "Life's been good with Doug and Diane. They've been great."

"That's good, kid," Dustin said, slapping Radley on the knee. "I'm glad. And you know what? Maybe it was a good thing for both of us that the old man got arrested. If he didn't, who knows? We'd probably be sitting alongside him in the slammer, busted for doing drug runs with the old bastard. Either that or we'd be spun-out potheads, livin' with our mother and ten other fried-out whackos in some cult compound somewhere."

"For sure," Radley said, smirking. *There, see? Dustin's okay — his words just proved it. He's okay because I wrote that letter and got our father arrested before he turned Dustin into a drug dealer.*

Radley leaned back on the shelf, allowing himself a sense of ease. This had been a weight on his psyche, an agonizing heaviness that had haunted him the past eight years and bogged him down. It was this very uncertainty that compelled him to visit, to get this very moment. He closed his eyes and savoured it, feeling the guilt and angst dissipate from his body.

Okay stop it. Focus on your brother, the here and now. The letter is not important anymore. It's over. Move on. He repressed the sudden concoction of elation, vindication and relief that he felt, and forced himself to sit quietly as he and his brother finished their beer.

Dustin stood up and let out a loud belch. "Well, I guess we better clean up all this paint dust." He grabbed a broom and started sweeping the garage floor.

"Right behind ya, bro." Radley bolted up and grabbed a dust pan and garbage bag.

Chapter 11

Radley decided to stay with his brother for an extra month – a decision the Trillamedes were happy to support. Dustin found Radley some casual work at the auto body shop, doing janitorial duties and assisting the technicians on various jobs. For the first time in his life, Radley felt like he had some meaning, a purpose. In the evenings, he helped Dustin in the garage, refurbishing cars for clients. He also enjoyed spending time with Abigail – the girl adored him, and her bedtime routine included Uncle Radley reading her a princess story from her Disney anthology.

It was the acceptance he felt with Dustin and his family that kept Radley at their home for so long. Dustin's boss even hinted there may be a part-time opening in the fall for Radley, with the intent he go to school in an auto-repair field. To Radley's surprise, Dustin and Jezzelle insisted that if he pursued such a course, he would be welcome to stay with them for the upcoming year. The offer was mind boggling – growing up, Radley wasn't accustomed to such favor from his brother, but now that he received it, he reveled in it.

His desire to impress Dustin heightened when he assisted him in the garage. Radley didn't see him much during the workday, so at night he volunteered to help his brother. He became an employee of Dustin's, though he never expected any pay. "Staying at your house rent-free is enough," Radley told him.

Radley learned a great deal about body mechanics this way, though Dustin never talked much about the intricacies of his business. Radley assumed Jezzelle helped him with the bookkeeping, but when Radley asked her one evening in private, Jezzelle said she had nothing to do with it.

"The side business, the cars and the repainting, that's Dustin's thing," she replied while washing the dishes; he dried. "He makes good money at it, I guess. That's his money, so he tells me. I think most of it's under the table – he has the guys pay him cash. We do claim some of it at tax time, just to stay honest, you know."

"Makes sense," Radley said.

"Your brother, he's a good provider for his family," Jezzelle said. "He's doesn't drink that much, doesn't do drugs. He works hard to make an honest living."

"He definitely doesn't get that from our father," Radley said. "The only thing our dad worked hard at was doing drugs. My mother usually had to pry him off of the couch to get him to go to his day job."

"So I've heard," Jezzelle said. "Dustin told me stories about your mother waking your father to go to work. You both carry the scars of those days, don't you?"

"We do." Radley nodded. The memories of those nights bothered him as much today as they did when he was younger.

As Radley continued to work for his brother, he noticed on

three occasions, the same individual, a Chinese man with a red sword tattoo, brought in three different vehicles – a Sonata, a Tempest, and an older Ford Bronco.

"How many cars does that guy have?" Radley asked Dustin after he brought in the Tempest. "He must be loaded."

"No, he's with the downtown dealership," Dustin said. "He's their runner boy. He brings in the vehicles and the work orders for me."

Dustin's clientele also included car dealers, who brought in used cars for him to refurbish, so they could sell them at a higher price. The dealers seemed like amicable fellows – Dustin insisted he meet with the dealers personally, even coming home early to be there. On his days off, Radley offered to be home for the delivery, but Dustin wouldn't hear of it.

"The paperwork is complicated," Dustin explained.

"Well, you can show me what to do," Radley said, "that way you don't have to cut shifts."

"I said no, Radley. I'll do it." Dustin was still very good at speaking with a finality that Radley dared not challenge.

That left Radley to work alongside his brother in the shop, ready to learn and eager to please. An older SUV had come in from a dealer the evening previous, and Dustin was asked to modernize the vehicle to include the newer sleek, streamlined panels, leather seating, and DVD wiring that would give the vehicle a more 'futuristic' feel.

"How do you make-up the cost of the parts?" Radley asked. He watched the special parts Dustin had brought in from the industrial sector of the city and started doing the math behind the merchandise Dustin picked up. It was a significant cost.

"It all comes back to me in the final sale, partner." Dustin winked to his brother.

Radley surveyed the vehicle – an older model SUV, still fairly reputable on the market as one of the more fuel efficient in its class. He had a hard time seeing the potential in giving it a face-lift. As for the prospective buyers, Radley couldn't imagine how the dealers would market a souped-up, used SUV.

The framing job went fairly well, covering two full days – Dustin even let Radley take the lead in pulling off the side paneling and replacing it with the sleeker design. The wiring job proved to be more complicated – Radley watched his brother closely but found it hard to follow. As Dustin fed a wire from the engine block into the cab, Radley hopped into the passenger seat to pull it through, but it wasn't coming.

"I don't see it," Radley said, feeling underneath the front carpet.

"Reach upward, behind the glove box," Dustin stated.

Radley still couldn't find the wire, and knew his brother's patience would soon wear thin. He couldn't reach behind the glove box – out of sheer desperation, he opened the glove compartment to see if there was an opening at the back.

"Whoa," Radley exclaimed when a stack of booklets, maps, papers, and an assortment of Chap Stick sprung out in front of him. "Hey, Dust, this glove box is full."

"What the hell?" replied Dustin angrily, "You gotta be

kidding me."

"No." Radley looked through the glove box. He pulled out vehicle insurance papers for a "Ron & Rose Pittman," registration papers, a couple of old photographs of what appeared to be a family vacation, and a ticket to a Kidsfest to be held next week.

"Hey, this stuff is important," Radley said, as Dustin came around to look. "There's addresses and phone numbers on these papers – I can give these people a call, let them know we have their stuff."

"No, let me take it," Dustin said, "I need to double-check the paperwork on this vehicle. The guys from the dealership … they're supposed to check this stuff before they bring the vehicle in. This … may not be for the dealership – it might be a private job. I'll review my records. Sometimes my jobs get mixed up. Happens every now and then."

"Yeah, well, I can give those guys a call for you, if you need," Radley offered.

"I'll see." Dustin looked annoyed, but left it at that.

That night, Radley finished sweeping out the shop. Dustin went in early to shower. Radley trotted up the stairs but was greeted by Jezzelle at the patio doors. She held a Styrofoam bowl filled with a brown, bubbly fluid in it.

"Radley, I'm putting you in charge of throwing out Abigail's 'worm stew.' It's starting to stink."

Radley laughed. He read the story 'Worm Stew' to her the evening prior, then the two of them made a worm stew for fun, gathering ingredients from around the house, and digging out the worms from Jezzelle's front flower beds.

He brought the stew to their plastic dumpster at the side of the garage. A couple of household bags and two smaller shop bags were in the bin. Not chancing the smell of the household garbage, Radley opened one of the shop bags and was surprised how light it felt. Most of it was paper, ripped into bite-sized pieces mixed in with grinder pads, grease rags, and rubber stripping.

But it was the colour of the paper that caught his eye. Radley took a handful and examined it closely. Blue and white paper, professional gloss, typed with numerals – Radley noticed the last name "Pittm" on one of the bits.

The insurance papers from earlier this evening. Dustin had ripped them up, thrown them away. Why?

Radley went through a number of possible reasons in his head. There had to be some legitimate reason his brother would do such a thing, but he didn't know what. He knew he better not quiz Dustin on it. Instead, Radley collected a small handful of the papers, and stuffed them into his pocket. It just felt like the best thing to do, but deep down, he couldn't ignore the sinking feeling in his heart.

Chapter 12

Radley kept the papers hidden in the bottom drawer of his room. Over the course of the next two weeks, he debated trying to contact the Pittmans or the dealership, but decided not to go there. Dustin must have had a legitimate reason for destroying those documents. In all likelihood, he made some sort of error with his original work order. The van was ultimately refurbished and brought back to the dealership, where Radley assumed it would be resold. He forced himself to have faith that Dustin knew what he was doing – his brother rebuilt his life, in spite of all the turmoil they had been through as kids, and that was inspiring to him. Radley's faith would last the full two weeks, until the two suits walked into the garage.

"Can I help you guys?" Radley asked. He was sweeping out the garage for the evening – the only job sat in the right bay, a Mustang that needed minor work from a fender bender. Dustin decided to take the evening off so he and Jezzelle could bring Abigail to a cartoon at the theatre – Radley had offered to sweep out the garage so Dustin could shower. Jezzelle took Abigail to the park to curb her impatience.

"Sorry, can I help you?" Radley repeated when the men didn't answer the first question. He assumed they were customers, about to show him a dented convertible or a new Cadillac needing a paint job. Instead, the one man stared at Radley with disappointed eyes while the other glowered at him. *The sympathizer and the destroyer* — Radley remembered those same looks so many years ago — from the scar-face man and the lunatic named Chain — both men stared at his father the same way. *The Devil's Minions.*

The events of that horrid night had been scorched into his memory, and once again brought to the fore by the presence of these two thugs. Both men stood before him with those callous expressions, that threatening demeanor, and it was then Radley knew exactly what his brother was doing. He had fought with himself to deny it, to rationalize it, but at that moment, he *knew*.

"Dustin, Dustin, Dustin," the first man spoke. He was short, stocky, with a dirty blond crew cut and five o'clock shadow to match his sandy suit. "I don't like to beat around the bush when I do business, especially with a talented guy like you, so I'm going to state this very clearly. You been screwing us around, pal. Cuttin' some corners on your jobs, taking some liberties with the work orders, beefing up your share of our profits."

Radley took a step back as the two men walked toward him. The second man was balding, heavy-set, almost too big for the grey suit he wore, and he looked like he wanted to rip Radley's head off.

I'm not Dustin. Was the first thing Radley wanted to blurt out, but didn't. He needed to stand up, be strong, if for nothing else than to confirm Dustin's role in all this.

"Yeah so," Radley said, mustering up courage he really didn't have, "take me to the Better Business Bureau then.

Their number's in the book."

The shorter man looked to his giant friend. As Radley suspected, it was the worst thing he could have said to these guys.

"Okay, so we got a tough guy, here, huh?" The shorter man's eyes turned wild. "Tough guy who likes to play games. Fine, let's play some games, then."

Like a cobra, the man shot forward and gave Radley an uppercut. Radley got his forearm up to partially block the blow, but not enough to prevent the wind from gushing out his lungs.

Dropping to his knees, Radley fought to catch his breath. The taller man stood over him, while Radley huddled into a turtle position, drooling spit onto the cement floor. It allowed him to take in air in slow breaths.

I gotta get outta here. Radley thought, and immediately crawled toward the open entranceway of the garage.

"Oh no, ya don't, ya little dickweed." The man grabbed him by the hair and rammed him up against the tool shelves, thrusting his left forearm against Radley's windpipe.

He tried to claw at the larger man's face, but the second, shorter one grabbed his hand and twisted the fingers back, causing Radley to yelp.

"The only thing that's stopping me from snapping these pretty fingers of yours is that the *Colaberro* likes your work, he likes your *technique*." The shorter man spoke centimeters away from Radley's left ear. "Now, if it was me calling the shots, and you were screwing me over, you'd be eating your fingers right now. What do ya think of that, tough guy?"

"I didn't – didn't do anything wrong," Radley said, wheezing.

"Luckily the *Colaberro* is a very forgiving man," the shorter man continued. "He figures you only cost him a couple grand. So this is just a warning. You screw him over again, we're not going to be so nice, you catch my drift?"

"Fine, just let me go." Radley struggled, trying to break free.

"Na, na, na." The shorter man tightened his grip. "You don't catch my drift. Let me spell it for ya this way – the next time I come here, it won't be you eating your fingers, it might be that pretty little girl of yours eating her fingers, hey?"

Those words ignited a rush of fury inside Radley. He pushed off against the shelf, breaking free of the shorter man's grip and struck the larger man in the jaw. Unfortunately, the two men were far more seasoned, and quickly wrestled him to the ground. They rammed his face into the cold concrete floor and pinned his arms behind his back.

"Now you're really pissin' me off," the shorter man spat into Radley's ear. "Maybe I can break –"

"Get the fuck off him!" a voice blasted through the garage, cutting off the mobster's words. Before Radley could turn his head, the larger man's weight flung off of his back. Rolling over to see the brute crash into the tool shelves, Radley watched the man clutch his mouth. Dustin had barreled into the garage, wet hair from his shower and dressed in black boxer shorts and tank top, holding a crowbar like a baseball bat, forcing the shorter gangster backward into the corner of his garage.

"Whoa, take it easy buddy." The shorter man held his hand up, no doubt sensing the crazed ferocity in Dustin. "Who the hell are you?"

"Your worst nightmare, you prick!" With lightning speed, Dustin charged forward and kicked the shorter man in the stomach, keeling him over. He brought down the crowbar hard against the back of the man's head. Radley saw blood burst from the man's nose before his face hit the concrete.

Ignoring the punctured feeling in his chest, Radley sprung up and grabbed a wrench from the tool shelves. They were firmly anchored to the wall, which was why the larger man stayed down after cracking his head on the metal support struts.

"You dickheads tell *Colaberro* I didn't take any of his money," Dustin said in a threatening tone. "I took what I was due to cover my costs. If he wants to see me about it, he can do it face to face, like a man!"

"I wouldn't recommend that," the shorter man muffled as he crawled up to his knees, leaving a puddle of red on the garage floor, his face and suit a bloody mess. He spit a red gob onto the garage floor, then spoke with in a stunted voice, his gritted teeth now scarlet pellets as he pushed the words from his mangled mouth. "If *Colaberro* comes here, he's comin' with his whole fucking army."

"Well, tell him to bring his whole fucking army, then!" Dustin shouted in the man's face, holding the crowbar to his throat. "And if I see you anywhere near my house again, you and your buddy'll be gagging on this crowbar!"

The shorter man stood and pulled up his larger friend, who spit out two teeth, and carefully placed them in his pocket. Despite the front of his suit being saturated in dark, red blood like his partner's was, the larger man still took the moment to straighten his jacket and cuffs. Both men completely ignored Radley, but he still clutched the crescent wrench, ready to defend.

The two suits walked out of the garage to their car in the alleyway. Before they got in, the smaller man turned to Dustin and waved his finger at him, "You watch your back, buddy. And mark my words; if I see you again, you better have something more than a fucking crowbar."

Dustin brandished his weapon, nodding. "Bring it on, buddy. I got a lot more than this – you come over and see."

The men drove off, leaving Radley alone with his brother in the open garage. The blood blotches stood out like sand dunes on the grey, concrete floor.

Dustin turned and looked at his brother. His hair still wet from having bolted out of the shower. "You okay?"

Radley gripped the wrench tighter. He motioned to the Mustang in the right bay. "These cars. They're all stolen, aren't they? These guys, they bring them to you, so you can change them, so they can be resold. You're not working for any dealership at all, are you?" His voice quavered as he spoke.

Dustin sighed. "Look, the cars aren't all stolen. Some of them probably are, most aren't. I don't know where these guys get the vehicles; I don't ask any questions; I just do the job they pay me to do."

"Yeah, and look where it's gotten you! Look at the blood in here!"

"Hey, it's not my blood! I can handle this. It's no big deal!"

"Those guys threatened your family!" Radley threw the wrench down on the cement floor. "They threatened Abigail! What kind of monsters are you dealing with?"

"Okay, calm down. That's just the way these guys work. They like to scare people. It's how they keep control. They're not going to hurt Abby."

"How, Dustin? How the hell can you be sure?" Radley shot back, the words, the emotions, the courage to stand up to his brother all came whirling out of him.

"That's none of your business." Dustin's tone turned vicious. "Just stay out of this, alright? I didn't screw those guys out of money. I took what was owed to me; I'm not going to let a bunch of clowns tell me otherwise."

"Listen to yourself." Radley rolled his eyes. "You're just like Dad."

"Don't you fucking compare me to him!" Dustin lashed out. "I'm not Dad. I don't do what I do because I'm some loser pothead. I'm supporting my family, and I'm doing a damn good job at it."

"Yeah," Radley said, pretending to applaud, "having some gangster threaten to cut your daughter's fingers off because you skimmed him two grand, yeah that makes you parent-of-the-year."

In a fit of anger, Dustin hurled the crowbar against the side of his garage, tearing into the drywall. The end of the bar jutted out of the wall like an ugly wound.

"Get the fuck out of here, Radley!"

"Does Jezzelle know what you're doing?"

"Get the FUCK outta here! Get out of my house!" Dustin screamed, close to losing control. His temper answered Radley's question.

Radley turned and walked out of the garage. He went into the house to pack his things. Dustin didn't follow.

With his duffel bag full of laundry and a suitcase in hand, Radley walked out of the house just as Jezzelle and Abigail returned from the park. Radley saw that Dustin had the garage doors shut and the lights off.

"Radley?" Jezzelle looked confused, eyeing Radley's distraught and disheveled appearance. "What's going on? Aren't you coming to the movie with us?"

No, because your husband is an out-of-control psycho who's screwing over the mob. Oh, and by the way, the gangsters threatened to feed your daughter her own fingers.

The words almost spilled out of Radley's mouth, but they didn't come.

"I don't think I can make it," Radley replied, "something came up. I have to go away for a while."

"Is everything okay?" Jezzelle asked, shocked. Abigail remained quiet.

"I'm not sure," Radley answered, turning away before he said something he might regret. "I hope so. I have to go." Walking away from his sister-in-law and niece at that moment killed him – he might as well have stabbed himself, it hurt so bad.

Chapter 13

For the next two days, Radley writhed in indecision back home with the Trillamede's. He told his foster parents the whole story. From the very beginning they had encouraged him to open up about his feelings, what was going on in his life, as a means to deal with anxiety, his emotions. They listened, offered advice, but this time Radley felt like he was on the edge of a cliff.

"This is your brother, this is the life he's chosen," Doug Trillamede told him. "You can't make decisions for him."

"Maybe he can talk to him, though, Doug," Diane disagreed, turning back to Radley. "Talk to him when you both have cool heads, and maybe Dustin will see reason. At the very least it'll get you boys back on speaking terms again."

It took a week for Radley to make first contact. Dustin would have nothing to do with him and hung up the phone. Radley called the next day while Dustin was at the shop and talked to Jezzelle, who invited him over to visit with Abigail.

"I have no idea what happened between you two," Jezzelle told him. "Dustin won't even talk about it, but I see no reason why you can't visit with your niece."

Radley didn't need to ask if it was alright with Dustin – he knew Jezzelle wouldn't dare tell him. There was no guilt to be had over that since Dustin had no intention of telling Jezzelle about the gangster attack, or what he was really doing inside that garage.

It was incredibly awkward for Radley to walk up the porch steps of his brother's house. Three months earlier he had done so with eager anticipation – now he felt as distant to his brother as he had ever been.

"Did he get mad at you? Did you damage one of his vehicles or something?" Jezzelle tried to pry more information from him.

"No, nothing like that," Radley said. "Look it's … best you don't know."

"Well, I don't know anything!" Jezzelle said, clearly exasperated. "Your brother won't even let me mention your name. He hides in that garage, and won't let anyone in."

"He's got a lot of work to do," Radley replied. "Things'll smooth over eventually." He suspected Jezzelle persisted so much because Radley didn't sound like he meant what he was saying.

Radley and Abigail played on the park equipment for about an hour: swings, teeter-totter, monkey bars. He enjoyed spending time with his niece, and forgot about the rotten situation with his brother. It would be on the merry-go-round that would remind him of it, and the words were not his own.

"Uncle Radley, is my family in trouble?" Abigail blurted out.

The question caught him off guard. "Why do you ask, Abby?"

"My dad gets phone calls late at night, while I'm in bed," Abigail replied. "He takes them on his cell and goes out to the garage. I hear him yelling outside my bedroom window."

"What does he say?" Radley's heart jumped into his throat.

"He says, 'if you come anywhere near my family, I'll kill you!' " Abigail mimicked her father. Radley wanted to jump up right there. Instead he forced himself to stay put.

"I'm sure it's nothing, honey." Radley rubbed her head. "I don't think anyone would want to hurt a pretty little girl like you."

Radley didn't speak to Abigail on their walk home – he said only six words to her and Jezzelle when he left. "I'll see you around sometime, okay?" He gave them each a hug, but both girls sensed his turmoil. Jezzelle told him to call anytime, but Radley didn't hear. He turned and walked down the empty street, through the archway of dry, late summer birches, away from his brother's house and the only biological family he had left. All he had with him was his own self-loathing, the feeling he was an ineffective pawn, unable to do anything to help his niece and sister-in-law. His entire adolescence played out before his eyes, and he was powerless to stop it.

Or was he?

Radley realized he had a decision to make, for the second time in his life.

Three Days Later

The chilly wind kept him focused on that very decision, and he was going insane trying to make it.

Leaning against the mailbox in front of the Trillamede's house, Radley noticed Doug's tall willow trees hovering over him. Their gentle swaying reminded him of the tides of life.

We were all like those trees, he thought, *rocking in the wind, losing our leaves, dictated by forces beyond our control.* He pictured himself swinging from the highest branches, leaping from one treetop to the next.

Okay, enough! This is real life now, and I have to make this decision again. Do I mail this fucking thing or not? Such a simple action, so many consequences.

He wondered how long he stood outside his foster parents' house. It wasn't long, but like every other agonizing moment in his life, it felt like forever. The letter took him two days to research and write and, like his note to Constable Roake, it was deceptively simple. He checked it again for the fifth time.

Crime Stoppers
Stolen Properties Division

A residence in 324 Springhill Lane, with a double-wide garage, is harboring stolen vehicles. The owner of the residence, Mr. Dustin Wycliffe, is accepting these vehicles, refurbishing them, and sending them back to the thieves, who are then re-distributing them to a network of crooked used-car dealerships and black market salespersons. Apprehending and questioning Mr. Wycliffe will likely lead you to the ringleaders behind this operation. Mr. Wycliffe's wife, Jezzelle, has no knowledge whatsoever of her husband's illegitimate activities.

Anonymous

Radley followed up the letter with a complete listing of the vehicles he and Dustin worked on, ten of which, as far as Radley found out, were stolen. The Ford mini-van owned by Ron and Rose Pittman, whose names and complete insurance information Radley listed next to the vehicle, topped the list.

Sending this letter meant Dustin would be arrested. Possession of stolen property over $5000 carried a maximum penalty of ten years in prison, though a typical first time sentence, Radley had read, would likely be more lenient. Either way, it meant a complete usurping of Dustin, Jezzelle, and Abigail's lives, and possibly a fine or lawsuit against Dustin, which would no doubt hinder the family's finances. This *wasn't* a decision Radley took lightly.

Jezzelle and Abby could stay with Jezzelle's parents, he rationalized. He also knew, even though he was lucky to have gotten away with his letter to Constable Roake, he likely wouldn't this time. Dustin would know Radley turned him in, and Radley would probably get subpoenaed to testify, given the fact he was the only person Dustin allowed to help him work on the vehicles.

Radley sighed as he sealed the letter. *Dammit, my life — Dustin's too — turned out for the better after I gave our father up, didn't it?* Dustin may not have learned the lessons Radley did, but his older brother would also be getting off light – this would be his opportunity to get back on the proper track.

Right?

Arrrghh!? Radley cussed as he leaned over the mailbox.

"Uncle Radley, are you coming?" Abigail's voice called out behind him. "We have to finish our game." She stood on the stairs with Diane Trillamede, waiting for Radley to return. He received permission from Jezzelle to bring her over to his house so Abby could see where he lived. But Radley really did it to confirm the reason he wrote the letter about Dustin's car ring and, for that matter, the letter about his father's drug-running business nine years earlier.

It's not about Dustin, or my father. Radley acknowledged. *It's about Abigail.*

And it was about me.

"Uncle Radley?" Abigail pleaded. "You said you just have to mail a letter."

"I'm coming kiddo," Radley answered. He plopped the letter inside the mailbox and marched back up toward the house, stirring up the fluttering, yellow willow leaves in his path. "Let's go finish that game."

Part III

Chapter 14

Seven Months Later – Age 24

Oh God, what have I done? Radley asked himself, burying his face in the cold water cupped in his hands. At this particular moment, he wished he could drown in it.

"Radley!" Diane knocked on the bathroom door. "Are you alright?"

"Yes." He sighed, knowing full well he'd been in there nearly an hour. Despite having showered, shaved, and washed his face twice with cold water, he could not stop sweating.

Just get dressed, he ordered himself. *Get going. I can't just sit and hide in this bathroom all day.* The thought of doing exactly that, however, greatly appealed to him.

"I'm going to get Doug to drive you, okay?" Diane spoke through the door, concern etched in her voice. They had argued about it the night before, and Radley insisted he drive himself – now he wasn't so sure.

"Fine," he conceded, looking at the clock above the toilet for what was probably the twentieth time. In two hours, he would be summoned to the witness stand, to testify against his brother. As much as he knew this moment would come, as resolved as he was mailing the letter that condemned Dustin, Radley realized no one could ever have fully understood what it would entail – the sensations, the fears, the sheer difficulty of having to face his brother in the courtroom, and say the things he was now obligated by the Crown Prosecution to say. The whole situation sucked.

And in the back of his mind, Radley once again wrestled with the doubt and regret that haunted him. He felt like the Prodigal Son, the tale he remembered during his first year with the Trillamedes, when they would bring him to church. Only in Radley's case, he earned vindication, only to abandon his family again.

Stop it! He closed his eyes to calm himself down. *This is the right thing.* He knew it wouldn't be easy, no matter how many times he had played the situation over in his head. Nothing could have prepared him for the sheer reality of what he'd done, or what he was about to do.

The corridor that led to the courtroom was open and formal. Radley sat alone on the hallway bench waiting for the clerk to open the mahogany doors, signalling the prosecution's official call for him to take the witness stand. He arrived at the courthouse twenty minutes early, feeling thankful Doug had driven him. His foster father dropped him off at the courthouse doors, where Radley scurried straight to the bailiff's office and hid, anxious to avoid anyone he knew who may have been in the foyer.

When the crowd cleared, Radley was asked to sit in the

hallway. It was the second day of Dustin's criminal trial, and Radley's first appearance. He was subpoenaed to testify by the prosecution, and had no choice in the matter once they discovered it was he who brought police attention to Dustin's activities. Knowing the police spent a significant amount of time investigating who wrote the letter, Radley decided to come clean with the lawyers, especially when it became clear he had become a suspected accomplice of his brother's.

The investigation leading to Dustin's arrest had been quick. Unlike the way their father had been set up in an undercover operation, the authorities simply went to Dustin's garage, found a vehicle inside that had been reported stolen, and brought Dustin in for questioning. A search warrant was issued, and automotive parts belonging to several stolen vehicles in surrounding cities were discovered in the garage.

Radley, during that time, had been completely oblivious about these events. It wasn't until eleven days after mailing the letter that he received a surprise, late evening phone call, then everything came crashing down.

Radley answered the cordless phone. "Yellow." He was raiding the Trillamede's fridge when the call came. Doug and Diane were out with friends, and he expected it to be for them, until the gravelly, desperate voice on the other end gripped him with fear and shock.

"Radley." The hurried voice was quick, quiet, and abrupt. "Radley, is that you?"

"Yeah," Radley answered, his heart plummeting to the floor. "Dustin?" He didn't need to ask.

"Yeah, Radley, listen." Dustin adopted a conciliatory, almost apologetic, tone. "I just got arrested. I don't know how or why it happened. I think those guys we fought may have turned me in."

"Really?" Radley swallowed. His words were slow, hesitant, controlled. "Oh crap. I'm sorry to hear that. What can I do?"

"Look, right now Jezzelle doesn't know what's going on. I want you to phone a lawyer for me. I don't trust the yahoo they said they'll bring in for me. I'm not tellin' the cops anything 'til I see a lawyer."

"Yeah, that's a good move." Radley fumbled for a pen and notepad. *My God, I'm Dustin's one phone call. Why is he phoning me?*

"I don't care who you get. Just get someone I can trust. And don't call Jezzelle."

"I won't." Radley said, starting to jot down anything he heard. 'No cops until lawyer' he scribbled. He felt like he had been run over, his head spun. He looked at the clock on the stove. It was almost 11:00. "Okay, it's probably too late to call anyone tonight … I'll … I'll do it first thing tomorrow."

"Goddamn it!" Dustin cursed over the line. It sounded like he slammed his fist against a wall or table. "I can't believe this is happening. I'm gonna have to stay the night here. Look, they got me at the remand center in the Southwest. You gotta somehow get a hold of me tomorrow morning, okay? Bring the lawyer in with you, if you can. I might need you to go to my house and get some things for me."

"Yeah, sure, Dust, of course," Radley answered. "Anything you need."

"Good, good," Dustin replied, then paused. The inevitable was coming. "Look, Radley, the cops might want to interview you. Ask you some questions. I need you to help me, okay? I didn't know where any of those cars came from. They were just brought to me, right? I was paid to do a job, nothing more."

Radley winced. He shifted on the balls of his feet. He didn't know what to say.

"Yeah, yeah, I know, Dustin. I can do that for you."

The relief coursed out of Dustin's voice. Radley hadn't a clue what Dustin had said – he was too busy trying to come to terms with what he'd just promised.

Dustin's apology came next. "Look Radley, I'm sorry about the way things went down, okay? You're a good kid, I'm sorry about the blow-up we had. Thank-you for doing this for me. I owe you one."

"Yeah, no problem Dust." Radley felt the uppercut thrust into his stomach. "Anything, man."

"This whole situation is total horseshit, bro," Dustin continued – his voice, his demeanor – had suddenly picked up. "When I get out of here, I'm gonna find the-son-of-a-bitch that set me up and I'm gonna kick his ass from here to the north-fucking pole. There's no way these charges are going to stick."

"Right," Radley said. The rest of the conversation was a blur. He remembered dropping to his knees on the floor after finally hanging up the phone. A mini-panic attack had set in.

Racing through a multitude of scenarios, he stayed up until

three in the morning. He fell asleep at some point, only to be waken by Diane, who informed him his brother's wife was on the phone.

Jazzelle had phoned at nine to tell Radley that Dustin was in custody. Frantic and scared, she pleaded with him to tell her what he knew about Dustin's business, but he didn't budge. All he could do was calm her down, and promise he'd look into it. He told her he would get a lawyer. She told him her father already hired one.

What a friggin' circus that day was. Radley shook his head, returning to the courthouse, and the empty court corridor he found himself in. He leaned forward and rubbed his face. It was six months since he talked to Dustin or Jezzelle – hadn't saw them until that fateful week when they discovered he had turned Dustin in, and would be the key witness to the prosecution's case. Unsure of exactly what their reaction was when they learned the news, Radley surmised that if he were in the same room with Dustin at the time, his brother would have lunged across it and choked him to death.

The thick, mahogany doors opened, and the courtroom bailiff appeared in the entranceway. Radley had never skydived before, but he felt he was being forced to out of an airplane, with a parachute improperly packed.

"The prosecution calls Radley Wycliffe to the witness stand," the bailiff said.

Chapter 15

The courtroom felt cold. He knew it wasn't. It was wide, bright, open. Feeling vulnerable and naked, he followed the bailiff up the aisle to the witness stand. The weight of the room, and everyone in it, fell on his shoulders. Refusing to make eye-contact with anybody, he stared down at his feet, walking in precise, controlled movements and doing everything he could to keep one foot ahead of the other. He lifted his head up only to see where he was supposed to sit.

A concrete arc framed the judge's bench and the witness stand. Heavily stained, gleaming wooden panels were lined vertically around the room, reflecting light from the florescent slat bulbs that were installed over every bench and sitting area in the court, from the public seating gallery to the judge's bench. The heightened courtroom murmurs of the small crowd were directed at him. He knew Jezzelle and her family were somewhere in the crowd, but didn't dare look.

Radley sat on a rolling chair in the enclosed witness stand, elevated about four feet off the ground. Ahead of him sat a row of court clerks who provided a buffer between the defense tables and the witness stand. He glanced at the judge, unsure if he was supposed to acknowledge the man or not. From the judge's solemn expression, Radley figured he shouldn't. An older man, the judge looked stern. His wispy grey hair, long face and hawk-like eyes penetrated through the small, rectangular spectacles he wore. He looked tall sitting in his chair, and provided an intimidating presence reinforcing Radley's squeamishness.

Radley turned away from the man, and found himself looking at Dustin. It was for the briefest of moments, but enough to tighten Radley's chest. His brother appeared well-groomed but uncomfortable; the grey suit he wore seemed out of place – Radley never knew Dustin to wear anything but sleeveless T-shirts and jeans.

Dustin's face appeared calm, stoic, but his eyes said it all. He glared at Radley, though his face didn't move. Wounded, Dustin was crippled by Radley's betrayal. Having expected bitter scowls, malicious glances, and even shouts of abject fury from Dustin, Radley did not get any of that. Instead he received what he least expected, and what he most dreaded – nothing at all.

I have to do this. Radley looked down at his knees. *I know why I'm doing this.*

He lifted his head to greet the Crown Prosecutor, whom Radley met with on three occasions. In a blur, Radley answered the man's questions. It was almost like an out of body experience. He identified his brother Dustin as the individual he spent three months with last summer, helping him refurbish used cars. In explaining his brother's operation, Radley finished with his vivid and controlled telling of the vicious mob attack. The words, descriptions, and explanations flowed out of him. His mind and emotions numb, as if someone else were in control of his body and words. Radley looked down after the prosecutor's final question. The man sounded pleased with the testimony. Radley felt relieved. He had condemned his brother, but in so doing, protected Jezzelle, Abigail, and ultimately Dustin himself. The hard, agonizing part was over.

Or so he thought.

"Cross examination, Miss Oakley?" the judge asked the defense attorney.

"Yes, Your Honor." The defense lawyer rose. An attractive lady with shoulder length, silky blond hair and a smooth face, nicknamed Athena by the lawyers in the Crown Prosecutor's office – an off-collar comment Radley wasn't supposed to hear but never forgot.

"Mr. Wycliffe, can you please explain why you chose to make your letter to the police anonymous?" she asked, her tone polite and professional.

"Yes, okay." Radley scratched his head, a nervous gesture, which he caught himself doing and abruptly stopped. "Um, well, I was hoping to draw attention to my brother's activities, to protect him and his family, without having to officially turn him in."

"Would it be a correct assessment, Mr. Wycliffe, that your intention, however noble you claim it to be, failed?"

"Yeah, I guess." Radley swallowed. He didn't know how to answer that question.

"Please explain why, Mr. Wycliffe."

Radley sighed. "Because here I am, having to testify against my brother."

"Would it be an accurate description to say, Mr. Wycliffe,

that you essentially betrayed your brother?"

Oh God, here we go. Radley cursed to himself. He was beginning to sweat again.

"Dustin may see it that way," Radley said, "but I don't. I like to believe I'm helping my brother."

Radley couldn't help but look at Dustin this time. His brother kept his face still, but was biting the inside of his cheek. Radley could almost hear Dustin tell him to "F-Off" in his thoughts.

"Mr. Wycliffe, are you aware of the timeline of events which led to your father's arrest, prosecution, and conviction nine years ago?"

"Objection, your honor," the Prosecutor spoke. "This case doesn't concern Tavis Wycliffe. Any testimony related to Dustin and Radley's father is irrelevant."

"Not when I'm trying to establish a connection between the two cases," the defense attorney responded. Radley had told his foster mother about the Athena nickname – Diane contacted a couple of friends who worked in the legal system, and began inquiring about her cases. Diane had found that Dustin's lawyer was known for presenting surprise testimonies or key evidence not known by Crown attorneys. It had given her a notorious reputation among legal circles, but made her very popular with wealthier clients, like Dustin's father-in-law.

"Overruled," the judge answered. "Please answer the question, Mr. Wycliffe."

Radley shifted in his seat.

"Yes, I'm somewhat aware," Radley answered. "I had just

turned 15 at the time."

"Please explain to the court why your father was arrested."

They prepared him for this question. "He was convicted for drug trafficking and the sale of illegal narcotics to minors."

For every question about his father she might ask Radley, the Prosecution prepped him to answer the exact same way, a tactic that would tie Athena's argument up.

"Any testimony you make concerning your father," the prosecutor told Radley three days earlier, "would be considered hearsay, and therefore non-admissible in court, because you were a minor and had been sheltered from your father's arrest and court trial." It was what Radley had banked on. To his heart's dismay, however, this was Athena he was dealing with.

"Were you a student in Rachel Macklin's Grade 9 Health class at Mayer Cross High School fourteen years ago?"

"Yes." Radley bit his lip. He wanted to swear. At the very least, delay his answer and stall.

Miss Macklin, was that her name? I can't remember, I really hated that fucking class. That phrase, and the bitter tone behind it, almost burst from his lips.

She reached into a white banker's box sitting on the corner of her desk, and took out a piece of paper, flattened out inside a sealed Ziploc bag.

"I have a letter, submitted at the time to Constable Dale Roake of the local city police service, which I will read to the court. Please note the date the letter was submitted by Constable Roake." She held up to the court. "Three days before the arrest of Tavis Wycliffe."

She read the letter in its entirety, word for word, the way Radley wrote it that fateful day. Radley glanced at his brother who sat at the defense table, with a bitter scowl on his face, as though he had just been forced to eat a handful of centipedes.

"Mr. Wycliffe," Athena said as she stared at Radley, almost with a dare in her voice. "Did you write this letter and submit it to Constable Roake 14 years ago?"

No, I did not. I have no idea who wrote that. It would have been so easy to deny, especially with Dustin sitting there, and several of his Wycliffe relatives in the courtroom. Of course, it would have also been foolish, because that also would give Athena the answer she wanted. She wanted Radley to lie on the stand, under oath, because she could have then ripped him apart, branded him a liar, a sensationalist who exaggerated the crimes of his brother so he could get attention for his own inadequacies. Whatever Radley's real motivation was would have been irrelevant – all she needed to do was smear his character, and make his testimony unreliable. It was all part of her strategy to discredit the entire case against Dustin, and tarnish the police proceedings against her client, a tactic that could very well have the charges against Dustin thrown out.

Radley was smart enough to realize it. He was smart enough to tell the prosecution beforehand, smart enough to allow them to prep him for that possibility, and smart enough to know he had to tell the truth.

"Yes, I did write that letter," Radley said. "I wrote it and gave it to Constable Roake. So, to answer what will be your next question, yes, I turned my father in as well."

The judgment never happened. Radley's testimony proved to be decisive in the case. It was clear Dustin not only had knowledge that what he did was wrong, but that he tried to cover up evidence. The defense gambled Radley would not want his childhood secret brought out into court, and their gamble failed. Of course, Radley didn't want it brought out in the open, but his testimony sent the defense reeling, compelling them to negotiate a plea bargain with the Crown.

The deal was quick, completed in the course of a day, and the sentence handed down one week later.

"You are being sentenced to three years and six months in a federal penitentiary for your involvement in these offenses." The judge spoke slowly to Dustin, with a tone that was a cross between a lecture and genuine sympathy. "Do you understand what is to be expected of you during your incarceration, Mr. Wycliffe?"

"Yes sir." Dustin stood straight at the front of the courtroom, dressed in a full length black suit. He never turned to look at anyone behind him. No one could read the look on his face.

"Mr. Wycliffe," the judge continued, "because this is your first offense, and in consideration of your young family, the Court is granting you an opportunity here — to think about what you've done, and to change your life for the better, so that, in the future, you will support your wife and child in a manner that benefits society."

"Yes sir," was all Dustin responded with.

"Good luck, Mr. Wycliffe," the judge finished. "I hope I never have to see you in my presence again.

The courtroom was a splash with whispers, shuffling, and mutters as the small audience stood and watched as they led Dustin away in handcuffs. Radley sat in the far right back corner of the courtroom, hidden but perfectly obvious to everyone in the room. He did not want to be there, but showed up because it felt like he must.

The judgment came as no surprise – Dustin was charged with 13 counts of possession of stolen property. The terms of the plea bargain were not announced, and Radley knew better than to dare ask anyone close to Dustin. It involved his brother pleading guilty and having the charges against him scaled down, either to obtain a reduced sentence, or agreeing to testify against his employers – Radley prayed it was for the former.

With Dustin gone, the court adjourned, and Radley dashed out of the room. Part of him hoped Dustin would be eligible for an early parole, but nothing in the judge's decision suggested it. Radley needed to leave the court house, and process everything he witnessed, everything he'd done. He never wanted to step foot in this place again.

"Radley, Radley Wycliffe!" a voice shouted to him from the courtroom doors.

Radley spun around and saw an angry Jezzelle storm toward

him, her purse in hand. As she approached, she took it off her shoulder, and threw it at him, hard. Radley put up his hand to block it. The zipper nicked his hand.

"Whoa–" Radley jumped back.

"I hope you're happy now," Jezzelle spat at him. "I hope you're happy now that you've put my husband – your brother – in prison! Because that's what you wanted isn't it? Isn't it?"

"No," Radley said. "It isn't."

"Don't feed me that line, Radley." The tears welled up in her eyes. "Don't you ever say that to me again. You could have come to *me*, Radley – I could have stopped him! I could've ended it!"

Radley shook his head. "No, you couldn't. He was in over his head."

"And where is he now, Radley?" Jezzelle screamed. She started slapping at him. "Is he over his head now, Radley, now that he's in fucking jail, and Abby's without a father! Does that make it all better! Does it!"

Radley put up his arms to shield himself from her blows. He tried to walk away from her but she continued lashing at him, yelling at him to look her in the eyes.

Several family members intervened. Her father and brother pulled her back. One of his Wycliffe cousins, Galen, stepped in to form a barrier between her and Radley. Jezzelle continued screaming and crying as she and Radley were separated.

"God." Radley spoke to Galen, who he hadn't seen in ten years. Galen was a year older and Radley remembered him as being a friendly guy. "Thanks for helping me out there."

"Just get the hell out of here, Radley." Galen held up his hand. The glare in his eyes said everything. "You've done enough damage for one lifetime."

"Hey, Galen, come on," Radley said.

"No," Galen replied. "No, Radley, you've turned against your family! You've betrayed them – that's the greatest sin of all, Radley, and you've done it twice."

"Galen, you don't under–" Radley tried to speak.

"Don't say anything more, Radley," Galen cut him off. "Just get out of my face, our family's face. Go, before I change my mind, and let the whole family come after you."

"For fuck sakes." Radley threw his arms up in the air, turned away from his cousin, and walked out of the main foyer of the courthouse. His heart dropped to his feet. He felt a surge of anger, of frustration, but reminded himself that he knew this would happen.

It doesn't make it any friggin' easier.

He'd been intelligent enough at the trial to tell the prosecution about the note – that gave him a small sliver of satisfaction. He was able to outthink Athena, and get his brother out of the problems Dustin had worked himself in. Even so, he didn't feel so intelligent anymore.

Chapter 16

Two Weeks Later

"I'm gonna burn every inch of your body," the scar-faced man said as he flicked a lighter under Radley's armpits.

"God, no, I don't know where my Dad keeps his speed," a 14 year-old Radley wailed, trying to keep his arms away from the sputtering flame.

"Get the fuck off him!" Dustin raced in with a crowbar. It was the adult Dustin coming out of the shower, dressed in a white T-Shirt and black boxers, with his slick, wet hair. He lifted the bar up and brought it down with a sickening thud, he brought it up a second time, a third –

"Radley," a female voice called from the kitchen. "Radley?" The voice coincided with Dustin's.

"Mom?" Radley muttered. Dustin kept swinging the crowbar, though he was no longer striking the scar-faced man. He was hitting Radley.

"You fucking pussy." Dustin kept pummeling him. Radley tried shielding his head and face. "Take the fucking gun."

Dustin, please stop! Radley wailed inside his dream.

"Radley!" Diane's voice thundered through the door, jarring him awake. "Are you still in there? It's two-thirty in the afternoon!"

The hammering on his bedroom door was almost as bad as the hammering inside his skull. Radley lifted his head from the pillow — it was the nightmare again. The scar-faced man had haunted his dreams for the past decade, but this newer incarnation, involving Dustin and the crowbar, was clearly the result of the past eight months. No matter how many times he had that friggin' dream, and how nonsensical it truly was, it felt as real as ever.

"Radley Trillamede," Diane repeated, a frantic and fiery tone in her voice, "if you don't unlock this door, I will knock it down with your foster father's sledgehammer! I swear to God I will!"

"Alright, alright already, I'm here," Radley muttered as he clambered out of his bed. He couldn't see the time on his alarm clock because it was covered with his sweater. "What do you want?"

"Radley Trillamede, it is two-thirty in the afternoon," Diane repeated, even more annoyed. "In case you've forgotten about the rest of society, the world wakes up no later than nine and is in bed by midnight. Last I checked, you aren't a raccoon or a skunk."

Tell that to my family. Radley felt like saying as he opened the door.

"Very funny," he grumbled to his foster mother. "What do you want?"

"Well, I want to make sure you're alive for one thing." She looked at him. He knew his hair was probably all over the place, and his eyes were bloodshot. "Second, I'd like to know why you need to be going to the bar every second night and staying out until five in the morning."

Radley rolled his eyes. "Aw look, get off my case already. I went out with my friends. What do you care, for cry'n out loud?"

"I care, Radley, because every night you go, you come home drunker than a loon. This isn't like you Radley, ever since your brother's conviction–"

"That's got nothing to do with it!" Radley snapped. "For once, I'm just trying to live my life, alright! I'm working right now, I'm paying you rent, can you please just let me live my freaking life!"

"Working as a gas jockey and spending your money in bars is no way to live a life." Diane pointed her finger in his face. "And as far as the rent is concerned, you and I know full well you'll never get the deal you're getting here anywhere else, buddy, and you know it."

"Yes, I know." Radley felt like pulling his hair out. "You never let me forget it."

A burning guzzle trickled up his esophagus, it was accompanied by the hops and barley from the dozen beer he drank the evening before.

"Oh, Radley, you stink." Diane waved her hand in front of his face. "Go take a shower, and use some mouthwash. There's lunch upstairs in the fridge."

"Whatever. Thanks," Radley said to his foster mother before shutting the door. *See, I am a bloody skunk.* He plopped back on his bed. Burying his face in the pillow, he knew wouldn't be able to go back to sleep – the scar-faced man and Dustin had made sure of that.

Two Months Later

"Dude, this is a biker bar from hell," his friend Mordecai laughed as they entered *The Rider's Hex* on the outskirts of the city.

"Why did you want to come here?" Brian, Radley's other buddy, seemed more intimidated than the others.

"Hey, somewhere different." Radley surveyed the locale. The bar was dimly lit, with Led Zeppelin's "Ramble On" blaring from the speakers hung from wire racks in every corner of the establishment. Posters from such movies as Easy Rider, The Deer Hunter, and Midnight Cowboy were displayed in framed plastic behind the bar tables. The atmosphere and customers offered a noticeable change from the country and western bars Brian always wanted to go to. A wire cage surrounded the stage where a red-bearded DJ sat, and a giant Confederate flag hung on the wallboard behind him.

The boys sat at a round table near the washrooms. Several pitchers of paralyzers and Radley acquiesced to the buzz he craved. Thoughts of his brother, sister-in-law, everything he'd earned back and lost, just went away.

"Where are you going, you fucking alcoholic?" Mordecai teased Radley as he wobbled off the chair.

"Get me a Slammer." Radley pointed to the washroom. "I'm going to make room for it."

Radley staggered to the washroom. The crowd in the bar was a blurry mixture of faces. He did not see the bald-headed biker three tables down who had stared at him since he came in. The man got up and followed him into the washroom. Radley went to the urinal and undid his pants, fighting sudden vertigo. He closed his eyes and leaning against a wrestling promo affixed to the wall. Feeling the urine spray on his hands and pants as it hit the porcelain, he knew it was gross but he didn't give a shit. The buzz was all he cared about – it helped him forget, at least for the time being. He would get the gears from the Trillamede's tomorrow.

It wasn't that he didn't care what they thought – it mattered to him greatly, but, for now, that was tomorrow's problem. As usual, he would sleep the hangover off, and his defense, which for the moment, had kept Diane and Doug off of his case, would be that he was still going to work, earning his money, so what difference would it make if he went out for some drinks every now and then?

"I'm no alcoholic," he muttered, not sure if he said it out loud. *I know what I'm doing.*

He turned to go to the sink, not noticing the older man in the biker's vest standing directly behind him – he realized it only when the man grabbed him by the throat and rammed him backward against the white tiled wall.

"You got a lot of guts showing your face around here, boy." The man was red faced, with a wispy salt-and-pepper beard, and tight, vengeful eyes. His breath carried a hint of whiskey. He was fatter in the face than Radley remembered, but there was no mistaking who he was.

"Get your fucking hands off of me, Cyclo!" Radley said,

trying to shove the man's hands away, but getting nowhere. "You have no idea what I've been through."

"Oh poor little Radley, is that it?" Cyclo thrust his palm under Radley's jaw, pressing him into the wall. His mocking, patronized. "My father was a drug dealer, my mother a junkie. Everybody feel sorry for me – my life's been hell. Is that going to be your fucking excuse for everything now?"

Radley struggled as he tried to pry himself from Cyclo's grip, but the older man's weight kept him wedged against the tile. Radley felt the anger surge up inside him. He braced his left leg against the tile.

"Get your filthy hands off of me," Radley cursed through gritted teeth. "I turned you in because I HAD TO!"

As he shouted, Radley pushed off the wall with his left foot, shoving Cyclo backward. The fist he threw became a slap, and connected with the older man's left temple. He made another punching motion, but again his fist became a flat hand, cuffing the back of Cyclo's bald, sweaty head. The texture felt like wet rubber.

I can't hit this man, Radley realized as he tried making another fist – the man had been like an uncle to Radley growing up. *God, what am I doing?*

Radley went limp as Cyclo hugged his waist and slammed him against the tile wall. Cyclo grabbed Radley's collar and pulled him down to the bathroom floor. Radley complied like a rag doll, and Cyclo returned the slap, connecting with the side of Radley's head.

Cyclo raised his hand to strike a second blow but hesitated.

Two bouncers charged into the bathroom and pulled him off. As one bouncer held Cyclo's arms, the second pulled Radley up to his feet.

Both bouncers said something to the two combatants, but all Radley could see and hear was Cyclo.

"You're so fucking pathetic, kid! After everything you did – everything you've done, this is what you've become? Poor, poor pitiful me, eh?" Cyclo said in disgust.

"Screw off." Radley shook his head. His tone no longer vicious, but defiant. *I am not going to take this shit.* "Look, I don't expect you to understand why I did what I did, Cyclo, but know this – you wouldn't have lasted a friggin' day in our house, old man. I was only a kid. I did what I did to survive."

"And where are you going to go from here, Radley, huh? What are you going to do now?"

"What?" Radley looked at the man. The bouncer started shoving him out of the bathroom. "What the hell are you talking about?"

"I've been trailing you for the last two weeks, boy," Cyclo said. "Watching you go from bar to bar, getting piss-ass drunk, stumbling on the street like some hobo and going home at five in the morning, only to go out again the next night. I've been watching you. All I can see, after everything you did to your father and Dustin–"

"Don't judge me for that!" Radley broke the bouncer's grip as he thrust a finger in Cyclo's direction. "You have no fucking idea what you're talking about–"

"I'm not judging you for that, let me finish!" Cyclo shouted over him. "I know why you turned Dustin in, okay, I get that! I'm glad you did it! But for everything – EVERYTHING – that you've done, Radley, as much guts as it took you, look at yourself now. You're wasting your life away, getting hammered every night, and going down the same Goddamn path your father did twenty years ago. Don't turn into your father. You can be so much more. You broke the cycle, kid – you got away from it, so why the hell are you starting another one?"

As expected, the bouncer threw Radley out of the bar. Mordecai and Bryan were stunned when they saw him and Cyclo dragged out of the bathroom. A third took Cyclo into the corner while the other two shoved Radley through the front entrance, and followed him outside. The bouncers said they wouldn't throw Cyclo out until Radley and his friends walked off of the property.

"Dude, who the hell were you fighting in the can?" Mordecai laughed as they walked across the street to Brian's car.

Radley slumped in the back seat, mind racing in a thousand different directions as he thought about the altercation with his dad's old friend.

"Seriously, man, who was that guy?" Bryan asked. "He looked like a Grandpa to the Hell's Angels or something. What were you two fighting about?"

"I don't know who he was," Radley said, trying to sober up so he could come up with a way to downplay the incident. "He started shoving me around for using his urinal."

"No kidding," Bryan snickered. "I'm glad you used the pisser before I did."

"Right," Radley replied, staring out the window. *Don't turn into your father, Radley.* Cyclo's words rolled inside him as they sped down the highway.

Chapter 17

"Radley, get up!" Diane knocked at the door. "Telephone."

"Who is it?" he grumbled and threw the pillow off his head. Glancing at the alarm clock, it cursed 9:14 AM at him. He had to double check if it was a Saturday or not. It was, so he didn't have to work. Who the hell would be calling him at this hour?

"Radley, your Aunt Dulcie's on the phone. She needs to talk to you."

"Who?" Radley asked. He heard Diane clearly, but asked again to register what she said.

"Your Aunt Dulcie." The frustration was evident in his foster mother's voice. "Come on. Up! Pronto!"

"Hold on, I'm coming," Radley said. His tone was polite. It had to be because he saw Diane watch from her upstairs bedroom window when he crawled into the house at 4:30 this morning. Why would his estranged aunt be calling him now?

He got out of bed slowly to prevent his head from boiling over. It was another late night, this time at a strip bar with a colleague from work. His encounter with Cyclo, as annoying as it was, did little to sway him from drinking. Once he thought about it – Cyclo the druggie chastising him for drinking – was like a stripper condoning him for sleeping in his underwear.

Trudging into the downstairs den, he picked up the cordless. "I got it," he called out to Diane. "Hello?"

"Radley, it's Aunt Dulcie." The urgency in her voice was evident. "Your mother is missing. She hasn't reported in to her case worker. No one knows where she's at."

Radley sighed. "What am I supposed to do about it?"

"There's a chance she may be in the Northeast somewhere. We need to look for her."

"Well, can't the case workers find her? I don't know where she is. I haven't seen her in years."

"I understand that, Radley," his aunt said. Her tone weak, defeated. "I can't get anyone to help me."

"What do you mean?" Radley asked.

"Your mother was released from the halfway house two months ago," Dulcie explained. "She's gone missing, and I'm the only one in the family who's willing to look for her."

His aunt picked him up two hours later. They drove to the city's east side; an area Radley had only been once before when bar-hopping. The place they wound up in was scuzzy, with less than welcoming clientele.

Oh Mother, what the hell have you gotten into now? Radley shook his head as Dulcie entered the shabbiest part of the neighbourhood. The houses were older, downtrodden, many of the residential lots nothing more than junk-filled yards. The occasional house did appear to be upgraded – the owners making an attempt to spruce up their home with newer siding and a garage, almost as if to cover something up.

Kind of like Dustin in his neighbourhood. Radley quickly expelled the memory.

His aunt navigated into a business area and pulled up to a ratty, two storey building made of brown brick with the cement layers cracking in between. A few of the boards nailed over the windows were broken, the busted edges of the breaks protruded outwards, as though someone had tried to pry the wood off from the outside. Had Radley been searching on his own, he would have driven right past, thinking the building condemned or abandoned.

"I'm too scared to go into these places by myself." Dulcie pulled over. The surrounding businesses consisted of pawn shops, liquor stores no larger than a shoe store, and the odd grocery store with bars on the windows.

Radley exited the vehicle and eyed his aunt suspiciously. "It seems to me you know exactly where you're going."

His aunt sighed, looking him in the eye. "Put it this way, sweetheart, we pulled her out of here once before. I wouldn't be surprised if she found her way back."

A broken runner at the entranceway appeared badly weathered. The door hung lopsided and when Radley tried to open it, he needed to lift it up. He realized the bottom jamb was caught on a rolled-up plastic carpet, wedged in the doorframe as if to prevent someone from storming in. When he wrestled the carpet away with his foot, he encountered a much larger problem, the door ran into the floor itself. The second he stepped into the landing, he caught the unmistakable whiff of burnt weed.

"What is this? A crack house?" Radley groaned, holding a hand against his face to block out the stench.

"No," his aunt said. "It's worse."

They walked down a badly worn, carpeted stairway that led to a dimly lit hall. Numerous, blotchy stains and kicked-in holes dominated the drywall. The hall carpet was torn up in places, and looked like it hadn't been vacuumed in a century. *People of all types must have tread here. God only knows what's inside the three rooms up ahead.*

Oh Mother, where the frick are you? The first door was knocked off its hinges, and propped up against the frame. Radley set the door aside, and could smell a hint of vomit ingrained in the rug. The room was disheveled and Radley could see the needle packages and Ziploc bags left haphazardly on the floor. In what appeared to once be a closet, an old man with a white, scraggly beard and no pants slept uncomfortably on a vinyl lawn chair. Radley could have started a chainsaw in the room and he doubted the man would have noticed.

The room across the hall was the bathroom, and Radley didn't want to enter it. The seatless toilet, with black circles swirling inside its badly stained porcelain bowl, looked as though it had been kicked off its seal. Junk littered the inside of the tub, but Radley looked no further — the sight of the room made him nauseous. Diane Trillamede drilled into him the importance of keeping a washroom clean and sterilized. She would have had a heart attack seeing the state of this room.

They opened the final door in the hallway. A small window,

half covered by broken blinds, offered a sliver of sunlight from the back alleyway. Several blankets lay strewn on the floor. Radley stepped over them to open the blinds to see if there was anything in the room. In doing so, he stepped on what felt like a rubber tube.

"What the —" He jolted, thinking he stepped on a squishy cucumber. It was a person's arm.

"Oh God, I'm sorry," he apologized. A person lay underneath blankets.

"Watch wer yer goin'," a woman's voice muttered at him.

"I'm sorry," Radley repeated. "I'm looking for someone."

"Well go fuckin' find him," the woman cussed at him. "Get outta my way."

Stupid crackhead. Radley cursed as he stepped over the woman. The light from the blinds revealed a blotchy old hag, with wispy, damaged grey hair and rotten teeth lying on the floor like it was a perfectly normal activity on a Saturday afternoon. He could smell the booze on her breath, and whatever else she was spun out on.

"Let's go." Radley stepped past his aunt. "What's up on the top floor? The drug dealers?" He couldn't help the sarcasm. Oh, how he hated being in this pathetic environment again. His entire childhood, the memories of his father's meth lab in the basement, came all flooding back into his mind. *It's fucking gross.*

He went to the stairs, and realized his aunt wasn't behind him.

"Dulcie?" he called, looking back to the room. He heard

her saying something through the doorway. "What are you doing? Come on, let's get outta here."

His aunt knelt down beside the woman. She helped her sit up, talking softly to her, calling her 'sweetie'. The woman responded by cussing and swatting her away. Dulcie told her to stop it, and ordered her to calm down.

"Aunt Dulcie?" Radley repeated, rolling his eyes. His patience wore thin. There were other places they needed to go to track down his mother, and he just wanted to get out of this dive, knowing a few more were likely in store for him. "Look I'm not here to play Sally Ann, okay? Do you know this woman?"

"Yes, I know her," Dulcie answered, annoyed. The woman was getting antsy, and appeared to be throwing a tantrum, insisting to be left alone.

"Well, does she know where my mother is?" Radley asked. "Because if she doesn't, she's no use to me, and I'm not in the mood for doting on some useless crackpot."

"Don't fuckin' touch me!" The woman slapped at his aunt. Her slurred snarl indicated she was still high.

"Stop it!" Dulcie said, grabbing her hand. "You're coming with us."

"No, I'm not!" the woman screamed. "Get the hell away from me!"

"Dulcie!" Radley hissed at his aunt. "Forget it. I agreed to come with you to find my mother, not to rescue the whole friggin' East side. This woman can stay here and rot for all I care!"

Dulcie looked at her nephew. Her eyes glared at him with a forceful intensity, and told Radley everything he needed to know. His heart sunk into his belly. Her words, at that point, were frivolous.

"Radley, this woman is your mother."

Chapter 18

"What?" His aunt's words numbed him.

"This is your mother," Dulcie insisted as she whisked him over. "Help me with her, please."

"What?" Radley asked a second time. He looked at the frail, dizzy woman in front of him. How could this pathetic, little stick be his mother? *She has no jaw!* Her bottom jaw was as flat as a piece of paper. *She has no teeth in her mouth,* he realized.

"Help me. Please, Radley!" his aunt repeated trying to pull Carla Wycliffe to her feet. His mother stumbled against the wall and cursed under her breath. Radley wedged between her and the wall to brace her up and secure a better grip.

It was then he realized she didn't have on pants. All she wore was a black sweater, which looked saggy on her – she was completely naked from the waist down. Radley reached under her right arm and propped it on his shoulder.

"Who are you? Get your fuckin' hands off me," his mother cursed him. Her eyes were wild and glassy, and breath smelled like rotten salami. Radley didn't feel so bad – she didn't recognize him either.

"Carla, this is your son." Dulcie spoke to her sister as if she was a five-year-old. "This is your boy, Radley."

Carla looked up at her son. "Radley?" she asked. He could see her teeth were worse than he first realized – black and badly rotted, poking through her blood-red gums like yellow maggots. As Radley and Dulcie carried her into the light, Carla's grey, blotch marks and her brown, leather like skin stuck out like fluorescent paint on her face.

"My God, Mother," Radley muttered. The last time he saw her was in a courtroom, but the last real memory he had of her was stroking her palm the evening the police stormed into their living room. She was on crystal meth at the time, and the cops had to wrestle her to the ground to subdue her.

Where are all the frickin' rabbits? He remembered her asking. That line disturbed him for years. The sight of her now would disturb him for decades.

Radley and his aunt tried to maneuver her out of the hallway.

"Where are we going?" Carla stopped and slapped at her sister. "I want to talk to my baby."

"You can do that in the car," Dulcie said. "We need to get out of this place."

"Is that really Radley, my baby?" Carla tried to put her hand on Radley's cheek.

"Yeah … uh, Mom." Radley pulled her hand away from him. He wasn't ready for this. "Look, we need to get you into the car."

"I can't believe it's really you." Her tone was sweet, loving toward her son, then instantly turned venomous towards her sister. "Why the fuck did you take him away from me?" Carla's anger caused her to stumble.

"Whoa, Mom." Radley caught her, holding her up straight, having to grab and support her bare, bony rear-end to do so.

"Nobody took Radley away from you, Carla." Dulcie resumed her adult–like tone. "We're going to the car – Radley's coming with us."

"Really?" Carla smiled, trying to caress Radley's face again. "Good. Maybe we can go to the bar and get a beer. Aunt Dulcie can take us to get a beer. Would you like that, baby?"

"No, Mom." Radley couldn't hide the disgust in his voice. "We need to get you home, okay." He looked at his aunt – for the first time all day, he and Dulcie finally understood each other.

They moved Carla forward, toward the stairway. They took a slight dip into the open doorway of the first spare bedroom.

"Hey, where are you going with my slut!" The slumbering man shot out of the entranceway, startling Radley and Dulcie.

"Oh God!" Dulcie jumped, startled. The man grabbed Radley's arm.

"Hey, what the hell are you doing?" Radley pulled his arm away in revulsion. "Get your filthy paws off me!"

The man appeared to be hung over – his breath reeked of old whiskey. *Single Malt. I recognize the honey smell. Hilltop or Reisers? Oh God, how pathetic is that? I can almost pinpoint the brand.*

"This slut owes me blow!" The man took a swing at Carla's face, grabbing at her hair.

"Back off, buddy!" Radley slapped the man's hand away.

"Fuck you, Leo!" Carla spat at him. "I don't owe you nothin' – you Goddamn cocksucker!"

"You owe me favors, slut." He grabbed the side of her hair hard enough to pull roots out. "Get on that floor!"

Reacting out of sheer rage, Radley pried the man's grip from his mother's hair and shoved him in the chest, tumbling him backward through the entrance of the bedroom. The man flopped to the ground like a broken sapling. He offered no resistance. Radley didn't know if he hurt him or not.

"Radley let's go!" His aunt's voice sounded panicked.

Radley tried to breathe. Fury welled up inside him. He wanted to charge into the room and stomp on the man's head.

Leo groaned and tried to sit up, rubbing his head.

Get him. Stomp the son-of-a-bitch's head in! Be the fucking devil!

He gave himself a mental smack. *God where did that come from?* Radley stopped himself.

"Radley, let's go! Let's get out of here!" his aunt shouted.

Leave him, Radley. Diane's voice popped into his head. *That isn't you.* For whatever reason, the thought of him cowering in his mother's arms as the scar-faced man burned his father with the cigarette lighter popped into his head. He repressed that image from his mind.

Let's go. Radley turned and left the man alone. The idiot yelled something out in anger. Radley heard, but it didn't register.

They stuffed Carla through the lopsided doorway and carried her down the stairwell.

"Here, Radley, you drive." Dulcie handed him her keys. "I'll sit in the backseat with her."

They lay Carla into the back seat of the car. Radley grimaced as he was forced to look at his mother's ravaged privates as she flopped onto the two seats. Dulcie went to the trunk and pulled out a dusty blanket.

"Yeah, good idea," Radley said, scowling. "Cover her up."

His hands still shook as he pulled away from the drug den and into the East End traffic. He flew out of the neighbourhood, not at all worrying about his speed. The thought of Leo running out of the house after them urged him forward. He started to calm as he hit the lights that led into the southeast.

"Where can we get a beer?" his mother said, lying on her side with her feet up on her sister's lap. Her voice was a cross between a whine and a polite request. "My baby boy wants to have a drink with me."

"Why can't we get a drink?" Carla continued a few minutes later, lifting her head up from the window ledge in the backseat. Her words were slow, slurred, but agitated. "It's only one fucking drink."

"I'm getting you some clothes." Dulcie cut her short. She ruffled through her purse, and pulled out a credit card.

"Here, Aunty." Radley reached into his wallet and handed her a fifty dollar bill. "Let me pay for them."

Radley pulled into a strip mall, in front of a discount clothing store. They had driven out of the bad part of the East end and decided that before they do anything else, they needed to get his mother some pants.

Dulcie took the money and nodded her appreciation, giving

Radley the impression she had probably spent a fortune bailing out his mother before.

"Do you see that, Carla?" Dulcie showed her sister the money. The derision in her voice was unmistakable. "Your son is buying you clothes."

"Are you, Radley?" Carla returned to her babyish, spiny tone, as if just remembering her long lost son was in the front seat. She completely missed her sister's sarcasm. "That's so nice that you'd do that for me."

Radley didn't bother to turn around. He couldn't bear to look at her. Quickly glancing in the rear-view mirror, he gave a short, polite smile to appease her, then looked straight ahead.

Dulcie could sense the awkward moment. "I'll be right back," she sighed. "Stay here," she warned her sister.

"Radley, honey." His mother's voice was sweet but purposeful. "I haven't seen you in so long. Where've you been?"

As far away from you as I could possibly get. But he didn't say it. He'd only been around her twenty minutes, yet her slurred words, the stench of her body, and that weepy, spun-out tone of voice, brought back a flood of uncomfortable, painful memories he would have preferred to forget.

"Radley, baby," his mother continued, "talk to me, honey."

"I'm fine, Mom." His tone was short. "Okay? I'm fine. I'm living with my foster family. I work full time, and I'm happy, okay? Happier than I ever was living with you and Dad." *And I'm a closet alcoholic. I have liquor under my bed, and sneak a shot of rum in my coffee every morning. I go out to the bar every chance I get, and get stinking, slobbering drunk, because I have no other purpose in life. So don't worry mom, I'm just like you. I'm just fucking like you.* He didn't say those words, the mere thought of them tasted like dog shit on his tongue.

"Tavis was such a jerk," Carla slurred. She rested her head against the hand rest of the backside passenger's seat door. "He ruined me, that bastard." She grunted. Radley wondered if she wasn't starting to sober up.

"How's your brother? How's my Dusty?" his mother asked. "I heard he was in jail. Dulcie told me that, I think."

Radley closed his eyes. "Yes, mother, Dustin's in prison."

"Is his wife okay? His daughter? He has a daughter, right? I worry about them all the time."

Radley looked at her in the mirror as if she told him she'd just won the Nobel Prize for Literature. "You worry about them?" He spun around and lashed at her. "You worry about them? What the hell have you ever done for them besides get stoned and naked in some crack house?"

"I'm addicted, Radley." His mother teared up. "I couldn't stop. I can't stop."

"Just don't say any more." Radley threw his hands up, then slammed the steering wheel, hard. "Just don't say anything ever again."

"Tell Dustin I'm sorry," Carla wept. "I'm sorry he got put in jail."

Yeah, tell him I'm sorry too. Radley shook his head. He wanted to get out, walk, think – instead, he remained in the vehicle with his decrepit, wretched mother, and his interminable guilt.

Dulcie returned to the back seat with a plastic bag full of clothes. She saw her sister sobbing, hunched over her lap.

"I got you some pants, underwear, a bra and a clean blouse," Dulcie said, completely un-phased at her sister's crying. She gently rubbed her sister's back. "I also brought you a brush and soap. We'll clean you up before we bring you into the home, okay, sweetie?"

Radley pulled back into traffic. His mother's wails blended into the routine hum of the vehicles and city noise.

They pulled over ten minutes later at a gas bar in the Southwest. Carla had retreated into quiet, guttural snuffles and moans. Dulcie managed to get her into underwear and pants, fitting the clothes onto her as though she were a newborn.

"Honey, you need to get a hold of yourself before I take you into the bathroom," Dulcie said. "What are you crying about?"

Radley rolled his eyes. He didn't want to hear his mother's sob story about Dustin anymore. It would just infuriate him further. His mother's next words, however, caught him off guard.

"I need some money. I need a fix, Dulcie. I don't have my speed."

"No, sweetie! NO!" Dulcie's tone was wicked, harsh. "I am not giving you one penny. You are going into the bathroom to get cleaned up, and then we are taking you straight to rehab, do you understand me?"

Carla retreated into her shallow, defeated sobs. "I need my fix," she repeated.

"Carla, get a hold of yourself!" Dulcie yelled. "Come on, your son is here! Is this what you want him to see?"

"D-Dustin is here?" Carla's head shot up. She slurred her words once more. She looked glossy eyed, confused, as if she had just gotten hit on the head with a hammer.

"No, sweetie," Dulcie said, sighing. "Radley. *Radley* is here."

"Oh, Radley is here," Carla said, looking at him wide-eyed. "Radley, baby, is that really you? How have you been, Sweetie?"

Chapter 19

Radley returned home that evening, as miserable as ever. They left his mother at a government-run rehabilitation center ten kilometers outside the city. The group home she lived in had kicked her out permanently, and none of the charitable agencies wanted her. The ones Radley talked to pretty much rolled their eyes when they heard the name Carla Wycliffe.

Not saying hello when he returned home, Radley instead walked straight to his suite in the basement. He knew Diane had waited up for him. He saw the dining room light on but didn't bother to go upstairs. The image of his ratty, decimated biological mother had contaminated his brain, and he didn't want to talk about it. To see that woman wither away to nothing, both physically and mentally, aggravated him like a festering wound. The thought boggled his mind as to how ten years with Doug and Diane helped heal the pain of his childhood, yet only one day spent with his biological mother could bring it all back – the drugs, the alcohol, the fighting, the assaults, the living in constant fear – The situation with Dustin.

He was certain his mother must have been told the story by someone. How Radley condemned his brother to prison, how he became shunned from the rest of the family. Word probably leaked out that her youngest son ratted Tavis out as well – that one he didn't feel as bad about, but who knew what his mother would think? It didn't matter anyway; her brain was so fried she couldn't even remember Radley being in the car with her. He clambered into his room and flopped face down on the bed. He needed a drink — should he go out? Call up Mordecai, or one of the guys from work? No, he'd rather just drink. He didn't need anyone to do that with. Reaching between his headboard and mattress, he pulled out the whiskey flask hidden inside the casing.

God, I'm such a loser. He tasted the strong, pungent liquid on his lips before it burned down his throat. It didn't seem possible he could ever drink water again.

A few swallows later, the thoughts returned. They started a few weeks ago. Everything would be so much easier if he would just take his own life. He could do it — had known enough from working with Dustin how painless it would be just to lock himself in a garage with the car running. Carbon monoxide poisoning would simply put him to sleep, never to wake up again. The alternative was pills, but getting the medication would be a pain in the ass. He could go out in a wave of glory — drive his car off a cliff and smash into a million little pieces. Anything would be better than living this.

You're wasting your life away, getting hammered every night, and going down the same bloody path your father did twenty years ago, Cyclo's words lashed out at him.

I'm a frickin' loser. Twenty-four years old, living with my parents because I'm too screwed up to get a decent job and do anything with my life.

You broke the cycle, Radley. You got away from it. Don't start another one.

Damn you Cyclo! What the hell did you know about life? A loser biker who helped Tavis build up a crystal meth business. If my father hadn't taken the brunt of the fall, your sorry-ass would still be rotting in prison. Radley grabbed his bottle and took one more swig. The whiskey tasted sour. It sat in his mouth.

I need a fix. His mother's voice repeated.

Radley spat the mouthful of whiskey against the wall. He could see the mess of brown drops against his white drywall. Diane would have lynched him if she saw that.

Never again. Radley slammed the flask on his headboard.

I am my mother, my father, my brother. His head no longer muffled up by booze.

Decisions. I can decide! He remembered the day he stood at his mailbox, amidst the willow leaves– the day he turned in Dustin. Mailing the letter that tipped off the cops – he did it because he chose to do the right thing, no matter the consequences. Now he was going to live with them, guilt and regret be damned. He wouldn't care what the Wycliffe family thought – this was his life now, and he wouldn't follow the path his biological mother and father took.

Decision made.

He charged over to his closet and pulled out the box of beer, gin, and half empty rum he had hidden in his duffel bag. Putting his whiskey flask into it, he charged up the stairs and into the dining room, the bag slung over his shoulder.

"Radley?" Diane was reading at the chesterfield. She stood up seeing the box of liquor. "Have you been drink–"

Radley cut her off. "Yes. But never again. I'm done. Do you mind if I smash these bottles on your garden rocks? I promise I'll clean up the glass, and hose off the liquid."

He could see his foster mother's hesitancy. No doubt she thought he was officially a lunatic.

"Be my guest." She gestured to the patio doors. "Just make sure you don't get glass in your eye."

"Right. Thanks," Radley said. It was getting dark outside, but he didn't care. "Six hours carting Carla Wycliffe all over the city would be enough to make Bonnie Prince Charlie go sober."

"That bad, huh?" Diane asked.

Radley whisked through the patio doors, straight to the giant-sized stones she had in the backyard. A tinge of hesitancy crept into him as he lifted the rum – this was a waste of money after all - $33 for that bottle alone.

This bottle represents everything I was, and everything I have gone through. The thought of his pantless mother, face down in the back seat, blasted into his mind.

He went backward a few paces, then threw the bottle full force against the rock. It exploded like fireworks.

Chapter 20

Two Months Later

Fuck, why did I get rid of all my booze? He hated thinking that way. Lying on his bed, he rubbed his hands over his face, then looked at his palms quizzically. They were moist. *God, I'm sweating.*

Radley had been sober since he smashed his stash of alcohol on Diane's backyard boulders, and it had been absolute hell from that point on.

He forced himself off the bed, and into the bathroom. It wasn't AA night – not that it mattered because he skipped the last two. There was no motivation to attend any more – the people were too flakey, the program too scripted, and everything got whacked-out religious, requiring you to place your faith in a higher power – whom everyone referred to as 'God," – putting Radley completely out of his comfort zone. No, he was done with AA, the only problem was telling that to his foster mother.

She's going to be home soon. Radley glanced at his watch. He knew that Doug was teaching a night class and would be home well past 11:00, but Diane went out to some feminist thing and would be back soon. *And she's going to wanna know what I did tonight.*

He had told her he would workout for an hour, then spend the rest of the evening studying. Having started Business Administration at the College, he had access to their universal gym, and wanted to take advantage of its location next to the food court, which in the evenings provided a quiet study area to work on his readings or homework.

Of course all of that meant getting off your ass, driving across town and getting on the exercise bike, Doug's voice entered his head, *and instead all you've done is lie on your ass, bellyaching because you smashed your casks. Poor you.*

Christ the urge to drink was killing him. He could taste the rum – his favorite - let it sit in his mouth, savor over his tongue, and burn down his esophagus as he swallowed it. The cravings made him want to pull his hair out, and he knew, without question, they were what kept him locked up in his room, all sweaty and with a big hate on.

The rum, it's almost as if I can smell it. Plopping down on the closed toilet seat, he rest his head in his hands. He couldn't get the taste – he felt like if he could just have a glass, just two minutes of the warm, numbing sensation to overtake him, to take the edge off, he would be able to get busy, get to the gym. All other substitutes he had tried – cola, black coffee, some weird Golgi juice Diane made him try – all of it just tasted so bland, so watery, unsatisfying.

The Devil is summoning me again. It had its ways, and certainly had tested him these past two months in different forms. Alcohol ads on radio and TV, far more numerous than he had noticed before. His friends also – Mordecai was constantly calling and texting him on phone to go out for a drink.

"Shit man, come out for one at least." He had phoned Radley two nights ago. "You're not a drunk, dude. Fuck, go downtown at 2 AM in the morning, and that's where you'll find the alcoholics, slobbering at your feet, begging for liquor money. That sure as hell isn't you."

But it is me. Radley thought of his biological mother once more. Of his father, sitting in a prison cell, and Dustin. *It's in the Wycliffe genes. Arrghhh!*

He stood up and made a motion to punch the wall, pound right through the gyprock. It was something he saw his father do twice when Radley was growing up. One hole Tavis instantly patched, apologizing to his wife and to the boys for an entire week afterwards. The second, a couple years later, Tavis never fixed. It remained in their downstairs drywall like a scar from a wound that was never treated.

Even if I could repair the wall, Radley thought, imagining himself putting his fist through, *Diane would throw me out of the house, or worse.*

Instead he went to the sink, took a handful of cold water and splashed it on his face, then did the rational, proper, and wholeheartedly insufferable thing he could do. Wearing only his T-Shirt and jeans, he exited his room, walked to the front door, stuffed his feet into sneakers, and left the house to walk. The evening had darkened and the air was cold, but Radley walked down his block and just kept walking, keeping himself moving.

Goddamnit, he cursed, shivering as he walked. Needing a jacket or a hoodie to cut the bite of the air, he didn't get either one. The faster he moved, the less the chill hurt. As he sauntered past the houses in the neighborhood, his mind, at least for this round, was completely off of drinking.

Two Weeks Later

Lift, lift. Radley repeated to himself in the college gym, bench-pressing the universal weights. He closed his eyes and put himself into a rhythm, the music from Metallica's *One* blaring in the portable, multidisc CD player he had sitting on the floor next to his bench.

The music soothed him, but the repetition of power-lifting the weights kept his focus, and his mind off of the drink. Every exertion - every thrust - he made helped him move forward. He was not really into the exercise for the muscle, and certainly not for the girls, the majority of whom he had met at college wanted only to go out and party; rather, he was in it because it made him feel good, and feeling good kept him away from the bottle.

That and the studying. He realized. I'm enjoying business management. The classes were interesting, the instructors were good, mature people. One thing about living with the Trillamedes, Radley became familiar with academic folk – all of the Trillamedes' friends were university professors or clerical staff. Business, even academia, seemed to have a calling for him, though he still wasn't certain exactly what field he would go into. Marketing was a possibility, maybe managerial work. Might be cool to run a franchise restaurant – a Moxie's or a Kelsey's, where families or coworkers would convene on a busy Friday or Saturday night, then the rest of the week would be a lighter schedule. There was some appeal to that.

Either way, you're searching for your purpose, kiddo, Diane's voice returned to his head. *That's what you need to find, and that's what'll get you away from that damn booze.*

Radley smirked as he finished his second set of repetitions, and stopped to rest. She was right, of course. Always was. It just took him awhile to see it.

He waited for the song to end, then the next one came on. Not realizing how loud the stereo was turned up, he glanced around the gym. It was still empty.

Good, he thought. It better be, it's 10:30 PM and closes in half an hour. Almost happy hour at O'Leary's Bar, where he frequented often with Mordecai and Brian.

And with that thought, the damn craving, the taste, the sensation all came flooding back into his brain, into his mouth. He winced, then closed his eyes again.

Lift, lift.

Radley's cell rang the next evening, just before nine. There was no desire to answer the phone, he already knew who it was. The person had sent two text messages earlier in the evening which Radley had ignored. He thought of doing the same with this one, but he was sitting at the dining room table with his Macroeconomics assignment in front of him, and the Trillamedes were lounging on the couch in the next room.

"Radley, your phone is ringing." Diane called from the den.

Yeah, thanks Ma, I know. There was no choice but to pick it up. He sighed as he grabbed his flip phone and hit the send button to answer it.

"Hello."

"Dude, what the fuck?" Mordecai's voice shot through the line. His voice was giddy even though his language was not. It was obvious he had already started drinking. "Why the hell are you not answering my texts?"

"Sorry. I've...been busy. Lots on my plate, you know."

"Well, what are you doing now? Why don't you come out with us, man?"

"I got tons of work to do, dude. Have an assignment due on Monday." That was a lie.

"Fuck man, it's Friday night! Who gives a rat's hiney what you got due on Monday? What the hell's wrong with you?"

This is exactly why I didn't want to answer the phone. Radley rubbed his forehead, trying to get out of this.

"It's a big project, actually. I haven't even started it yet." Another lie. "I just want to do well this year. Forked out quite a bit of coin for college. Can't really afford to mess it up."

"You won't mess it up. Man, it's just one night. Come out tonight, have a drink. We're set up with these hot babes from outta town. Might go over to their hotel to…well, you can imagine, right! Come on, get your ass out here."

And there you are. The thought entered Radley's head. There was something about his words, the goading. *I know exactly what you're doing with my friend, you son of a bitch.*

"Look man, I'm sorry but I'm saying no." Radley said. "Maybe we can go out later in the week, catch a movie or something if you like." He cringed at the comment, knowing how it would be received.

"What the—" Mordecai made as guffaw, as though Radley had told him he was joining a monastery. "Go to a movie? Holy fuck, what are you, six? Hey boys!" He started calling to his compatriots in the bar. "Hey Brian, hey boys – Radley doesn't want to come out and drink tonight because he's got to stud-eee. Doesn't want to come out and get laid, but he wants to go and watch Star Wars with us one night. You believe this shit?"

"I'll see you later." Was all Radley said before he hung up. His heart sank. It hurt to know they were laughing at him. There was a part of him that missed the excitement of the bar. A rum and Coke on ice would be so tantalizing right now.

And that, he thought resolutely, *is why I'm not going out.*

Diane stepped into the dining room entranceway. "That sounded a lot harder than it should have been."

Radley leaned back in his chair, and gave an empty laugh. "It was peer pressure. Worse than high school."

"How long has it been since you had a drink?"

160

The question surprised him. He did a quick calculation in his head, based on the date. "Well, I guess it's been two months, 13 days, since I smashed those bottles."

She smiled. "And we're proud of you. Just wanted you to know that." She gave him a wink, then returned to the living room.

"Thank-you," he called out, knowing she could hear him, then leaned back in his chair. He licked his lips. There was sweat on his face. *Goddamn it.*

Two Hours Later

It was midnight. Radley stood over a part of the city called the Hallows – it was the pinnacle of a large hill that offered a vantage point of the entire city. On a clear night after dark the view was spectacular because the city lights lit up the night sky and you could see to the outer edges of the city from either side of the peak. He decided to walk up the hill along the roadside – most people drove to the top, and only the brave few were daring enough to hike, especially at this hour.

There's my childhood neighborhood, Radley noticed to the far west of the city, then quickly dismissed it. *I don't need to think about that shit right now.*

The ping of his cell phone interrupted the quiet. There were only two people on the planet who would be texting him, and he was certain Mordecai was done with him.

Where are you? It was Diane. *You said you were going for a walk! Just at the Hallows. Needed to think.*

The Hallows?! That's a hike, not a walk!

It was a fair statement. He had been gone for two hours,

161

and left right after Mordecai's accosting about staying in on a Friday night.

Yeah, and the real reason I'm out here is because I feel like a friggin' loser studying in my parent's dining room on a Friday night when I could be out at a bar with friends and out-of-town, pretty girls. And why aren't I?

Because I'm a recovering alcoholic and could cave any second. He didn't type any of that. Instead, he simply wrote, *Heading down the hill now, and clearing my head. Fresh air's better than a Rum Hurricane, if u catch my drift.*

Indeed, Diane instantly texted back. *I get the joke. And it's you, not u!*

As he walked down, a white truck zipped past him on the road, going way faster than it should have this late at night on this particular incline. He noticed the make and model.

Dodge Ram, Pickup, 2500 series. V8, 8 Cylinder. The 2000, 2001 model, a couple years old. The newer models have a rounder hood and a wider bed.

He named two more vehicles that passed him, down to their exact specs, finally stopping himself when the third, a small, four door Chevy Prizm, drove past and he realized there was no way in hell he could have named that vehicle, let along describe it, five years ago, or any other point in his life, for that matter.

It was my time with Dustin. I learned so much about cars with that guy, I…enjoyed it. Miss it, even.

He started pacing on the road, rubbing his lips as he thought. *Holy shit.*

It was obvious from his conversation tonight, and the fact that he trekked up a frigging mountain in the middle of the night that the bar scene, or the restaurant-that-served-alcohol scene, or any other 'scene' where there were happy, liquored up people, wouldn't be a good fit for his career, or his soul.

No, I think I know something better.

He had found his purpose.

Chapter 21

Twenty Two Months Later – September – Age 26

The final rivet was tightened, securing the railing to the bridge. The children's playground stood completed.

"Congratulations, team." Winston Denault, the dealership owner, came around each of the picnic tables, and shook the hand of every one of his employees. The last hand he shook belonged to Radley Trillamede's.

"Radley, your first official playground. Good job buddy!" Winston slapped his arm. Despite being in his late 60s, he was a trim, fit, and energetic owner, with carefully styled, spiked gray hair that seemed odd for a senior citizen. His energy and enthusiasm rubbed off on everybody.

"Thanks, Captain," Radley said, smiling at his boss. *Actually it's my second playground, but who's counting.*

Radley withheld the correction to his boss. He tirelessly volunteered for Denault Motors during the summer of last year, showing up at charity functions and doing odd jobs around the dealership, hoping to get his foot in the door. Finally noticed, they asked him to work part-time in the parts department in the New Year. With a two-year business administration degree under his belt, Radley accepted the offer to take a training course at company headquarters, which led to his full-time hiring as a sales person.

"For the first time in my life, I have a career, not a job," he told Doug and Diane when he finally moved out of their place in the spring. He rented a two bedroom apartment in the north end of the city, six blocks away from the dealership. It was enough for the Trillamedes to take him out to dinner to celebrate.

As expected, Winston pulled out the champagne and poured all the volunteers a glass in a plastic, disposable wine cup. Radley accepted the drink, having anticipated that the head honcho would be serving alcohol this time around. He had hoped he could conveniently disappear, helping put tools away when it came to this part, but there was no opportunity to, and the boss man had been insistent that all volunteers be called in for his closing, celebratory speech.

Come on, kid, he heard his boss's voice inside his head, feeling Winston slap him on the side of the arm, like he usually did when speaking to employees. *It's just a cheap dollar-store cup of even cheaper champagne. Cut yourself some slack, you just spent the whole day volunteering to put up a playground for kids, for Christ Sakes.*

Just drink it, Mordecai's voice was next. *It's fucking baby Pablum compared to what you're used to.*

It's just a small, six ounce glass, Diane was the last to goad him. *One swig isn't going to matter.*

Nice try with the fake foster mother advice, Radley thought to himself, in a mocking, defiant tone. *There's no way in God's Green Earth Diane would ever say that to me.* Whenever he came around alcohol these past two years, the internal dialogue had been commonplace. The temptation was there, the craving returned

- not so much for rum anymore but just for the strong sharpness of booze – one sip of weak champagne surely wouldn't put him over the edge.

"This playground is for the kids of this community"–the real Winston completed his announcement to the entire group–"and the tireless volunteers who make this tradition a success. Where's our new guy? Radley? This is your first playground with us. How are you going to feel, ten years down the road, driving out here and seeing kids who haven't even been born yet, climbing these monkey bars?"

Radley tried to ignore the smirks on his co-workers faces. He had been asked the exact same question by Winston last year, when he helped the sales team build their annual playground in the south-end.

Playing along, Radley held up his glass. "Actually, I will feel just as good as I do when I see those kids on our south-side playground roll gravel down the slide."

The laughter ensued, and Winston had the typical, taken-aback look whenever he laid a goose egg. "Were you with us out in Ridgeway last year?" The razzing of the boss continued. "Sorry buddy." Winston threw his arm around his employee. "That's why I love this kid. He's tactful, not like the rest of you clowns. Let's get those barbeque grills lit. Food and Champagne are on me, everybody. Drink up."

The teasing, laughing, and eating eventually gave Radley his chance. As the attention fell on the boss, Radley snuck around to the back of the dealership van and pretended to tie his shoe. As he did so, he set his champagne cup down on the grass, and tipped it over. The grass soaked up the alcohol like a sponge.

"Thanks, Cappy," Radley said, returning to the barbeque, and setting his glass in the garbage. That subtle gesture had allowed him to keep his streak in-tact – two years, two months, and 14 days alcohol-free.

"Where are them burgers?" he said. "I'm famished."

The dealership's annual playground set-up was a community event. Denault Motors invited church leaders, community groups, and the local police to help out. That's why it wasn't a surprise for Radley to see a uniformed officer at the event, but it caught him off guard when Winston and that same officer approached Radley after supper.

"Hey, Radley, let's talk for a moment," Winston said, plopping himself down in the empty lawn chair next to Radley. The officer, middle aged with a blond crewcut, chose to remain standing. "This is Staff Sergeant Donaldson." The two exchanged an awkward introduction – the officer was polite enough, but his firm handshake overpowered Radley's flimsy, wet-fish grip. The presence of a police officer still made Radley uncomfortable – more fallout from his childhood.

"Listen, Radley," Winston continued, "we were talking about some initiatives going on in the city right now and your name came up."

"Really?" Radley answered, surprised.

"Yeah, I remembered the story about your birth mother and how they found her a few months back. You mentioned to me she was a drug addict."

"That's right." Radley looked down. No matter how hard he tried, his mother and her final fate would forever haunt him. Discovered underneath a bridge in the outskirts of the city, Carla was found naked, hands and feet bound, a rip cord wire around her neck. The autopsy showed she injected heroin shortly before her death, after which time someone raped, killed, then raped her again post-mortem. It didn't come as a shock or even a surprise to Radley – he was called into the coroner's office to identify the body. He saw the bruises, the burn and needle marks in her arms and neck. There was difficulty identifying her – the body rotted in murky water for a few days before two boys fishing in the river stumbled across her corpse. In the end, Radley recognized her hands, the freckled marking on her bony, withered right hand gave him the cue. All he needed to do after was look into the eyes of her bloated, decomposed face, and see the anguish, addiction, and sadness there to be able to identify her as Carla Wycliffe, his biological mother.

"Yeah." Winston could see the turmoil in Radley's face, and his tone changed. "I remember you telling me your mother's drug use had a real rotten impact on your life. Drove you to alcohol, and all that stuff. Well, it looks to me like you've picked yourself up from all that. The constable and I were talking about a program we're sponsoring in the schools, getting former drug users or family members to talk to the kids about drug abuse, its impact on people, and why they shouldn't get involved."

"Yeah, I'm familiar with that program," Radley said. *Oh, and by the way, Winston, did I mention my drug-dealing father to you? He's currently in prison — been there for the past 15 years because of my previous involvement in that program.*

"You should think about going out to the schools, talk about your experiences. The city police are running the program; I'm one of the chairpersons. You would partner up with a city officer, go to each class, tell your story. The officer would do all the nitty-gritty stuff with the kids. You present one — maybe two — days a week — I'll give you the time off. What do you say?"

All Radley could do was picture himself in a grade nine health class, the same one he attended way back when, standing at the front of the room like Dale Roake, handing out slips of paper and saying, "Okay guys, only serious questions today, alright?"

"Come on, Radley." Winston gave him a slap on the arm. "Great opportunity here, hey buddy?"

As much of a worker's boss that he knew Winston Denault to be, Radley also knew he wasn't a man you say no to, especially for a request like this one.

"Yeah, okay, sure," Radley said, smiling to hide his uncertainty. "I'll do it."

Chapter 22

Okay, Radley thought as he sat in his new car across from the playground he had fond memories of. In his lap sat 10 advertising fliers and a ruffled, dirty newspaper bag. *Time to deliver some junk-mail.*

The Infiniti, purchased from Denault motors, was his first ever car – silvery white, all-wheel drive, plush interior – certainly nothing a paper delivery boy would be driving. Today was payday, and after Radley finished work, he deposited his cheque. Sitting in his hand were three, crisp $100 bills. He placed them in a plain, security-lined envelope with the typewritten words A GIFT FOR YOU on the back and sealed it. He dressed in his routine disguise: dark glasses, fake moustache, low ball cap, and earphones. Wearing a dark hoodie, an LA Raiders jacket, and grey jogging pants, this was an outfit no one would catch him dead in, but it had become a valuable part of his new operation.

The newspapers were a guise – he employed many different ways of carrying out these transactions. This was the cleverest of his schemes. He would take a stack of leftover grocery flyers from the local Safeway and place them in his bag, tucking the envelope in the eighth newspaper of his bundle, and always started eight houses down. The eighth house got the newspaper with the cash in it. The first few times he tried it this way, he was paranoid about missing the house, but deep down he knew there would never be a chance of him consciously failing to make the delivery. By far the most daring way to deliver the money, also became the one he preferred the most. The sheer closeness of returning to the house again, to the double garage, the hint of catching a glimpse of either of them made it all the more appealing.

He approached Dustin and Jezzelle's place, trotting up the stairway. No one appeared to be home, though the mysterious white truck was parked in front of the garage. He had seen it there last month when he did a quick drive-by to check things out. Despite being curious, he placed the newspaper in between their screen and wooden door so it would spill onto the floor when they opened it up, forcing them to pick it up and find the envelope.

Radley hadn't delivered the money this way for a couple of months – he had relied on less conspicuous ways – Jezzelle's office mail, an anonymous post package, even a fake parking ticket on her hatchback, with hand-written instructions on the back telling her to look behind the front tire. Not at all convinced that his covert actions were foolproof, he hoped his creativity at least kept them wondering. Aunt Dulcie mentioned that Jezzelle had been having financial problems – her father sold his business and could no longer assist his daughter. When the second Radley heard the news, he started devising ways to secretly help her out. Figuring by now he would be considered a suspect for the mysterious money delivery, his unwavering persistence – $300 a month since he started working at the dealership – might have diverted the suspicion somewhat.

Shoot, no Jezzie, no Abbie. Radley frowned as he turned away from his sister-in-law's porch, without so much as a distant glance of either special lady. He knew Jezzelle would never speak to him again, and that little girl had grown up so much. It made him wonder about the things she would be into now. Two years had passed since he last saw her. The hard part, unfortunately, was knowing his not being around worked out for the best.

He sighed and finished his now pointless, but important, routine - delivering paper numbers 9, 10 and 11 to the final three houses of his fake route.

Three Months Later

Radley walked through the school hallway with the projector bag anchored over his shoulder. The snowmen crafts on one of the hallway bulletin boards reminded him of another life time. His days in elementary school were as foreign to him as life in a faraway country – the only real memory he had of that age was of his parents fighting, their occasional camping trips to the lake, and the odd time playing computer games with Dustin. He couldn't even remember the names of most of his elementary teachers – he had either been away from school or had too many problems on his mind.

God, what the hell am I doing here? Finding the Grade 5

classroom he was to present in, it was empty as the kids were currently on recess. An integer number line was strung across the room, and student stories and spelling words were stapled to the walls.

Grade 5, what are they 9 or 10 years old at that age? The target audience had gotten younger. Radley was in Grade 9 when he first encountered Constable Roake and the DARE program, but as Sergeant Donaldson told him at his orientation a couple of months back, *the problem kids get younger and younger every year.*

The female officer he was partnered with entered the classroom with the teacher a couple of minutes later. Radley hadn't worked with her yet. On the email schedule Winston's secretary had sent out to all presenters, her name was listed as Constable Clark.

"Hello, it's Radley, right?" The officer shook his hand.

"Yeah, Radley Trillamede." Radley smiled, maintaining a tone of professionalism "And it's Constable Clark, correct? Are you presenting with me today?"" His voice trailed off as he finished the question, realizing how stupid it sounded. Obviously she was there to present with him. As usual, his nervousness around police came to the fore.

"Yes, I will be." The constable smiled, unphased by the awkward question. "And you can call me Claire. Great to work with you today."

"Absolutely." Radley nodded, silently chastising himself for his unease. *Come on, man, you've done ten presentations with these officers, you think you'd quit acting like a criminal in front of them by now.*

To calm himself, he hooked up his laptop and slideshow to the classroom projector, while the Constable discussed their talk with the teacher. There were two uncertainties stressing him out.

How much detail do I go into with these kids regarding my biological parents' drug abuse? What will this cop think? Will she try and shush me? Two of the officers he'd worked with up to this point interrupted his presentation, cutting off his story about Carla and Tavis's drug abuse by deliberately interjecting general statements about citizens' duties to obey the law and not getting caught up in the 'wrong crowd,' whatever the hell that meant. Radley took the hint, and was told bluntly by one of the cops after his presentation that he shouldn't 'frame' his parents' stories in a way that suggested that the justice and rehabilitation system failed them. Attempting to defend himself, he insisted that wasn't his intention, but his intimidation of the officers pushed him to concede his point.

Tavis would just tell those pigs to fuck off. He smirked at the thought, then quickly rebuked it, hearing the break bell signalling the fifth graders to return from recess. *Knock it off you idiot, you're in with little kids.*

The children quietly came into the room and immediately went to their desks, sheepish at the sight of the two new people in their classroom – a strange man and, even more intimidating, a uniformed and fully armed police officer.

Radley knew the feeling.

"Good morning Grade Fives," the Constable took right over and introduced herself. "I'm happy to present our program to you today." She opened with some stories of her police work, made the kids laugh with some of her descriptions, and looked quite comfortable speaking to this age group, something Radley was getting more anxious about, watching how dynamic she was with them. Talking about the program, she drew on her own experience to summarize the types of drugs in the city, and what people who abused them did to either get arrested, or get pulled off the street by officers. The common thread to all of their stories was that the users were addicted, broke, homeless, and desperate. Radley found it engrossing – he had never heard such stories told from the police perspective before.

"At this point, I would like to introduce Mr. Radley Trillamede, my partner for this presentation, who's here to share his own story with drug abuse – Mr. Trillamede."

Oh shit. Radley thought, forcing himself to come to the center of the room. Turning off the screensaver on the Smartboard, he suddenly felt uncomfortable with the opening slide of his show, which displayed his title 'My Mother Against Her Demons: A Life in Pictures' and showed the two photographs of Carla that he received from his Aunt Dulcie – one was her a picture of her in high school – she was young, short-haired and slim, standing with a 35 mm camera around her neck against a rustic fence, laughing at whoever had taken the picture. She looked like the type of girl who could light up a room simply by entering it. The second photo was recent, taken within the past three years, of her in a hospital bed. Having been found passed out in the parking lot of a highway motel an hour out of the city, Carla was taken to the psych ward. The photo was of her the next morning - her bloodshot eyes, hair like a bird's nest on the top of her head. One could make out the ends of her bones in her gaunt face and pale arms. After listening to Claire's engaging stories, to hit these kids with Carla's woe-filled tale seemed rather dispiriting.

Radley looked at the faces – so innocent. He froze for a moment. Everyone in the room awaited his start. Even though he had rehearsed this presentation to the letter, from the timing of his pauses to the inflection of his voice at key points in the show – all with Diane and Doug coaching him, it felt like he was leaning over the edge of a skyscraper. *Do I really do this? What the hell am I going to tell these kids?*

The problem kids are getting younger, Sergeant Donaldson's voice cut into his head.

"Do you have everything you need, sir?" The teacher asked from the back of the room, addressing the uneasy silence.

This is what you do then Bud, Diane's voice spurred him on, *you tell it like it is, and pull no punches.*

"I'm fine, thank-you," Radley said. *Here goes nothing.*

Chapter 23

"Carla was a horrible parent to me," Radley said, closing out his talk with the class. "As brutal as her death was, as *tragic* as her life was, I could not shed a tear for her at the funeral. My own mother, and I couldn't do it."

He finished his talk with the usual message, making it clear to the children his mother had died a junkie, and she had been beaten and murdered as a result of her chosen lifestyle. Using the terms 'beaten' and 'murdered' was a gamble with Middle School, but he want to be honest with them. As it was, the kids didn't appear upset or rattled but rather sombre and thoughtful. Modifying the presentation only slightly, he left out the explicit details of his mother's prostitution and death, but still, he felt, he was able to get the message across to the kids.

"Mr. Trillamede will be happy to take any of your questions," Constable Clark said. She never interrupted his talk, and didn't appear irritated about anything he had said.

There, I got away with it - easy peasy. Radley thought. He clapped his hands in a welcoming gesture. "Okay, guys, question time. Ask me anything, fire away." *I have no blessed idea what these kids would want to know. Should be interesting.*

An oriental girl in the middle row raised her hand. "Do you miss your mother now?"

"Absolutely." Radley nodded. "I miss the lady she was

when she was sober, I miss the lady she could have been." That answer was scripted — he had answered it several times before.

"Have you ever been in jail?" another boy asked. "For drugs or anything?"

"No, I have not." Radley shook his head. "I've made my life choice. I made it a long time ago, thanks to my mother." Junior-high kids always asked that one. Radley started to recognize a pattern — Senior-high kids typically asked issue orientated questions about drugs; the younger ones were more curious about him.

"Is your Dad still alive? Do you talk to him?"

"I haven't talked to my father recently," Radley said. "But he knows how I feel about him." *Good open ended response, thank Diane for that one.*

"Why did you change your last name from Wycliffe to Trillamede?" a girl in the back row asked, jolting Radley from his script. *Where the hell did that question come from?* He rubbed his forehead. *Definitely haven't had that one before.*

Crap, he thought, *did I introduce myself as Wycliffe again?* He'd done that once before, the second time he ever presented to school kids, and it was when he presented with one of the tight-ass constables who had glared him down as he introduced himself, making him nervous.

The class could sense his hesitancy, the awkwardness at the question. A dozen responses raced through his mind — when had he said his Wycliffe name? He looked over at Claire, who looked just as confused as he did.

Wait a minute, Claire introduced me. I couldn't have introduced myself as Wycliffe. He always avoided saying his birth name in his presentations. Did he slip somewhere else?

The cat was out of the bag, either way. He acknowledged the question. "I decided not to use my birth name. I left my mother when I was a little bit older than you guys."

The kids in the class seemed confused.

"I have another question." The same girl raised her hand again. She was a chubbier girl, dressed in a brown hoodie with a headband which matched her auburn hair.

"Go ahead," Radley answered, trying not to appear unraveled.

"So why did you put your brother in jail when he wasn't guilty of stealing anybody's cars?"

Radley's heart leapt up his chest. The kids all turned their heads, and started speaking at once, their attention directed to the girl.

"What you talking about? He never said that!" a boy at the front of the room said to her.

The kafuffle meant little to Radley. Everything else in the room faded away and he honed in on the girl, who glared at him with daggers in her eyes. He knew the second she asked that question – the words, the tone of voice, and the sheer venom that spewed out with them. Radley knew *exactly* who she was.

Abigail. It had been almost five years. The girl who asked these questions was his *niece.*

Radley hadn't noticed, let alone recognized, her sitting

amongst the rest of the class; he was more focused on himself whenever he spoke. She sat quiet at the back of the room, no doubt listening to every word he said. *My God, four years,* was all that raced through his mind. *Had it really been that long?*

She stared at him as if to say, "Are you going to answer my question?" She seemed older, far beyond a fifth grader. All of this Radley garnered from looking at her eyes, they were all her mother's. They glared at him with impatience, attitude, and anger.

Diane isn't here to help answer this one. Radley took a breath. The attention shifted to him – everyone in the room stared in discomfited silence. He rubbed his brow, wanting to answer before he started sweating. *Stay in control,* he heard Diane tell him. Through the years, it became her prime advice for helping him deal with difficult situations that caused him anxiety which, in the past, typically turned him to the bottle.

"I did … I did what I did to protect you … and your mother," Radley said, swallowing. "It's nice to see you again, Abby." He winced at the last comment. Did he really need to say that right now?

"My Dad says I didn't need protecting," Abigail announced, her voice calm. "He said that you overreacted and blew things out of proportion and that you lied at the trial–"

"Abigail Wycliffe." The teacher rose from her desk, recognizing the direction this was going. "Come over here for a moment, please, sweetie."

"Okay, we want to bring everyone back to our lesson today." Claire stepped in, drawing the kids' attention away from the back of the room and lifting the weight of the universe off of Radley's shoulders.

As Claire closed the presentation, Radley watched the teacher speak quietly to Abigail at the back of the room. Radley could not keep his eyes off of his niece. He had no idea she even went to this school, but realized he was in the same city zone that Dustin's neighbourhood was in. There must have been four or five other middle schools in the area — the idea he hit Abby's was a total fluke, compounded by the fact his presentation was about a grandmother she never knew, and likely wouldn't want to after today.

"Alright, class," the teacher spoke before the lunch bell went. "Let's give a big thank you to Constable Clark and Mr. Wycliffe – Oh, I'm so sorry." She closed her eyes in embarrassment. "Mister … Trillamede." Her face went tomato-red.

"It's alright," Radley said. As the rest of the kids left the room, Radley approached his niece. She stood, waiting for him at her desk. Radley knelt down to speak to her quietly.

"Hi Kiddo," he said to her. She resembled her mother. Smooth, freckled skin, red cheeks, and long auburn hair clipped with fluorescent pink berrettes. "I'm sorry you've been told all of those things about me."

"I'm not supposed to be talking to you," Abigail announced. "My parents both say you're a liar. You made my dad look worse than he really was. And you put my grandfather in jail, too."

Radley swallowed, feeling Claire's eyes watching him. He

had hoped they spoke quietly enough that Claire nor the teacher could hear what they were saying.

"I know why your parents told you that," Radley said, "but your dad and I were both attacked by a group of men that threatened to hurt you. Men that reminded me about the gang members that attacked your grandfather and dad when I was a little boy. I swore I wouldn't allow anything like that to happen to you, no matter what."

And that's probably why your parents don't want you talking to me, Radley wanted to say. *Yeah, and these same men, threatened to cut off your fingers and make you eat them, and you know what your father said? He said I worry too much.*

Don't you dare say that, Diane's voice entered his head, *you are the adult here.* He was her uncle, and had to be the better man, but it just killed him to think Dustin and Jezzelle were talking about him that way to Abby.

"I don't expect you to understand everything I just told you." Radley patted her arm, the same way he did years ago. "I thought it would be fair if you at least heard my side of the story. When you're older, we can talk more." He rose to his feet, and gave her a smile. "Say hi to your mom for me. And the next time you see your father, tell him I'm sorry, and that I still think about him."

"I'll see him tonight," Abby said.

"Yeah?" The comment caught Radley off guard. "You're going ... to the prison tonight?"

"No," Abby said. "My dad's home. He's out of prison."

"What?" Radley asked. Dustin still had another year on his

conviction. Every day, Radley counted. "Did he get early parole or something?" Radley calmed himself, trying not to sound too surprised.

"They let him out because they knew he wasn't guilty." Abigail shrugged. "That's what my mom and dad told me. He's been home for a month."

Radley felt like he had been hit on the head with a hammer. He had no way of keeping tabs on Dustin's progress, and all but divorced himself from the Wycliffe extended family.

"Good. That's good news." Radley gripped his niece's hand, then left her at the desk to take out her lunch bag and head to the cafeteria. His head still spun when he thanked the teacher. As they left the classroom, Constable Clark handed him his projector bag. She had unhooked the hardware and packed it away for him.

"I thought you could use some help," she said, "given the unexpected audience member."

"Thanks." Radley took the bag as they walked down the empty school hallway. "Yeah, she's my niece. I haven't ... seen her for quite some time."

"I garnered that." She nodded. "It sounds like your story doesn't just include your 'woefully addicted mother'."

Radley gave her an uncomfortable smile. *Damn,* he hated talking to cops. "It's definitely a lot more complicated than that."

She gave him a business card. "My voice mail is on here. If you ever want to talk, I'd like to hear more about your story. You know, so I can bail you out the next time you give a presentation to a surprise family member."

He took the card. "Thanks." He dismissed the notion. "That'd be nice, but I'll be really busy these next couple of weeks."

"Yes, I am too," the Constable answered, "but evenings are fine. We can meet at a restaurant, go for coffee or something."

"Oh, okay." Radley. *Hello, Earth to Radley,* Diane's sarcastic voice leapt into his mind. "Um, well, are you doing anything tonight?"

"Tonight would be fine," the Constable said. "Your story fascinates me. I find it more intriguing each time I hear it."

"Yeah ... okay," Radley said, bumbling for words. *What else could he say?* She was a cop for Christ's Sake. "There's a ... bistro on the South end – my co-workers take me there for staff functions, if you want."

"Sounds good," she said. They finished making arrangements in the school parking lot. Radley watched her get into her police car.

"Thanks, Constable." Radley's head didn't stop spinning. "I'll see you tonight at ... seven, right? That's what we said, right?" God, what a crazy afternoon.

"Yes, seven o'clock." The Constable smiled. "And Radley?"

"Yeah?"

"Call me Claire."

Chapter 24

Seven Hours Later

As Radley entered the bistro that evening his mind whirled. *Oh Lord, what have I gotten myself into?* He didn't go too casual — wearing what he normally would to a work function. A grey, button-down shirt, a blue cartoon tie, and slacks. Was he overdressed? He didn't know — he'd never really gone on a date before. The only girls he ever felt comfortable around were the college or under-aged girls at the bar — the kind who seemed to be impressed with any older and more established guy.

Radley, in his alcoholic stage, did a good job of pretending to be *older* and *more established,* but never got past second base with any of the girls who caught his attention. He did not exhibit much confidence around women — the only ones he knew growing up were his mother and his Aunt Dulcie, and he certainly didn't learn anything from them.

Top it all off, Claire's a cop. You idiot. He purposefully arrived fifteen minutes early to peruse the place and get mentally ready for the date, if he could call it that.

Of course it's a date, Diane's voice popped into his head, though he wouldn't have dared tell her where he was going this evening. *Anytime a single man and a single woman go out for dinner or to a movie, it's a date. There's no getting around it.*

He ordered water for the table and a ginger ale. *Need to be careful about what I say. How do you talk to an off-duty police officer anyway?* He could feel his father stare down on him with that intimidating glare. *What the fuck are you doing going out with a cop? Are you fucking retarded, boy?* Tavis's voice drilled him.

Screw you, Dad. He calmly sat at the table, forcing himself to wait and not bolt out through the bistro kitchen. For whatever reason, hearing his biological father's voice echo in his mind made him more resolute to stay the entire evening, and, heaven forbid, enjoy himself.

Claire arrived on time, wearing a sleeveless blue dress with a gold chain around her neck. She looked so different out of uniform – Radley hadn't noticed her long, flowing brown hair earlier in the day, nor her trim, muscular arms. She was a fit lady – no doubt, given her profession.

"Hi Radley."

"Hi." He stood up and pulled a chair out for her. He had taken that bit of courtesy from Doug who, to this day, continued to do so for his wife whenever she took a seat.

"Quite a day," Claire said. "So, you didn't know that was your niece's class?"

"No." He hoped not to delve into this too early, but it was the only thing they had in common. "I hadn't seen her in a while. I'm not very close to my brother anymore. He got into some trouble a couple of years back – blames the world and everyone else for his problems. You know how it is."

"Sounds complicated." Claire sat with arms on the table and hands under her chin. She seemed genuinely interested.

"It's alright, actually." Radley said, not believing it for a second. "My niece harbours her father's guilt, and turns it into blame. That's what she's been taught. She'll get over it, and my brother will too."

Having spent far too much time this afternoon ruminating over the incident with Abby, he decided to finally get ready for this meeting, enjoy himself, and not let the situation with his Wycliffe side bother him any further. "That's the way families are. Everything's fine - we just gotta work the bugs out, you know?" He hoped his words didn't sound as artificial as they felt.

"Yes, I know a thing or two about that," Claire said, nodding. He could tell she wanted more detail, but also understood limits, and he was grateful. The last thing he wanted to obsess about was whether she was working undercover to fish out information about Dustin or God knew what else. He was normal, damn it, and he was going to prove that to her tonight.

And to myself.

"Hey, they have great appetizers here." Radley grabbed a menu, changing the subject. "Might I recommend the zucchini bruschetta?"

After dinner they walked around the south end, but it was too congested – traffic, kids running on the street, the occasional peddler eyeing them for money. Claire confessed it felt too much like work.

"Mason Park's just outside my building," Radley offered. "Be pretty quiet on a night like tonight, I'd imagine."

They drove in separate vehicles and arrived within minutes of each other. Radley parked in his stall and walked out of the parking lot to meet her. She drove a four star, black Volkswagen Jetta, which Radley playfully ribbed her about.

"Nice car," he told her, winking. "Makes a great taxi in Europe."

"You sound like a North American car salesman," she said, playfully punching him in the arm.

The entrance to the grounds was a log archway with the letters 'Mason Park' carved out on stained cedar wood, draped with vines and surrounded with artificial flowers.

Playground equipment lay strewn about the park entrance, making it appealing for parents and kids. Deeper into the park were lit trails that navigated through city-planted pine trees – at the center was an artificial lake fed by Mason Creek, which ran through a section of the city. It *should* have been a romantic walk, but at nine thirty they both knew it wasn't going to be a long one.

"I know this park," Claire said, as they walked through one of the inlaid trails. "I've had to come here once or twice. The local clientele have been known to shoot up by the lake on occasion."

"I've never been in this park," Radley admitted. "I always wanted to know what it was like at night – I thought, here's the perfect chance, I can walk through here with a police officer."

"You're such a dork," Claire laughed, jabbing him in the ribs. The park's reputation of late night parties and drug use was well known, but the police and a local security company ramped up enforcement in recent months, after syringes and plastic bags were found in the lake.

Radley jabbed her back – this was what people called flirting. They did more of it on the playground as Radley pushed her on the swing.

"I wish we didn't have to work tomorrow," Radley groaned as they made their way to the entrance twenty minutes later. "We should do this again sometime. How about tomorrow?"

Claire laughed. "Mr. Trillamede, you are forward. Alas, I'm working nights."

For the first time, the thought of this woman working as a police officer petrified him. "Why did you become a cop?" He was serious, and fascinated.

Claire looked at him coyly. "We all have our reasons, Radley. We all have our demons to fight."

"True enough." Radley recognized her hidden message - *take me out again and you'll find out more.* It was fair enough, considering he felt the same way.

They left the park entrance and walked to the mouth of his driveway. Her VW sat across the street. He would be the gentlemen and take her to the door.

The small squeal of tires caught his attention first, then the bright headlights prompted them to jump backward on the apartment lawn. The white pick-up charged angrily, the driver slammed on the brakes directly in front of them, sliding onto the sidewalk a metre away. Radley put himself between Claire and the truck's grill, shoving her backward, knocking her off balance onto the grass and out of the way in the split second they might have been ploughed into. Had they been, Radley would have taken the worst of it, but he had no time to play hero.

"You Goddamn fucking, son-of-a-whore!" Dustin bolted from the driver's side, his truck still running. He leapt over the hood and lunged at his stunned brother, smacking the side of Radley's head with an open hand. "You gotta lot of nerve lying to my daughter!"

"I never told her anything!" Radley spat back, holding his arms up as Dustin slapped him again. He could feel the force of his brother's blow even through his leather jacket. "Did you set that up just so you could sabotage me again? Did ya?" Dustin shouted at the top of his lungs.

Everything happened so fast, Radley didn't know how to react. He got a quick look at his brother — he was bulkier, larger than Radley had ever seen him, but seemed flabbier around the waist. Wearing a plain black shirt, and sporting a large tattoo on his arm, Dustin appeared more sinister than Radley had ever seen him.

"You get the hell out of my life, you understand me you little fuck wad?" He grabbed Radley by the ear.

Radley pushed his hand in his brother's face to hold him back, but couldn't break his grip. His brother was powerful, intense.

"Dustin, I didn't do anything to Abby!" he yelled, not at all sure what he said. "You did everything to her!" Dustin rammed Radley against the grill of the truck, winding him. "She hates me to this day because of you!" Hot breath and spittle pressed against Radley's face – the grill and the running engine vibrated against the back of his head.

"Just when I was getting her back, Radley, just when she started coming around, you fucking show up again!"

"I told her the truth," Radley spat, knowing full well that was the one thing he shouldn't have said.

"Fuck YOU!" Dustin's grip tensed with a wild, ferocious rage and he tried ramming Radley's head into the grill, but Radley braced his hands against the metal. Just then he felt a force tumble into Dustin, cutting him down at his knees. His brother yelped. Radley fell face first onto the grass, then looked up.

Dustin rose and swatted at Claire, who dove low to shield herself, hitting him in the midsection. Grabbing at her hair, Dustin didn't appear phased by her initial strike, but she swiftly shot up and rammed an elbow just under his jaw, causing him to stumble backward onto the sidewalk. The shoulder of her dress came off, exposing bare skin and a bra strap. He lunged a second time, breaking her necklace as she fought him off. Radley sprang forward and tackled his brother in the belly, his momentum enough to send them both to the grass. Landing on top of Dustin, Radley used his leverage to pin his brother's arms onto the ground. Realizing Radley was on top of him, Dustin fought like an animal about to be eaten alive and wrestled free, using his bulker frame to flip Radley to the side. Radley tried to scramble to his feet, but Dustin beat him to it, about to deliver a closed fist that would have struck Radley in the face unimpeded.

Oh shit! Radley thought, seeing the sheer malice and hatred in his brother's eyes. But the blow didn't happen – mid-swing, Clarie reached in and blocked his punch. Seizing her arm, Dustin tried to throw her down but Claire broke the grip and twisted his fingers backward. Dustin gave a painful shriek, as she shoved him forward with her foot, sending him face-first back to the ground. Staggering to his knees, he looked with a wild, stunned expression at Claire's face, then scrambled to his feet and sprinted to his truck, clutching sprained fingers. Diving into the driver's side, he slammed the door.

"Hold it right there!" Claire shouted with an authority that startled Radley. She bolted toward the sidewalk and appeared ready to charge at Dustin in the vehicle. All Radley could think of was his brother's temper.

"Claire, get down!" Radley grabbed her around the waist and pulled her back onto the lawn. The vehicle didn't drive forward as Radley feared. Instead, Dustin backed off of the sidewalk, then screeched forward down the street, out of sight in a matter of seconds.

"Get his license number!" Claire broke free from Radley's grip and shouted down the street, into the empty air, but no one was around.

"Claire." Radley's voice faltered. He touched her shoulder.

She spun around and grabbed his hand with a vice grip, the intensity and adrenaline coursing through her.

"Ahhh!" Radley winced. He thought she was going to rip his hand off.

Claire glared at Radley with a ferocious anger, then calmed herself, releasing his hand.

"Was that … your niece's father?" She bled from the lip.

Radley took a breath. He could feel wetness trickle down his face, then touched his scalp. Blood. A scrape, probably from the grill of the truck. The side of his face felt raw.

"Yes." Radley tried to keep his heart from spilling out of his mouth as he spoke. "That was Dustin. My brother."

Chapter 25

"I can't believe no one in your building saw that!" Claire cursed, throwing the cold cloth into Radley's bathroom sink, splashing water on the mirror. "That was aggravated assault with intent to maim! The front lawn of your apartment is all torn up, for Pete's sake!"

She still fumed, her finger gingerly touching a fat lip. Dabbles of blood stained the outside rim of the white porcelain sink. *You almost killed us - Fuck Dustin what the hell is wrong with you?* Radley was a basket case, the sink the least of his worries. Hand on forehead, he paced the bathroom. *You hit a cop, tried to run us over. You looked like a madman with murder in your frigging eyes.*

He finally registered the bloodied cloth in the sink. *Claire, take care of her,* he thought in a slow, rational voice. *I'm the only thing stopping her from sending a team of cops into Dustin's house to nail his ass to the wall.*

"No, hey, keep that on your lip." Radley took the cloth, wrung it out and held it to her face, but she broke away from him, shoving his hand back down.

"I can't believe you didn't let me call a car!" She glared at him. "I should have done it 20 minutes ago, and I can still do it now! Give me his address, you know where he lives!"

Radley rubbed his forehead. It felt like his brain would explode.

"Claire, I can't do that." He tried to keep his voice calm, to counter hers. "Dustin overreacted. He didn't know what he was doing."

Claire shook her head and threw her hands up. "He's an ex-con who threatened his brother, recklessly drove his vehicle over private property, and struck a peace officer! He knew damn well what he was doing!"

"No, he didn't. Look, his temper gets the better of him. He was in a rage. It was all a part of a misunderstanding between him and me. Let me just talk to him. Please."

She paused and stared at Radley with a mixture of disbelief and disgust, as if he had stuck needles up his nose. She shook her head and spoke through the facecloth. "I'm calling the station. I have to."

Charged into the kitchen, she picked up Radley's cordless phone, and started dialling. Radley went after her and tried to grab the handset. She blocked, pushed his arms away, giving him a deadly glare, daring him to take the phone away. Incredibly powerful for her size, he could see in her intense expression and defensive posture. She wasn't going to give it up without a fight.

The station answered.

"Yes, this is Constable Clark, please get me to Staff Serg —"

You've turned against your family. His cousin Galen's words echoed in his ear. *You've betrayed them. That's the greatest sin of all, Radley, and now you've done it three times.*

Radley lunged for the phone, bumping into Claire to grab the handset. She flung him backward into the hallway wall, his head striking the picture of a red corvette hanging there, but not before he hit the red "off" button which severed the link. Radley lost his balance from the push, and landed hard on his ass, shaking the apartment. The picture slid along the drywall behind him, scratching the paint, landing on the floor with a crash.

He looked up at her and shot to his feet, pushing the picture away as he did so.

"I'm sorry," he said. "It's just … it's just that I've turned him in once already, and I've hated myself every single day for doing it. I can't do that again."

Tears welled up in Claire's eyes. She shook her head and threw the phone at him. He wasn't ready for it. The antenna nicked his ear, and spiralled against the living room wall, where the plastic casing broke in two.

"Ow, hey!" Radley said, more startled than anything. "Jesus."

Claire held up her open palm to his face, and turned away from him. She stormed out of his kitchen and out the apartment. Her silence, and the look on her face, was enough. The slam of the door told him not to dare follow her.

Chapter 26

He paced along the sidewalk for fifteen minutes, waiting for the police car to pull up. The rain fell sudden and fast. In a weird way, the downpour helped ease his nerves. He could blanket himself behind the rain. It offered comfort, allowed him to psych himself up

As expected, the car pulled along the avenue and parked at the corner of 10th and 1st Street in front of the downtown Good Earth cafe. Radley stopped pacing and instead stood underneath the awning of a closed book store – a silly thing to do now that the car had arrived. It was one day after his disastrous date with Claire – not a word passed his way from Dustin or Jezzelle, or anyone in his family. Nor did he expect them to. Not that he cared.

There was only one thing Radley needed to do – make peace with the only person in the universe who mattered right now.

He snuck into the cafe and signalled for his two cappuccinos to be made. They were prepaid, and the clerk placed two berry and white chocolate scones in the bag as per his instructions. He took the bag, then a deep breath, before jaunting into the rain. With his hood up, and approaching the squad car cautiously, he noticed there was only one person inside.

Where's her partner? That was who the second drink and

scone were for. He waved his hand before tapping the passenger window.

The officer inside rolled her window down. "Can I help you?" she asked.

"Actually, you're the only person who can," Radley told her, taking off his hood and holding up the paper bag. "I came to make peace."

"Radley?" Claire said. "Omigod, you're soaked. What are you doing here?"

"Nothing really, just stalking you … that's it, pretty much."

"Just a minute, you clown." She spoke into her dispatch, typed something into the laptop computer that jutted out of the center console, then her parked unit car. Radley backed himself onto the sidewalk, underestimating how much she needed to follow police procedure even by just talking to him.

Oh well, at least she didn't tell me to get lost, or arrest me, he surmised. She came outside and stood with him under the Good Earth awning.

"I'd never seen the inside of a cop car before." Radley said.

"I'm on duty, but I guess you knew that since you were stalking me."

"No partner today?" he asked, holding up the bag once more. "These were supposed to be for the two of you."

"My regular partner is sick and we're short on officers today." She smiled and took one of the coffees, and the bag. "Who told you where we take our breaks? You're lucky I didn't get a call, or pull over a speeder. You'd have been waiting here a long time."

Radley looked at his watch. "Fifteen minutes as it was. You're ten minutes late."

"You're lucky it's raining. Usually means less action on the streets. Why didn't you just call me?"

"I needed to see you in person. I thought it was the least I could do for taking you on the world's worst first-date."

They both chuckled. Claire nodded. Her lip was still puffy, but the swelling had come down. She had a small scratch on her neck Radley hadn't noticed the night before.

"It definitely would have made for some good Reality TV. I have to say, your family makes shitty first impressions."

Radley shook his head. "He's not my family. Not anymore. I just hope you understand why I couldn't bring myself to turn him in. Not a second time."

Claire sighed. "I still can't believe I didn't call that in."

"Claire, please—"

"I'd only do that for you," she said. The look on her face kept Radley in check. "Against all my better judgment, against my civic duty, against public safety, I would only do that for you."

"Thank-you," Radley said. "And I'm glad … I didn't call you in for breaking my cordless phone."

"Oh, God." She turned her face down. "I'm sorry about that."

"That's okay, I deserved it. I hated that phone – doesn't dial out very fast, as you found out."

"Yeah," she said, flushed. "I have a bit of a temper. Serves me well on the job."

"And I have crappy reflexes, as you saw. Any bozo would have known you were going to throw that phone at me from a mile away."

"Oh brother, you're making me realize what a horrible first impression I've made." She leaned her head against the driver's side window. "I bled all over your bathroom sink, shoved you against your living room wall, busted your phone and your picture. What a supportive date I was."

"Again, my fault – totally. If we ever do this again, let's just make sure we go to your place after so I can return the favour."

They laughed amidst the rain and the occasional squawk of the police radio on her belt. Radley felt the tension leap off his shoulders.

"Well, I'm glad you brought coffee." Claire opened the bag. "No – cappuccinos, and berry chocolate scones! Radley, who did you talk to?"

"All the criminals you busted. They're friends of my brother."

"You're such a dork." She took a scone wrapped in a napkin, then noticed a square, gift-wrapped box in the bag.

"Hey, what's this?" she asked.

"It's for you," Radley told her. "I didn't know how you'd react to me tonight, but at the very least I thought it would be appropriate to give you this."

He held her coffee as she opened up the box. It was the necklace Dustin had torn off her.

"When you left, I knew I better not go after you. But I did

go down to the lawn to find that necklace. I had it repaired today. I even took the morning off to do it."

"Thank you," she said, and grabbed his hand. He took hers.

They sipped their drinks under the awning until she was called to a fender bender five blocks down.

"Sorry I have to go. Do I have to leave you in this rain?"

"My car's close by. Go get 'em, girl."

The moment was awkward. Both of them knew she needed to get going, but neither wanted to leave.

"Call me," she replied, before driving off.

Radley walked down the street in the downpour, letting the water fall on his face. Rain had become his new favourite weather.

Chapter 27

Four Months Later – Age 27

"Thanks again, for all your help," The customer said, shaking Radley's hand.

"No problem." Radley opened the door for the man's wife. "Enjoy your vehicle."

The bay doors opened, and the brand new hybrid rolled out of the showroom, its owners smiling as they left the lot.

"Well, that sucker just depreciated in half," Shane, the sales manager, joked as he slapped Radley's back.

"Don't tell them that. They were a tough bunch, but they're leaving here happy."

"That's good. Happy customers mean more customers. More customers mean a happy boss."

"Everybody likes a happy Winston."

"And you, sir, have been the only salesperson this month to move any of those hybrids. Happy Winston may be eyeing you up for a promotion if you keep this up."

Radley rubbed his chin. He was having a good month, and working damn hard, too. Driven and motivated, he had an insatiable desire to do well for himself, the dealership, but most importantly for the Trillamedes. Ironically, in spite of finally realizing the success he was starting to achieve, he felt uncomfortable with praise.

"I don't care about climbing ladders," Radley said. "I'm

happy just doing what I'm doing."

Winston Denault appointed Radley salesperson of the month. His name was plastered in the Denault Motor website and newspaper ads for the next two weeks. Diane and Doug had a cut-up of a newspaper flyer with him on the cover on their fridge. None of it mattered. Radley was in a great relationship with Clare, now four months strong, and he would be seeing her tonight. Sure he was happy with this life, but more than anything, he was happy having stability.

An announcement blared over the intercom. "Radley Trillamede, customer at the front desk."

"Aw, come on," Shawn said to the loudspeaker, "give the kid a break." He turned to Radley. "You spent all morning with the hybrid folks. Tell you what, get outta here and take lunch. I'll tell the front desk you just left before they called."

"No, I'll take it." Radley closed the showroom doors. "More customers make for a happy Winston, right?"

"And a happy Shawn too," he gave Radley a playful slap on the behind. "You're a good man, Rad."

Radley left his office for the front lobby. He took his responsibilities seriously – customers started to ask for him by name. With his reputation growing, he did everything he could to make it a good one. If people asked for him, he gave it his all to treat them cordially and fairly. Radley Trillamede was becoming someone even he was starting to like.

He approached the front desk and stopped dead in his tracks. Twenty feet away, standing in a grey hoodie and dirty blue jeans was a bald, stout man with a grubby white goatee and a three stud earring in his right ear. The beady brown eyes were unmistakable, together with his slightly hunched, crooked posture.

Tavis Wycliffe stood conversing with the phone clerk. He was making her laugh, having likely rehearsed everything he would say. Just another customer to her, looking for a small pick-up truck to take the grandkids out fishing, or some stupid line to get her to page him to the front.

Radley made eye contact with his father, who was clearly scouting the showroom for his son. He sighed and shook his head. Completely oblivious to it all, the clerk saw Radley and called out.

"Hi, Radley, this gentleman's looking at a van. He'd like your services."

"Yes, I'm sure he would," Radley said. "Unfortunately, I'm busy right now."

"I'll only be a few minutes," Tavis said. "I already know what I want."

"Well, maybe the other salesmen can help you. I have customer satisfaction calls I need to make."

"Oh, I'll make those calls, Radley," the clerk offered. "Just email me the client list and I'll do them for you this afternoon."

Tavis smiled at his son. "There you go. I won't take much of your time."

"Karen, I won't be serving this gentleman today." Radley turned and walked back to the offices. "One of the other salesmen can have the displeasure."

"You can't just walk away from me, boy." Tavis raised his voice. "You owe me a hell of a lot more than that."

Radley spun around. He could not have this conversation on the open floor of the dealership showroom. "Come to my office," he hissed. "Follow me."

He turned, glared at the clerk whose mortified expression told him she realized this was about more than just buying a van.

Radley stormed to his office, the top of his desk barren except for a paper tray, laptop, and two picture frames - one of he and Claire in front of a waterfall and the other of he and the Trillamedes on a winter hike last Christmas. He thought about putting the pictures in his bottom drawer before Tavis sat down, but he refrained.

"What do you want?" Radley slumped in his chair.

Tavis sat in the chair at the front of the desk. "I want to see my son. The last time I saw you, you stormed out on me–"

"That was supposed to be your first clue that I was done with you–"

"Oh, I figured that out fine and well, Radley. Do you know how long it took me to find you? What the hell is this Radley Trill-a-meed crap? Why did you change your birth name?"

"That's none of your business." Radley stayed firm, but his voice quivered.

"It's none of my business, what the hell is that?" Tavis threw his hands up. "My son changes his God-given name – the name I gave him. I would think that's my damn business. I gave you life, boy."

"And for the first fifteen years of it, you made it a living hell!"

"Oh come on, you and your brother had everything you could have wanted as kids. I provided a home, food, big screen TV, any friggin' thing–"

"I don't remember things, Dad. I don't remember years. I remember moments. You wanna know what 'moments' I carry around in my head from my childhood? Hauling in drug supplies from your van. You beating my mother and brother senseless while I hid under a blanket in my room. I remember being handed a gun and told to 'man up' in case you needed me to shoot one of your–"

"You gonna throw that in my face, are ya?" Tavis cut him off with a vicious and angry tone. His face swelled red. He bit his lip, then looked down at the floor and took a deep breath. "Fine, okay - you're right." He held up his hand in a concessionary manner. His words trickled out slowly, deliberately, with an underlying desperation. "I made mistakes, Radley – terrible ones. And I will carry that regret forever. But I also served my time. Almost eighteen years in the barnyard. Do you know what that does to a man, huh? I'm 53 years old for Christ's sake. Did you even know I got out?"

"I heard something about it." After the surprise of Dustin's early release, Radley contacted his Aunt Dulcie for more information, and discovered his father had been released one month earlier. He was relieved he hadn't heard from Tavis since, thinking his father was officially out of his life – until now.

"I get out of the slammer and find out from your cousin Galen that it was you who turned me in. Imagine the argument we had, Radley, just imagine how defensive I got, claiming my boy would never have done such a thing ... until they told me about the note you wrote at your brother's trial."

"Is that what you're here for?" Radley slammed his fist on his desk. "Are you here to throw that in my face? Punish me for it? Well, don't bother. I've done enough of that on my own for the past 18 years, but before you go making any more judgments about me, know this. I turned you in to protect your family, and I turned Dustin in to protect his family, because neither one of you were competent enough to do that job yourselves!"

Tavis closed his eyes, and took a breath. "Radley."

"You were the ones who screwed up your families! Not me!"

"Radley, I'm not here to argue with you." Tavis tried to speak calmly, the way he did when Radley started visiting him in prison a few years back. "I ain't here to punish you, either. Eighteen years in jail taught me not to hate, not to lay blame on anyone else for what I did. I'm here because of your brother. Have you talked to him lately?"

"Dustin?" Radley asked. "I haven't talked to him since he tried to run over my girlfriend and me on the front lawn of my apartment, which, by the way, we could have – and probably should have – pressed charges against him for, but didn't. So in that respect you could say he and I are even!"

Tavis sighed. He looked at the pictures on the desk, and

held up the one of Radley and Claire. "Is this your girlfriend? She's pretty." He put down the picture and picked up the next one. "Who are these people? The folks the government put you with?"

Radley shot across the table and grabbed the pictures from his father and threw them in the bottom drawer.

"What do you want?"

Tavis squirmed in his seat. "Look, Dustin's in trouble. Big trouble, and there's nothing I can do about it."

"Oh God." Radley threw himself backward in his chair. "What now?"

"I don't know the fine details, but he owes money to the *Rouge*. They're a national gang now. Heavy into drugs, prostitutes, big guns. Nasty buggers, always have been."

"Yeah, I know. Radley sighed. "I remember full-well who they are. How did this happen? What did he do?"

"I think it stems back to that car racket he got caught up in a few years back. The one that put him in jail."

"I know about that too, believe me." Radley rolled his eyes. The agitation festering inside him.

"From what I hear, he owed money to the *Colaberro*. You know, Patillo Rivierra, out of the West Coast? He got at Dustin in prison, threatened his wife and little one. Dustin paid him prison money, but it was nowhere near enough. The guy lost a pile of revenue when Dustin went to jail, and the cops started linking the stolen cars to his dealerships, so he really had it out for Dust."

Radley took a deep breath. *What I did was right. What I did*

213

was right. But he wasn't sure who he was trying to convince anymore. Radley collected his thoughts, not allowing the guilt to rankle him a second longer.

"Look, Dad, Rivierra had it out for Dustin well before Dust went to jail. Dustin was skimping on parts for the cars, then overcharging the *Colaberro's* people for his work. They were on to him before the cops were, and they threatened Jezzie and Abby on two separate occasions before I decided to turn Dustin in."

Tavis looked suspicious. "You know that for sure?"

"Yes, I know that for sure!" The question shot up a surge of rage inside. "Rivierra's cronies came after me first, thinking I was Dustin. I heard, and felt, every one of their threats. I think you know a thing or two about what that's like."

"Yeah, I do," Tavis said, with a defensive edge in his voice. He showed Radley his right arm, which still harboured the red, distorted burn marks where his skin bubbled up from armpit to elbow. "You think every time I look at this arm I don't think of what happened that night?"

"Yeah, well, the *Colaberro* didn't want to just burn Dustin with a lighter. What they said they would do to Abby was horrible. And the only friggin' thing Dustin kept saying was 'don't worry, I got it under control.' He didn't have a bloody thing under control, the same way his father had no bloody control fifteen years earlier!"

"Okay, now who's punishing who? Huh?" Tavis said, snarling. Radley could see the anger build up in his father, but he didn't care.

"Don't even get me started about Mom," Radley added.

"Your mother was a slutty, little pothead–" Tavis shot back.

"You made her that way! You got her hooked!"

"The hell I did." Tavis leaned over the desk, his face beat red. "Your aunt Dulcie's been feeding you that line! Your mother was hooked long before I met her. She was the one who pushed me to make the meth, sell it on the market. 'It's easy money, you lazy ass,' was always her favourite line."

"Whatever." Radley lifted his hand, disgusted. He expected no less from his father.

"My memories are what they are. You ruled the roost and kept my mother so high she didn't know her ass end from her forehead, and you did it so you could go on runs, get high, play video games, and keep her from nagging you to be a real husband and father. Anything else you tell me is irrelevant because, from where I sat, it was perfectly clear you were more interested in getting spun out than you ever were about your wife or kids."

Much to Radley's surprise, his father didn't respond. Instead, he gazed at the floor. It appeared as though Radley just placed a 300 pound weight over his shoulders.

Radley shifted in his chair. For half a second, he almost felt sorry for his father.

"Carla's death hit me hard," his voice rasped, as though the words that came from his throat were sharp barbs. "I never thought it would end like that."

Radley stopped him. "I said not to get me started on Mom, and I meant it. Get back to Dustin. Is the *Colaberro* still after him?"

"No," Tavis said, his annoyance returning. "But the *Rouge* is. They make the *Colaberro* look like the Pope. I guess when he got out, Dustin cut a deal with them — I don't know what he did — move drugs, steal cars, rough up people, I don't know — but they paid off the *Colaberro,* and got him off of Dustin's back."

Radley rubbed his temples. "And now they want their money back, plus interest."

"That's only part of the problem." Tavis shook his head. "The police have been investigating the *Rouge* the past few months, and they forced your brother into a corner. I think he gave them info he shouldn't have and the cops just busted one of their ringleaders."

"I heard about that." He remembered Claire mentioning something about it last week, and how excited the cops were about the bust. *Score one for the good guys,* he told her at the time. "So now they're blaming Dustin for the arrest?"

Tavis nodded. "That and, like you say, they want their money back, with interest. And they want it back yesterday. Your brother's screwed to say the least."

"Can't the cops protect him or something? He gave them the information they needed."

"Come on, Radley," Tavis said, his words laced with sarcasm. "You know how the pigs work. How the hell are they going to protect your brother from a nationwide gang that runs three quarters of this city's underground?"

"I don't know, Tavis. That's not my department. I sell cars

216

in case you haven't noticed. I make a legitimate living, unlike the Wycliffes."

He might as well have stabbed his father with a knife; his words did their job, only this time Tavis didn't respond with silence but fury.

"You wanna be a little prick, Radley? Fine. You wanna insult your family name, go ahead. But you might wanna get some balls and help your brother out a little, okay? Since you're doin' so well, Mr. Legitimate, maybe you can cut him some cash! Give it to me if you don't want to see him yourself. It's the least you can do for what you did to him … and to me!"

His words spilled out like acid. Radley rolled his eyes, looked up at the ceiling, and made a snarky laugh loaded with disbelief.

"Wow," he said, shaking his head. "That's rich. A real good one, Tavis."

"What are you talking about?"

Radley leaned across on his desk, and looked his biological father straight in the eye. His words were slow and calculated.

"I've been giving Dustin and his family $300 a month – every month – secretly - for the past two years."

It was the truth. Radley almost stopped giving it after the attack on he and Claire, but rationalized the money wasn't for Dustin, it was for Jezzy and Abby, and he refused to punish them for Dustin's stupidity. He was no longer going directly to their house, instead he had the cash delivered in the mail with no return address, even bribing the postman who did

Dustin and Jezelle's route to see to it personally that the cheque made it to their mailbox. All this time, Radley didn't know if they suspected who was giving them the money – either way, they were accepting it – that was over $7000 in two years Radley had given them, and in spite of it all, Dustin still found himself in a whack of trouble.

The expression on Tavis' face looked as though he had bit into a rotten piece of fruit. Radley could tell this was news to him. Had Dustin been sitting in the room with them, Radley suspected Tavis would have stood up and smacked Dustin across the head. *'Ah boy, you're so fucking stupid!'* Tavis would have hollered, just like he did at Dustin from the bathtub that night of Scar Man and the home invasion. The memory made Radley wince.

There was an awkward silence. Tavis finally spoke.

"Well, I suppose that makes you the hero then, doesn't it?" His words matched the spite in his eyes. "So what Mr. Big Shot-with-his-own-office, does that make you better than the rest of us, then your Wycliffe blood? I suppose in your mind, it does, huh?"

Radley gave himself a couple seconds to respond. *I will not be intimidated by this man.* He leaned forward and spoke methodically, his sarcasm intentional. "Tell me one thing, Dad. How did Dustin get set up with the *Rouge* in the first place?"

The question further caught his father off guard, as he knew it would. Tavis shifted in his chair.

"Look, Radley, I don't know, alright?" Tavis shrugged.

"The kid won't talk to me. Won't have anything to do with me."

"Gee, I wonder why? Who was it that set him up with the *Rouge* in the first place? Hmmm, I wonder ..."

"I said I don't fucking know, Radley!" The old Tavis, the big, towering bully came out as he raised his voice. "He probably had a contact in prison. How the fuck should I know? Do you think I'm a—"

"Get out of my face! You're not getting a DIME from me. Neither is Dustin anymore. You dumbasses have sailed your own fucking boats. You're not dragging me through your wake! Never again!" He had no idea how loud he and his father were, but others in the dealership could hear them now.

Tavis pushed off against Radley's desk. His wide, feral eyes suggested he was talking to someone other than his biological son.

"You and I know damn well who gave Dustin that contact," Radley continued his assault. "I also know what you've been doing since you got out. There's no other way you'd know this about Dustin."

"And what the fuck are you going to do about it, Radley?" Tavis shot up in his chair. "Turn me in? Put me in jail again? Huh?"

"Go back to your employers and tell them to lay off your son. Or better yet, why don't you contact your old bosses and tell them to pay a visit to the *Rouge*? Tell them to bring their lighters."

"That's the way it's going to be then, is it?" Tavis asked.

"Well, that's fine then, Radley. When your brother and his family are found dead, stuffed in some trunk — their blood will be on your hands, just as much as on mine. You started this mess when you wrote those fucking letters, and don't you tell me anything different."

The anger and adrenaline surged through Radley's arms and neck. His hands shook, and he trembled with rage. The fury welled up inside him, paralyzing his ability to speak. Fortunately, Shawn came into his office area, the concern evident on his face.

"Radley, is everything okay here?" He glanced uneasily at Tavis.

"Th-this g-gentlemen was just leaving." Radley's voice stammered. He struggled to speak, but forced the words out.

"Sir, why don't you come with me?" Shawn grabbed Tavis's sleeve.

"Get your fucking hands off me!" Tavis pulled his arm away. He turned and headed out of the showroom.

Shawn gave some distance, but followed him out. He came back to Radley's office, giving Radley an important two minutes to let the anger and adrenaline drain out of him.

"Who the hell was that guy?" Shawn asked, taking a second glance down the hall to make sure Tavis was off the lot.

"Disgruntled customer," Radley answered. "The usual. Wanted to get something for nothing."

"Jesus, why the hell was he shouting at you? Did he want the car for free?"

"Doesn't matter, I stood my ground," Radley said. He

220

ruffled some papers on his desk, and gave a false, hollow chuckle. "I think I'll take that lunch break now, though."

Chapter 28

The card game at the Trillamede dining room sounded more like a Las Vegas casino than their typical games night. As if it were right out of the Twilight Zone, there was chatter, raillery, and playful bantering at the table, and it was obvious that the source of unusual livelihood had everything to do with the special guest who, for the first time ever, Radley had brought to the house.

Radley watched her interact flawlessly with his foster parents, making them laugh, and bringing out their giddy side.

"And did he tell you the time he wore a Wonder Woman costume to his school's Halloween Party?" Doug asked "That's when we really saw him come out of his shell."

Diane patted his shoulder, and tried to stifle a laugh. "He looked so cute in his star-covered mini-shirt and lasso rope. He used paper towel for his brassiere and to round out his hips." Diane couldn't control herself. "The funny part was when he went on stage, the paper towel stuck out of his chest." She snorted trying to finish her story.

"I'm trying to picture that image." Claire closed her eyes and shook her head. "It's not coming to me."

Radley rubbed his forehead, knowing where this was probably going. "Hey, you have to admit, I did look pretty hot – I even shaved my chest for it."

"Wait, I've – I've got pictures. I'll get them." Diane snorted again. "Oh, there I go, once I get started, I can't stop."

"For God's sake woman," Doug said. "Get control of yourself or you're going to scare the poor girl away."

"Too late for that." Radley rolled his eyes. Yup, he called it – Diane going to bring out the photos. He grabbed Claire's hand. "I knew bringing you for supper was a bad idea."

"No way," Claire said. "Supper was incredible. I'm getting tons of information I can blackmail you with."

"Sorry son." Doug winked across the table.

"Couldn't you have just showed her your Shakespeare collection?" Radley asked his foster father.

Diane called from the den. "Oh Heavens, the last thing Claire wants is to feel like she's in high school English class again – these are way better." She returned to the table with a stack of photo albums. "Doug, clear a spot on the table for me, will you?"

"Aw Ma ... Not all the albums. I thought you were only bringing the picture."

"Hush now." Diane set them on the table. "There's too many photos of you and your high school shenanigans for me not to share them."

"Remember what I told you way back when, kid?" Doug said. "Act like an idiot and it'll come back to haunt you, especially when you have a camera-happy mother."

"Right," Radley answered.

"Scoot over here girl." Diane grabbed an extra chair at the head of the table for Claire. "You're going to want a front-row seat for these."

Claire got up and squeezed Radley's shoulder. "I wouldn't miss this for the world."

"Oh God." Radley knew bringing Claire home was a bad idea ... an idea he couldn't have been happier with.

"Earth to Radley, your turn." Diane gave him a smack on the arm.

Radley looked at the chips on the board. "What, already? I just played, didn't I?"

"Duh, there's only four of us," Diane said. "When Doug decides not to take half an hour to make a play, the game moves along pretty quick."

Radley looked at the cards in his hand. Much to his relief, they had moved away from the embarrassing photo albums and delved into card games. They played a game called *Sequence,* a fun, easy, family card game the Trillamedes introduced him to when he first started living with them. He and Doug were on a team, playing the two ladies. Claire seemed to be enjoying herself — the evening couldn't have worked out better, but since the game started, Radley's thoughts shifted back to the encounter with Tavis at the dealership, and the impending situation with Dustin.

Their blood will be on your hands, just as much as on mine, his father's voice reverberated in his head. *You started this mess when you wrote those damn letters, and don't tell me anything different.*

Actually you started this mess when you decided to sell your speed to two rival gangs. Radley had the perfect comeback for his father, but thought of the response well after the fact. *Never mind that I've been giving Dustin's family $300 a month while the two of you sat in the slammer, so go to hell, asshole!* As much as he wanted to wash his hands of the Wycliffe line, he continued to dwell on Dustin and his problems with the *Rouge*.

I warned you, you idiot! He wanted to tell his brother. *I even sent you to jail, all to prevent this very thing!* He could imagine what the *Rouge* threatened him with. Two *Rouge* cronies were arrested last year for torturing an informant with a metal grinder and a welding torch. The victim wound up dying four months later resulting in the men being charged with first degree murder, torture, confinement, and just about every assault charge available. But the authorities couldn't make any hard connections to the gang leaders, and instead tried the two thugs individually. The men received life sentences, but not a thing was done to the big bosses who ordered the hit in the first place.

See what they're capable of you imbecile? Radley cursed Dustin again, throwing a chip on the board. *Do you see what I was trying to protect you and your family from? And how do you thank me?*

"Are you on Jupiter or something?" Claire kicked his feet under the table. "You need to put your card down if you're going to play there."

"Oh, sorry." He didn't even register what card he played. Because the game was a strategic one, the room was stone quiet, allowing him to ruminate over his brother's predicament.

God, no matter where I run, or hide, there's my family, stuck to my soul. He remembered camping as a kid, rolling around the birch leaves, and how, even after brushing them all off, he'd still find bits of them embedded in his pockets, under his shirt, and in his hair afterward. That's the way he felt with the Wycliffes – *I just can't shake them off.*

Okay, stop this. Now. He forced himself back to his game. *No more Dad and Dustin. They're out of my head. Out of my life.*

He threw his next card on the table. At least when the photo albums were out, Radley kept occupied by trying to defend himself.

"Shoot, I was hoping you had a wild card," Doug said to him. "We could have won this game."

Radley refocused on the game – he actually had the wild card they needed in his current hand. Doug would have a fit.

"Are you alright?" Claire picked up on his inner turmoil. "You seem out of it."

He could feel Diane eyeing him as well.

"Yeah, I'm fine." Radley forced himself to keep his composure, and picked up a replacement card from the deck. It was a two of hearts, which did nothing for his team. He did not tell Claire or his adopted parents about the encounter with Tavis, or Dustin's problems, nor did he intend to. "I'm mulling over a few things from work, but nothing this wild card I just picked off the pile won't solve."

He won a groan from both ladies and a wink from Doug.

Just after midnight that same evening, Radley pulled his car in front of Claire's apartment.

"Sorry to keep you out so late on a work night," Radley said. "My parents can be quite long-winded at times."

"Don't worry about it." Claire smirked. "I had a lot of fun tonight. Your parents are great. I like them better than your brother."

They both laughed.

"God, what a gong show that was." Radley shook his head, then looked at her. "I'm worried my crazy family is going to scare you away."

"Your family *is* scary, your biological one, anyways. Thank God for the Trillamedes, hey?"

"Yes, thank God for the Trillamedes."

"I never had a Doug or Diane in my life, but like you, I do have a crazy biological family."

"Really?" She never told him much about her parents, other than the fact they were separated and living in different cities.

"My father's been in trouble with the law and my mother continues to struggle with alcohol and depression."

Radley could tell it was hard for her to admit.

"My Dad was arrested for fraud 12 years ago, has violated probation twice, and spent some time in the pen as a result. He's been getting his life back on track, but I worry about him constantly. He's proud of me, proud of my decision to go into law enforcement. My mother is too, though she's usually too distracted to say much — either from the sauce, or one of the loser husbands she keeps marrying."

"That's sucks." They talked for almost two hours in the vehicle, stories about their childhood, growing up, fears about their parents, where their own lives were heading. It didn't take long for Radley to realize Claire's career choice was intended to make up for the misdeeds of her father, though he didn't say it out loud.

"So why were you so pensive during the card game tonight?" She asked. "You seemed distracted."

"No, no, I was fine," Radley replied. "Just thinking about work. Sales were down this quarter. Looks like there's going to be a safety recall on one of last years' lines, and we sold several of those models so we're going to get a flood of phone calls — angry customers, media, that sort of thing, you know."

"Radley, be honest with me." She responded. "You sure this has nothing to do with your brother?"

"What? No," Radley responded. "No, it… I told you I'm done with him, with my whole Wycliffe family. What Dustin did to us, that was inexcusable, and the only reason his sorry ass isn't back in prison is because I stopped you from arresting him, something I had no right forcing you to do."

She slumped into the passenger side chair, crossed her arms, and sighed heavily. "You're lying to me," she said. If the annoyance in her tone wasn't clear enough, her change in demeanor certainly was. "If we're ever going to make this work, please don't ever lie to me."

"Godamnit, Claire, I'm not…" *fucking lying to you,* was what he was about to say, but his words tapered off. She had caught him, there could be no denying that. Radley had been too quick to answer the first time, too shifty – she probably saw it in his eyes or body language. *Serves you right, boy,* Tavis's voice spoke, *you're the shit-for-brains who was stupid enough to date a cop.*

He paused, took a breath. "Had to cut myself off because I realized the words about to come from my mouth would have been Wycliffe talk, not Trillamede." Shaking his head, he rubbed his hand over his face. "Sorry. This is hard for me … you're right. I was lying. I am worried about Dustin."

Like a dam releasing its overflow, Radley opened up and let it all out. He told her his biological father's visit at the dealership a day earlier and everything that Tavis told him.

"Oh, my God," Claire said. "We've been after the *Rouge* for years. Get your brother to call it in. We can protect him."

Radley knew it would be problematic to tell her. He didn't want her anywhere near this. *I just want this whole mess out of my life, forever.*

"Look Claire," he said, hoping to get through to her. "Dustin would never go to the cops, especially if I or Tavis or you, for that matter, told him to."

"Radley, do you know what the *Rouge* do to people?"

"Oh, yeah." Radley massaged his temples.

"We can't nail the leaders. We barely have enough to nail their thugs. The courts have let so many walk. My God, Radley, if you cross the *Rouge* they rip you to pieces. Doesn't your brother know that?"

"If he does, he's too pig-headed to do anything about it. Remember, I've been down this road with him before. I practically put him in prison because he was so stubborn."

"With the refurbished cars. Yeah, I know."

"So, are you sure my crazy family hasn't scared you away yet?"

"No, no," Claire said, holding her finger up to him. "You're different from them. You're not your biological family. I love how you're standing up to them, building your own life. Sometimes I wish I could do the same."

He grabbed her hand, and embraced her. They kissed softly, slumping over the gear shift of his Infiniti. It was almost three in the morning. Time, as it often did when he was with Claire, flew.

"If you can somehow get through to that whacko brother of yours, get him to call us. If he's acting as an informant, we can protect him. We *have* to protect him. For his family's sake."

"I know." Radley closed his eyes and smelled her hair. He needed to let her go, it was late, but the thought of Dustin, and Tavis, and all the crap they put him through made him want to hold her a little longer.

"I know," he repeated.

Chapter 29

Three Months Later

The phone call came at three in the morning, jolting him out of bed and setting his heart in a surge of panic.

Oh my God, Claire, raced through his mind. *Please, no.*

He read the digital call display. The police. His heart dropped.

The tone of the dispatcher braced him for the worst. *We will be sending two officers to your building. They will arrive within five minutes.*

God, he hated her being on the police force. He did nothing but worry about her, wanting so badly for her to stop but knowing this was her life's mission, the very essence of her being.

He paced the bedroom floor, the hallway, the living room, kept looking out his balcony window. Every light flicked on in his apartment.

But the police force wouldn't necessarily know she was dating him, would they? Surely, he wouldn't be listed as her emergency contact, right?

It's the Trillamedes. Picking up the phone, he hesitated. Diane and Doug did very little most nights besides stay at home, watch TV, or read. He knew if he called them he'd only disturb their sleep.

No, it's Dustin. The *Rouge*, the *Colaberro*, God knows who else — finally got him. Or he killed himself. *Or maybe they got Jezzelle or Abby? Fuck. I stopped sending them money months ago. Dustin probably got desperate, did something stupid. Damnit, what was I thinking?*

Two short rings of his intercom signalled the police had arrived. They couldn't have gotten there soon enough.

The two officers, a male and a female, stood in his doorway, caps removed. Radley thought it was the male who spoke, but he couldn't remember for certain.

"Good evening, sir." The female officer spoke. "Are you Mr. Radley Wycliffe?"

Trillamede, he wanted to say. The question caught him off guard. "Yes."

"The son of Mr. Tavis Wycliffe." She listed Tavis' address, some communal hostel Radley had never heard of.

"Yeah, sure." He answered with impatience. "What's going on?" Both officers removed their hats.

"Sir, we regret to inform you that it appears as though your father, Tavis, was found deceased in a location east of the city. Because no paper ID was found at the scene, we require a family member's identification of the body."

"What?" Radley replied, mind numb. "How certain are you that it's him?" *It wasn't Claire or the Trillamedes* was his next thought, though he forced himself to set aside the relief he felt to focus on the present.

"We can't legally tell you we're 100 per cent certain, sir, until you help us identify the remains." The male officer answered. "The investigators in charge are familiar with your father's incarceration, and the information that was in our records was used to corroborate markings on the body. We just need family to provide confirmation for us that this information is correct."

What are they not telling me? Radley thought. He was learning more about police procedure from being with Claire. The officers' choice of words were too legalistic, too deliberate.

Identify the remains. Corroborate markings.

"Oh Christ," Radley sighed, looking up at the ceiling. "He was murdered. You found him in pieces or something, didn't you?"

"We can tell you that at this stage of the investigation, the possibility of foul play is being considered."

"Perhaps you should come down to the pathology lab with us, Mr. Wycliffe." The female office said.

Radley quickly put pants and a sweatshirt on. The police offered to take him in their cruiser, but he decided to follow in his own car, head spinning in a hundred different directions.

Got to call the dealership, he reminded himself. He found himself on the city freeway, following the cruiser. *Tell them I won't make it to work this morning. Or at all today.*

My father's dead.

The body was still dressed and wet, though the clothes were tattered, torn, and soggy. The face pale, puffy, bloated, but unmistakably Tavis. His body had been found in a sludge pond on the outskirts of the city's east side. A couple out walking found him floating face down, and upon removing the body, police divers declared him deceased, keeping the corpse as they found it, given that his death was instantly deemed a potential homicide. Plastic ties bound Tavis' hands behind his back, while a ream of duct tape was wrapped around his head and face. For Radley's visit, the coroner cut the tape around Tavis' eyes, nose, and mouth, revealing an anguish-filled expression that indicated his father's death had been anything but peaceful.

Radley stared at the corpse but could conjure up no

emotion, in spite of the gruesome sight in front of him. His reaction, at least, matched the callous mood of the room, as both the medical examiner and the lead investigating officer seemed impassive and matter-of-fact. *They're just being professional,* Radley reminded himself, throwing back to his own business training. *This is not their father on the table, and they have an investigation to conduct.* The truth was their indifference made things easier for him. It gave him permission to be insensitive, at least for the time being.

This is still my Dad, he thought. *A man I spent the first 14 years of my life with,* and in Tavis's face Radley could envisage his father's anguish-filled, final moments.

There was no question his father had been murdered — tied up, wrapped and thrown into an industrial run-off pond. Whether he was dead before or after he hit the water would be for the autopsy to determine.

So this is the end of Tavis Wycliffe. He thought the same thing the day of his mother's death, though he'd braced himself for that one. This one came out of the blue, especially having only seeing his father alive and well three months ago. Remembering that meeting, the angry words exchanged with Tavis sparked a tinge of regret within him. In some respects his father deserved some credit for serving out his term and, in recent months, attempted to help out Dustin.

For all I know, that might even be what got you killed, Dad. Radley noticed his father's distended belly jutted upward on the gurney; his hands still bound underneath the lower back. The body looked uncomfortable and awkward.

Can I at least straighten him out? Radley wanted to ask but knew he could not.

The door to the room opened, breaking the silence and jarring Radley's attention. His heart clenched when he saw an officer lead Dustin into the room.

"Is it Dad?" He looked at the body himself. "Yeah, it's him."

"We'll leave you two alone for a minute," the officer replied. "All that we ask is you do not touch the body." The officer accompanied the coroner out of the room.

"Who the hell would touch that?" Dustin said as the men shut the metal door. "Stupid old bastard. What the hell were they doing?"

"They?" This was the first time he had seen Dustin since his stunt on Radley's condo several months back. "Who's *they?* What are you talking about?"

"Cyclo's missing too," Dustin answered. "The cops didn't tell you?"

"No."

"Dad was apparently last seen alive leaving some biker bar downtown, the one where Cyclo hangs. They left together, but no one knows what they were doing or where they were going. For now, the cops have Cyclo listed as a person of interest."

"What? Cyclo wouldn't have done this—"

"No shit. Cyclo's probably floating belly up 40 yards down the same bank they found Dad in. But you know the pigs, they gotta waste ten friggin' years investigating the people who didn't do the crime instead of going after the ones that did. In the meantime, the real killers are moseying down the highway to the next city, snuffing the next person that crosses their ringleaders."

"Dustin, if you know something about Dad's death, get out in the hall and tell those cops right now."

"Know something about his death?" Dustin's eyes went wild. "What the fuck makes you think I know what happened to him? Oh, it's because I'm the ex-con, right? With all the mobster ties? You know what, Radley, you can go fuck yourself."

Radley shot his hands up. "I'm just saying, if you know something for God's sake tell the police, because they're here to—"

"To what? To help me? You know what, kid, maybe it's time you pulled your head out of your ass and saw the real world for a change!"

"I know what the real world is," Radley snapped.

Before he could continue, the lead officer opened the door. "Everything alright in here?" He eyed both men suspiciously.

"Yeah, fine." Dustin shook his head, scowling at Radley. He turned and headed for the door.

"We need statements from both of you," the officer announced before Dustin could walk past him. "We can take them out in the hallway."

Radley took one last look at his father, and his pathetic, horrible fate. It all felt surreal and numb. There would be no tears to shed.

Goodbye Tavis, he thought, waiting one last moment for some sort of emotion to swell up inside him. It didn't. Instead, he left his father's pasty, lifeless body in the cold, dark pathology lab, because the chief investigator wanted to take a statement from the victim's two sons, both of whom hated each other's guts.

Well Dad, there's your legacy, Radley thought bitterly as he followed his brother out of the room.

The officer spoke to Radley and Dustin in the hallway. "Alright, so your father was living in a hostel unit in the

Southeast. You may want to contact a lawyer and discuss getting in there. I'm not sure what kind of estate he would have had, but that's a family matter for you two to discuss."

"I can tell you right now he didn't have a will," Radley said with a sigh, handing the last of his paperwork to the officer. He made the comment to the officer, but it was intended for Dustin.

"I don't care." Dustin waved the papers away. "I don't want any of his crap. I didn't want Mom's, and I sure as to hell don't want his."

Mom didn't have anything, Radley felt like saying, but didn't. He and Aunt Dulcie spent more time *disinfecting* the place Carla called home, than salvaging anything out of it.

"I don't suspect he'd have much anyway," Radley said.

"My team will be at the residence within the hour," the officer said. "They'll want to look the place over for any clues as to why anybody would want to harm your father. You won't be allowed to go there until their investigation is completed."

Both Radley and Dustin looked at each other. Radley decided to speak.

"You said you guys will be going through his place?"

"That's correct, yes. We're treating this as a homicide investigation."

"Better send the narcotics unit, too," Dustin said, exhaling heavily.

"Was your father still using?" the officer asked. "I know he was an ex-con. In prison for drug crimes."

Radley didn't know how to answer, but Dustin did. "Yeah, he was still using. I'm sure the narcs will find a gold mine at his place."

The two brothers chatted with the officer for the next

twenty minutes about their father's activities since his release. Dustin did most of the talking, while Radley only relayed his story regarding Tavis' visit to the dealership, but he said nothing about his concerns regarding Dustin's problems. When it was all said and done, it was clear neither brother knew much about their father.

"I'm sorry for your loss," the officer said. He turned and left them in the hallway.

"Did Dad want money from you?" Dustin blurted, the cold, calculating tone returned to his voice.

"No, he just wanted to talk," Radley answered.

"Did he say anything? About me and my family?"

Radley fought back the urge to lie. Instead, he put on a bold front. "I don't know, should he have told me anything?"

"What the fuck is that supposed to mean?"

"I just want you to know"–Radley chose his words carefully–"regardless of what you think of me, I am there for you, for Jezzie, for Abby. If you need anything, I can help you–"

"I don't. Need. Anything," Dustin said through pursed lips. He looked to the room that once held his father. "Whatever he told you was a crock of shit." In spite of his brother's quick words, Radley could sense a weakness, an uncertainty in Dustin's tone.

"Dustin, listen, I–"

"Radley?" A soft voice came from behind him. He turned his head.

Claire hurried down the hall, in full police uniform. "Oh my God, I heard. I got here as soon as I could." She gave him a hug.

Dustin looked like he had just been forced to swallow poison.

"What! Is this your girlfriend? She's a *cop?*"

"Yeah, look Dustin, that's not important right now. Listen I–"

He held up a hand, glaring at his brother to back off. "We're done here. I don't want to hear another word out of your mouth."

"Dustin, wait–"

"Whatever the old man told you, it's horseshit, okay? We're done, Radley. You never have to see me again, and vice versa. After today, our ties are cut, got it?"

"Aw come on, Dust."

"Just … frick off, Radley. It's over. I'm done pulling knives out of my back because of you." He turned and walked away. Radley knew better than to go after him.

"What the hell is going on?" Claire asked him. "What was that all about?"

Radley threw his arms up in the air. "She's the girl you slugged on my front yard, you friggin' imbecile!" Radley hollered, but Dustin barrelled forward, and pummelled through the double doors at the end of the hall.

"Look, if you want to go after him," Claire said, "go ahead. I'm sorry – I didn't mean to interrupt."

"No, no." Radley wrapped his arms around her. "No way. You heard him. We're done. If that's what he wants, then fine. I'm done too."

He gave her a big hug and closed his eyes. She returned the gesture.

"Let's get the hell out of here," he said. "I just need to get out of this morgue and sit with you for a few minutes. You can stick me in the back of your squad car if you have to; anything would be better than this friggin' place."

"Yes, of course. Let's go."

With that, they walked out of the morgue, leaving his father and the entire Wycliffe name behind.

Chapter 30

Christ, I forgot all about it, Radley thought as he walked into his old room in the Trillamede's basement. Doug was teaching a summer class and Diane was outside in her garden. *I bet it's still down here.*

The basement hadn't changed at all since he moved out. Most of it was finished, except for the laundry room, which housed a sump pump and the furnace. The largest room was Radley's – a dated bedroom suite with dark stained, brown wallboard, red shag carpet, and a queen sized bed the Trillamedes had bought exclusively for him. He never complained because the room was as big as the entire living room in his childhood home. The real perk was having his own bathroom, something that guilted him in recent years, realizing that every other member of his immediate Wycliffe family had to share one in some capacity or another for their entire lives.

Mr. Big Shot-with-his-own-office. Tavis had called him during their final meeting together. Radley could just imagine Tavis' spin on what he had with the Trillamedes: *Mr. Big Shot-with his-own–bathroom.*

Screw you, Tavis. Radley thought, understanding he was only cursing what he thought Tavis would say. It was one week after his wake, which was sparsely attended by a few Wycliffe relatives. It was held in a union hall that he and Dustin agreed to split the cost on, but that was all they discussed. They sat on opposite ends of the hall. Radley greeted Jezzelle and Abby, introduced them to Claire, and said nothing to any other Wycliffe family member. He caught Dustin's glare only once, said an uncomfortable hello to their cousin Galen, and the only other person he and Claire talked to was Aunt Dulcie, whose comment about the family 'only getting together for funerals' was intended as a joke, but the reality of it stung Radley. The whole wake was awkward.

I'm glad there wasn't a funeral. He thought, bringing his attention back to the present, to his basement suite at the Trillamede's. An old mahogany dresser, which still sat in the same spot on the wall underneath his window, was what he honed in on. The only light in the room came from the late afternoon sunlight that squeezed through the closed slats of his horizontal blinds.

The dresser had a stylish, ornately-curved bottom which needed reinforced backing to keep it sturdy. It contained 10 drawers and two Cabinet-style doors that opened up into larger compartments. Radley had used the drawers for his clothes – the two larger spaces were for towels and whatever else he wanted. He stored mostly books and magazines in them – one of the biggest changes living with the Trillamedes was the introduction of books and reading into his life. There was so much reading material they had bought him over the years that during his high-school grad year, he noticed the cumulative weight of the books caused the bottom board of the right compartment to sag – so much so that a space was created at the back wall between the shelf and the reinforced backing, big enough to fit your hand through. Having discovered it when Diane made him clear out his used books to donate to the public library, he was careful not to tell her or Doug about it. Remembering the time well, it was his experimentative years.

He opened the right side Cabinet – there were mostly spare blankets and quilts Diane stored in the event of company.

Taking them all out, he reached his hand to the back wall, pushing his right hand down on the shelf with just the right amount of pressure.

And there you are. A sudden rush of nervous excitement and tension mixed together overtook him. He grabbed one, then reached a bit further in the opening. *And there's your buddy.*

Pulling his hand from the compartment, he fished out two long-forgotten about mini-bottles of whiskey. Having hid them from the Trillamedes, they were unopened leftovers from a summer graduation party, and had survived his great liquor purge from over two years ago.

I wasn't a big whiskey guy, he recollected as he stood up, looking at the label. This stuff wasn't so bad though. He opened one of the bottles, and remembered the flower-like smell. The liquor still kept, retaining its amber color. The sheer possession of it felt scandalous to him – the thought of drinking it, after all the shit he'd been through with his father's death, the difficulty of dealing with his bitter brother, and balancing all of that with the day-to-day stresses of work - appealed to him. Surely, if anyone deserved just a taste, it was he. Even if it was to just savor the thick, buttery flavor and hold it in his mouth.

"Radley, what are you doing?"

Jesus! He jolted, and turned towards Diane's voice behind him. As he did so, he slid the closed mini-bottle into his vest pocket, but there was no way to hide the second, which he had opened.

"Oh, well ..." *Don't lie, Radley,* Claire told him. "I, uh, was looking through my old drawers and found this old stash of whiskey I hid after one of my grad parties." He held up the bottle and gave a forced, clumsy laugh to downplay the situation.

Diane eyed him suspiciously, her tone curt. "So what are you going to do with it?"

"Oh nothing, I didn't even know it was still hidden there." *You're lying!* It was Claire again. "I, uh … I don't know, maybe get rid of it. Maybe give it away as a gift at a work party – I don't know." *I'm sorry, my love.*

"No one's going to want a bottle that small. Give it to me, I'll show you how to get rid of it."

Radley handed to her. She immediately headed up the stairs. Like a hapless duckling ambling behind its mother to the pond, he followed her to the kitchen, watched her pour it down the drain.

"There. Done. Remember how good that feels?"

"Sure." Radley uttered. His hands sat in his pocket, his right clasping the second bottle to keep it steady in his vest.

Diane put a tiny drip of dish soap into the first bottle, filled it with hot water, shook it, then set it on the counter. "Cleaning it for the recycle bin," she said, then motioned to the patio doors. "Come sit with me outside."

Radley sat on the patio stairs, arms crossed over his knees, head down. Diane sat next to him, rubbing his shoulders.

"So Dustin saw Claire, saw her in her uniform, and what, just snapped?" she asked.

"It was like he thought I was dating Adolf Hitler or something," Radley replied. "He was repulsed by it. We were actually starting to make headway, you know, talking to the cop about our dad and his drug habits. For about 15 minutes, it was like Dustin and I were on the same page."

"You were," she agreed, "but unfortunately he still sees you as the reason for his imprisonment, not himself, and harbors that anger as a result."

"I never expected him to forgive me. I knew that would be impossible, but deep down, a part of me always hoped he'd at least understand why I did it."

"You know, when we first took you in, you were a scared, confused little boy. Yes, I know you were fifteen, but inside you were a terrified eight-year old. Guilt ridden to the core, so worried that you'd done something so horrible it turned you into a shy, withdrawn little hermit, too frightened to do anything wrong."

Radley put his hand on her knee. "You guys helped me out of that shell."

"Not really, no." Diane sounded firm. "We didn't do a damn thing. We kept a roof over your head, kept you well fed–"

"And gave me stability and structure and let me speak my mind, encouraged me to try different things. You guys turned my life around."

"Oh hell," Diane said with a scoff.

"What?"

"I shouldn't be telling you this, but we didn't know what the hell we were doing, Radley. It's not like Doug and I said, 'Well, we're going to turn this kid's life around by doing this, that, and the next thing.' The truth is we were just as terrified as you were. We never had kids of our own; we didn't know the first thing about parenting. I built my counseling career at the university, and Doug spent his time writing about 20th Century poetry! What the hell did we know about raising kids? I think the reason the agency gave you to us was because we could give you that one-on-one attention, with no other kids getting in the way."

"You're too hard on yourself. You guys were fantastic foster parents."

"Ah." Diane waved her hand at him. "I guess my point to all this, Radley, was that you were away from your Wycliffe family – your parents, in particular. That's what you needed most as a teenager, to get as far away from them as you could. And look at what happened when you finally did. You became a good student in school, you helped Doug do volunteer work, you came out of your shell – you dressed as Wonder Woman for Pete's sake."

"Not proud of that one." Radley rubbed both hands over his face, embarrassed.

"The point is you started living. You escaped, and you were finally free to explore, to learn, to search for yourself, because God knows you didn't get that chance as a kid."

Radley looked out at Diane's backyard. He sat with arms resting on his knees and chin resting on his clasped hands.

"I tried to go back to them, make amends. Had to reject my father because he was still making drug deals in prison, then I went to Dustin and we know what disaster that turned into. And my mother, well … it's no wonder I became a bloody alcoholic."

"You got burned, kiddo. Every time you tried to reclaim

your family, it left you scarred. With each family member the results were the same. Dustin included. Dustin especially."

He turned to face her. "Okay, now maybe your point is eluding me."

She grabbed his arm. "Your family, Radley. The Wycliffes. They're *toxic*. They destroy you – mentally, physically, emotionally. All they've done, and continue to do, is drag you down with all their baggage, and their piss-poor choices they make - choices that have ruined, and are ruining, their lives."

"The Devil's got them," Radley muttered. He stared past her.

"What's that?"

He told her the story of their camping trip in the Windbender Valley when he was ten years old, of Carla giving him weed, of the most chaotic family picture in history, and of him lying under the trees to get the hell away from his whacked-out parents, and their raging bonfire.

"I always thought they acted the way they did because the devil got them." Radley never told anyone this before. "I wanted to think they were good people, that deep down, they cared about Dustin and me. It was their addictions, the cycle they were in – the devil as I called it then – that turned them into the buffoons, criminals, monsters of our childhood." *And now the devil's got Dustin too.*

"It's funny you mentioned trees," Diane said, with a subtle laugh. "You were always enamoured with them. You'd sit in our front yard for hours looking up at our willows, or the birch trees when we took you to the park. In that respect, I compare you to our apple tree over there." She pointed to the full, lush common tree in their back yard – tiny green buds were starting to sprout on the branches. "That tree's your life right now – whole world in front of you, numerous possibilities ahead. The choices you made so far in your life – escaping your Wycliffe house, getting sober, going to college, working at Denault's dealership – allowed all these branches of opportunity ahead of you. But opportunities, like the fruit on that tree, don't last forever. You gotta work to make those branches grow healthy, and if you do, then you have to know when to grab that fruit at just the right time before it spoils. If you do grab it, then you damn well enjoy the hell out of it because you deserved it. This is what I tell all the university kids I counsel. Some get that lesson, most don't."

"Good one." She knew how to speak to him. "Doug would be proud."

"Want some Golgi Juice?" She stood up.

He frowned. "I'd sooner drink what's currently in my mini bottle that you're recycling."

"Smart ass." She smiled. "I'll make some iced tea."

When she left, he immediately took out the second mini-bottle from his pocket. The lure was still there. He clutched the whiskey in his hand and held it to his lips. *Come on, just one drink.* He remembered a line from some poet guy named Oscar Wilde that Doug often quoted whenever he ate a second piece of dessert: "the best way to get rid of temptation is to yield to it."

Get rid of that bottle, he told himself. *Dump it in the grass.* That was an action far easier to do with Winston's cheap champagne than with a bottle of aged Canadian whiskey. *I could just smash it on the rocks like I did two years ago* - but back then he had ridden the utter resentment of his mother that shattering those bottles had been an easy call, a sure-fire way to guarantee he would never turn into her. He must have smashed at least $200 worth of booze that afternoon – some of it, at least for this moment, he wished he could have back, if only for a taste. It had been naive, he understood now, to have thought he could lick his addiction in a blaze of broken glass and simply be done with it.

Placing the bottle back in his pocket, he realized he wasn't ready to get rid of it yet. *Why? I can't answer that.* Instead, he shifted his focus back to the tree. Not all the branches were plush and budding – strung amongst the healthy, green leaved branches were a few withered, dead ones that protruded out like witches' fingers. Perhaps they had been neglected – in spite of Diane's speech, neither she nor Doug were avid arborists, they kept their trees watered but that was about it. Either way, those branches were in need of pruning - there would be no apples, buds, or life of any kind, popping out on them.

Radley thought about that, as well as Diane's words. She returned with the iced teas.

"Dustin's the only member of my immediate family still alive." Radley spoke after the first sip. "Maybe he can still be saved?"

"The point is, you saved yourself, kiddo." Tears welled up

251

in her eyes. "You got the heck away from them. That's what's important here, and that's all that's going to matter in the end."

"Yeah, you're right." He gave her a hug. "I still think – no, I know - that I couldn't have done it without you guys."

She returned his hug, and gave him a kiss on the forehead.

"Move on, Radley Wycliffe-Trillamede. It's time for you to enjoy your life."

"I know," he said, taking a sip of tea. As he set his glass on the patio stairwell, he forearm brushed against the whiskey bottle hidden in his pocket, reminding him that it was there.

He sighed, realizing how watery the tea tasted in comparison.

And that is why I'm haven't gotten rid of this bottle yet.

Part IV

Chapter 31

Six Months Later – Age 28

Radley lay prone on the sub shop bench, his eyes partially shut. He would open and close them at random, and take deep, heavy breaths. The pungent smell of alcohol emanated from his overcoat and marinated his skin, hands, and hair. Customers, who walked in, stared at him repugnantly, only to be assured by the restaurant manager the police had been called. The man, the owner insisted, appeared not to be a danger or threat – he'd wandered into the sub shop, and passed out on the restaurant bench.

"Public drunks." One lady shook her head at him in disgust. "They should take you people to the tank and clean you right out. Drain the blood from your body, and fumigate your liver. I'd have no problem with that."

I'm homeless, Radley wanted to say, but instead ignored her. He hadn't showered for two days, rolled around in garbage, and smelled like a sewer plant.

Through the sub shop window, he saw the police car double-park in front of the restaurant. Its lights on, two officers exited, one male and one female. They came in and the male motioned for the female to approach the drunk while he headed to the counter to speak to the sub shop owner.

Radley turned away from the officer, and buried his face in the bench.

"Excuse me, sir." Claire's voice sounded professional and firm, with that sexy, all business attitude he loved. "You're sleeping in a private business establishment. The owner has called us to the premises and would like you to leave."

"No," Radley answered defiantly, keeping his head down and speaking through the bench, muffling his voice to sound like an older man. "Go away."

"Sir, I'm not giving you a choice." An edge of annoyance tinged her voice. "Either you agree to come with us and leave the premises, or we'll physically remove you. I'm sure neither of us want that, do we?"

"I said, go away. I'm busy!"

"Sir." Claire put her hand on his shoulder. He could sense she'd caught a whiff of the stench exuding from his body and clothes. "Sir, I really don't need to ask this, but have you been drinking?"

"I got something important to do!" Radley repeated, making it clear he wasn't going to get up.

Radley turned his head slightly and saw Claire look at her partner, who simply shrugged his shoulders and gave her the signal to haul him up.

"Alright, sir," she replied, grabbing him by the shoulders and the leg. "You've left me no choice but to forcibly remove you." She pinned his leg down and jarred him up.

"I said I got something to do!" Radley hollered, keeping his head low.

"What exactly do you have to do, sir?" Claire asked, raising her voice.

"I have to get on the floor." Radley still didn't make eye contact with her.

"On the floor?" Claire's patience wore thin. She released the grip.

He pretended he was going to look under the bench, but instead dropped down to one knee in front of her. She looked confused and on guard, her hand on her Tazer.

Staring up at her, his face went serious. He removed the ball cap and reached in the inside pocket of his overcoat. Her eyes nearly popped out of her head.

"I have to ask my beautiful, wonderful, brilliant girlfriend if she'd make me the happiest man alive and marry me." He opened up the box and lifted the ring.

"Radley!" Her hand came off of her Tazer and straight to her mouth. "Oh, my God, Radley!"

"I thought I'd better ask before you Tazer me," he said.

"Oh, you dork!" She looked at the ring. "It's beautiful."

"You're supposed to give an answer, Claire," her partner chided from the counter. He and the sub shop owner were in on the plan, which had consumed Radley's life the past week.

She turned to look at the men behind her. "You jerk. You're all jerks."

"Give the poor guy an answer," her partner goaded. "He's dying over there."

"He already knows the answer." She turned back to Radley and smiled, her eyes watering.

He stood up and grabbed her hand. "Thank-you." He smiled back. "I'd hug you right now, but I don't think you wanna hug me like this."

"Yes, I do." She gave him a quick hug, then pushed him back. "You're right, maybe we'll hug after."

He placed the ring on her finger. Two customers in the restaurant had seen the whole thing, and applauded.

"I should taze you for this," she said, face flushed.

Radley smirked. "You better let me shower first."

"Okay, okay, enough of the shenanigans," her partner joked. "Congratulations buddy." He shook Radley's hand. "Now we gotta throw you in the drunk tank."

One Month Later

"Yeah, I liked those invitations," Radley said, flipping through what felt like the fortieth wedding magazine he'd looked through the past month. "No, the frilly style is fine – who cares? An invite is an invite." He lay on the leather couch, feet propped up on the coffee table with the cell phone tucked under chin.

"You sound like my father," Claire laughed, mimicking her dad's low, gruff voice. "Nobody cares what invites look like – they just wanna know where it is, what time, and how to get there."

"Wise man." They had decided to get married in the

summer, which was only five months away, so almost from day-one the wedding hoopla invaded their lives.

"You do remember my father served time in prison," Claire reminded him.

"I know, but I need to take his side. My goal in life is to get him to call me something other than 'the car salesman'."

Within the past month, Radley met both of Claire's biological parents. They drove four hours to spend a weekend with her father, Carl, and several visits with her mother Sophie, whom Radley found to be pleasant enough to him, but crude and sarcastic to her daughter. Both of her parents were odd ducks – Carl encouraged them to elope rather than have a wedding, providing them with a contact to buy into the time share business while Sophie condemned marriage entirely, going on a raging rant that got worse with four glasses of wine.

"I'm sorry about that," Claire said. "*Now* who's worried about parents scaring their fiancée away?"

"You know that's not going to happen. If I can handle your job, I can handle your parents." *At least I got to meet* your *biological parents.*

"Yeah, about my job," she sounded dejected. "My shift starts in an hour, and you have to work tomorrow. Come over tomorrow night – I promise no wedding talk."

"For an entire hour?"

"For the entire evening."

"If it's our wedding, I can talk about it all night if you want," he insisted, though the thought of looking at anymore floral-arrangements made him cringe.

"I love you, Radley Trillamede."

"I love you too. Stay safe out there tonight. I want my bride in one piece for the wedding."

"Depends how good our gun control laws really are," she said with a laugh. "But I always wear my vest. At the worst, you may have a one-armed or one-legged bride."

"I'd marry her anyways."

Radley brushed his teeth and climbed into bed an hour later. He flipped through the invitation magazine hoping it would make him tired. When that didn't work, his mind took to playing out the wedding, the ceremony, the fun, how happy Diane and Doug would be, and his first dance with Claire — oh, he had to work on that one. He needed lessons.

The raucous ring of his cordless phone jarred him awake, and one look at his alarm clock told him why. He'd only been asleep twenty minutes.

Please, please not about Claire, the fear once again entered his mind. *No, she just started her shift.* He glanced at the call display and didn't recognize the number. It looked like a cell area code.

"Hello?"

"Uncle Radley?" a sobbing, female voice pleaded on the line. "Uncle Radley, is this you?"

"Yeah." Radley shot out of bed. "Abigail? What's going

on?"

"My Dad." Her voice dropped to a frightful whisper. "He's drunk and he's fighting with my mom. He's yelling and breaking things. He's going crazy."

"Are you in trouble, Abby? Are you in danger?"

"No, but my Dad hasn't been himself. He's locked my mom and me in the garage for two days, won't let us go anywhere. He's got guns in the house. That's why he and my mom are fighting."

"Do I need to call the police? Is he hurting your mom?"

"No. He's trying to protect her, that's what he keeps saying. They started fighting when she said she was going to call the cops."

"Abby, I'll be there as soon as I can, okay?" He could hear Dustin and Jezzelle shouting in the background. Jezzelle screaming and sobbing.

He heard her say, "Is that what happened to Tavis? Is it?"

"Abby, let me stay on the line with you." Radley tore his sleep pants off. "Don't hang up, okay?"

"I've– I got to go," Abby said. "I need to help my mom."

"Abby, wait!" The dial tone buzzed. Not even thinking about the consequences, he got dressed and flew out his apartment door.

Chapter 32

Ignoring stop signs and red lights as he raced to the Southeast in under twenty minutes. *I hope Claire doesn't pull me over.* He sped through another intersection.

An unfamiliar gray Jeep Wrangler sat parked in the driveway of Dustin 's house. Every light in the house poured through the windows, backlighting a commotion in the kitchen. Radley leapt out of his car and sprinted to the porch landing, slowing as he approached, sensing the awkwardness of being gone for nearly five years.

I'm not dropping off cash and I have no disguise. As he jumped onto the porch steps, the sound of glass breaking startled him. He paused a moment outside the door, his heart pounding as his brother 's rage echoed through the house. A second adult argued with him.

Radley opened the screen door to a scene that catapulted him back to his parents ' house 20 years earlier. Shoved to the corner off the room, the kitchen table had an empty whiskey bottle overturned on top of it. Three chairs lay kicked over, spread amongst bits of shattered glass from a cup that had presumably caused the smash seconds before.

"Don't come here and tell me what to do in my own house!" Dustin threatened a man who appeared to be about 30 years old. Radley thought he looked familiar – heavy-set, with a buzz cut just starting to grow back, and glasses. He was dressed in a black T-shirt and sweat pants, and like Radley, appeared to have just gotten there.

"Ya kicked the damn table and ya bust the damn glass, it only makes sense that you clean it up, ya Goddamn drunk!" the man yelled.

"Will both of you just shut the hell up!" Jezzelle screamed. She stood by the sink, face bright red, eyes bloodshot, cheeks tear-stained. The entire house appeared unkempt, looking nothing like it had five years earlier, though the kitchen and living room layout appeared the same. Nobody noticed Radley.

"Hey," Radley said, voice shaking from the awkwardness of the moment, "what's going on here, guys?"

Dustin reacted like he saw the military bust through his front door.

"Who the fuck called him?" he screamed at Jezzelle. "Why is he here?"

"I don't know!" Jezzelle threw her arms up, then turned away sobbing. "I don't know and I don't care anymore!"

"Abby called me. She was scared out of her wits. Where is—"

"Well, good, I'm glad someone from his family is here," the man said, referring to Dustin, but pointing to Radley. "You can stay here with your lunatic brother! I'm going to take my sister and niece and get the hell out of here."

"You're not taking them anywhere!" Dustin shouted, moving toward Jezzelle's brother. "You can't keep them safe, Jonah!"

"Aw come off it, Dustin." The brother stood his ground,

motioning to the overturned table and broken glass around the kitchen "You think they're any safer here with you? All pie-eyed and acting like a psychopath?"

Dustin charged his brother-in-law and rammed him against the side wall, rattling the entire house. Jonah clawed at Dustin's face.

"Stop it, Goddamn it. Stop it now!" Jezzelle hollered, trying to pull Dustin away. Radley stepped around her to grab Dustin's left arm, just as Jonah shoved him back.

"Get your fucking hands off me!" Dustin spun around and punched Radley on the side of the mouth spiralling him off balance. The same side of his face struck the edge of the kitchen table. He landed on the floor, the taste of blood saturating his mouth. Pain shot through his cheekbone and pulsated into his forehead.

"Goddamn it, Dustin!" Jezzelle screamed at her husband.

"He had no right to touch me!" Dustin shouted. "Him of all people!"

"You hit him with your ring," Jonah said. "You probably knocked him stupid."

"I'm okay." Radley held up his hand, slowly getting to his knees. He spoke with a mouthful of blood, trying to save face, but he could tell something wasn't quite right. He spat blood into his hand.

"There you go, Dustin," Jezzelle said. "You've been waiting five years to do that, there you go! You done it, you done it good!"

"He grabbed me!" Dustin shouted at her. He frothed at the

mouth.

Radley crawled over to the garbage next to the fridge, and spat more blood. He glanced at Dustin 's hand and realized he had been struck with a thick, silver plated biker's ring. The gums around his top left molars bled – he couldn't tell exactly where. Wiggling the teeth with his tongue, he could only taste metal as the swelling numbed his cheek. Glancing down the hall that led to the bedrooms, he spotted his niece huddled in the darkness, against the wall. Her face beat red, she was dressed in a pink tank-top and shorts shivering.

"Well, he's your brother, Dustin – you take him to the hospital," Jonah said. "I'm taking my sister and Abby."

"You do that and they'll be dead in a week."

"Damn it, Dustin, will you quit fucking saying that!" Jezzelle screamed. "Who are these people?"

"They're the ones who killed my Dad, and they're after us now."

"Why? Why?"

"I don't know why!" Dustin threw his hands up. "I gotta finish paying his debts." He looked down at the ground, shaking his head.

"And why haven't you called the cops yet?" Jonah glared at his sister.

"Mind your own Goddamn business, Jonah," Dustin threatened. "Get the hell out of my house!"

"Believe me, there's nothing I wanna do more. I'll leave when my sister and her daughter are ready."

Dustin turned away from his brother-in-law and took a

breath. He appeared to be walking away. Radley knew exactly what he was doing, and shot up to one knee.

With lightning speed, Dustin spun around and charged Jonah. The men slammed against the kitchen sink, sending a dish rack crashing onto the tile panel. The piercing racket of smashing plates amplified the chaos in the room.

"Dustin!" Jezzelle shouted.

Radley pulled his brother away, this time hugging the back of his frame, staying low to avoid being clocked a second time. Jonah shoved them both backward, the intensity in his face showed he was done talking.

"Daddy! Daddy! Stop it!" Abigail ran from the hallway, sobbing. She stood between Dustin and Jonah, holding her hands up.

Radley held Dustin 's arms back. He felt like he was riding a wild bull, but Dustin loosened up with Abby's presence.

"Abby, Abby honey, come here." Jezzelle started crying again. She grabbed her daughter, then glared at Dustin. "We're going with Jonah. If you follow us, I'm calling the cops."

"Jezzie, you can't," Dustin pleaded, then caught himself. "Fine. Go then! I don't fuckin' care." He broke Radley's grip and turned away from them. Marching down the hall, he rubbed his hands through his hair, muttering.

"Your brother's been sleeping in his garage for three nights now," Jonah said to Radley. "He locked Jezzie and Abby in there with him for over a day. Wouldn't let them out – made them use a porta potty and everything while he sat in a lawn chair and slept with a shotgun in his arms."

"Your brother, he ain't right in the head anymore, you know?" Jonah finished, glaring at Radley with an accusatory look. "And now he's just a crazy drunk."

Radley didn't respond. Instead he watched Jezzelle help Abby put her shoes on as if she were a two year old. She scooped her up, and Abby clung to Jezzelle's neck like a baby Koala.

"Come on," Jezzelle said, "you got your keys?"

"Damn straight, I do," Jonah replied, pulling them out of his pocket. "Let's go."

Jezzelle left through the porch, carrying Abby. Radley noticed she took no luggage, hadn't even bothered to put on shoes.

The house went stone quiet. Radley stood alone in the kitchen. He felt like there was a rubber ball in his mouth, as the inside of his cheek continued to swell. The rumble of Jonah's Jeep was the only noise that could be heard. It took three seconds for his Wrangler to pull out of the driveway.

"Where did they go?" Dustin marched back down the hallway with another whiskey bottle in his hand. "Where the fuck did they go!"

"They left," Radley answered with a muffled voice. It was hard to talk and he could taste blood on his tongue as he spoke. "What the hell is going on?"

"They're not leaving." Dustin ignored him, tossing the whiskey bottle down the hallway, where it thudded on the linoleum floor but somehow didn't break. Agitated, irrational, he turned into the bathroom.

"Where are you going?" Radley followed him, keeping his guard up.

He watched Dustin pull the shower doors back. Sitting in their white, porcelain tub was a pump-action shotgun.

"I'm going after them. Bring them back here."

"With that?" Radley said, panic drove into his chest. "Are you crazy?"

Dustin pulled out a case of shotgun shells from the medicine cabinet.

"Jesus, Dustin, what's going on? What the hell are you doing?"

"Nobody takes my family away from me. I'll do whatever I have to ta protect them."

He pumped the action with a loud snap. "I'm not letting that SOB. put them in danger." He tried to shove past his brother, but Radley held his ground.

"God, Dustin, listen to yourself," Radley pleaded. "You can't do this."

"Get the hell out of my way, you fucking pussy!"

"I'm not letting you do this." Radley stood between Dustin and the door, exasperated. He grabbed the barrel of the gun.

"Get your fucking hands off me, Radley!" Dustin pulled the gun away. "You're a pussy! Always have been, always will be! Now get the fuck outta here!" He shoved Radley backward and into the bathroom doorframe and thrust his arm into Radley's face as he stepped by him.

"No!" Radley grabbed the gun barrel a second time, and pulled it toward the wall. He used every ounce of force left in him. "No ... Goddamn ... WAY!" His right hand grabbed his brother's chest and pushed him backward.

"Is that what you want, Radley? Ta fight me? Is that it?" Dustin screamed, but before he could register anything else, Radley struck him in the nose. Dustin tried to react but Radley charged and rammed him square in the chest, sending him backward and through the shower doors with a thunderous spray of plastic and metal. Dustin's head smacked against the ceramic tile landing awkwardly in the tub, the metal frame of the shower doors underneath him.

Radley followed his brother into the tub, fists flying.

"I'm ... not ... a ... God ... damn–" Radley was over his brother, striking him in the face, the forehead, under the eye. The anger, the fury, the frustration gushed out of him.

Radley stopped himself, holding his fist in the air for another blow. He looked at his brother's bruised and bloodied face.

'Hey you little assholes, stop it, stop it, right now!' Carla's voice shouted in his head. Not for a long time had his biological mother's words come to him.

What the hell? Radley unclenched his fist and dropped his hand. Dustin wasn't fighting back. He was letting Radley beat him. The look on his face said why.

"Just kill me, Radley," Dustin muttered, his eyes red, glassy, defeated. Blood dripped from his nose and trickled over his lips. "Just end it, already. You owe me one."

"Arghhhh." Radley pulled away, shooting up to his feet.

Dustin was on his back, head against the corner of the tub.

The path of cracked white tile along the wall traced the trajectory of his fall. He was covered in pieces of acrylic glass, bent metal frames, broken tile, and drywall dust. On the floor lay the loaded shotgun. Radley couldn't remember how it got there.

"Oh God, Dustin." Radley looked around the bathroom, and down at his brother.

"I fucked up, Radley – fucked up real good this time." Dustin closed his eyes, rolling over a piece of broken glass and a mess of tile shards to lay on his side in the tub, curled up in a fetal position. He muttered in a drunken stupor, "My life is over."

Chapter 33

Eight Hours Later

Radley sat on the bathroom floor taking a break from the clean-up. He removed the acrylic glass, which thankfully didn't shatter the way normal glass would have. Most of the grout and dust was swept up, though he still found the odd, tiny bit embedded in the baseboards or behind the toilet. Propped up against the wall, he dozed for a couple minutes, but the dull ache in his mouth didn't let him sleep for long.

He jolted awake, remembering where he was. Not wanting to be caught sleeping in the event Jezzelle, her family, or God knew who else, came barreling through the door, he paced the room. His mouth ached with a persistent throb that felt like a screw was being drilled underneath his bottom, right molars.

Snatching his plastic ice bag from its dish towel wrapper, he pressed it against his cheek. Mostly melted, the salve still felt cool and helped dull the pain, at least temporarily. Radley headed to the bathroom, knowing full well the disaster waiting there. But he needed pain medication, badly. Scrounging though Dustin's medicine cabinet, he found a bottle of extra strength Ibuprofen, right next to a second box of shotgun shells.

Fuck Dustin. Bullets and shells in every corner of this house. No wonder Jezzelle was losing her mind. Trying to dismiss the thought, he opened up the bottle and popped two pills, washing them

down with tap water cupped in his hands. He closed his eyes
to let the pills do their work and temper the drilling sensation
inside his mouth and cheek.

Also don't want to look at the room we destroyed. Small and
practical, the bathroom was nevertheless Jezzelle's joy —
Radley remembered her telling him years ago how she hand-
picked the tile, the mouldings, the shower doors, and
cupboards for her and Dustin to install themselves.

Not going to be able to shut this out forever, sunshine, Diane's voice
scolded him. *You gotta deal with it.* Sighing, he opened his eyes
and looked at the bare, wounded tub. It was empty now -
shortly after his fight with Dustin, he helped his brother out
and escorted him to his bed, where Dustin immediately passed
out. Finding a screwdriver, Radley then set to work, removing
the broken and twisted sliding door frame and crumpled it up
in the backyard while it was still dark and the neighbours
weren't watching. Several pieces of tile had been torn off, so
he removed the ones that were cracked, revealing blank
blotches of gray underlay to scar the backdrop of what was
otherwise white, glossy, ceramic tiling. He also cleaned up the
mess in the kitchen and hallway, sweeping up the broken glass
and mopping the floor with whatever he could find in
Jezzelle's cleaning closet.

It was seven-thirty that morning when Radley finally
decided to call Shawn, his sales manager. He took a sick-day,
telling Shawn he had "a wicked toothache."

"No problem at all," Shawn said. "You've never taken a
sick day before, so you're due." Radley reacted with

trepidation to those words – he had never wanted to take a sick day, and was proud of his streak, but felt better with that call out of the way.

He hung up the phone, and plopped down on the couch in the living room. Set underneath the coffee table was Dustin's shotgun, the one he'd previously hidden in the bathroom.

Good God, Dustin. Not this again. He shut his eyes, massaged his cheek, and just tried to get away for a moment – hoping this was just another nightmare he would wake up from … he drifted into an uneasy, uncomfortable micro-sleep.

"Radley! Hey!" Dustin's dazed and gravelly bark jolted Radley from the couch. Radley rushed through the kitchen and down the hallway to see his brother leaning against his bedroom doorframe in an open robe and black boxers.

"Where's Jezzelle? Abby?" he muttered, stumbling against the door and leaning on the knob.

"They called around six." Radley grabbed his brother helping support him. He caught a whiff of stale whiskey on Dustin's breath. "They said they're okay. Staying at Jezzie's parents' place and for you not to call. She said if you do her parents will call the cops, no questions asked. I said I'd stay with you for the night – Whoa, hey!"

Dustin's hand slipped off the doorknob and he gripped Radley's shoulders for balance.

"You gotta lie back down." Radley supported his brother's weight and set him gently on the dark blue towel draped over the bed.

"There's a bandage or something on my back." Dustin

gazed at his shoulder. "Am I bleeding?"

Radley checked. It was blood-stained.

"Yeah, you got a nasty cut on your shoulder. I put a dressing and treatment on it. If it keeps bleeding you're going to need stitches."

"Not right now." Dustin squirmed. "I don't have time for a hospital."

Radley didn't argue. Instead, he went to the bathroom, grabbed the first aid kit, and put a second dressing on his brother's shoulder.

"Just stay propped up on the bed and keep pressure on it." He took a closer look at his brother's face. The minor scrapes on his face and neck were already healing. A hint of black haloed Dustin's puffy, right eye.

"Looks like we both gave a shit-kickin' to each other, huh?" Dustin grunted as he eased himself against a pillow.

"Your house has definitely looked better. I cleaned up best I could."

"Yeah, I think I heard you taking out my shower doors, but my head was jackhammering. I couldn't get off my ass to give you a hand."

It's called a hangover, you idiot, Radley lashed out in his mind. "It's alright. You weren't in any shape to help me anyway."

"How bad's the damage?" Dustin closed his eyes.

"You'll need new shower doors. Some of the tiles need replacing. I'll help pay for the repairs. Even help fix it if you want."

"You?" Dustin laughed. "You can't even look after

yourself, let alone help me."

Look who's talking, you fucking moron. Radley again held back. "You want some coffee?"

"Yeah, I don't want to sleep anymore. The coffee's in the canister by the stove. Pot's by the fridge —

"Already have it brewing." Radley went to the kitchen. Two minutes later, having collected his thoughts, he came back with two mugs and his mind better braced for his brother.

"Thanks." Dustin winced as he sat up. "I'm surprised you had it ready. Must be the car salesman in you, huh?"

"Jezzie had it in the same spot she did five years ago.

"Right." Dustin guzzled half his mug, then took a deep breath.

"I'm serious about the shower," Radley repeated, ready for an argument. "I'll help you fix it."

"What?" Dustin asked. He appeared distracted

"Your bathroom. I said I'll give you a hand to help fix it."

Dustin waved his hand and scoffed. "That's the least of my worries."

"What's going on? Why did you have a shotgun in your bathtub? You locked your family in the garage? My God, Dust!"

For once, his brother did not argue or get defensive. Rather, he rubbed his temple and answered the question.

"In the trunk of my car are a bunch of pharmaceuticals. I only have half of what I was supposed to run. I gotta deliver them to the *Rouge*, but it's not going to be enough."

"Pharmaceuticals? You mean like prescription drugs?"

Dustin nodded. "Valium, Percocet, Tylenol 3's – a whole whack of them. I got them from a supplier who has moles working in pharmacies and drug companies. He promised me a full shipment but only got me half."

"Do you owe the *Rouge* money or something?" Radley asked, not-at-all surprised by his brother's predicament, even though he pretended he was.

"I owed twenty grand at one point." Dustin closed his eyes. "They promised to cut it down to fifteen if I did some runs for them, so I did. I paid them another three, from some odd jobs I done out of prison – that was all legit, but this last twelve has been killing me. This drug shipment was supposed to cover four grand, but it's only worth about two."

How did you get into this mess, you idiot? After all you've been through? Radley bit his tongue. He'd finally gotten his brother to talk. The last thing he needed was to judge or criticize him.

"Can't you just give them what you got? Pay the two thousand from the drugs in your trunk and then only owe ten grand?"

"I gotta pay it all. They think I snitched to the cops about them, got one of their ringleaders – a guy I became friends with in jail named Daniel Wannick. Got him thrown back into the clink. They think I did it as some kind of payback for Dad bein' killed. Gave me seven days to pay the rest of my debt. That was a month-and-a-half ago. Haven't paid them a dime yet."

"Have they threatened you? Your family?"

"Why do you think, genius?" Dustin snarled.

The anger bubbled up inside Radley. "God, Dustin, why don't you go to the police?"

"Goddamn it, Radley, it was the cops that probably set me up!" Dustin said. "It had to be. I didn't turn on the *Rouge*. They gave me money when I got out, helped me pay off the *Colaberro* and the car debts he held against me – I wasn't about to turn on them. I don't know – maybe I blabbed information to an undercover officer, someone I thought I could trust. There've been a ton of guys I've had dealings with – ex-cons from jail, guys I've done straight deals with. One of them could have been a narc, I don't know. I mean, I did vent about a falling out after I got released, but I sure as fuck wasn't trying to get him arrested." He rubbed his hands over his face in a sign of duress. "All this hit me at once, y'know, like a friggin' tornado!"

"Couldn't you at least get the cops to protect you? You were a material witness–"

"No, no, no, Radley." Dustin turned his head away from his brother. "I was still doing runs for the *Rouge* affiliates – guys who wouldn't turn me in if I ran shipments for them. I figured it was still my best bet to pay the big guns back. The money was good. All under the table. That's how I was able to fool Jezzie – used the drug money to pay bills, buy nice things for the family, take 'em on trips – make up for the past two years, while all my legit money paid off my debt. The cops might have protected me, but I'm no rat, and they would've been on me twenty-four-seven. I had drugs stashed in my garage, under my trailer – merch they didn't know about, merch for other dealers that paid well. I sure-as-shit didn't need the cops on my tail. The *Rouge* were bad enough."

My brother, the professional criminal. Radley's head spun from the information.

"Problem was I didn't realize how much the *Rouge* had the hate out for me. Dad and Cyclo didn't have a chance."

"Whoa, wait a minute." Radley held his hand up. "Dad and Cyclo were connected to this?"

"I told Dad to get lost, mind his own Goddamn business." Dustin's tone became defensive again. "But he caught wind of my problems. Started goin' to people, trying to bum money off them to help me. I'm surprised he didn't ask you when he saw you at the dealership."

"No," Radley reacted. He wanted to lie, then stopped himself. "Well … arghhh."

"What? Did he come to you?"

"Yeah," Radley answered slowly. "When he came to my dealership. The last time I saw him before he was killed. He told me you owed money to the *Rouge*. We got into an argument about it–"

"I knew it!" Dustin shouted, slamming his fist on the bed. "That stupid, fucking asshole. He went to you? Fuck, Radley, if you were the one who went to the fucking cops about me, I swear to God I'll–"

"Hey, no!" Radley shot back. "I never said anything to the cops!"

"You probably blabbed something to that woman of yours–"

"No. No way! I didn't tell Claire anything. All I did was argue with Dad, and told him I was done with you, him and the Wycliffe name. I swear to God, whatever the cops know, they didn't get from me!"

Dustin eyed him suspiciously. Radley's words were genuine. *Except I did tell Claire.* But only what Tavis had told him about Dustin's money problems with the *Rouge*, nothing that could incriminate Dustin or the people he owed. *Get your brother to call us,* he remembered Claire finishing off their conversation, *if he is acting as an informant, we can protect him.*

Radley calmed himself, and tried to think rationally. "Besides, the cops were on to you by the time Dad told me about your problems. There was no way I could have sent them your way before then." *At least, I think that's right, isn't it? God, I couldn't have been responsible for this yet again?*

"Ah, doesn't matter anyway." Dustin shook his head, moving on. "I fought with Dad too. Told him I didn't want help from a spaced out druggie, begging for money on my behalf. But he kept doing it anyways. Said he felt responsible for my problems, and wanted to help his granddaughter. So he started doing runs for the *Rouge*, trying to pay off my debt."

"Dad did that for you? Really?"

"Yeah, well, don't pin a medal on his tombstone yet. The stupid, idiot junkie that he was, wound up undercutting the *Rouge's* supply, skimping money off the top for himself. He even snorted some of the coke he was running, which may have fooled the dealers back in the 1980s, but this is the 21st Century and the *Rouge* are high tech with their own bar codes and spy gadgets. They knew right away he was ripping them off. You saw for yourself what they thought about that. I'm just sorry he dragged Cyclo down with him. God only knows what the hell they did to him."

"Can't you tell any of this to the police? I mean, they can nail these guys for murder!"

"I can't prove nothing. And I'm not exactly 'Mr. Innocent' either, Radley. The *Rouge* have enough on me to put me in the clink for 20 years. So they're threatening me by forcing me to pay up, with interest. I can do it; I just need more time. But the longer I wait, the more they press me. I don't know what I'm going to do."

Radley squeezed the water bag tight against his cheek, the pain in his mouth nothing compared to the angst in his chest. Virtually all of Dustin's problems started with jail connections gone horribly wrong. Jail connections set up because Radley turned him in five years earlier. Every predicament Dustin found himself in – from the financial problems that forced him to turn to the *Rouge,* right through to their father's murder – Radley could trace back to that damn letter he wrote. The guilt struck him like a sniper's bullet.

For the last thirteen years he lived the sheltered life the Trillamedes gave him, paraded around with a successful job in car sales, and now was engaged to the woman of his dreams were nothing more than shameful ends he gained as a result of his selfishness. All the good in his life had come at the expense of his real family. He'd destroyed them so he could live, so he could vindicate his past.

Poor, pitiful Radley, he thought with Dustin's voice, *you force your family into these pitfalls, and it's you who comes out with all the opportunity, security, and happiness while all hell breaks loose amongst the family you betrayed.*

Hell that you unleashed.

And God, for all I know, maybe my discussions with Claire set this whole new chain of events into motion.

"What you're going to do, is pay these guys off and end your debt to them." He closed his eyes as he said the next six words. "And I'm going to help you."

Chapter 34

Five Hours Later

The Home Depot parking lot was the last place Radley expected to be spending the afternoon. They had purchased a new set of shower doors, a dozen white tiles, and grout. Somehow they managed to stuff it in the back of Radley's Infiniti after pushing his back seats down. A great feature he'd have to remember the next time he had a young college student at the dealership.

If there is a next time. Okay, stop it! He massaged the inside of his cheek with his tongue. The bleeding had stopped – all he could taste now was the raw, swelling of his gum line, as if someone stuck an air pump underneath his top molars and overinflated them. It hurt to touch the swelling, but he kept doing it to keep his mind off of the absurdity of whatever the hell he was doing here.

"Yeah, okay. I'll see you soon. Goodbye," Dustin said over his cell phone, ending his second conversation of the morning with Jezzelle. Most of the morning he spent on the phone. He talked to Jezzelle two hours earlier while Radley napped on the couch. It was mostly small-talk – Dustin had lied to her about having paid off most of what he owed, without getting into any specifics. They agreed that Jezzelle and Abby would stay at her parents for the next few days. Dustin didn't belabour the point at all, wanting to fix the bathroom before she came home. They even dropped off a suitcase of clothes, toiletries, and shoes for the girls – Dustin went as far as the front door. He gave his wife and daughter a hug before he left.

The next half hour he was on his cell with the "mole" who stole drugs from pharmacies. When Radley pulled into the store lot, Dustin was still trying to arrange another deal, talking in some sort of code. Apparently they were to wait in the lot for someone to arrange a pick-up point.

"Okay, it'll be at least an hour," Dustin said to Radley when he finally hung up. "We're just going to have to wait."

"Who is this guy we're supposed to meet?"

"I don't know."

"How are we supposed to know it's him?"

"We'll know."

Oh God, here we friggin' go.

For the next half-hour they spent most of the time sitting in silence. Radley killed the stretch by trying not to use his tongue to nudge at the swelling inside his mouth. He watched the clock – in half an hour he should have been finishing work and heading over to Claire's. He'd definitely have to cancel their date tonight.

A red Sapphire pulled into the space ahead of them. A middle aged man in a white golf shirt and khaki shorts stepped out of the driver's side while a young boy, maybe nine or ten, went out the passenger side. The man sent the kid to go get a cart. He signalled to Radley.

"Who the hell is this now?" Radley lurched in his seat, muttering so only Dustin could hear. He rolled down the driver's window, "What do you want, dude?"

"Excuse me, sir." The man pointed to the front end of Radley's car. "I noticed your left headlight is broken."

"Yeah, thanks," he said with a tinge of annoyance. "I got a rock chip a month ago. Been meaning to get that fixed–" *Not now, Buddy. Get lost.*

"I know a guy from Delmedia. Works on an acreage, but runs his own repair shop out of his sheet barn. Nice little business. Does solid work. Here's his card."

No cards, guy, get outta here! "Thanks." Radley held up his hand. "But I work at a dealership and I can–"

He felt Dustin tug on his arm. His brother reached over and took the card.

"Thanks for the contact," Dustin said. "We'll check it out."

Radley glanced at the card. It appeared to be a business card. There was a time on it, written in blue pen with bold letters: 11 PM.

The man glanced at Radley suspiciously, then spoke to Dustin.

"Good. I appreciate it whenever I can get my friend some business." He winked and headed toward the store. His son met him in the parking lot with a shopping cart.

"What the hell was that?" Radley asked.

"That was our rendezvous." Dustin studied the card before turning to his brother. "My God, you really are green, aren't you?"

"What, he uses his kid for a cover?" Radley watched the man enter the store with his son. "Just a regular Joe, going shopping on a Friday afternoon, picking up some lawn fertilizer, huh?"

"Yeah," Dustin replied, turning his eyes back to the card. "Didn't you learn anything from Dad?"

Radley paced the kitchen and bathroom, trying to calm his nerves. He felt more composed when he and Dustin were installing the new shower doors – the task gave him something to focus on. They did a good job. The doors were a slightly different design than the old ones, but they had the same brass frame and mirror partitions. Radley wasn't certain if Dustin told Jezzelle what happened, but he should. There was no doubt she'd notice the difference.

Dustin insisted he repair the tile himself and started scraping the back shower wall, leaving Radley nothing to do but sit and ruminate. And second guess himself. In about five hours he and his brother would be leaving for Delmedia to pick up a stash of stolen pharmaceutical drugs and bring them to God knows where. He looked at the clock and realized he couldn't put off his phone call to Claire any longer.

"I gotta use your cell again," Radley said, his stomach feeling like a blender. He'd already called the dealership to take tomorrow off.

"Yeah, go ahead," Dustin called from the bathtub.

"Hello," Claire answered the phone suspiciously. She obviously didn't recognize the number on her call display.

"Hi, it's me." Radley swallowed.

"Radley, what's going on? How's your tooth?"

Tooth? What? Radley panicked in his head. "H-how did you know about my tooth?"

"Detective work." She chuckled over the phone. "I like to run stakeouts on men I'm in love with which, in the last five years, has only been you, so it's pretty easy."

God, what is she talking about? A surge of panic rushed through his body.

"Really?" he replied, realizing just how stupid that must have sounded.

"Radley, are you alright?" Claire caught on fast. "Whose number are you calling from?"

God, she must have gone to the dealership today. "Did you come in to see me at work?"

"Yeah. I was at your end of town and thought I'd surprise you. Shawn said you called in sick with a toothache. He told me to arrest you if you came over this weekend and nothing was wrong. Ha, ha. He's such a dork."

"Yeah," Radley replied, somewhat relieved. God, he didn't want her to know anything. "Listen, I can't make it over tonight. Probably not tomorrow either. Hopefully Sunday, okay?"

"You didn't answer my question earlier. What's wrong? Is your tooth bothering you that much?"

287

"Yeah, my gum is bleeding and starting to pus. I think I got an infection." *If I don't see a dentist soon, that probably won't be a lie.* "It's kind of embarrassing."

"Sounds like you need emergency surgery. There's a clinic on the South End. I think they have a twenty-four hour hotline. I can pick you up."

"No, I can't – have some things to do tonight."

"Radley, what's going on? You don't sound like yourself. Whose cell is this?"

"It's my new work cell. And I'm fine. Please, I just need a few days to myself. If I go to that clinic, I'd rather be by myself. Look, I need to go. Gotta get some ice on this. I love you, okay. Bye."

"I love you, too," she said not hiding the worry in her voice. It killed him to hang up.

He walked back into the bathroom and set the phone on the counter. Dustin set the last of the new tiles.

"I just need this glue to dry and then I can grout." He stared at the tiles. "Most of them are pretty level."

"Yeah." Radley stared at the shower wall, but wasn't focused on it at all.

"You're a terrible liar, by the way." Dustin pushed on the last tile, making sure it was secure.

"Tell me about it." Radley pushed on his cheek to feel the soft pain shoot into his temple, helping him feel something in his moment of sheer stupidity.

The cell phone rang. He was relieved to hear it.

"I'll get it," Radley said, knowing full-well Claire wouldn't have let it rest at that. She was persistent and tenacious. That was part of why he loved her. Dustin's call display read Private Number, which was what Claire's unlisted phone number always registered as.

"That's what you get for dating a cop," Dustin said. "She probably thinks you're banging some other woman right now."

"Oh God." Radley stepped out into the kitchen, making sure he was well out of his brother's earshot this time around.

"Hey," he answered. *Come clean with her, man, you have to.* He could hear Diane speaking to him in his head, offering that advice.

"Twelve grand, plus interest, you little bitch," a sharp, angry voice tore through the line.

"Whoa, what?" The voice caught Radley off guard. "Who is this?"

"Gonna play dumb now, hey sunshine? You think you're little drunken-stupor act, havin' your whole family over at your house is gonna protect you, huh? It ain't. We decided to ante up the interest, because you keep jerk-wadding us around. Just like you jerked Sly Dan around. Just like you jerked Ho-Jo. Well, you ain't gonna jerk the organization, buddy. You think your family's safe, huh? We know you, man. We know where they are."

Radley's heart pumped through his chest. "What do you want me to do?"

"You know what we want, you dumb fuck. We ain't playin' games no more. You saw what happened to your junkie old man. You know what happened to his bum buddy. And your sweet little girl? You wanna see how a garrote can cut off her head? We'll show ya. You wanna hear your wife scream as we dunk her head in a pot of boiling water, huh? We'll show ya that too, you son of a bitch, right before we put you on the chains. You got me? You bring us the money you stole, and the merch you're keeping for Winslow. We want it all, you little quiff, no more games, no more stalling. You come to us, and you bring everything, 'cause if we come to you, it's over. You got me?"

"Yeah, I got you."

"Consider this your last warning."

The caller hung up. Radley stood alone in the living room. He looked at the cell phone in his hand.

"Are you done, already?" Dustin came out of the bathroom, wiping his hands with a towel.

"Yeah," Radley answered, turning to face his brother. "Everything's fine."

"Good. Hey, there's some frozen pizza in the freezer. Why don't you get it ready for us? I'm starving. I got some beer in the garage; we can eat supper before we go."

"You still want me with you?"

Dustin paused and looked back at Radley. He shrugged his shoulders. "Only if you want. It's up to you."

Radley may have been a rotten liar, but he was very good at reading people. His brother needed him. He had no one else.

"Yeah, I'll be there. Don't want any pizza. Not really hungry."

"Fine"–he motioned to Radley's hand–"you better give me the phone. I might be getting a call here soon. Best let me take it."

"Yeah sure, here." Radley handed him the cell, understanding, perhaps for the first time, what kind of hell his brother had gotten himself into.

Chapter 35

They drove off a rural route onto a winding, gravel road in Delmedia County, on the far outskirts of the city. Radley had never driven his car on anything other than pavement, and could feel the rocks kick up against the side of the vehicle, chipping paint.

As they approached the rendezvous for Dustin's payout, Radley drove slowly – partially because of his car, partially because he had no idea what they were getting into. This wasn't even the *Rouge* they were going to see – God only knew who these guys were that Dustin had set up this deal with. The back of his Infiniti was loaded with boxes of the stolen pharmaceuticals. They were going to deliver the drugs on behalf of a man named Winslow, a name Radley recognized thanks to the horrid phone call he received a few hours earlier.

According to Dustin, he was to get paid $4000 for this delivery. Winslow paid him $2000 up front when he picked up the merchandise, while the remaining $2000 was to be paid by the receivers upon delivery of the shipment.

"There's the farmhouse." Dustin pointed to the left of the building. He'd been quiet most of the trip. "There's the sheet barn."

Radley held a bubble of air on the inside of his cheek – doing so numbed the pain slightly. The barn was completely dark, but as they approached it two sets of security lights affixed to the building turned on.

"Somebody's home," Dustin said to himself as Radley pulled up to the barn entrance. Two men walked out of the barn. They looked to be Latino or East Asian, Radley couldn't tell for sure. One was heavyset, dressed in a checker hunting jacket with a thick, round face and razor thin moustache. The other was a much younger man, late teens – lanky, dressed in a Black Sabbath concert shirt and torn jeans. He had a buzz cut, and appeared quite shy, not wanting to look Dustin or Radley in the eye.

I hear ya, kid. God, it was 11:00 on a Friday night. *I should be over at Claire's place sitting on the couch, eating popcorn and watching a movie, laughing. What the hell am I doing here?*

"You got a bad head light," the older man said in broken English. His accent sounded Spanish.

"Yeah," Dustin replied. "I have the replacement parts in the back."

Radley popped his trunk. The older man motioned for the boy to help grab the boxes. Radley shivered and wished he'd brought a coat.

I guess I don't have the experience of doing 'deals' at night. He kept his bitter thoughts to himself as he helped unload the boxes to keep warm. They set them inside the barn.

"Here's your pay." The older man handed Dustin an envelope. Radley went back to his car to warm up.

Good, now let's get the hell out of here, but he noticed his brother counting the cash.

"Hey, there's only a thousand!" Dustin flared, flipping through the bills. "It's supposed to be two-thousand even!"

"Late fee." The man shrugged his shoulders. "You're a week late with the merch."

"Things came up!" Dustin said. "I had the cops on my back. I was protecting your merch."

"Not my problem." The man held firm. "I have my customers. I lose business when supplies are late."

"We had an agreement!" Dustin yelled.

"Your agreement was with Winslow." The man held up his hands. "Not me. I deal my own business."

Radley gripped his steering wheel. *Crap. What the hell's going on?*

"You're gonna pay me my other grand. I gave up too much for this delivery."

"You got your money, that's what you deserve." The man waved his hand. "Now, get the hell out of here."

Like lightning, Dustin lunged at the teenager, spinning him around and grabbing him under the throat, pinning the boy 's left arm against his torso. The kid yelped in terror. Dustin pulled a pistol out of his inside jacket pocket and held it to the kid's temple.

"You give me what I'm owed, right fucking now!" Dustin shouted.

"Whoa, what the hell are you doing?" Radley stuck his head out of the vehicle, wise enough not to shout out Dustin's name. *Remember, never use our real names,* Dustin said on the way out here, a lesson Radley recalled from going on runs with their father.

"Stay in the vehicle!" Dustin snarled. Sure enough, a second man emerged from the side of the barn, aiming a rifle at Dustin.

Oh Shit. Radley crouched low in his car, peeping under the dashboard, ready to hit the floor. Not that it would help much if everyone started firing.

"You wanna shoot me or my partner?" Dustin threatened. "Go ahead! The boy's brains get splattered either way. You give me the extra grand, we all walk away nice. *Comprende?*"

"Si." The man nodded. He signalled for the other gunman to lower his weapon. He reached in his back pocket and took out a roll of bills.

"Just hand it to my driver." Dustin ordered, keeping the boy as a shield between him and the men. The kid breathed heavily, nearly in tears. He was way too young for this shit.

"Then put the rifle down." Dustin motioned to the other gunman. "And walk away backward, nice and slow."

The old gentlemen handed Radley the roll. He scurried through it. Ten, crisp one-hundred dollar bills, like they had just been pulled out of the ATM.

The men retreated as instructed. Radley started the car and began to back out of the driveway, turning his vehicle around. Dustin backed up with him.

"I'd tell you, you're a dead man," the older Latino hollered. "But you're on the *Rouge's* list, so I think you know that already. I'll collect my money by picking it off your carcass. "

Shut up, you idiot. Radley glowered. Dustin was probably crazy enough to shoot all three of them. Completing his 180 degree turn, Radley had the car facing forward. He cranked the passenger door open. Dustin shoved the boy to the ground, and bolted.

Before Dustin could even say a word, Radley spun out of the driveway and down the gravel road. He could feel the rocks pummelling the finish, but that just wasn't important anymore. His heart blasted holes into his chest – no less than what those guys might have done.

"Don't lose control on these gravel roads," Dustin said, saying nothing about what transpired. Radley didn't know he had the gun.

At this point, I can't say I blame him for carrying one. Radley kept the thought to himself, recognizing that starting a fight with Dustin would only distract him from what he most wanted to do – get as far away as possible from that barnyard.

Radley pressed a fist against his cheek, massaging the raw gum line with a knuckle. *You bring a gun hopin' like Hell you never need ta use it,* the Tavis from 20 years ago instructed. *But if things go south then you "ll be glad you have one.* He and Dustin also removed the license plates from his Infiniti before turning onto the gravel roads – another rule of drug running they learned from their father.

Thanks, Dad. Thanks for all the wonderful, practical things we learned from you.

Chapter 36

One Hour Later

Radley paced back and forth inside Dustin's double-bay garage. Simply being inside it made him anxious. The last time he stood there two of the *Colaberro's* thugs mistook him for Dustin and nearly beat him to a pulp. After being "rescued" by Dustin, Radley was involved in the explosive confrontation with his brother that compelled him to turn Dustin in to the police. It was an ugly time and memory, one Radley had long since shelved in the back of his mind.

The garage hadn't changed much. It was junkier – his brother no longer used it for auto body repair. Dustin's metal shelves still lined the left side of the wall. There was more pegboard on the far wall. One piece covered the hole in the wall where Dustin threw his crowbar during his argument with Radley. An other painful memory, compounded by the fact that now, five years later, the two brothers stood in the same garage, this time facing a threat far worse than anything the *Colaberro* could do to them.

"I'm sorry I drew the gun," Dustin grumbled, pulling a ladder out from the bottom of one of the shelves. "I thought I had a good relationship with that outfit. I can't believe they tried to skimp me – now of all times."

"Okay, so you got four-thousand." Radley ignored him. He was agitated, and wanted to get out of that garage, as far away from Dustin's house as possible. "Subtract that from the twelve you owe the *Rouge*, that leaves you with eight grand to pay back."

He watched Dustin set up the ladder at the back of the garage and climb to the top. From there, Dustin pushed up the roof panels a few feet away from the garage door opener.

"Dust, what are you doing?" Radley asked. "You just pulled a gun on a drug dealer's kid. God, what are we even doing here? We gotta go. It's not safe."

"It hasn't been safe here for a month." Dustin strained himself, trying to reach for something in the roof. "And that guy wasn't a drug dealer. He was just a storage rat. He was trying to undercut Winslow. That money was ear–marked for me."

"Whatever." Radley threw his hands up in frustration. "It's not like you could take him to the Better Business Bureau!" He watched as Dustin pulled what sounded like a heavy sack toward him.

"I know, Radley." Dustin glared at him, annoyed. "Why do you think I pulled the gun? Here, give me a hand with this." He hauled out a sack, wrapped in brown plastic, and handed it to Radley. It looked and felt like a sack of flour, but Radley knew instantly what it was.

"What the hell is this?" he asked, though really didn't need to.

"Another four grand, " Dustin said. "Cocaine. It's pure."

"Pure?" Radley's jaw dropped. "How do you know that?"

"I just do." Dustin climbed down.

"Where did you get it?"

Dustin folded up his ladder. "Don't ask me any more questions."

"Don't ask you any questions!" Radley shouted. "Goddamn it Dustin, what the hell are you getting me into?"

Dustin threw down the ladder. It slammed on the floor with a piercing crash, though neither of them really noticed. "Damnit, Radley, you're already in! The second you pulled out of my driveway with that shit in your trunk, you became a runner, okay? You were with me when I threatened to splatter that kid's brain's all over his Dad's barn. You're an accomplice. You drove the getaway car, Mr. Car Salesman of the Year! You 're guilty as fucking charged! " He turned away in anger.

Radley didn't react. He didn't yell back. Dustin's words hit like pneumatic-powered nails flying at him, but Radley recognized the irritation in his brother's voice – irritation with his own self.

"This coke isn't yours to sell, is it?" Radley said. His tone was calm, matter-of-fact.

"I've dragged you into this." Dustin sighed. He kept his back to Radley. "The less you know, the less you have to lie to anyone who asks you."

"Goddamn it Dustin, you're just gonna keep owing drug dealers one after the other–"

"I'm trying to protect my family!" Dustin shouted, his face turning red, the agitation and frustration mounting inside him. "Right now, that includes you, too."

"You have a bizarre way of doing it." Radley set the bag down.

"Whatever, Mr. Big Shot!" Dustin sloughed him off, eyes beginning to tear up. There was a definite dent in his armour. "What the hell do you know? You turn Dad in, you go onto to live the high life in the Hamptons, while I'm left on my own to finish school, find a job, figure out how to live life with a con for a father and a junkie for a mother, neither one of whom gave a rat's ass about me. The contacts I ma de, the crooks I dealt with – that was all I knew. I didn't know how else to function in the world. It was a way to make money."

"You were an auto-body specialist. You did detailing, painting, you were skilled."

"And who the hell do you think taught me?" Dustin gritted his teeth as he spoke. "You think I taught myself? You think I had money and went to school on my own? I didn't have no foster parents who paid my way, Radley. The dealership – the *Colaberro's* people – they took me in, set me up with a journeyman, actually got me my first job with Jezzelle's dad. I was groomed to be their patsy."

Radley looked down. More repercussions. This time from the first letter, so many years ago. *The fucking devils had their way.* Radley allowed the thought to enter his mind, then dismissed it.

"It was a foolproof operation." Dustin laughed, though there was no humor in his voice. "I made more money in my side-business that I had ever made in my life. Top it all off, I was being paid well doing the legit work. We were never going to get caught."

"Until me." Radley sighed.

"No," Dustin said. "Until me. I realized how much I was being used by them. I was nothing more than their whipping boy, and I got greedy and stupid. I *was* undercutting the *Colaberro*. I was cocky and thought I could take on the world."

Radley looked at his brother. A pang of sadness struck him.

"I'm not going to say I was glad you turned me in," Dustin continued, taking a heavy breath. "I know why you did what you did, but don't ever expect me to forgive you. My life sucked after you turned Dad in. It's sucked even worse after you turned me in."

Radley tried not to react, but felt himself wincing.

"But that's enough of that," Dustin said, waving his hand. "I think I can get four grand for this coke. It's pure. It's rare. That'll cover the debt."

Radley could have asked a dozen sarcastic questions and comments. *Yeah, and how do you know it's pure? Did you snort some? Hey good job, Dust, now all you have is a $4000 debt to some coke cartel that 'll only kidnap Abby for ransom money rather than strangle her with a garrotte. Man, you are a great problem solver.*

Instead, Radley made a simple, clear-cut comment he knew would be equally as vexing to his brother.

"You also owe them interest, Dust. Twenty percent."

Dustin shoved the ladder across the floor and wedged it back into the space under the shelves then slumped against the wall, closed his eyes, and put his head down.

"How did you know about the interest?"

"They called you on your cell, and I answered. God, Dust, these guys sound like psychos. "

"They are." Dustin placed his hands over his face, speaking through them with a muffled voice that didn't sound at all like him. "And I don't have the money. I won't get more than four for the coke. I'm all out of options."

"So how much interest is it?" Radley did the math in his head. "Twenty percent of 12 grand … twenty-four hundred?"

"That's not how these guys work." Dustin said. "It's twenty percent of the original debt. I owed twenty grand to pay off the car debt to the *Colaberro*."

"That's four-G." Radley rubbed his forehead.

"Thank-you, Mr. Car Salesman. Unless I start whoring myself at gay bars, there's no way I'm going to get that kind of money anytime soon. I got no more contacts who don't want my friggin' head on a platter."

Radley sucked on his cheek, wrestling with his conscience. He could once again taste blood in his mouth. Finally, he spoke.

"I'll pay it," he blurted. "I'll pay it out of my savings."

"You have eight grand?" Dustin looked up at him.

"Yeah. I have it, and we 'll use it to pay off the *Rouge*."

Dustin laughed and shook his head. "I don't wanna owe you anything."

"I'm doing it for Abby, and for you. Think of it as a gift."

"You have eight-Gs and you're willing to help me out? Where did you get that kind of money?"

It's for my wedding. He'd saved religiously for the last couple of years as part of his financial plan. Since Dustin was released from prison, he was able to incorporate the $300 he had been giving to Jezzie and Abby every month into his savings, and wound up leveraging it through his financial planner to make even more money. Since he proposed to Claire, he had earmarked that money for their wedding expenses and honeymoon.

"That's not important. I'm doing this to protect my family." He looked his brother in the eye. "I want you to go hide out in a motel the next couple of days. I'll drop you off, don't do anything or go anywhere. My money is saved in a money market. I'll need a couple of days to get it."

And with that, Radley realized how deep he had become entrenched, and his heart dropped knowing what he would have to do because of it.

One Day Later

Radley sat at the table, biting his lip, body numb as he held his handwritten letter. This felt like the most appropriate way, though the thought of doing it rotted his soul.

He set the letter carefully on the table, and glanced over it one last time.

My Dearest Claire,

These past few days I haven't been myself, or maybe I should say that I have been myself. Too much of myself, the old me, the boy who just wouldn't die, who needed to prove something to the world, to his family.

I don't know if this makes any sense at all to you, but I suspect that nothing I have done, or will do in the immediate future, will either. I cannot, could not, and will not, drag you into my misery; you're too good for that. You deserve so much better than me. I cannot marry you. I cannot see you anymore. I am so sorry.

Just know it is absolute agony to write these words. Please take solace in the fact that no matter where you are, where you go, I will always love you. Take the rings, sell them if you want, they're yours. Please don't call me; it will only make things harder.

Goodbye, my love,
Radley.

I have to do it this way. This was the hardest letter he wrote in his life, and he had written some doozies in his time. But he couldn't face her – he was too ashamed of himself, of what he did, and what he was about to do. And for that reason, he would end it this way, rather than humiliate and betray her – something Radley realized would be far more painful to them both in the long run.

He smacked the table in frustration. He was saving his brother just as much as himself. The love of his life would be the sacrifice for his core being, his dignity.

"When your brother and his family are found dead, stuffed in some trunk — their blood will be on your hands, just as much as on mine," Tavis' voice echoed in his head. *You started this mess when you wrote those fucking letters, and don't you tell me anything different.*

He placed the rose at the top of the letter, and the wedding bands at the bottom, by his signature. With the pen, he neatly wrote underneath his name.

> P.S. Your key is underneath the doormat.
> R.

Standing up, he looked sombrely at the clock. She'd be home in about two hours. It took him the entire afternoon to write that letter. He opened her front door, placed the key under the mat, and locked it from the inside, shutting Claire out of his life forever.

Chapter 37

Five Hours Later

Radley checked his email. He received the message he'd been waiting for from his financial advisor's secretary. The $8365.00 he invested in the money market would be transferred to his bank account within two business days. That wasn't the greatest situation for Dustin, the faster he paid off the *Rouge* the better, but that was the drawback of registered investments. *Better than keeping it stuffed in a pillowcase inside a bedroom register,* he thought back to Tavis' old hiding places for cash and drugs.

Regardless, he and his brother had high-tailed it out of the garage after the disastrous deal in Dalmedia. Dustin gathered up a few things for a prolonged stay anywhere but inside his house, where the *Rouge* or the Dalmedia Latino were sure to come. Radley dropped him off at a Motel Six out by the airport, where he was to hide out for the next two days. He had no vehicle and $25 cash, nowhere near enough to live on for two days. Too paranoid to use credit cards, Dustin insisted he'd be fine.

Yeah, I've heard that line before. Between the two of them, they managed to scrounge up $200 in cash to cover the room.

"Look, if you start getting stir crazy take my condo key." Radley reached into his pocket. "You can come to my place if you want food or whatever. You can even take my credit card to cover the cab, if you want. " He tossed the key and the card on the bed.

"No." Dustin shook his head. "I'm gonna stay here and figure things out." He unloaded his travel bag on the bed. Radley noticed he had two flasks of whiskey laid out with his toothbrush and deodorant. "I gotta make sure Jezzie and Abby don't go home. It's probably being ransacked as we speak."

Radley said very little. This was his brother's show. He finished watching Dustin unpack.

"I'll be back in two days." Claire's bright smile and the letter he wrote to her flashed interchangeably in his mind.

Don't think about that anymore. He returned to the present, ignoring the up-swell of regret surging through him. He rose from his chair and paced the floor. *What's done is done, at least you'll be able to face her again. She'll be your ex-girlfriend – ex-fiancé – but NOT the love of your life that you betrayed, humiliated, and lied to.*

He repeated those lines to himself, not entirely certain he believed them, but knowing no other way.

I can't worry about her. She's no longer relevant in my life, and it's for the best. It was a mistake to get involved with a cop in the first place, you dipshit.

Enough. Focus on the here and now. With Dustin's cocaine, plus the $8000 in cash, they should be able to kill off most of Dustin's debt to the *Rouge* and end the nightmare. Then his brother could worry about picking up the pieces. So far Radley managed to minimize the damage. He hadn 't told the Trillamede's anything, and if everything went smoothly, he'd never have to. Having called in to take the next three days off, he used up the last of his paid sick days to help organize this chaos. As far as work was concerned, he was getting his tooth pulled because of this "rotten infection". And he made a clean break with Claire, ending their relationship on his terms, cutting her out of his life. All he had to worry about was keeping his brother in one place for the next two days. With Dustin drinking, he worried his brother might do something foolish, like go see Jezzie and Abby. Maybe he better check his credit card account to see if Dustin purchased anything with it.

A knock at the door surprised him. Was that Dustin? He could hear the key tumble in the lock.

Just don't be drunk if you're coming here. Radley charged through his kitchen to main doorway. *Damnit, I should have taken those whiskey bottles.*

The door opened just as Radley went to grab the knob. He took a step back. His heart sank.

Claire stood in the doorway in full uniform, her eyes red. Past tears formed subtle, dried pathways down her cheek.

"Here's your stupid letter." She tossed it at his face. The paper hit just under his nose, causing him to step back.

"Whoa, hey." He put his hands up, catching the paper before it hit the ground.

"Here's your damn key, I guess, too." Her voice quavered as she pulled the key from the door and threw it at him, though not quite as hard. He blocked it with his hand, knocking it on the floor, but it still stung. "Now do you mind telling me what the hell this is about?"

"Claire, I'm sorry I can't." Radley swallowed. "It's just me, I–"

"You what?" Her face flushed, angry. "Everything was going fine. Perfect, I thought. And then this? Come on Radley, this is kinda out of the blue, you know?"

"I understand. But ..." He bit his lip, suddenly unsure.

"And this?" She tore the letter from his hands and waved it in his face. "This is how you do this? You write a letter? 'I will always love you' and 'Goodbye my love?' What the hell is that?"

"I meant everything I said."

"Then why are you doing this?" What? Is it someone else?" She continued when he didn't provide an answer. "Is that why you were so weird on the phone Friday night?"

He looked down at the floor.

"Yes." He tilted his head up, ever so slightly, ashamed to look at her. "Yes, I cheated on you. I had an affair with a colleague, a girl who works in sales with me. I'm kind of confused right now. I'm sorry."

He might as well have slapped her in the face, seeing the hurt and shock creep over her features. Her eyes went glassy from the pain, she shook her head, frowning at him as she did so.

"Alright then, thank-you for being honest and up-front," she stated calmly, rationally, then shoved the letter back into his chest, hard. "And thank-you for ruining my life."

"Claire," he said softly, unsure of what to say. "This letter,

I–"

"I don't want it." She closed her eyes. "God, Radley, why would I want that? Why would you want it? Every time you write a letter in your life you wind up regretting it. Take it and rip it up. As noble as you think your intentions are, the actions behind it speak volumes. It's a betrayal. You're ending us, Radley. *You* are. Not me. Why on earth would I want to keep that letter?"

He glanced away from her. She was giving him his out. Part of him felt relieved. Part of him fell apart. But he had to let go. He had to let her go.

"Goodbye, Claire." He swallowed.

She turned and walked out, sobbing, slamming the door behind her. He ached to go after her. It took every ounce of his being not to.

Slinking out his patio door and onto his balcony, he watched her pull out of the parking lot. He gripped the railing as she drove away, disappearing down the thoroughfare.

I need a drink, was all he could think. *Rum. Straight up. It's the only thing that could take this away.* He had been so controlled watching his brother guzzle the whiskey earlier in the week, had rejected any remnant of temptation he had seeing Dustin drink. His sole focus had been on helping his brother, but this moment, this pain - it was too much. *I can't do this anymore.*

He dropped his head. *My streak, it's been nearly three years now, I can't break it.* None of that mattered now. *I screwed everything up.*

Shifting uncomfortably as he pushed on the rail he noticed

the dead leaves under his feet. They had blown in from the Hawthorns and Paper Birch trees planted in Mason's Park. Scrunching his feet over them, he drug them against the vinyl decking, where they disintegrated into a thousand little pieces. Flashbacks from his childhood discharged into his memory. Gritty leaves. Dustin's anger. *'Give me that fucking gun!'* Dustin pummelling him with blows.

Fuck! Radley kicked the pile into a scatter of dust off the deck, kicking so hard he banged his foot against a rung of the aluminum railing. Pain shot through his big toe, up though the foot to his leg.

Ow! He stood on one leg to rub his foot. *Son of a bitch!*

He plopped down on one of the patio chairs on his deck. As bad as his foot hurt, it was nothing compared to what was happening in his heart.

Chapter 38

Two Days Later – 2 PM

Radley called his brother at the motel. The call he dreaded, and ruminated over for two days.

After the seventh ring, Dustin answered the phone.

"Yeah," his voice was hoarse.

"Dust, are you okay?"

"Yeah, yeah." He sounded as if he was waking up.

"I got the money. It's been wired into my account."

"Okay."

"I just need to go to a bank machine to withdraw it."

"Yeah, okay."

"What's the matter? Are you … stoned or something?"

"I ain't no druggie, Radley!" Dustin's tone instantly defiant, defensive. "Don't ever think me a pot-head, okay? Don't ever!"

"Okay, okay. You just sound out of it, that's why I'm asking. It's two in the afternoon."

"I had too much to drink last night. It helped me kill the time, try and forget about this fucking mess. There was nothin' else to do."

"I understand." *More than you'll ever know.* At least, his brother's seeming sincerity against the drug use relieved him. Though Dustin had been involved in drug-running, Radley wanted to believe his brother hadn't been a user himself. The current disaster Dustin had gotten into was in order to make money, help his family, and not to get high, which had been their father's sole motivator. "So are you going to contact them? Tell them you got the money. Set up a meeting place? What? How do we do this sort of thing?"

"It'll be a drop-off. Probably within the hour I call them. The only thing I'm not sure of is the coke. I can't one hundred percent guarantee it's pure. If it is, they'll want it for sure. If it's blended, they may not want it at all. God, it might even be worth as much as six grand, I don't know."

"Well, we can't worry about that now. They'll be getting enough cash to get them off your back either way."

"Just let me do it, Radley. This is gonna be dangerous. They want my head. The only thing that may stop them from lopping it off completely is that I'll have the money and the coke. I can't guarantee what they'd do to me – or *us* – if you come with me."

His brother knew how to persuade him. Radley closed his eyes and spoke to the contrary.

"No, Dustin, I'm coming with you. I've given up too much not to. I'll bring my money, every penny of it, and I'll be there by your side the entire time."

"God, Radley, you don't know what you're getting into."

"Maybe I do, maybe I don't." Radley felt the vindication seep through his chest, neck, veins. *This is why I'm doing this.* These were the words he needed to speak, and he'd been waiting to speak them for a very long time. "But I'm going to be there either way."

Two hours later, the slow, rolling ring of his cordless sent him back to the table. It was Dustin.

"They want us at the Dregs Mine, in the Northwest in one hour. It's in the St. Pierre outskirts, by the old coke ovens. Dad used to do his dumps out there."

"Yeah, I remember the place. One hour, eh?" Radley rubbed his forehead then looked at his watch. "The Dregs Mine? The Northwest? Nothing like cutting it tight."

"They'll probably make us wait. You know how these things work."

"I just … I don't think we can get there in an hour. There's no way, with traffic and lights and–"

"They know that, Radley, they just want to put the pressure on us. Look, just drop off your car – I can go myself."

"No, Dust, we've been through this. I'm coming. You need me there."

Dustin went silent. Radley could imagine him grimacing.

"Dustin. What's the matter? Talk to me, man!"

"I just want you to level with me, brother."

"What is it?"

"This money. You taking time off work. Away from your lady friend. Paying for this motel for me. You're doing all this shit to help me."

"Yeah, I know. What about it?"

"Why, Radley?" Dustin's voice went tight. "Why are you

doing this? Is it because you narked me to the cops again? Level with me, man!"

"Whoa, what?" Radley's said. *And here I thought he was going to say thank-you.* "Dust ... no!" His words piped with exasperation. "We been through this man. I never went to the cops. I couldn't have. Come on, we been through this already!"

"I know, I know. I just ... I spent all morning lying in bed trying to figure out how I got into this fucking mess, and I don't understand what went wrong. Who I blabbed to. Who might I have told – if I told anybody. I don't frickin' get it. Somebody must've told the cops what I was doing, told them about Wannick."

"I did it once to you, Dust," Radley said, closing his eyes and swallowing while conjuring up his next words. "And we both paid the price. I wouldn't do that to you again."

"I just gotta stop belly achin' over it." Dustin's voice dropped. He sounded tired, sad. "Maybe Dad did it. Cyclo. I don't friggin' know. Bottom line is that it's my mess, and I gotta deal with it."

"Look, I'll be there in ... twenty minutes. Then St. Pierre Outskirts. Dregs Mine. One hour. We'll get there and we'll end this, okay, bro?"

"Yeah, thanks," Dustin muttered. He hung up the phone.

The old Dregs Mine. It seemed a fitting locale. Quiet, isolated, lots of trees, in the middle of no-where. Radley remembered it well – too well.

The place where my life is going to end, he thought, only half joking.

They rolled over the coarse, dirt road, which was not in the slightest bit suited for an Infiniti. Rolling hills and thick pine trees which, together with the grey sky, swallowed them up. Radley winced with every bump and jar they hit, constantly glancing over to gauge Dustin's reaction. His brother stared straight ahead, looking occasionally out the side window as the rows of Pines thinned out, replaced by empty space, peppered only with tall, yellow grass and thistle weeds.

The terrain brought back a flood of painful memories – Radley had completed his first drug run out here with his father, Cyclo, and Dustin, so many years ago. Dustin had said some nasty things to him – Radley wondered if his brother remembered that night – probably not.

The irony was now, almost twenty years later, Radley and Dustin travelled down the same road, this time to pay a vicious drug gang nearly $10,000 in cash and cocaine – the same gang they believed were the prime suspects in the murder of their father and Cyclo.

Dark clouds obscured the grey sky, though no rain was forecasted. Dustin stayed quiet the entire drive.

Radley didn't ask him anything else until they arrived in the St. Pierre outskirts. He couldn't remember which of the dirt roads he needed to take to get to the old coke ovens. Dustin seemed to know the route by heart. At least it got him talking.

"Keep one wheel on the grass, the other in the middle of the dirt," Dustin suggested early on. "That way you won't bottom out."

"Thanks," Radley replied.

Dustin didn't respond. Instead, he stared straight ahead, as though in a hypnotic trance – not at all the kind of person Radley wanted to be with when they were about to hand over $8000 in cash and narcotics to drug lords and murderers.

He maneuvered his vehicle over the uneven terrain, dodging the potholes and large pieces of gravel that littered the road. The Infiniti was only a front-wheel drive, so every once in a while the back wheels would hit a rut or a large rock rattling the back end of his car, sending a dissonance of awkward sounds and vibrations from the trunk on through to the front of the vehicle. Radley kept glancing over at his brother. Dustin seemed oblivious to it all, continuing to stare straight ahead at the road in front of him.

"Rough road," Radley said, feeling like he should talk, trying not to sound nervous. The silence gnawed at him. "I have a bunch of vehicle reports from work in my trunk; I should have left them at home."

"Yeah," Dustin muttered, then leaned his right arm against the passenger window and massaged his face. He said nothing more.

Radley hoped it was just a hangover – one that would pass quickly. After all, Dustin was about to eliminate a big debt, a debt that had burdened him for weeks – it would be over within the hour. That alone should bring Dustin back to the world of the living.

No. Radley suddenly understood. He hit the brakes, jolting the vehicle. A rolling thud at the back told him perhaps he hit the brakes a little too hard.

The jolt jarred his brother's attention. "What are you doing?"

"Sorry," Radley said, glancing at the back end. He shook his head, and got his bearings, then turned to Dustin. "Damn road. Don't worry about it, I'm fine. But I need to ask you this. Are you being completely level with me?"

"What do you mean?" Dustin asked.

"That cocaine. Does it belong to the *Rouge*? Is that where you got it from?"

"Just let me do the talking, okay?"

"You were holding it for them? You're gonna give them back their own drugs?"

"The *Rouge* leader I inadvertently put away – Dan Wannick – it was his," Dustin said. "He had me keep it for him. I don't think the rest of them knew he had it. I was storing it for him."

Radley put his hand on his forehead.

"I mean, the guy already has it out for me. Put it this way, if do wind up in jail, they won't throw me in the same cell as him. Only one of us would be walking out alive."

"And what happens when this guy gets out? Then what?"

"That won't be for another five years."

"You got out early."

"Yeah, but he won't."

"How could you possibly know that? Friggin hell, Dustin!" Radley slammed his hand on the steering wheel in frustration.

"The coke ovens are just up ahead." Dustin's tone went dark. "Just get us up there."

"Whatever." The Delmedia Latino, the *Rouge* informant. God knows who else had it out for his brother. As he drove up the road, Radley realized even after tonight, his brother wasn't going to be free from anything. He wasn't going to be free from anything at all.

Chapter 39

Half an hour later

Radley kept his head down, breathing deeply. Waiting parked in front of a row of ovens, once used for baking coal into coke, a hard grayish version of coal with the water and gas burned out of it, Radley couldn't help but stare at the leftover husks. The ovens were old and withered – there were at one time a dozen lined up and embedded into the hillside, but only four remained that hadn't been torn down or collapsed in piles of rubble. Grass and weeds covered the igloo-sized, clay-brick structures that remained, the insides of which retained their carefully constructed, arc-shaped openings. The hills the ovens were burrowed into had slumped into hanging crests that reminded Radley of hunched up old ladies huddled over their walking sticks. Remnants of an old mining track lay in the grass in front of where the ovens were situated; the imprints of the rails embedded themselves in the caked-in, mudded earth, just like the way Radley remembered it. The entire locale was surrounded by tall spruce and poplar trees whose rustling branches formed a thick, dense canopy of leaves and needles that hovered over them, sealing them off from the city, the sky, and the rest of the world.

"I told you these guys'll make you wait," Dustin muttered, shifting in his seat. He was much more alert now, but restless, fidgety. Radley could relate. They'd been sitting for thirty minutes. Radley fought the urge to pull out, get the hell away from there, but he knew at this point, he had come too far. Leaving now would mess everything up, apart from the fact bolting away meant running into the *Rouge* cronies on the way out. Anxiety and dread danced in his stomach, sending tingling sensations to his neck, back, and legs.

He played out different scenarios of what might happen over and over in his head. Every noise, every rustle of wind, made him jolt in his seat. *Remember, just give them the damn money and drugs, and it'll all be over. For me, anyways.*

A dirty, dark grey Yukon truck turned onto the road behind them. The vehicle took up the entire dirt roadway. Radley's heart stopped. With his Infiniti facing the coke ovens, there was no way for them to get out.

"They've pinned us in," Dustin said, seeing Radley spin around, looking at their surroundings. "The only way we're leaving here now is on their terms."

"I guess that's why they make you wait," Radley said. Dustin's tone was complacent, not at all like the stubborn, pig-headed brother Radley was used to. He didn't know if he should feel relieved or petrified.

The Yukon came to a stop about five metres away from the back of Radley's car. The hum of its engine and glare of angry headlights made the front end look like a giant predator ready to snap up Radley's Infiniti in its jaws.

Dustin quickly reached into the back seat and grabbed the bag of cocaine. "I'll take the coke. We gotta step out of the car before they do. Keep your hands up so they know you're unarmed."

And so they can shoot you in the chest. Radley grimaced as they stepped out of the vehicle, the cash already stuffed into the inside pocket of his leather jacket. They emerged from the car.

The air was cool and they brought coats to ward off the chill. Radley probably exaggerated his unarmed look more than he needed to, holding his hands high in the air with fingers straight, while Dustin kept his at shoulder level. Radley lowered his when he got a good look at what Dustin did.

A second later, four men emerged from the Yukon, two from the front, one from the back, and a fourth from the hatchway of the vehicle.

Four of them, shit. *Why four of them?* This couldn't be good. He scanned them – they were worn and weathered men of varying ethnicity. All were brusque, cheerless, daunting individuals. One of them, a bald, aboriginal male with a black goatee, carried a weapon under his light brown leather coat. A lanky oriental man with sunk-in cheeks, cropped hair, and a right arm covered in medieval tattoos, stared at Radley as though he wanted to tear him apart. The other, a younger, bulky Caucasian man with a tanned, bullish face, seemed the most professional of all in a loose, blue vest and beige golf shirt. Both front men appeared to be hiding something, probably firearms.

The Four Horsemen. Radley glanced at his brother. *The four Devils. God, Dust. You better not have brought that gun.* Dustin glared at the men. Surely Dustin wouldn't be that stupid. These were clearly not people you pulled a gun on.

The tallest of the men stepped forward and glared at Radley, who inadvertently took a step backward once he recognized the man.

Oh no, not you, Radley thought, feeling his chest tighten. *You've got to be friggin kidding me.*

The man was clean-cut, dressed in a black jacket and brown slacks, with wispy, feathered-back salt and pepper hair, and a smooth, leathery face, tarnished only by an unmistakable scar that started above his right eyebrow, continued on with a small nick on his nose, and finished on his left cheek, just above his jawline. This was the same gang enforcer who burned his father with the lighter so many years ago. The same man who terrorized the Wycliffes in their home. The same man who still haunted Radley's dreams. He was twenty years older, but the same man.

The Devil himself

He eyed Radley. "Who's this?" The man's mere appearance, coupled with that cold, tight voice made Radley cringe, the same way it did when he first heard it twenty years ago.

"My brother."

"Why's he here?"

"He leant me money to pay you dicks off."

"Search them." The man eyed Dustin suspiciously as he motioned for two of his men — the red-faced, balding man, and the lanky, oriental fellow in a bandana — to search the two brothers. The oriental man searched Radley, grabbing his legs, crotch, feeling up his back. He rubbed his fingers under Radley's shirt, over his chest, arms, pressing so hard Radley winced – no doubt he searched for a weapon or wire.

Oh God, just hurry this up already. Radley closed his eyes, letting the man practically molest him. He put his hand down the front and back of Radley's pants.

"You ain't gonna find anything." Dustin went through the same routine, voicing the same complaint. "I told you all I wanna do is clear my debt."

Both searchers signalled their boss that the two brothers were clean. The scar-faced man waved his finger at Dustin. "You didn't tell me nothing. You told my employers, not me."

"Radley, give him the money," Dustin ordered. Radley reached into his jacket and took out the envelope. The oriental man snatched it out of his hands and flipped through it.

"Eight," he said to his boss.

The scar faced man looked at Dustin.

"I have the coke." Dustin held up the package. "I'm giving it back. It's pure, I haven't touched it. It's all here."

The oriental man took the package. The scar faced man nodded to the other Caucasian man who went to the back of the vehicle. He took out a garbage bag.

"Not good enough," the scar-faced man said. "You clear a twelve-thousand dollar debt by paying us eight in cash and what? Three, maybe four grand, in our own coke? Dustin, Dustin, Dustin. You are just as stupid as your old man."

"That coke was mine to deal!" Dustin fumed. "I got it fair and square from Danno–"

"Who you promptly squealed on and got sent to the clink!" Scar-faced man hissed.

"I didn't fuckin' squeal on him!" Dustin shouted back. "How many times do I have ta tell you fucktards that!"

"Whoa, Dust." Radley stepped in front of his brother. Both the Chinese and tall Caucasian stepped in, glaring at Dustin, daring him to act.

"Oh Dustin, there are conditions when you deal with us, friend. Even more conditions when you piss us off."

Radley stepped back, feeling his heart sink. This wasn't going well.

"Fortunately, we're fair and equitable men. One more job for you, Dustin. One more job and your debt is cleared. Forever."

"Go to hell. You got your money, you got your coke. Get out of my life."

"You owe more than just money, Dustin. You betrayed the *Rouge*. You betrayed our family."

"For the last fucking time"–Dustin glared at Scar-face man with an angry, wild frustration that almost bordered on pleading–"I didn't narc on Danno!"

"It'd be a God awful tragedy to lose your father, daughter, and wife all in the same year. If you want to prevent that, you'll carry out this job."

Dustin paused, took a breath then shook his head. "What is it?"

From the inside of his jacket, Scar-Man removed a Glock and tossed it to Dustin, handle first. The aboriginal with the goatee pulled out the sawed-off shot gun from his jacket, and aimed the open end at Dustin's chest just as he caught the pistol in mid-air.

"Now, shoot your brother, right between the eyes." Cougar-fast he lunged forward and walloped Radley in the gut with a hard-uppercut. Scar-Man acted so fast Radley didn't have a chance to brace himself. The blow keeled him forward, dropping him to his knees.

"Ohhhh—" Radley heaved. The wind sucked from his lungs, followed by a surge of pain that shot under his ribcage. Hacking for air, he spit onto the dirt, trying to cough. Collapsing into the fetal position with his left hand over his gut, he heaved, with little air getting in. There was no chance to recover. Scar-Man grabbed the shoulders of his jacket, forcing Radley to his knees.

"Fu—" Radley gasped. "Get off." He needed to vomit.

"Stifle it, boy!" Scar-Man hissed in his ear. Grabbing Radley by the hair, he spun him around to face Dustin. Radley straightened his back, feeling the shock of the punch subside in his stomach and chest, and his lungs eek in short breaths of air. He saw Dustin in front of him, holding the gun in his hands, staring at it like a live hand grenade.

"What the hell is this?" Dustin's jaw dropped as he glanced at his wounded brother, then to Scar-Man. "What the fuck are you talking about?"

"You heard me." Scar-Man stood behind Radley, answering with a casual tone. "The cartridge is full, but don't even think of aiming that sucker at me. If you do, Jack here'll fill your face with shells. And after we get through with that little girl of yours, your old lady'll be scraping her off the sidewalk."

"When did you guys start smokin' what you're dealin'?" Dustin glared at the men. "You expect me to shoot my own fucking brother?"

"Shouldn't be too hard, should it? Isn't this the same brother who testified against you a few years back, hmmm? Here's your chance to get revenge. Danno said you hated his guts for turning you in and ruining your life, so here you go."

Radley winced. His chest, stomach, and lungs were still numb from the blow, but a surge of fear ignited his body. He'd acted out a dozen different scenarios in is head for this deal. Not once did he ever think this would happen. The Aboriginal guy kept his shotgun aimed at Dustin, looking every bit like he'd use it. This was not part of the plan.

"He only turned me in to save me from pricks like you," Dustin said.

"Well, Wycliffe junior"–the man slapped the back of Radley's head–"looks like you did a pretty shitty job of that, huh?"

Radley didn't answer him. Instead he stared at his brother looking at the gun in his hand.

"Come on, Dustin, shoot him – right in the head," Scar-Man goaded, flicking himself in the forehead for his own, twisted attempt at effect. "You can do away with this little bastard, once and for all. We'll even destroy the body. We'll give you an alibi and the cops won't have nothin' but an abandoned car. For all they know, junior here went for a drive in the country, had a little weed on him, got pie-eyed and lost wandering into the woods. Probably fell in the river, or got eaten by a bear. Either way, he won't be nothing more than a missing person's report."

"They won't believe you," Radley pushed out. "My family knows I'm no junkie."

"Shut up!" The man pulled something out of his jacket and clubbed Radley on the head.

"Ahhh!" Radley yelped. He caught some of the blow with his hand, but whatever it was caught the right side of his head, just above the temple. The pain was sharp but receded quickly. Radley glanced up and saw the object was the butt end of another pistol.

"Come on, Dustin," Scar-Man spoke, waving the gun in a circle. "Do this lippy little cunt, right here. I mean, you put a gun to Subió's kid in Delmedia, for Christ Sakes. He didn't like that very much, by the way. As you can guess, he told me that if we don't gut your family, he will. But we can make all that go away. We can roll Subió back into his acreage. We can clear your debt with the *Rouge* and protect you, the last living Wycliffe. Hey, you guys are an endangered species, right? Your old lady rotted to shit on meth and the pricks of every homeless junkie on the East End. Your old man, meanwhile, just couldn't figure out that you don't undercut the people you work for, even after twenty years in the con college. And what about your old man's bum-buddy, Cyclo? Whatever happened to Cyclo, boys, hmm? Show them, Jack."

The young, bulky Caucasian man tossed open the garbage bag, and spilled its contents in front of Radley.

"Oh God …" Radley closed his eyes the second he saw the

head roll into the dirt in front of him.

"Look at it!" Scar-Man pulled Radley's hair, forcing him to open his eyes.

Cyclo's head appeared to have been torn from the torso. His eyes ripped from a grey, pasty head. Dirt ground into the skin and the scabby dried-out openings where the eyes should have been. Looking at the rotting, wretched face of his father's friend, Radley couldn't begin to comprehend the horrid fate of the man who'd been like an uncle to him. He could see Dustin share the same reaction. Radley couldn't help but think of the last words Cyclo had spoken to him two years back. "Don't wind up like your father, kid."

"Oh, what the fuck did you guys do?" Dustin held his arm up to his nose, his voice filled with disgust and horror.

"I didn't do this. The people you owe money to, the people you betrayed, Dustin, they did this. And they want to do this to you. And your family. But these guys are my *compatriots, mes peuples.* I can stop them from doing this to you." He motioned to the dried out, rotting head on the ground. "And I just told you what to do to make that happen."

Dustin turned away. He rubbed a hand through his hair and stared at the gun.

"I know how your organization works. I know this game. This is how you get me to join. To prove my loyalty."

"We didn't care much for Danno anyways," Scar-Man said. "You're a good company guy, when you don't have your family sticking a knife in your back. This is our way of owning you, Dustin. Making sure you stay a *Rouge* man the rest of your life. It ain't so bad being a *Rouge* man, is it boys?"

The three cronies muttered in agreement. Radley tried to think of anything he could say to get out of this. Dustin sounded like he actually considering the offer.

"Don't do it, Dust. They just want you to do their dirty work. We're both dead anyway."

"Shut up!" Scar-Man clubbed Radley with the pistol a second time, knocking him forward.

"Just like your fuckin' old man, kid, talkin' outta turn to people you shouldn't talk outta turn to."

Radley stayed on his knees and touched the back of his skull. The second blow was a lot harder than the first. His eyes were watering, and he could feel the goose egg form through his hair.

He hit me harder because I'm right. Dustin and I are both dead. I just hope, Dust, that you see it too.

"So all I gotta do is kill my brother." Dustin looked the scar faced man straight in the eye. "And he disappears. You give me my alibi, and Jezzie and Abby are safe, forever."

"There are always conditions when you deal with us. That would be one of them, though. You've got our word."

"But then I pretty much became the *Rouge's* little whipping boy. You guys need drugs run or stored, I gotta do it. You say bend over, I say how low, is that it?"

"There are always conditions," Scar-Man repeated. He pointed to Cyclo's rotting head. "But I can guarantee you, that won't be you, or any member of your family. Save except Junior here."

Dustin looked down at Radley.

"Now you, Dustin, I can own," Scar-man said. "But baby brother, I can't trust. He has to go, and I need you to make that happen."

Dustin hesitated for a moment. He took a slow, deep breath.

"I'm sorry, Rad."

"Dustin, what the hell are you doing?" Radley pleaded. He needed to plead. This was it. "Look, don't do this. There's other ways we can clear this debt! We'll cut a deal with them. I can sell my car, look." He reached into his pocket and took out his keys. "My Infiniti can still cut us ten grand, we'll give it all to them. Every penny, please."

"I'm sorry, Radley," Dustin repeated. His voice dropped, torment smeared all over his face. He pointed the Glock at Radley's forehead. "You're right, they'll kill us. And Abby, too. This is my only out. This is all I got."

Then he pulled the trigger.

Chapter 40

Radley flinched as the click of the chamber echoed in the cool, evening air. His eyes were closed.

Oh my God, he shot me!

The second click was louder than the first. *He shot me again!*

Radley opened his eyes, and saw his brother's face tighten. He looked at Radley, keeping the gun barrel at his forehead, then turned his head up to Scar-Man. Radley slapped the gun away from his face, more in self-defence than anything else. He glanced at Scar-Man, who simply shook his head, smiling.

"Holy shit," he said to his men. "He would'a done it. And here I thought for sure he would'a turned the gun on me. Shit, Dustin, and to think your brother was going to give you his car." Scar-Man held up his gun and shot Dustin in the head.

"Ahhhh God!" Radley yelled. The loud crack detonated over his head. The sheer shock of the gunshot and watching his brother fall backward put him in a panic. So much blood.

"Want your money back, kid?" Scar-faced man held up the envelope, unable to resist goading Radley. "Never trust a drug dealer. Especially a Wycliffe."

Radley charged the man, and went for the gun, relying on pure instinct.

He hit Scar-Man in the chest, knocking him slightly off balance, then lunged for his gun hand, clutching it to keep him from using the weapon. Scar-Man grabbed the back of Radley's hair and yanked it. Radley howled but leaned into the man, keeping him off balance. The two twisted in a struggle with Radley using his leverage to gain a better footing. Desperate, Radley pulled out his car keys and stabbed Scar-Man's wrist, raking it over his arm. A strip of red shot across the soft part of Scar-Man's forearm.

"Arghhh, you little fucker!" Scar-Man's strength, however, was too much. He grabbed Radley by the hair, snapping his head back and away from his bloodied wrist. Losing his grip on the gun handle, Scar-Man managed to keep it in his hand, trying to right it so he could get a finger on the trigger, but not before Radley utilized the one, sole advantage he had remaining.

With his left hand, Radley hit the trunk button on his keyless entry.

"Police! Freeze!" Two SWAT members, in full riot gear, burst out of his trunk, guns raised. Radley hit his alarm. Plan B came into effect.

"Goddamn, it's a sting!" the aboriginal man screamed. He raised his sawed-off shotgun and fired. Radley didn't see where. The goon went behind the van, reloaded, and fired a second round as the SWAT members ducked for cover. One of them staggering with a hit.

"We checked them!" Jack screamed. He pulled out a gun. "Goddamn it, we checked them for bugs!"

The oriental man drew his weapon and pointed it at the red-faced Caucasian. "Drop it, Jack." He pulled out police identification.

"Holy shit! Ola, you Goddamn gotta be kiddin' me?

Undercover? You!" Ola shook his head, then pointed his gun at the undercover officer, who immediately shot Jack point blank in the chest.

POP! POP! POP! A gunfight exploded between the SWAT members and the aboriginal man behind the van. Over a barrage of yelling, Radley tried dropping to the ground, but Scar-Man grabbed him around the neck and pulled him backward. The loud din of the gunfire equalled the roar of a train, each harsh, piercing discharge felt as though the bullets flew in his direction, knocking him backwards and into Scar-Man's arms like a rag doll. With his head spinning from the unfolding chaos, Radley froze, paralyzed with fear. No matter how much he had prepared, the violent outcome he had tried so desperately to prevent happened anyway.

God no! Scar-Man's gun burrowed into his temple as the man screamed at police – the words white noise from the pulse of the background gunfire. Radley couldn't make out any of it. *What the hell have I done?*

Chapter 41

THREE DAYS EARLIER

Radley stood on the balcony of his apartment. Darkness gradually overtook the skyline but it already devoured his soul, as he had just confirmed to Claire he was ending their relationship. His heart plummeted watching her drive off into oblivion.

I need a drink. Rum. Straight up. He didn't want to. It was pointless. There was no benefit doing it, but he felt compelled nonetheless. Thoughts of Dustin's drinking, the smell of his whiskey, of everything he tried to do to help his brother out barraged his mind. Abandoning Claire, destroying her. The pain was too literal, too real. *I can't do this anymore.*

A war of epic proportions was going on in his head. *My streak, it's been nearly three years now.* He needed every inkling of his being to fight the craving, the sudden, powerful urge to regress into an alcoholic debauchery. *I can't break it. I screwed everything up.* His mind was all over the place.

It was then he noticed the Hawthorn leaves and Birch leaves at his feet, crunching like popcorn as he shifted on the deck. Mashing them with his feet, a sudden memory brought him back to his adolescence, of being in the fetal position, his brother overtop him, walloping him with blows. Dustin was trying to grab the gun. The gun he would have used to shoot the Militiamen.

Fuck! Radley kicked the dust off the deck, striking the rail as he did so. *Ow!* He leaned on his good foot, tending to the shockwave of pain that propelled off his foot.

He pulled up a chair from a patio set Claire encouraged him to buy. Never having owned deck furniture before, he had come to enjoy sitting on it with a coffee or cold pop. Especially sitting on it with her. He quickly purged that thought – it hurt far worse than his toe did.

Serves you right, idiot. He chastised himself, though he wasn't thinking about his foot. *You stopped Dustin that night with the Militiamen, started a fight to do it. It was that night that finally got me to write that second letter to Constable Roake, the one that condemned Dad. The one that saved Dustin and I, saved us from Tavis and his drug running.*

I stopped him with that letter to Roake. Dad would have gotten us killed had he kept forcing us to go with him.

I saved my life. My life with Claire.

He jerked in his seat, a swift but clear revelation overwhelmed him. *What the fuck am I doing?* He grabbed his coat, and tore out the front door, straight for his vehicle. Any pain that he had dissipated into sheer desperation to get to his destination. Arriving at Claire's twenty minutes later, he was at the intercom of her apartment. The light was on in her living room window.

"Claire!" He hit the buzzer. Stopping himself, he realized the mad panic boiling inside. *Calm down. Get to her, now.* He hit the buzzer a second time. *Come on, pick-up.*

"Hello?" In that one word, Radley could hear the

confusion, frustration, anger, and sadness that had snowballed inside her. Her voice still every bit as crackly and tearful as when she stormed out of his condo.

"Claire, it's me."

"Radley? What are you doing?"

"I haven't been honest with you. I didn't have an affair. God, you know I could never do that to you. There's so much more going on."

The click to release the door lock prompted him to bolt up the stairs, faster than he ever had in his life, three at a time. Heading straight to her door, it stood open. He careened inside.

"Radley, what the hell is going on?" She came to the entranceway, police jacket off, city-police shirt ruffled and unbuttoned to her sternum. The sight of her red and tear-stained eyes was like a needle through his chest.

"It's Dustin," he told her. He took a deep breath, then let it out. "Everything I've done this past week has all been for my brother. He's in deep shit, Claire. He's in bad, and I don't know what to do anymore."

She let him in. He told her everything.

"Radley, we gotta take you in." Claire grabbed his arm. For most of the evening she sat on her couch while Radley paced her living room. At three in the morning, she finally got him to sit down.

"I'll take you straight to Narcotics. Sergeant Mike Relone. He's a good man, Radley. He can help you. He's been after these guys for a decade."

"Oh God, Claire, I don't know." Radley hunched forward, holding hands over his head, closing eyes tight. "I can't betray Dustin. Not again. Not a third time."

"Radley, he's in way over his head. And if he's in over his head, you're already five feet under. You wouldn't be here otherwise."

Radley wanted to react, but couldn't. She was right, and they both knew it.

"There's no way either of you are going to come out of this alive. Let us take your brother into custody–"

"No, no. Dustin will go AWOL. He has a gun in that hotel room – I can't predict what he'll do if you try and take him in. That damn *Rouge* just keep threatening to kill Jezzie and Abby–"

"It's their game, Radley. They do it to intimidate him."

"They're serious, Claire. They killed my Dad and Cyclo, I'm sure of it."

"Radley, let's go to Relone, okay? Dustin doesn't have the money to pay them back. If you want this to end once and for all, the police need to be involved, alright?"

"Okay." Radley sat up. He looked at her strong, beautiful face. "Okay," he repeated, rubbing a hand over his eyes.

"Good Lord Almighty." Sergeant Mike Relone took a big breath, then leaned back in his chair, rolling hands over his neatly trimmed, military style crew-cut. "I've been waiting ten years for this chance. The only question is what the hell do I do about it?"

Radley and Claire sat on the other side of the Sergeant's desk in his private office. Relone was a bulky man, with a baggy face and withered, tired eyes suggesting he put a lot of heart into his job. His buzzcut and the subtle presence of a five o'clock shadow suggested the man was concerned less with his appearance and more on practicality. He dressed in full uniform even at the ungodly hour that Claire knew he would be there. But nothing prepared Radley for the bomb this man detonated on his lap.

"I know who your brother is, Mr. Trillamede," Relone said. "We've been monitoring Dustin's activities for quite some time. I'll admit to you, Crime Stoppers was contacted about his involvement with the *Rouge* five months ago, and that put us on his trail. If I may be perfectly blunt, once I started investigating your brother's file, I'd assumed that you, once again, were the one who gave us the information."

"Oh, God." Radley held his hand up. "I can't believe this. And no, I didn't contact Crime Stoppers. That's exactly what Dustin thought too. I swear I didn't."

"Regardless," Relone continued, "we've been infiltrating the *Rouge* for almost four years now. We currently have an undercover operative working with the highest levels of the city sect – people your father and brother have been dealing with these past eleven months."

"Good God." Radley shook his head. A roulette wheel of emotion coursed through him, finally settling on anger. "And what about my father, Sergeant? What about Cyclo? Couldn't your undercover operative do anything to protect them?"

"Let me tell you something about this organization – the *Rouge*." Relone leaned over his desk, looking Radley straight in the eye and speaking with a finality he decided to back away from. "I have been after the ringleaders for over ten years. They're shifty, fluid. They have a lot of money and even more influence. I liken them to a cheap Teflon pan, they don't let anything stick and when it does, it just flakes away. They change henchmen frequently and always produce rock-solid alibis for those that become suspects.

"We've worked damn hard to get inside that group, and I won't tell you to the depths we've sunk to get there, but essentially we've nailed it down to three hitmen – Paul Lanton, Claus Stavinsky, or Manuel Darga. I know these are just names right now, but these are their key henchmen, and one of these men killed your father. Lanton is my best guess, and I have good reason to believe he's in the city right now. I'm not sure who they'll send to deal with your brother, but if I can nail any one of these guys with the information you've given me, it'll be a big blow to these scumbags, and will give us a doorway to work with the RCMP and go after the top brass, several of whom operate out of province."

From the discussion, Radley garnered that Relone knew nothing about the current threats the *Rouge* made against Dustin. Relone apparently hadn't heard from his operative in a while, but the situation brought before him – that of a pending drop between Dustin and one of the *Rouge* leaders –

seemed to give the Sergeant an intriguing possibility. They had gone to Relone to voice a complaint, but he was clearly presenting something much bigger, also much more dangerous. An uneasy silence lingered in the room.

Claire finally spoke. "Let's take Dustin into custody, Sir. Get protection for him and his family. That needs to be our ultimate objective here."

"And let the *Rouge* walk?" Radley cut in, glaring at her. "These guys won't stop, Claire. They won't stop until Dustin pays them back which, at the rate he's going, will be never."

"Constable Clark's assessment of the situation is correct," Relone said. "Bringing your brother in would be the wisest course of action. We have enough on him to justify an arrest. But doing so doesn't end the threats against him or his family. It also jeopardizes four years of undercover work – work that we hoped would lead to a situation just like this one."

The Sergeant shifted yet again in his seat, rubbing his lips intently as if he were about to pull them off of his face. Radley saw the dilemma stirring in the Sergeant's head.

"I'm willing to do it. To set up the sting," Radley blurted, before Claire could stop him.

"Radley–" Claire warned.

"You heard him, Claire. My brother is a dead man walking. I want – no I need – this to end. If it means me putting my life on the line, if it means signing a waiver, whatever I have to do, let's do it. Let's … set up this sting, the ambush, whatever it is. I have to do this for Dustin. I owe him that much."

Claire folded her hands and shook her head. "You don't

owe anyone, Radley."

"Once again, Constable Clark's right," Relone cut in. "Mr. Trillamede, you have to understand the risks. We can't make you do this."

"My brother and his family are in danger. This undercover guy you say you've got working for the *Rouge*, you say he's confirmed they have Dustin on their hit list?"

Relone looked agitated. Radley thought he could see the man's face redden before his eyes.

"I've already compromised my operative's mission enough, Mr. Trillamede. But yes, I will confirm what I've told you. The *Rouge* have targeted your brother, though that could mean anything at this point. We have no definitive way of knowing."

"Targeted? Sergeant, that can't be a good thing. They've targeted his family too, and believe me, I've been 'targeted' by these guys in the past, it's no tea party! God damn it!" Radley slapped his hand on Relone's desk. This agitated his inner cheek from Dustin's punch a few days back – the swelling had gone down but it was still sensitive. Even more disconcerting was how much the Sergeant knew about Dustin's problems. Radley learned Dustin had been on their watch list for quite some time as a known drug runner for the *Rouge*. "I know your frustration, Mr. Trillamede, but I need to make a play here, and I'm not going to risk contacting my man unless I can get a definitive lockdown on where these guys are going to be."

"Radley, if Dustin isn't willing to cooperate then there's very little the police are going to do," Claire said. The tone of her voice was tired, knowing full well what her words would mean. Radley could tell she didn't want to say them. It was like she knew what he would say next.

"Then we do it without Dustin's cooperation. I'll work with your office, tell you guys everything you want to know – the meeting site, what they tell Dustin. Everything."

"I'm throwing the ball in your court, Radley," Relone said, staring him down across his desk much in the way an owl would an intruder who landed on its branch. "If you can give me a rock-solid meeting point, and you can deliver your brother to the *Rouge*, then we wire you, record their conversation, get them to threaten you, talk about your Dad's murder, getting Dustin to do their runs – hell, even get them to say all those things they told you on your brother's cell phone, and we might just make some charges stick. It's the only way I can bust those guys. I need their hand in the cookie jar – hell; I need them taking the whole jar – to entice the Crown to move against these scuz-buckets. Either way, it's your call, kid."

"Fine, I just made it. Do the sting. It's the only way. Get the SWAT Team – I'll get Dustin to take us to them."

He thought he spoke with a decisiveness that would keep Claire's protest at bay. By doing this, by taking this whole Gong Show to her and the police, he was making his commitment to her. The last thing he ever wanted was to put her in danger because of some stupid, damn thing with his Wycliffe side.

"Fine then," Claire said, sitting forward in her chair, and

leaning into the table. "Sergeant, I want in on the SWAT Team."

Chapter 42

Three Hours Later

"I don't know how you pulled this off, you little fuck, but they ain't takin' me alive!" Scar-Man pressed his gun against Radley's temple and dragged him into the surrounding bush.

"Hey! Put the weapon down and your hands in the air, Lanton!" A sharp voice hollered at the two men. Another crack from the aboriginal man's shotgun sent the police scrambling.

The blast jolted Radley from his temporary paralysis. He decided to cooperate with Scar-Man Lanton, shuffling his feet as they trampled over twigs, thistles, and branches. The man loosened his grip on Radley's throat as they moved together, but he kept the gun embedded into Radley's right temple.

They ran onto a makeshift pathway that ran parallel to the coke ovens. Two shots in the distance pierced the silence — one was another shotgun blast, the second sounded more like a rifle.

Lanton grabbed Radley by the hair and pulled his head back, holding the pistol at his throat.

"How many cops are there?" he whispered. "Where are they stationed?"

"I don't know. They wouldn't tell me."

"Bullshit! You little fucker, you're wired aren't you? My man Ola, he was a fucking narc! Searched you and your brother, then lied to my face."

"I'm wired, but you'll never find it." Radley said through gritted teeth. The truth was Radley didn't have a microphone when he arrived, but when 'Ola,' Relone's undercover agent, searched him, he clipped a wireless listening device in the front waist of Radley's jean, just behind his zipper. The officer's name was John Lim, who was Relone's informant for four years. Relone stayed in Radley's apartment all morning, awaiting the confirmation call from Dustin on where the meeting was going to be. Once confirmed, Relone immediately coordinated the SWAT teams, which he had organized 24 hours prior, and ordered them to the Dregs to secure any possible position they could establish around the Coke Ovens. Radley initially wanted nothing to do with having the two officers in his trunk, but Relone had insisted it was a non-negotiable, safety precaution in case the *Rouge* decided to change the locale at the last minute. 'Just make sure Dustin doesn't go into the trunk,' Relone had told him, 'and you'll be fine.'

"The cops have you, Lanton," Radley said, reacting to the man's silence. He wasn't certain where his brazenness was coming from, but he continued, "the police – city SWAT and the RCMP - are all over the place. They've got you on camera. Everything you did -"

"Shut up, you little asshole!" Lanton said, snarling. He ambled along the path dragging Radley with him, but it was obvious they were just blundering together in the dark.

"Freeze, Lanton!" A voice shouted from the woods along

the same path they just barreled over. "We already got you for Murder One, so let's make this easy on yourself. Drop the weapon and release your hostage."

"Fuck you!" Lanton screamed, pressing the gun into Radley's scalp. A puddle of red started to pool and smear from the key gouge Radley had given him.

"There's nowhere for you to go, Lanton." The SWAT officer emerged from the bush, fully outfitted, a helmet covering her face. She held up a Glock of her own. Radley recognized her muffled voice right away.

"You're letting me outta here, or his brains go sky fuckin' high!"

"You're in control, Lanton," Claire said through her helmet. She lowered the weapon, but Radley could tell by her stance she had it at the ready.

Lanton stepped backward, bringing Radley with him. Radley still had his keys in his hand gripping them between his fingers. Sweating profusely, he refused to panic. Two more officers skirted along the top of the coke ovens toward them. He could tell Lanton didn't' see them. In a couple of seconds, he would.

"I'm walking out! I'm takin' the kid with me! When I hit the tracks, I'll leave him–"

"No!" Radley yelled, thrusting his fist and keys upward into Lanton's wrist, pushing the gun away from his face. The weapon fired, blinding Radley. He could feel the heat and powder whip against his face. The noise and vibration struck his nose and lanced his eardrums, but he forced himself to push forward against Lanton, shoving him backward.

"Down, Radley!" Claire screamed as she stepped past him and fired her gun. Striking Lanton in the upper shoulder, she made him drop his weapon into the grass. He lunged for it. Radley dove on top of it, pinning it under his stomach. Claire charged forward, slamming her forearm into Lanton's throat and driving his head backward into the rocky pathway. Her right knee fell hard on the centre of his chest while her left pinned down the other arm. Within two seconds the other officers leapt down from the coke ovens and helped subdue him.

"You fucking bitch!" Lanton screamed, writhing on the ground like an injured animal. "That fucking bitch shot me! Fuck me!"

Radley looked up to see Claire press Lanton's chin upward against the ground, while she pulled out a set of cuffs. Her right knee wedged farther into his gut.

"Owwww, Fuck!" Lanton shrieked – his voice high, raspy, and pained. "Get off of me!"

Radley pushed away from the man, thrashing on the ground as though he was drowning in a lethal undercurrent. Another officer lunged onto Lanton's right arm, pinning it down with his knee, shoving Radley forward as he did so. Radley pushed the gun out from under his belly, sliding it along the ground in a maelstrom of dust, as far from Lanton as possible. The gangster freaked out behind him, still pinned down by officers. By Claire.

Radley struggled for a breath, burying his face into his arm.

He tried to calm himself, the fear and realization of what had just transpired exploded inside him. Closing his eyes, he could feel the shock rivet from his heart through his entire body. He vaguely noticed the other officers sprinting up the pathway, guns drawn as they surrounded Lanton.

"Paul Lanton." He could hear Claire speak through gritted teeth. "You're under arrest for murder."

The world spun around. Radley's surroundings, the stars in the sky, the tops of trees hovering over him like watchmen. Everything turned clockwise, spinning circles overlapping each other.

Dizzy, Radley told himself. *In shock.* He lay on his back in a pile of twigs and dried up leaves.

Radley, get outta those shit leaves, his mother called out to him, her stoned voice from his childhood, raspy and slurry. He remembered the smell of smoke and sweat as she sat by a campfire. It was one of his earliest memories - she had handed him something. *Come here and have a toke with your mommy.*

Hey Mama.

He came-to abruptly, yanked out by the cold and shock. He was confused, disorientated, his arms tied up in the cotton blanket the Medics had given him. Scrunching the blanket in a tight ball over his chest, he struggled to keep the core of his body warm. He vaguely remembered stumbling over to his car from the coke ovens and collapsing on the grass where his

Infiniti sat. Claire was with him, helping him over, but she wasn't here now. Against his wishes, she joined, part of the SWAT team. The thought agitated him, made him dizzier. Where did she go?

She took a step back so that the Medics could examine me. They'd sat him up, checked his vitals, blood pressure. *You're traumatized,* they told him. *Just rest. Try to breathe and keep warm. If you need anything, yell.* They laid him down on the grass and gave him the blanket, then they were gone, Claire with them. There was so much commotion going on, it had swallowed them all up.

We're still at the Dregs … where all that shooting happened. It was the thought of the gun fire that kept him down. He remembered the sharp, piercing Pop-Pops of bullets between the police and the *Rouge.* He closed his eyes and felt the cold metal of Lanton's gun pressed up against his throat. It was the second time that evening he faced a barrel of a gun – the first had been an inch from his forehead, held by –

No, I'm not ready to think about that. Radley stopped himself. Instead, he turned his head back to the commotion.

He saw several paramedics, three, no four of them surrounding a body. Medical equipment and portable flood lights cast dark shadows. There were other attendants tending to a couple of injured officers, but Radley honed in on the most serious of casualties. He could tell from their words: "gunshot wound to the head" and "not able to breathe on his own," that they were talking about his brother. The fact they were talking about him at all had to be a good sign. Could

Dustin have survived?

Oh good God, Dustin's been shot! He closed his eyes tightly, then turned his head back to the treetops – they pointed up to the clear, black sky, peppered with sprinkles of starlight affording him the peace to breathe, to settle the nausea that threatened to overtake him. At some point he turned his head again and saw Dustin being loaded into the ambulance. He had a blue mask over his face. Radley tried to process what he saw, but was still too traumatized to get up.

He had no idea how long he lay there. It was probably close to midnight by now – hard to judge as the intensity of the flood lamps lit up the night's sky. Every instance thereafter that Radley turned to look there seemed to be more investigators, forensic experts, and ambulance attendants scurrying about. Everything blurred – he drifted in and out of consciousness.

"How are you doing?" Claire knelt and rubbed his right shoulder. She had a second, heavier blanket with her.

It took him a moment to register her presence. Once he did, he remembered he needed to lash out at her. "Good Lord, Claire. Why did you put yourself in danger like that? I wanted to protect you–"

"No,"–she held up her hand silencing him–"we're not doing this now. I did my job. Yes, I did it for you, but ultimately it's my job and that's all I'm going to say about it right now."

She laid the second blanket over his chest and tucked it around his neck. He knew better than to start arguing with her. The thought made his head spin.

"How are you doing?" She repeated, then motioned to the attendants and police behind them. "They want me to check on you."

"I'm fine." He tried to swallow but his mouth was dry. Unable to escape the sensation of being on a Tilt-A-Whirl, her presence comforted him. "Thank-you for being here," he muttered.

"I'm sorry I had to leave you alone over here," she said. Radley noticed she still wore her SWAT gear, minus the helmet. Her long hair remained in a tight bun at the back of her head – how he longed to be home to run his fingers through it. "We had to debrief with our commander, and I had to start the paperwork on why I shot that creep. I came back as soon as I could."

"I'm okay." He took a slow breath to keep his voice calm.

"Don't talk." The concerned look on her face told him he wasn't fooling anybody. "Just take it easy." She explained to him all of the *Rouge* members were accounted for. Lanton had been arrested. The red, bull-faced man was dead, and Jack – the sawed-off shotgun lunatic – had been killed by a police sniper during his shootout with the SWAT team. The ambulance had taken Dustin to the hospital – miraculously he was still alive, but in grave condition.

"You need to call Jezzie," Radley said. Claire hushed him. Everything would be taken care of by the police.

They sat quietly for the next ten minutes. Claire held his hand while Radley let his body go numb. He was shivering even with the two blankets – Clare finally placed her bullet-proof vest overtop the other layers and the weight of it on his chest felt warm, secure. Then the hallucinations started. He was climbing trees again, using the branches for leverage and the leaves for grip as he pulled himself up to the sky. *Swing,* he kept telling himself, *I want to swing.*

"Radley, come here baby," his mother's voice came back to him. "You're gonna have your first toke, honey bun."

Get the hell away from me! Turning away from his mother this time, he sprinted into the woods, down a crooked, rackety trail that curved into the tanned brick coke ovens of the Dregs. Upon seeing them, he stumbled, falling flat on his face.

A hand reached out to him. Radley took it, looked up and saw Scar-Man looking down smiling, the way the bastard did when he shot Dustin.

Here I am kid, Paul Lanton said with his twisted chortle, engulfed in a backdrop of red and black. *The Devil.* "And to think you were going to give Dustin your car." The man took out his gun and slammed it down on Radley's head.

No! Radley hollered. *Not you. No–*

"Radley!" Claire shook him, jarring him awake. His mind jolted from the roller coaster ride.

"You were wailing. Listen, we're going to get you out of here soon. Leone wants to get a statement from you. Do you think you can do that?"

"Yeah." Radley rubbed his eyes. So that was the reason they were keeping him here.

"Are you sure? You and Lim are the key witnesses to

everything. Relone can wait until you're ready – he'll have to wait."

"No, bring him over." Radley forced himself to sit. His neck and back muscles were stiff and achy and a swarm of pain shot into his head, but he kept upright. Claire supported his shoulders. He kept a hand gripped firmly in hers. It had to be early morning now, the sun surfaced and a cool mist sat in the air.

Radley looked at the scene around him. Crime tape and two bodies in white bags about to be transported out of the woods, but all he could think about was his brother.

"Good God, Claire, what did I do?"

"You did what you needed to. The only thing you could do."

"But Dustin…" His voice wavered, he felt remorse crawl up his throat. "It wasn't supposed to happen like this–"

"I know, I know. But listen, we got Paul Lanton. We think he was responsible for your Dad's death. He's an evil, evil man, Radley, and we finally got him for First Degree, thanks to you and Dustin. Now if you want to help your brother, help his family, you have to tell Relone your story. Tell him everything that happened here tonight."

She motioned the investigator over. Relone knew the larger background already. Radley took a breath, trying to process everything that happened during the whirlwind of the past three days. The real problem, of course, was the sickening sensation festering inside him, knowing everything he had risked these past few days had come to an utter failure with his brother being loaded up in that ambulance, fighting for every inch of his life.

Chapter 43

Twenty-Eight Hours Later – Present Day

Radley sat in the hospital's Intensive Care waiting room. Jezzelle sat across from him, face cradled in her hands. Dustin wasn't dead. The doctors somehow managed to keep him alive. Apparently the bullet struck his head straight on, just above the left eyeball. Its damage was localized to the left hemisphere of his brain. They could not remove the bullet, but rather performed two surgeries to cut down the damage. All dead tissue surrounding the wound was removed, including his left eye. A portion of his skullcap was incised then detached, and a drain placed inside his head to relieve the fluid and swelling around the brain.

Either way, Dustin would never be the same again. The doctors explained everything from his speech to his memory, his understanding to his motor skills, would be significantly impaired. They projected he'd lose as much as ninety-five percent of the strength and coordination in the right side of his body. Years of rehabilitation would be required and the extent of the injury, simply put, would be life-changing for Dustin and his family.

Radley glanced up and saw Claire standing in the doorway. Relone stood beside her. Relone shifted his feet, while Claire looked at him with sympathy. Both she and Relone appeared uneasy being there, but it was obvious they needed to speak with Radley.

He stood up and laid a hand on Jezzelle's shoulder. She didn't lift her head, or even acknowledge him, just stared at the floor with a blank, emotionless expression.

"I'll bring you another coffee, Jezzie." Radley's voice was raw and scratchy. He walked into the hall. His eyes briefly met Claire's, but he could tell this was to be all business.

"I talked to the prosecutor," Relone said. Presumably he'd been updated on Dustin's most recent prognosis. "She figures we got enough on Lanton that we won't need you in court, or to testify."

"Good," Radley muttered, his voice laced with relief and resentment. "The guy was only driving around with Cyclo's head in his backseat. What more evidence do you need?"

"Well, it comes down to who made the killing blow in that particular case." Relone said, grimacing. "We'll have to see if Lanton confesses, or wants to implicate any other *Rouge* members for us. Either way, we should have sufficient evidence for at least two indictable counts."

"I hope Dustin's going to be one of them. You both saw Lanton shoot him in the head."

"Lanton'll definitely be charged with attempted murder and—"

"Attempted murder?" Radley raged at Relone. "The guy shot Dustin point blank in the face. It's only a fluke miracle my brother is still alive, never mind the fact that he's now a fucking vegetable …"

"Radley." Claire gestured to the entrance of the waiting

room, only ten feet away from where they were talking. "You know how the legal system works. Believe me, Sergeant Relone wants the same thing you do. We all want to see Lanton locked up for the rest of his miserable life."

"Yeah." Radley bit his lip. He couldn't look her in the eye. "Sorry, Sergeant."

"It's alright, don't worry about it. Like I said, the Crown has enough hard evidence from our cameras, your wire, and John Lim, our undercover guy, to take down Lanton. We do, however, want to be able to get a hold of you if we need to, especially given the shape your brother's in. You may have to fill in some blanks for us."

"Of course. Whatever you need."

Relone looked at him and Claire, sensing the unease between the two. "Okay, then. Constable Clark will make sure we have your up-to-date contact information. It might be a good idea to keep a low profile for the next little while, alright? Please don't talk to any press. We're gonna nail Lanton to the wall, okay?"

Relone turned and walked away, disappearing around the corner, leaving Claire and Radley in the hall alone.

"Radley, I–"

"Claire–"

Both stopped themselves. Radley spoke first. It was hard to get the words out.

"I'm sorry to have dragged you into this. I'm sure it's been awkward having to deal with this in front of your colleagues, your superiors. I feel terrible."

"No, no," she insisted.

"This is a major bust for you guys. This is going to be high profile, and will stay that way for the next hundred months before they put this guy away. And I ... I can't do this to you. You were an arresting officer – you shot the guy for God's sake. You can't have this connection to me. If the press, or the defense attorneys, the *Rouge* – anyone – finds out about our relationship, it could compromise the trial, and put you in the gang's crosshairs."

"We can just keep it quiet."

"You know that's not going to work. You're going to get scrutinized as it is, having fired that gun. If his defense team catches any inkling of our relationship, they will condemn every action you took as a member of that SWAT team. The *Rouge* will claim you had a personal vendetta against them, start threatening your family, and all that crap again. This whole mess has the potential to jeopardize your career and put you in danger."

"I don't care about any of that. I did what I did to protect you."

"I know ... I know you did," he said, wanting to touch her, but resisting the urge, "and I owe you everything for it. But we have to see this through – Lanton has to be convicted."

Claire stared at him. He recognized the pain in her eyes. It was unmistakable – he had seen it earlier in the week and it was easy to spot – he felt the same pain, like a thousand daggers spearing his heart.

"It doesn't have to be this way." But her words fell flat.

"Yeah, it does." He kissed her forehead. "Goodbye, Claire. I'm sorry. I so wish things could have been different."

She didn't say anything. She walked away, unable to look at him.

The embarrassment he had caused her from this ordeal was enough to make him turn away and let her go. She would be called to testify against Lanton, whose trial could possibly implicate other *Rouge* members. Her having any connection to Radley and Dustin not only threatened the integrity of the case against Lanton, but also put an eternal target on her back – one that Radley couldn't bear her having. *Deep down, I know she understands that too.*

He treaded over to the coffee machine, to get a strong, black coffee for Jezzelle. His hands shook as he tried to hold the cup still underneath the spout.

"Ow, dammit!" Radley cursed as he spilt a few drops of hot liquid on his inside palm. "Jesus!" He punched the machine with the palm of his hand.

He took a breath to calm himself, and closed his eyes.

It would be a very long road for the Wycliffe family.

He sat alone in the Trillamede's living room, feeling sorry for himself. One of his foster father's Scottish tumblers, with a picture of Edinburgh Castle on it, sat a quarter full with single malt.

Drink it, for God's Sake. If any bastard on the face of this earth deserves a taste, it's you. Besides, you poured it, you imbecile. It's Doug's liquor, not yours, and you stole it. Now you have to get rid of the evidence.

Fair enough, he thought, *picking up the tumbler. Just one drink. Christ, Scar-Faced Man held a gun to head, my own brother tried to shoot me, Dustin himself got shot and will never recover, and I wound up losing the love of my life. Have a drink, for fuck sakes.* He took a sip and held it in his mouth.

No! What the frig am I doing? This is bloody gross! Catapulting himself off the couch, he took the tumbler with him. The thick, warm-syrupy fluid tasted raw and pungent on his tongue. He shot over to the sink and spit it out, then dumped the remainder of his glass down the drain.

Get this shit out of my sight! He put the cap back on the bottle and stuffed it back in the liquor cabinet Doug and Diane had under their breakfast nook. He had wanted to dump the whole bottle down the sink, but it wasn't his booze to drink. Doug or Diane could never know he'd tried it.

And you, he reprimanded himself. *You stupid shit. Quit making these fucking excuses.* His point of view shifted, but he was still self-berating. *My dry streak is almost three years, and I'm not going to blow it. I at least owe Claire, the Trillamedes, myself, that much.*

He went back into their living room, plopped on the couch, and held up the Wycliffe family picture he had taken from his apartment, the one his Aunt Dulcie snapped in Windbender Valley so many years ago, when Dustin was fourteen and he ten. The day he had his first marijuana joint. It was also the day of his last. The only other thing he could remember from that campout was Tavis screaming at Dustin to get in the picture, *Because I'll fucking kick yer ass if you don't!*

My mother gave me that joint. Radley gave a hollow chuckle, shaking his head. *Oh Dustin, what wonderful parents we had.*

And how it cost us. Cost them both. Dustin lying in a near vegetative state, and Radley on stress and personal leave two weeks after the shooting at the coke ovens. It was all Radley could think about – that night – the events before it, the shooting itself, and the crucial minutes afterward. Radley obsessed over them: Should he have told Claire? Involved Relone? Maybe he should have clicked the trunk of his Infiniti a few seconds earlier, when Dustin first aimed the gun at him. They had produced Cyclo's head at that point. He learned from Relone, however, that the officers weren't certain what the head was when Lanton's crony rolled it out the garbage bag, so they didn't intervene and continued to wait for Radley to pop the trunk. "The prosecution is going to try to link Lanton to Cyclo Mcyestra's murder," Relone told him in a conciliatory tone. "But there's no rock-solid evidence as to who delivered the killing blow yet. If anything, Lanton and the *Rouge* have been ingenious in covering their tracks over the years – our best hope is whatever John Lim can try to piece together for us. The real smoking gun we have is, unfortunately, what he did to Dustin, and I promise you we're going to crucify him for that."

Regardless, Radley surmised, *that doesn't save my brother. I should have just let Dustin handle it, Lanton might only have scared him – the whole-shoot-your-brother-thing might have just been a game.*

No, no, he shot Dustin, point blank in the head. Radley had to keep reminding himself of that. Lanton shot him deliberately – the sickening sight, the painful blast of the gun, permanent fixtures in Radley's psyche that would follow him to the end of his days. Lanton had intended to kill Dustin. Everything Radley did, bringing in the cops, arranging the set-up, getting the SWAT team involved, was done out of necessity. If nothing else, it ended the danger to Jezzelle and Abby. Dustin was bound and determined to face down the *Rouge*. There was no talking him out of it. *I made the right call. I just have to live with myself for doing it.*

"Arghhhh!" Radley stood up. He had spun around in circles all week. Desperate to get out of his apartment, he stayed at Diane and Doug's just to get some order and stability back in his life. It wasn't good for him to be home alone.

All alone now, Radley reminded himself. Diane took the past few days off of work to be with him. He'd talked over the evening's events with her a hundred times. She had finally gone back to work when he told her he was okay.

Bullshit. Radley ran his fingers through his hair. The booze called him. The pain called him. The Wycliffe family picture sat on the coffee table.

Dammit! Radley stood up and hurled the frame, face down on the floor, shattering the glass into a dozen pieces.

He took a breath, letting the anger drain through him. At least he had enough of Diane's training in him to ensure he threw the picture face down on the laminate rather than the carpet. The clean-up was easy. The photograph was damaged;

a piece of glass had torn the centre of it. Radley ripped it in half and threw the pieces in the trash.

That part of my life is done. It has to be. My childhood, adolescence, everything to do with drugs, and the impact my Wycliffe parents had in my life, is over. There's nothing more I can do, or get sucked back into. It's time to heal, to move forward.

Leaning back on the couch, a sudden, rare moment of clairvoyance came to him.

I know what I need to do.

Chapter 44

Four Months Later

"Pass me some tacky-tack, please?" Dulcie asked, standing on a step stool. She held the corner of a white banner that read "Welcome Home Dustin" in bold, red letters.

"Here you go." Radley helped her straighten the banner. They put it up over the living room entranceway of the new home Jezzelle's father, brother, Dulcie, and Radley purchased for them. The new house was a one level bungalow, with no stairs, wide rooms, and two wheelchair ramps leading up to the front and back entranceways. The house previously belonged to a homemaker with ALS, who was confined to a wheelchair with little mobility in her arms and legs.

Like Dustin. Though his brother was no homemaker.

Nor would he ever be, even if he wanted to. The thought jarred Radley's heart.

"I just want to make sure the banner's straight." Dulcie stepped back to look at the banner. "It's straight, right?"

She's obsessing over this. Radley could see the wear on her face. "Yeah, Aunty, it is."

She rubbed her face, hiding the tears, which quickly turned into sobs.

"Hey, Aunty, come on." Radley gave her a hug, glancing at the banner, just to make sure it really was straight. They worked hard the past two weeks, getting the house ready for

Dustin's arrival. The banner was a frivolous gesture. *Dustin won't even notice it, let alone read it.*

"It's not easy, I know," Radley said, patting her back.

"I have this picture I took, oh, about seventeen or eighteen years ago. It was of all four of you – your mom, dad, Dustin, you. We were at Canyon Creek camping. You guys – it was the only family picture we had of the Wycliffe's. I think I gave your mother a copy." She wiped her cheeks.

Yeah, you did. It was actually at Windbender Valley, not Canyon Creek. "I think I remember it," he said.

"This is not the future I envisioned for you, or your brother, or your family. I curse my sister and her husband for doing this to you boys." Her voice shook as she spoke.

"There's nothing anybody could have done, Aunty." The past four months Diane and Doug Trillamede had become his only true parents. They had counselled him through this, were still getting him through everything that happened since that horrible night at the coke ovens.

"I should have taken you boys in after your father got arrested. I just couldn't at the time. I had devils in my closet, you know?"

"Oh goodness, say no more, Aunty" Radley held up his hand. "I've come to terms with the past. All of it. And you know what? None of it matters anymore – all that matters is who we are now. And how we move forward."

"You're a perceptive man, Radley." Dulcie grasped his hand. "The fact that you're here, helping your brother, after everything he's done – done to you – these past few years.

You should hate him, Radley, hate him to the core, and yet here you are, at his side, helping purchase this house. How do you do it?"

By fighting a never-ending battle with my own devils, Aunty, and they're all bastards if you really want to know. Radley exhaled, then paused for a moment. "Let's just say I want to believe there's more to being a Wycliffe than just selling drugs, stealing cars, and screwing up your life."

"That's incredible Radley, you know that?"

I'm trying, Aunt Dulcie, I'm trying with every breath and ounce of my being.

"Thank-you." He leaned forward and hugged her a second time. Glimpsing at the clock on the wall, he saw that Dustin and Jezzelle were scheduled to be home soon.

Radley ignored the pang in his chest upon seeing his brother, helpless and feeble, roll up the ramp of the walkway.

"He's home!" Dulcie pushed the open button on the automatic door and Jazzelle rolled him in.

The extra wide porch accommodated the wheelchair with the attached oxygen tank, which Dustin needed on occasion. Radley stood in the oversized, arch-shaped doorway that led from the living room to the kitchen, trying to stay low key. A few members of Dustin and Jezzelle's extended family greeted them on the porch; Dustin made no motion or acknowledgment to any of them there. He sat in the wheelchair, the space where his left eye had been completely closed shut, his right eye rolling toward the floor, a string of drool trickling from the corner of his mouth.

"This is home, baby," Jezzelle said. They rolled him into the living room where the welcome banner and its red shimmering letters were the first thing everyone noticed.

Should've ripped that stupid thing down, Radley thought, cringing. *What the hell were we thinking?*

"Nice," Abigail said, walking behind them, carrying a suitcase of clothes for her Dad. "Who's the genius who put that up?"

"Abby, not now," Jezzelle said, as the rest of the family came in. An awkward silence followed.

"You have a beautiful home, Dusty," Dulcie said.

Abigail rolled her eyes. Only Radley noticed.

"Thank-you, everyone." Jezzelle's voice wavered. "All of you. For everything."

"Anything for my big sis," Jezzelle's brother, Jonah, said, giving her a hug. "We wanted to help." He reached over and tried to give Abigail a hug.

"Don't touch me,' she said, pushing him off. "Get the hell away from me."

"Abigail! What the hell is the matter with you?" Jezzelle shouted.

"Look at this place!" Abby bellowed back. "Look at this house. We're going to have to live here forever. My father is going to be this way forever!"

"Abby, baby," Dulcie said. A few family members tried to

intervene.

Abigail turned to Radley and pointed. "And why the hell is he here? What the hell has he done for us? For my father!"

"He's done more than you'll ever know!" Jezzelle hissed.

"Hey, wait, Abby," Radley said. *What do I do here? Stay? Turn away and leave?*

"He let my father get shot! He brought the police to set up my father, and all they did was get him shot!"

"Abby no!"

Radley didn't say anything. Abigail spun around. Her mother tried to grab her, but Abby shoved her away. Dustin remained docile in his chair, staring at the floor. The drool from his mouth hung over his chin.

"Get away from me!" Abigail screamed, storming out the front door, leaving the house in a loud silence.

Radley looked at Jezzelle. "Let me talk to her." He sprinted out the door after her.

"Abby!" Radley bolted down the ramp and onto the front lawn. Abigail had already stormed across the street and turned into an alleyway, breaking into a sprint the second she heard his voice.

Don't call out to her, he told himself. *Don't make a scene, just go to her.* He crossed the street, following her into the alley. It was paved, with high fences and trees from the houses that surrounded them.

She stopped and turned, knowing he was there. He stopped a few paces away from her. "Get the hell away from me! You're the last fucking person on Earth I want to see right now!"

"Okay, okay." Radley saw her red face, the anger, and watery eyes. *She's lost her father. She blames me for it. Okay.*

"Abby, I'm sorry for everything that's happened. Please understand, everything I tried to do I did to save your father. To protect him, you, and your mom. I know it's hard to see that, but your father–"

"Oh, God, stop it already! My father tried to shoot you!" she yelled.

Her words were like running into a brick wall. Radley took a breath. "You know about that?"

"Of course I know; do you think I'm stupid? I hear everything! I know you faced down the *Rouge*! Tried to help my Dad. Well, you know what, he deserved everything he got! Did you hear me? He fucking deserved it!"

"Abby, you can't mean that."

"Of course I mean it! I did everything I could to stop him … I tried to be like you."

"Be like me?" Radley shook his head. "What do you mean?"

"It was me, Uncle Radley," Abigail said, breaking into tears. "It was me who phoned Crime Stoppers and told them about my Dad and his deals with Danno. That bastard threatened Dad. I told them everything."

"Oh, God, Abby." Radley froze as a wave of clarity swept over him.

"I wanted the police to arrest him, put him in jail. To make him stop doing runs. When they actually did, I thought, 'Oh good, now he's safe.' Only the stupid police just set him up, and instead all it did was get the *Rouge* angry at him. So you see, Uncle Radley, I'm the one who caused my Dad to end up like this. It is all my fault. I tried to be like you, to have the guts to turn him in, to protect him from himself. And I failed!"

"No, no, no, sweetie." Radley reached out to her. She let him come closer. "You did what you needed to. You tried to protect yourself, your mom, and your dad. That's exactly what I tried to do – and I spent too much of my life trying to make amends for it. I've learned that we can't take responsibility for other people's choices, least of all our parents. We can only do what we can to protect ourselves."

"But if I hadn't called Crime Stoppers, my Dad would be–"

"He would be dead," Radley said, he was right up to her now. "He would have died horribly – at the hands of the same men who killed your grandfather. And there's no guarantee they wouldn't have done the same to you, or your mom. You did the right thing, Abby." He took her hand, and leaned forward to hug her.

"No, no I didn't–" She tried to pull away. Radley held on.

"You did the right thing, girl. Abby, you did the right thing. One day you'll understand that. You did the right thing." He drew her toward him. Abigail started sobbing. He held her close against his chest and let her cry.

"You did the right thing," he repeated. "I know it, and some way, somehow, and I think your Dad knows it as well."

Chapter 45

Three Months Later – Age 29

"On top of your game, Buddy." Shawn gave Radley a thumbs up through the doorway of the staff room as he left for the night. "Miss over a month of work and you're still tops in sales this year, by a country mile I might add."

"Yeah, thanks," Radley replied, giving his boss a customary salute. "Have a good one." As Shawn trotted down the stairwell, Radley was officially alone in the staff room, sitting at the table over half a cup of lukewarm coffee and an uneaten submarine sandwich that was supposed to be his lunch. He hadn't eaten all day. Too much on his mind.

The two bombshells dropped on him were the reasons why. The first was Winston's offer to be sales manager for a new dealership on the West-Coast. Somehow Radley had managed to pull a fast one over his employers – having taken two weeks off work for dental pain, all of which covered with a dentist's note as he did have his tooth replaced and gum work done. He took an additional two weeks due to a family accident, mentioning only that his biological brother was seriously injured and required hospice care, but thus far any mention of Paul Langdon's arrest and impending trial didn't seem to register with anyone at work during the past seven months. It had become a larger jurisdictional matter, which certainly helped keep it out of the local airwaves. Either way, Radley felt like he was living a ruse – he buried himself in work, told no one of his biological father's death, and gave only vague answers as to how his brother was holding up, stating he'd suffered serious head injuries from "an accidental gunshot wound to the head."

It is a ruse, buddy, quit trying to sugar coat it. It's so easy to lie when you're so busy you don't even realize you're doing it. Miraculously, he was pulling it off – the promotion offer from Winston this morning came right out of left field. He had no forewarning, no real understanding why.

"You're ready, kid," Winston had told him. "I need people like you out there, get the new dealership credibility and my nephw Jon's name some exposure in a brand new market – let the young, up-and-comers look to someone like you as a role model. You got the people skills, Radley, now it's time to hone that into leadership." He slapped him on the shoulder, told him to think about it, and he had forty-eight hours to give him an answer. So far, it had been nine, and he hadn't told anyone yet – not Shawn, not the Trillamedes, not Jezzelle or Abby, and not Claire. He so badly wanted to tell Claire, but knew he had to keep his distance. His mind was a spinning roller coaster of pros and cons about what life on the West Coast would be like. Yet this wasn't the bombshell that monopolized his thoughts – that bombshell sat on the table in front of him, next to his uneaten ham & provolone submarine.

It was his cell phone, and the text that was supposed to be coming in the next minute, one of three texts he had received in the past thirty-six hours that sent ice-chills up his spine and into every corner of his body.

The phone buzzed on the table at 5:25 PM, exactly when he expected it to. It still startled him.

He grabbed the phone and opened his webmail. *Let's just get this over with.*

> **To:** radley.trillamede@hotmail.com
> **Subject:** Location
> **From:** thetyrannicalmonkey@sh0345.org
> **Time:** Friday, 5:25 PM
>
> **Message:** I'm ready to meet. Pub on 32nd in NW
> – Malckey's. 6:00. I'll have a green hat on.

Radley had anticipated a message like this – it had consumed his mind for the past day, overlapping even Winston's offer, which should have been all he thought about. Instead, he agonized over possible scenarios and outcomes to this email, and his response to it.

No way, Tyrannical Monkey. He began typing, his mind completely made up. *This will be on my terms, not yours.*

Radley typed back:

> Negative. I'm not meeting you in some remote pub in the boonies. Public place. Sunridge Shopping Mall, late night shopping until 9 PM tonight. Meet me in Food Court at 6:30. You have until 7:00 to tell me what you need, then I

walk. Deal or no deal. Keep in mind, "no deal" means we don't meet again. Ever. Period.

It was probably wordier than necessary, but Radley had no idea who he was dealing with. He figured this couldn't be good – whoever it was had gotten his private email somehow and hounded him the past two days.

Radley had no idea what to do. The person wouldn't say his or her name, leaving Radley to speculate anyone with the nickname "The Tyrannical Monkey" couldn't be a reputable character. Who was this person? Radley could only assume a member of the *Rouge*, someone perhaps affiliated to Daniel Wannick, Dustin's old cell mate and *Rouge* connection who Dustin had admitted stealing the cocaine bag from right before he and Radley drove into the coke ovens that fateful night. But why contact Radley, and insist on meeting with him? Probably some kind of extortion scheme, perhaps more threats against Jezzelle and Abby? The police seized the cocaine during the SWAT sting, so there was no chance Wannick would ever get the drugs back. Wannick no doubt still accused Dustin of turning him in, but what vengeance could possibly satisfy him at this point? Radley and Dustin had already suffered enough, Dustin's consequences were life-altering.

God, Dustin, your web of lies, deceit, and shady dealings still friggin' haunt us even after everything. What the hell do these guys want from you?

Radley could only theorize. All he really wanted to do was

tell the Monkey to suck an egg and stay the hell away from his brother and family. He certainly wanted to after the first email, but the content of the second email gave Radley no other choice but to play this slime ball's game.

I know why your brother put that gun to your head and pulled the trigger. I can tell you why. I can tell you everything.

Radley had read that email sitting at his desk at work, just before a couple came in asking him to take them on a tour of the showroom. Radley had been distracted the entire time, thinking only about the statement.

He knows what Dustin did. He's close to the situation. Close to me. Has to be a Rouge Militiaman.

Who the hell are you? Radley had written back.

Someone who knows, was the response. *I need to meet with you. In person. Will contact u at 5:25 PM sharp this Friday. We'll meet that night. It's important for u, and ur brother.*

Use proper English asshole, Radley had wanted to type, but restrained himself. Instead he replied *OK,* if for no other reason than to buy himself time to think. And think he did, but he came no closer about deciding what to do, other than to see what this scuz wanted.

Radley leaned back in the staffroom chair, waiting for the response to come. *Whatever this is, it needs to go through me first, and I'll do everything I can to handle it myself this time.*

He hit the refresh button on his phone, and the return email downloaded instantly.

Alright. Sunridge Food Court. Youll definitely be

there, right? Dont ditch me, Im risking my neck coming to u. Come alone, dont bring any1. We need to do this man 2 man.

Yup, it's Rouge. Fuck! What the hell do they want?!

Fine, I'll be there.

But mark my words you son-of-a-bitch, I'll be ready.

Radley sat in his car in the parking lot of the shopping centre, a hundred options racing through his mind. He was about to meet with a *Rouge* – a *Rouge* what? Informant? Current member? Someone who wanted to strap Radley to a chair and drill holes into his skull?

Do I phone Claire? Do I tell somebody where I am? He gripped the can of pepper spray he put under his coat. *Will this be enough?*

I moved this to a public venue. A food court in a major shopping mall on a busy Friday night. There were always people in the mall on a Friday night. If this guy jumped him, or a group of them came out of nowhere to try and kidnap him, he could make a scene, fire the bear spray, someone would call mall security, and the police. He would be safe, right?

Damnit! He cursed himself. *What the hell have I done?* He refused to phone Claire, and hadn't spoken to her in a while.

It had been awkward between the two of them of late, talking only small talk and a little about Lanton's trial, which started this week. It was no coincidence this Tyrannical Monkey freak had contacted him a day after the opening hearing.

He looked at the clock – 6:25. *I gotta do something.* He had been there for ten minutes, paralyzed in his seat; the uncertainty of what he was walking into kept him on edge. *I'm gonna text Relone.* He hadn't talked to Sergeant Relone in two months, but telling him was the only way he was going to get out of the car and meet whoever this Tyrannical Monkey was.

Radley typed into his phone:

Sergeant Relone,

I am meeting with a Rouge informant about Dustin, not 100% sure about what, but I think it's a threat against Dustin's family. I'm going to find out what. If you don't hear back from me in 30 min, I'm at Sunridge Mall Food Court – security cameras will be on me.

He hit the send button and didn't bother to check to see if the Sergeant replied. Relone would probably try and stop him.

And that's not going to happen. I'm going to meet with this creep. I need to know what this new threat against Dustin is, then deal with it promptly.

With that, he put the phone in his belt holster and got out of the car. He remembered to take a breath when he went through the mall entranceway and headed toward the food court.

Chapter 46

Godamnit, you gotta be friggin' kidding me! Radley fumed when he saw the man in the green ball cap, uncertain from the shock as to whether he said the words out loud or not. The man sat at an isolated table a few seats away from a Subway Restaurant, and rose to his feet the second he saw Radley.

"You gotta be friggin' kidding me!" Radley repeated, knowing this time for sure those words were heard. "What the hell, man! Thanks for wasting my time. I'm leaving."

"Wait." His cousin Galen following him. He had a shoulder bag on him, which he made sure to grab before leaving the table. "Hear me out, please. I've got information."

This is going to be a scene. Radley calmed himself. He supposed, if anything, he should be relieved it wasn't a member of the *Rouge* waiting for him. Turning to face his cousin, he noticed there were about fifty people in the food court around them, mostly eating and having their own conversations.

"Did you have to play Spy Games with me, Galen?" Radley said, spinning around to confront his cousin head on. "Jesus, you gave me a heart attack with those emails! The Tyrannical Monkey? Seriously? I thought you were a member of the friggin' gang that shot Dustin!"

"Really?" Galen said, the first civil-word the two cousins had said to each other in five years. "I never thought of that. The Tyrannical Monkey is my *World of War* nickname."

"Good God, Galen. Give your friggin' head a shake! After all I've been through with Dustin and the *Rouge* this past six months! What the hell were you thinking?"

"Well, shit, Radley." Galen's tone got defensive. "I knew you weren't gonna wanna meet with me any other way!"

You got that right. But Radley motioned to an empty table next to an overfilled garbage can nobody else wanted to sit by. "Gee, I wonder why?" Radley didn't hide the sarcasm. "You only blame me for every friggin' calamity that befell our family in the last twenty-five years. I have nothing to say to you and I can't imagine what the hell you'd have to say to me!" He paused, then sighed. "But since you got me here, you've got five minutes – you bring up anything about me putting Dustin in jail and I'm out of here!"

"Fine." Galen sat. He immediately opened up the shoulder bag on his lap. He pulled out a grey, hardcover book and handed it to Radley. He'd never seen it before. On the cover was the picture of an older, balding, heavyset gentleman with a thick face and bushy eyebrows posing in a professional portrait. The title of the book was *Unchained: My Liberation from a Life of Crime, Violence and Evil.* The author's name was Real Cormier.

"What is this?" Radley asked, flipping through the autobiography. Galen had read the whole thing, and had several pages bookmarked with different coloured sticky tabs. "Am I supposed to know who this guy is?"

"He's Real 'Bullethole' Cormier, one of the country's worst gangsters of the past fifty years – used to be a frontline enforcer for the *Rouge*, and other gangs out here in the West. Anyway, got busted about twenty-five years ago, spent time in the slammer, and now he's clean as a whistle. Goes around to church's and shit, telling people how he's reformed, found Jesus, all that stuff. A buddy of mine was tellin' me about him – he beat my friend's dad stupid when my buddy was a kid. The kid tracked the guy down and it turns out Cormier's the real deal – genuinely turned his life around. Even the *Rouge* went after the guy for a time, tellin' him to shut his yap because he'd been telling the public too much about how they roll."

"Well, that's a nice, feel good story, I guess," Radley said, impatient. "What the hell does this have to do with me or Dustin?"

"Turn to page one-sixty-three – blue sticky tab. Read the section I highlighted."

Radley looked at him suspiciously, then turned to the page. Galen had the first paragraph marked with a star. The following two pages of text was all underlined.

My time with the *Rebel Rouge* coincided with my occasional contracts with the Dragons. I was playing a dangerous game, working for one gang while dealing with another. How dangerous? Well, I knew what the *Rouge*, in particular, loved to do with 'Doublespeakers' as I liked to call them. I was what you called an educated criminal. I read Orwell. I preferred sophisticated names for 'informants' or 'traitors' than the typical, arcane names my colleagues had given them – names like 'narcs' and 'rats.' Our methods, however, for dealing with these people were no less brutal. There was a game these guys would play with Doublespeakers. I knew because I had seen it done six or seven times in my career – I called it 'Double Talk.'

The premise behind 'Double Talk' was to test informants' loyalty – often these 'Doublespeakers' – once confronted by their mother gang – would beg their former employers for a second chance. So the hitmen or enforcers – and I certainly had a direct hand in this in at least three occasions, all three of which I have been prosecuted for – would offer up a second chance to the 'narc' in a mock show to prove his loyalty to his home gang. The Doublespeakers would be given a choice – betray one of their family, either by turning them into police or, in an ultimate test of loyalty, harming them. Kill them, beat them, rape them, sodomize them – any Godforsaken concoction of mental torture the enforcer could cook up. The intent, of course, was to never really grant the Doublespeaker his loyalty back. It was nothing more than sheer glee for the hitman – who himself was usually some sort of sick, twisted, sociopathic son-of-a-bitch. The Doublespeaker was as good as dead, but in a show of utter humiliation, the idea was to have the narc give up every facet of his being in a pathetic attempt to grovel for a spot in the gang, and quite often his life. I say every facet of his being, because the intent was to destroy the individual – if the narc, for instance, refused to turn on his family, quite often the Doublespeaker would be left alive to watch the *Rouge* hitmen personally kill, rape, torture or sodomize that family member. There is no question it was pure, unadulterated evil, and I can honestly say I was ashamed to have ever been a part of it.

Radley read the last line and set the book down on the table. *What the hell?* he thought, then looked at the back cover and read the description blurb, which told more about the author. This Cormier guy had been around the block, serving in the criminal underworld for a thirty-year career. On the back cover, a mug shot of him as a young man and a picture of an older version of him in prison. He was a one-time enforcer, a hitman for the *Rouge. Did you know Paul Lanton?* Radley wanted to ask the man.

"So, wha'd ya' think?" Galen asked, his tone curious, eyes boring into Radley like a dog eager for a scrap of food from the table.

Radley flipped to the front of the book again to look at the copyright date. The book was written four years ago. "How would I get a hold of this guy?"

"That's the thing," Galen said. "Apparently he died of cancer two years ago. I guess he wrote that book once he found out his diagnosis. His widow and his step-kids are still alive, but that's it. My buddy went to his funeral."

Radley shut the book and dropped it on the table in front of his cousin. "Well, fat lot of good that does me."

"Whoa, what do you mean? Come on, Radley," Galen said. "Don't you see? That *Rouge* technique they do. This Cormier guy described it to a T. I've attended Lanton's trial all week. And I know that Dustin put the gun to your head – all of this was released on the first day of testimony. Lanton's defense tried to object to it but it got overruled."

"No, I'm not doing this." Radley shook his head, anger bubbling up inside him. "Look I'm trying to come to terms with what Dustin did with that gun, and I'm almost there. He was desperate. He was backed in the corner. I get that, and guess what, Galen? I forgave him. I helped buy him and Jezzelle a new house for Christ's Sake!"

"I know that, Radley," Galen said, leaning forward and tapping his finger on the table. "But that's my point; there may not be anything to forgive. Dustin knew what Lanton was going to do. He was protecting you."

"Galen, you weren't even there!" Radley hissed, raising his voice, not worried at all as to who heard him. "I saw the look in Dustin's eyes. I saw him look at me with pity and regret. He pulled the … fucking … trigger, Galen. Dustin was going to kill me."

Galen opened up the book back to the passage and pounded on the page for emphasis, his own voice high. "That's what the damn book is saying, Radley. Dustin pulled the trigger because he knew that if he didn't, Lanton would have shot you instead. Dustin knew this game, Radley. He knew what Lanton was doing. It was either going to be him or you. Dustin saved your life by squeezing that trigger!"

"You don't know that. There's no way Dustin could have known Lanton's gun wasn't loaded. He wouldn't have brought me there if he knew they were going to be playing that game."

"That's my point exactly. Dustin didn't know. He probably only figured it out when he saw Lanton pull out the gun and make the offer."

Radley shook his head. "No, no. There's no way you can know that, Galen."

"And there's no way for you to know that it wasn't, is there? Tell me, how deep do you think Dustin's involvement was with the *Rouge*? I'm talking about after he was let out of prison? Do you even know?"

Radley shook his head in disgust. "Now what are you saying? That Dustin took part in these *Rouge* schemes? What are you kidding me?"

"I've done the research, Radley. I've talked to people. Why do you think he had the fallout with Daniel Wannick—"

"I don't want to hear it!" Radley stood up. He could see other patrons looking at them, some with alarmed expressions on their faces. "Time for me to go!"

"Yeah, run away, Radley. Don't bother giving your brother the benefit of the doubt. That's what your good at, isn't it? Just get up, run away, and throw your family under the bus while you do!"

This is why I picked the food court. Radley glared at his cousin. He clutched the bear spray under his jacket. *So I didn't unleash this can on your sorry ass.* He pulled his hand away from his coat. Taking a breath, he paused, then spoke calmly and rationally.

"Look, I'm not running away. This is too much for me to take right now. I want this friggin' trial over, I want Lanton's ass in jail, and I want to get on with my life! I am helping take care of my brother, and always will. I don't know what to think about this book, and this idea that Dustin pulled the trigger to save me. I don't know if you, me, or anybody else will ever know for sure, but I'll think about it, okay?"

"But I know it, Radley," Galen said, holding the book up. "I know for sure."

"Well, that's good for you," Radley said, then turned and walked away. Not the greatest response, but that was all he could give at the moment.

He walked back to his car and pulled out of the mall parking lot, his mind a swirl of emotions and scenes of the past six months. For whatever reason, he couldn't get the image of Cyclo's severed head laying at his feet. The image of Cyclo's head and face haunted him since the event, a blot in his vision he couldn't wipe away from his line of sight. There were many blots from that night – Dustin's decision to pull the trigger probably being the worst of them.

As he pulled onto the freeway exit to the overpass that would lead to his neighbourhood, his heart stopped as he saw a police cruiser speed past the off ramp.

"Oh shit!" Radley yelled. He immediately pulled over to the

side of the road and turned on his hazard lights, then yanked out his phone. His conversation with Galen lasted over thirty minutes. He opened up his text messages. "Oh shit," he repeated again. *I texted Mike Relone.* The Sergeant had responded and, as Radley feared, was in a panic.

> Radley, where are you? Can you contact me? I'm sending officers to the mall right now.

Radley texted back.

> No, no! Everything's fine. I'm alright. False alarm. It was my cousin Galen. All is good.

He hit send, then placed the phone on his forehead. Cars flew by him, drivers going about their daily business, completely oblivious to the anguish gripping him. Closing his eyes, he felt his heart race like a belt sander. This whole month had felt like riding a speed train about to go off its track any second. Lanton's trial was to resume Monday.

I need to get the hell out of here. I need to get out of this city. I need to start over.

Chapter 47

ONE MONTH LATER

TheSlam.com Private Chat Room

User Logins: car-salesman319, VicWarshawski-rules-my-world

car-salesman319: nice name. never heard of her til I met u (sorry, *you!*)

Vic-rules-my-world: Thanks. Other than the capitalization, my only other complaint is that it's until, not til. Nice name yourself, BTW. LOL

car-salesman319: Ah, yes. I thought that would be a fitting name. Thanks for keeping me in line. Everyone on the West Coast talks like this. Everyone has a cell phone or Blackberry, and seem to be texting every minute of the day. You learn to talk like this after awhile. I prefer chatting on my knew computer rather than texting, though.

Vic-rules: Your knew computer?

car-salesman319: Gotcha. LOL. I did that on purpose.

Vic-rules: Dork.

car-salesman319: Yeah, I no. (kidding! ;-) So what happened in court today? Did they let him off on a technicality? Because you didn't wear your hat when you shot him, or something?

Vic-rules: God no. He's still locked up. Today his defense lawyer asked for a delay because two of his key witnesses are in jail and he needs to make arrangements to speak with them. One of them is Daniel Wannick, who the *Rouge* accused Dustin of ratting on.

car-salesman319: Oh yes, good old Wannick. What good would he do on the stand? How could he help Lanton? You'd think he'd only make things worse, given his hatred for Dustin.

Vic-rules: It's just another stall tactic by his defense team. They know we have a ton of evidence to lock Lanton up for life. They're also trying to discredit John Lim. My guess is they're going to try and get any testimony John gives to be thrown out of court.

car-salesman319: Great. Then the Prosecution will call me in. Just what I need, another chance to condemn my brother. Might as well kick him while he's already down. Bad enough, this is turning into the longest, flippin' trial in world history…

Vic-rules: Hopefully it won't come to that. Like I say, there's lots of evidence against Lanton. We've got him for other murders, including your Dad's and his friend.

car-salesman319: Yeah.

Vic-rules: Sorry to bring that up again. How is your brother doing?

car-salesman319: Not bad, if you call being able to nod your head and the ability to say "ow" progress.

Vic-rules: That is progress. It's a miracle he's even alive.

car-salesman319: I know. It's just so sad. He's my big brother, you know? There was a time when I looked up to him. And now, I don't know what to think. He's just so helpless. Actually, I haven't called Jezzelle in awhile. I really need to do that, and get a more recent update.

Vic-rules: She is one good woman. I can't imagine what she's going through.

car-salesman319: You got that right. She's more of a nursemaid and therapist than his wife. She's stood by him, thick and thin, and right now it's more thin than thick.

Vic-rules: Unbelievable.

car-salesman319: Yup. Well, thanks for the update. It was so good to hear from you again.

Vic-rules: Yes. Keep in touch out there on the West Coast. Are you finally settling into your new place?

car-salesman319: Almost. It's been a little overwhelming, a little scary, but yeah, I'm starting to get a rhythm out here. Everyone I work with seems decent. My new condo overlooks the west side. If you squint really, really hard you can see ships on the ocean.

Vic-rules: Awesome. I still have a hard time believing you're actually out there now.

car-salesman319: I know. Well, I know next to no one out here, so I'll probably be spending long nights sitting either in front of my laptop, or the TV.

Vic-rules: Well, if it's the laptop, drop by my page, and see if I'm on. Or post me a message. We can definitely do this again.

car-salesman319: u bet, and eye promis to use good english

Vic-rules: dork.

car-salesman319: Hey, that should be capitalized – "Dork"

Vic-rules: Dork. There, happy?

car-salesman319: LOL Only because I got to chat with you. It was good hearing your voice (sort of) ;-)

Vic-rules: Yes. You know where I'm at. I miss you.

car-salesman319: I know exactly where you're at, Vic. And yes, I miss you too.

Vic-rules: Logged off 10:34 PM

car-salesman319: Logged off 10:38 PM

Chapter 48

One Month Later

Radley sat at his manager's desk of the new Denault dealership, glossing over hard copies of three different flyer advertisements. The differences were subtle, but layout and eye-catching slogans were key hooks for the target area of his new market on the West Coast. One of the problems was that the ad layout he liked didn't have the correct financing rate on the used models they were selling, which meant having to delay that run another two days if he decided to go with it.

These are all nit-picky details, Shawn's voice spoke to him in his thoughts, *but that's your job now, hey Mr. Manager?* Radley could almost see his old supervisor give him a customary, affectionate thumbs up, the way Shawn always did whenever he'd given Radley a piece of advice.

"I have two customers here," the young secretary informed Radley, speaking to him from his doorway.

He stood up and stacked the layouts on the back shelf behind his chair. Biting his lip, he hadn't yet made his final decision on the ad choice, and wasn't in the mood for customers, but it usually meant a successful sale if they made their way to him. Desperately wanting to boost sales for the first quarter in management, he was willing to do whatever it took to get those numbers up, even if it meant putting on a fake smile and turning up the charm.

"Oh, God." His hands went up when he saw his parents walk into the office. "You guys aren't supposed to be here until tonight."

"I know." Diane gave him a hug. "We caught an earlier flight. We wanted to check up on you. Make sure you really are working and not gallivanting on the East side, getting into trouble."

"Very funny," Radley muttered. He kissed her cheek. It had been difficult explaining everything to the Trillamedes – they weren't happy with his decision to jeopardize his career, and life, in order to help Dustin, but they didn't blow up at him about it. Dustin's fate made it perfectly clear just how dangerous and insane Radley's actions were.

"We really just wanted to see how clean you kept your office," Doug said, shaking his son's hand. "It looks way cleaner than your room ever was."

"Yeah." Radley glanced around his office. It sat on the second floor of the dealership and was enclosed with a big bay window overlooking the showroom. He had a black desk with marble countertop, white walls with pictures of the most recent line of Infiniti sports cars and Nissan SUVs, and wall to wall shelving that helped him keep his desktop tidy. He even had air conditioning; that alone was a giant step up from his office back home.

"You guys have thrown me for a loop," he said, glancing at his watch, "you should have texted me. I was planning to pick you up at the airport after work tonight."

"You know Doug and I don't 'text' on holidays," Dianne

said with a shrug. "Besides, we didn't want to bother you at work. We took a cab from the airport. Our luggage is sitting at the receptionist's desk in the front."

"Besides, you're the big boss man, can't you take us for a ride in a new sedan or something?" Doug asked.

"Yeah, Big Boss Man," Radley said with a sigh, though nothing could be further from the truth. There was one person at the dealership above him, not including Jon Denault, the owner and Winston's nephew. Radley had, however, worked extra hours this past month and won favor with everyone there. Cutting work an hour early probably wouldn't be a big deal, just this once.

"Just let me talk to the dealer principal." The truth was, he couldn't be happier to see them. All he did this past month involved work. Eat, breathed, and slept it – trying to impress in his role as sales manager, but also to make up for the work he neglected by helping Dustin four months earlier. If he buried himself in his new job, he felt he buried his guilt along with it. He also buried the horror. Lanton's gun exploding above his head, the shock of the moment, seeing Dustin's head snap back and his lifeless body on the ground, the trauma of having Lanton's gun to his throat – all of it haunted Radley's evenings, his non-working hours.

He returned a few minutes later, getting the okay to take the rest of the afternoon off. No other time had he wanted to be with Doug and Diane more than tonight. He needed to be with his family.

"Big Boss Man is going to take you for a ride in a new

sedan," Radley said. He tapped on the framed picture of a four door, sleek, grey car that hung next to his door. "My new sedan." This would be his big surprise. "The Altima."

"You got a new car!" Doug's eyes popped out of his head.

"Good salesman I know sold it to me." Radley winked. He traded in his Infiniti when he arrived on the West Coast. Too many bad memories associated with that car.

His parents followed him down the stairs. He introduced them to the dealer principal and a few of the staff members on the floor. After a brief tour, he brought them out to his car, and loaded their bags in the trunk.

"I'm going to take you to the best seafood joint I know on the West Coast"–he paused–"it's the only seafood joint I know, mind you, but it's a good one."

"Radley, can I see you a moment?" Jon, the dealer principal, came out of the side doors.

"Uh, yeah, just a second guys," Radley apologized to the Trillamedes, then walked over to see his boss, unsure of what he wanted.

"Hey, Radley, looks like you screwed up on a deal for a customer earlier this week." Jon thumbed through some papers. "She just came in, pretty upset about her new Pathfinder. Her sales-slip and vehicle description are showing all of the wrong features for the model she bought. This is your screw-up, man."

"It's one of the new models she bought?" Radley looked at the paperwork, confused.

"The sales-slip listed it as a 4 wheel drive, V-6, 22 miles to the gallon, with a trailer hitch and a 7000 pound towing capacity."

Radley glanced over to the front parking lot and saw the vehicle – it was a dark grey Pathfinder. He remembered selling it to a middle-aged lady named Wilma McGivens. She wanted an SUV so she could have more room for a home delivery business. One of his salespeople reeled her in, and he made the final sale.

"Yeah, I remember that vehicle," Radley said, biting his lip. Something wasn't right here. God, this was awkward. "These weren't the features. Where did she get this from?"

"She claims you gave them to her," Jon repeated, clearly irritated at the mix up. "This is what she bought the vehicle on. It's actually a 4 wheel drive, V-6, 18 miles to the gallon, and a 5000 pound towing capacity, so she can't haul the cooling units she needs for her refrigeration business. That's a five-thousand buck difference. You need to go to this woman and make it right – she's sitting in her car now, quite upset and ready to call her lawyer."

"Oh God." Radley rubbed his head. *How the hell did this happen?*

"This is your fire, kid." Jon gave him a stark glare. "You damn well better put it out or we're in for a world of pain."

"Yeah, I will." Radley swallowed, with no clue where to begin. *Why did this have to happen now of all times?*

"Radley." Diane approached him. She always could sense his anguish. "Is something wrong?"

"No, of course not," Radley insisted, smiling, even though

he knew Diane would know differently. "One of my salespeople made a mistake. I just … have to explain what happened with the customer. Say, maybe you and Dad can take my car and go hang out at my place? I promise I won't be long."

"Your father can't drive in this big city," Diane scoffed.

Oh God, kill me now. Radley wanted to roll his eyes but didn't. "Well, maybe you guys can hang out in my office for a couple minutes. I'll try not to take too long, okay?"

He felt bad having to sluff her off, especially being so happy to see them. Maybe he could make this quick.

Walking outside to the grey Pathfinder, he conjured up a dozen scenarios to present to the lady. If he remembered correctly, she was a firecracker. She'd insist on getting her money back and not accept any alternate arrangement, despite the dealership's pledge for "100% customer satisfaction with every transaction," Radley knew he would be sunk. He wouldn't get canned over this, but he would have to work his butt down to his pelvic bone to make it up to Jon and the rest of the dealership. Either way, this was probably going to ruin his night, despite his best efforts to enjoy himself with his family.

He bit his lip while approaching the vehicle, a blinding glare from the sun stretched across the front windshield. Composing himself, he knocked gently on the Pathfinder's passenger-side door. He took a breath and opened it, ready to face the full wrath of Wilma McGivens.

And instead saw the face of the woman he loved.

Claire sat in the passenger seat, smiling sheepishly. She was dressed in a brown leather jacket and navy blue denim jeans. Her hair styled with subtle curls, hung loose at her shoulders. Wearing a tinge of make-up, her face was radiant, brightening up when she saw the surprise on his face. Having dressed up to see him, she sported a new look. Her skin was lightly tanned, matching her sand, velvet tunic – the collar of which was unlaced giving her a sleek, stylish appearance. She looked stunning, but she would have looked stunning in just about anything at that moment.

"I just wanted to come in with your parents and surprise you." She held up her hands, seeing the relief and surprise on his face. "This prank was all their idea." For once, she didn't have a wisecrack to greet him with. He turned and saw Jon, the dealership staff, and Diane and Doug waving at them from his Altima. Jon gave him a thumb up and a coy wink.

"You guys are all jerks," Radley called out to them, but couldn't hide the smile on his face. He turned back to Claire. "And I'm sure they had to twist your rubber arm to do this."

"At least I showered and don't have fungus growing on my jacket," she said.

"God, it's so friggin' wonderful to see you again." They'd chatted every night when he got home. The only other thing he did besides work these past three months.

"You too, car-salesman319."

He slid into the car, shut the door, and gave her a hug. They kissed, and everything was right in his world again.

Chapter 49

One Year Later – Age 30

Radley spun around on the dance floor and lifted Claire in his arms, reveling in the shrieks of excitement and surprise in the crowd. They had rehearsed their first dance for months, and spent more time on the moves than the wedding preparations. The work had been worth it. They started off with a slow, typical wedding song. People smiled at first, pictures were taken, then the audience seemed to lose interest, beginning side conversations, yawning, the young people in the crowd turned on their phones and started texting.

Then the music shot up in tempo, signaling their cue. Radley dipped Claire in his arms, and the two proceeded into a Latin salsa, catching everyone off guard. He picked Claire up and spun her at the hips, that move alone took three weeks of practice until he was comfortable holding her up – she already had the upper body strength to hold herself up in mid-air and keep her body rigid. They finished with a flourish of twirls and spins, and a mock rumba, in which Claire showed off her garter as she clung to Radley's body, winning the applause and laughter of everyone in the room.

Radley wiped the perspiration from his brow – he hated

sweating in the tuxedo, but it was well worth the exertion. He looked over to Diane and Doug, who were both laughing – Diane shook her head in amazement. There was nothing better than catching her off guard.

"You realize your mother's going to put this in her album," Doug called out from the dance floor.

"Claire's already seen me as Wonder Woman," Radley laughed, turning to his bride. It was the look on her face that made everything – the after-work dance lessons, the sore ankles, and the sweat – all worthwhile.

"You looked sexy in that outfit." Claire smiled, hearing Doug's comment. They embraced on the dance floor, kissing one more time under the light of flashing cameras and pot fixtures above their heads.

Radley kissed her again then twirled her over to her father, who walked onto the floor for the parent dance. He walked over to his mother and hooked arms.

"Thank-you, for everything." He smiled to her as he guided her into a slow waltz.

"I only paid for the limos."

"You know what I mean." He winked at her.

As they steered around the floor, Radley spotted Abigail giving him a subtle wave. Sitting behind her was her mother, father, and Aunt Dulcie. They appeared to be enjoying themselves. Dustin sat awkwardly in his wheelchair, rocking slightly while staring at the floor. He had an eye patch over the empty crater that once contained his left eye, and was dressed in regular, loose-fitting clothing. There was a drool tray attached just above his collar, and an emergency oxygen tank he hadn't needed since he could breathe on his own again. He appeared to be leaning his head toward the music while Jezzelle and Dulcie watched the dancers and chatted.

"Have you talked to your brother yet?" Diane asked.

"Not yet." Radley smiled, but this was Diane, and there was no point in telling the lady he called his mother anything but the truth. "I'm delaying."

She didn't respond. They just kept dancing.

"I still can't believe they came all the way out here for this," Radley continued, talking quietly in her ear. He and Claire had given them a token invite, not thinking in a million years they'd actually attempt the three hour trip to Claire's hometown for a wedding, but they travelled in Dulcie's motorhome, and drove slowly, taking just over five hours to complete the journey. They arrived two days earlier, and were staying in a spacious RV campground with a pool for Abigail and lots of space and walking trails to push Dustin around on.

"I talked to them about it," Diane admitted. "I guess Abigail was so excited, she absolutely had to come. Jezzelle said her family was ready for a vacation, and she had a contingency plan ready to transport Dustin to the nearest hospital any minute if need be."

Radley bit his lip as he glanced over at them one more time.

"Radley, look at me." Diane stared him down. "You go by Radley Trillamede now, but Radley Wycliffe is still inside you. That's still your brother."

"I know, Ma. I'm just … still trying to think of what to say."

"Hey"—she pointed her finger in his face—"we've been over this. You know where I stand. I'm in your cousin Galen's camp. God knows I've talked to enough people in that case now to believe your brother was looking out for you at those coke ovens."

"I know. I've been over that night a thousand times, thinking about the way it played out, I just wish I could remember everything that was said. At the very least to give me some clarity – oh never mind, we've been over this …" He paused and looked up at the roof, blew out a heavy sigh, then looked back at her. "I am too – in Galen's camp, I mean. The problem is … every time I look at Dust I see the guy who aimed that gun at me and pulled the trigger."

"And that son-of-a-bitch Lanton made him pay for it." Her words surprised him. That was the first time he'd ever heard her speak that harshly, with that much repugnance for someone. "And now Lanton's put away, where no one has to worry about him ever again. This is how you move forward. This is how you survived every one of those Goddamn devils that have haunted you since you were a little kid. You be better than them all!" She pressed a finger into his chest for

414

emphasis.

"Geez, two cuss words in under a minute." Radley nodded, smirking at her under the dance floor nights, well aware people were watching them dance. "Maybe you're getting some Wycliffe in you." Of course, she was right about everything. She was the only one who knew about his devil analogy, and he had survived them all – his parents' addictions, Tavis and Dustin's criminal activities, his own drinking. *And the grand devil himself.* Paul Lanton – the scar-faced man – who haunted his nights for almost two decades.

The wedding put a big spring in Radley's step this past month, but so too did Lanton's conviction, which was upheld even after his appeal. Multiple counts of first-degree murder, attempted murder, torture, indignity to a dead body, forced confinement, kidnapping, drug running. They successfully convicted him on Cyclo's murder first, which got him life in prison and no chance of parole for twenty-five years, then procured evidence that garnered him two more life sentences. The other counts added an additional sixty years onto his sentence, but were pretty much frivolous at that point. Lanton's conviction opened a floodgate of litigation against the *Rouge,* which led to several raids and arrests of key members, sending much of the gang's operations in disarray.

"Very funny"–Diane gripped his arm–"but like it or not, that Wycliffe shadow follows you wherever you go, Radley Trillamede. But remember, you broke free. *You* escaped."

Radley thought about the letters he wrote. The chances he took. The lies he told. The guilt.

"It put me through hell." He shook his head.

"And now your brother's going through hell," Diane finished. "That's my point. You escaped. He didn't. Everything he did, even when he put that bloody gun to your face, was because of the crap your parents put him through. He's paying for his mistakes, and theirs. He'll be paying for them the rest of his life."

Radley sighed as he looked at her.

"Time to let it go, this time for real," he said with a smirk. *I can do that. I can also choose to believe my brother tried to save me, not kill me. Regardless of what may have been going through his mind. I'll probably never know for sure, will I?*

"God, I don't know what the hell to tell you anymore." She caressed the side of his face. "Mostly because I know I don't have to."

He gave her a big hug, then walked her back to her seat. Heading immediately over to Abigail, he extended his hand, and brought her onto the floor for the chicken dance, and a fast song. She seemed happy, even if it was slightly awkward. Today was about him and Claire, so he had little opportunity to ask Abby how she was doing, coping. For a young girl her age, she carried a lot of weight on her shoulders. Radley wished he could do more for her, because he understood the guilt riding around in her heart, understood it far better than

416

anyone.

"I'm so happy for you, Uncle Radley." She hugged him on the dance floor as their song ended.

"And I'm proud of you, sweetheart," he said in her ear. "For everything you've done to help your Mom and Dad." Taking an uneasy breath, he followed her to Dustin and Jezzelle.

"Hello, Radley." Jezzelle hugged him. Radley noticed Claire scootch in behind him. Jezzelle also hugged her. "Congratulations, you guys."

"Thanks." Radley smiled. He noticed how trim his sister-in-law was, the slimmest he had ever seen her. Jezzelle must have shed the pounds taking care of her husband.

"Man, Jezzie, you look good," Radley complimented.

"Thank-you," she answered, looking down at the floor. "It's been a tough year. Your brother keeps me on my feet. Dustin, say hello to your brother."

Dustin glanced up at Radley, but turned his head, apparently bothered by the dance lights.

"He's getting tired," Jezzelle observed. "I think he's had too much excitement for one day. I better take him home."

"Do you mind if I take him for a walk outside?" Radley asked. "I haven't had a chance to talk to him yet. Would that be okay?"

Jezzelle shrugged her shoulders. "The fresh air might be good for him. Maybe wake him up."

Radley wheeled Dustin out the French doors that led to a

patio. The Greenwood Golf and Country Club was expensive, but it allowed their wedding guests to enjoy a short walk in a well-kept garden of trees, flowers, and shrubbery. The sky was dark but the cobblestone pathways were well lit. Green ash trees lined the view of the valley below, while professionally pruned, lush Cypress grew inside the courtyard surrounding them. There were enough flowers at their feet Radley could detect a faint, sweet smell. A couple of wedding guests were outside having a cigarette, and smiled as they saw Radley wheel his brother onto the path.

He pushed Dustin to a bench just out of the light of the jade lampposts that hid amongst the greenery. He placed him next to the bench and sat down. They were completely alone. A half-moon offered a sliver of white light.

"Well, Dust, I finally did it." Radley put his arm over his brother's shoulder. "I took the plunge."

A slight groan emanated from Dustin's lips. It was a tired groan, nothing more. If Dustin hadn't been injured, he could just imagine what his older brother's reactions to his marriage.

"Yeah, well just be careful to keep the missus happy," Dustin would have quipped, *"she could kick the shit out of you."* Radley smirked at the thought.

"Do you ever wonder if Mom and Dad can see us?" Part of him liked to think Dustin understood everything he said. Jezzie and Abigail liked to say the same, but his Aunt Dulcie was far more realistic. *His brain is all scrambled,* Dulcie told him two days ago, when they arrived in their RV. *He has no function on one side of his head. All he does is take in input, but he has no way to process it.* Dulcie was no expert, but it was difficult to argue with her given the time she spent with Dustin, and the fact that his brother, for all intents and purposes, was now an invalid.

"Sometimes I think they can," Radley continued. "I like to think Mom and Dad would be proud of us. How could they not? After the childhood they gave us, huh?" He looked at his brother, who turned his head to glare at Radley. It was like clockwork, it seemed he had struck a chord with him.

"What?" Radley asked, a spark of interest built up inside him.

A string of drool dripped from Dustin's mouth and hung like a yo-yo.

"Oh." Radley used the drool tray to wipe his brother's face. Dustin gave another tired groan.

Radley frowned. Once again he caught himself wanting his brother to be someone he was not. He wanted that of his entire Wycliffe family, even now. Even the idealized "bread-winners of the family" he tried to justify Tavis and Carla as being, stemmed from the same habit. His Wycliffe family was who they were, and there was nothing he could have done, or could do today, to change that. He had escaped, as Diane told him, and he would just have to accept that.

"Hey, what are you songbirds doing out here?" Claire snuck

up behind, giving him a kiss on his cheek. He was her groom, and even in the dark enclave, she was absolutely glowing.

"We're just sitting here under the trees." Radley smiled. Dustin glared off into the darkness, breathing heavily.

"Well, have fun." Claire smiled at him, saying nothing more. She knew this was their time. "I'm going in to dance."

"You go, girl." Radley blew her a kiss. "Save one for me later, will ya?"

"Dork." She laughed, turning down the pathway, into the light of the hall.

Radley turned and put his arm around his brother's shoulder once again. He looked up at the rustling green Cypress leaves above him, with the moonlight trickling through the foliage. It was a beautiful sight.

Michael Saad, author of All the Devils Are Here (Tumbleweed Books, 2016), has practical experience fighting devils and demons, and almost never swears or cusses. His writing appeared in Orange Magazine, Open Minds Quarterly, B.C. Historical News, Halfway Down the Stairs, Nil Desperandum, SQ Mag, Under the Bed Magazine, eFiction Magazine, The Cross and the Cosmos, Youth Imagination Magazine, Non-Local Science Fiction, and Dark Passages Publishing.

Michael won 'Best Short Story' in the First Light: New Writing from the Elk Valley anthology for his piece "A Sort of Second Nature" in 2000. He is currently a dedicated high school teacher in Alberta, Canada, and a member of the Writer's Guild of Alberta.

Michael holds a Bachelor of Arts and a Bachelor of Education, both with distinction, from the University of Lethbridge.

The author and publisher hope you enjoyed this novel. Please take the time to either review or rate it on GoodReads.